Frances Elliot

The Diary of an Idle Woman in Sicily

Frances Elliot

The Diary of an Idle Woman in Sicily

ISBN/EAN: 9783337192006

Printed in Europe, USA, Canada, Australia, Japan

Cover: Foto ©Raphael Reischuk / pixelio.de

More available books at **www.hansebooks.com**

COLLECTION

OF

BRITISH AUTHORS

TAUCHNITZ EDITION.

VOL. 2038.

THE DIARY OF AN IDLE WOMAN IN SICILY

BY

FRANCES ELLIOT.

IN ONE VOLUME.

TAUCHNITZ EDITION

By the same Author

THE DIARY

OF AN

IDLE WOMAN IN SICILY.

BY

FRANCES ELLIOT,

AUTHOR OF "AN IDLE WOMAN IN ITALY," ETC.

LEIPZIG

BERNHARD TAUCHNITZ

1882.

TO

MY FRIENDS AT MANIACE

THIS DIARY

IS

AFFECTIONATELY DEDICATED.

CONTENTS.

---

8 CONTENTS.

CONTENTS. 9

THE DIARY

OF

AN IDLE WOMAN IN SICILY.

CHAPTER I.

PERHAPS it was six o'clock in the morning, perhaps seven—the sun was shining brightly.

It woke me. I sat up in the solitary *compartimento* .where I had passed the night coming from Rome to Bari and Taranto, down the coast line of Calabria, rubbed my eyes, dashed down the window, and looked out.

Was it clouds? Or a mirage? A dream? Or a vision of that paradise to which all good people are hastening? Ah! let me gaze at it before it melts away!

That anything so lovely could be real, never came into my head!

Across the sparkling sea, some twenty miles ahead, the island of Sicily rises before me, purple and blue, and opaline, shaded in tints no human hand can paint, a stupendous mass of piled up mountains, sweeping down in heavenly lines to meet the azure sea. Nothing but mountains, not a span of level land, with Etna throned in the blue sky—a dome of dazzling snow, towering above all!

Along the golden sand just tipped with creamy surf, town after town, village, burg, and tower, bluff, cape, and castle-topped headland, rocky promontory, bay, and bight —come gradually into view like a procession. To each curve of the beauteous coast answers an echoing curve of beauteous sea, spread over with masses of flitting light and shade, soft morning mist and purple mysteries lingering from night. A hundred arcs answer to a hundred indentations and wide sweeps; rocky barriers break into needle points, and there are broad forelands of rich and glowing hues, brown, porphyry-red, and sage.

Weary as I am after nearly forty hours' continuous travelling, I mentally decide that I would willingly perform the distance twice over to behold such a sight.

At this moment we are slowly steaming along the sandy coast of Eastern Calabria, amid an undergrowth of cactus and tamarisk, close to the sea. As each moment brings me nearer, the more does the beauty of that Sicilian shore grow upon me. Where the gods lived and walked like men, cannot surely be a mere work-a-day world like any other. Sorrow and pain and death can never enter this island of the blest, as fresh, and fair, and young as when Proserpine gathered flowers in Enna's perfumed woods, and Ceres lit her torch at Etna's cone.

The clearness of the air, the brilliancy of hues, the ever-changing form of that Neptunian chain—Poseidon's mountains, with their mysteries of rift and fissure, Cyclops-haunted cave, and Nereid-dwelling grotto, the great volcano opposite with its familiar memories of

Ulysses and his fleet, Æneas, Empedocles, the Giant Enceladus—ah! who can paint it?

I hate my pen for being so incapable.

I would fly with the wind to be across, but on *this* side, at all events, I am in a prosaic world.

Our train, as if weary of its long journey, is horribly deliberate; it stops at every miserable little station, and creaks and groans through many a rocky tunnel, from which it is a blessing to escape, and have a fresh peep at Sicily.

Pallizzi, Bova, Salini Lazzaro, Pellaro, San Gregorio, (Hercules must have had "a bad time of it," driving those wilful cattle of Geryon's along this weary shore), the best but dirty villages, sometimes only one house— when will it end?

Elysium is in front, and we are dawdling on in an earthly purgatory of ugliness!

We pass Pentedattilo, the station below, the town poised aloft on a dolomitic rock, shooting upwards like the pointed fingers of a hand, the houses nestling in the slits; then we glide among prickly pear hedges and yuccas, exotic flowers flash out on the red earth, and glossy thickets of orange and citron shut out the sea, over which the purple mountains of Sicily rise sweetly.

This Calabrian coast seems to be riming itself to meet its beautiful island-neighbour, as they draw nearer to each other. Olive trees come fluttering down from the hard-lined rocks, umbrageous carobbias throw a sombre gloom, aloes stand forth in dignified reserve, and a palm, here and there, raises its rounded head.

The scent of some late-blooming jessamine is in the air, and the fiery globes of the pomegranate light up the groves. Behind frown the dark flanks of Aspromonte, where Garibaldi lay wounded on the mountain-side, to the eternal shame of Italy!

But what matters Aspromonte—a sturdy, ilex-planted, mountain ridge, running like a backbone through the centre of the Calabrias, or Garibaldi, or patriotism, or anything, with entrancing, fantastic Sicily dazzling my eyes in front? Sicily bathed in the morning sunshine, the golden lights playing upon peak, ravine, and cliff, and the eleven thousand feet of Etna glistening like some huge diamond set in blue! Shall I ever get to Reggio? Shall I ever see Messina?

I cannot look down the Straits, there are so many curves, and capes, and bays; but I can guess where the harbour of Messina must be—hid behind the arm of a sweeping promontory ahead, and I feel that the sight of a *city* would give just that touch of human interest, wanting in this scene of vague delight.

My eyes becoming accustomed to the glittering island before me, I see that where Etna uprises above the Cape of Passaro running out in one long continuous line into the sea, all other mountains shrink back abashed, that its base is so enormous—(a hundred miles)—it detracts from its height; that the side nearest me, the poetic side of the Cyclops, Odysseus, and Æneas (Æneas was more fortunate than I, for he saw the Cyclops fighting on the shore as he sailed by) forms the horn of the Bay of Catania; that there is not the smallest vestige of smoke, and that, but for the depression of a well-marked crater, three miles round, one would only think it, of all mountains, the most grave and impassive.

By-and-by, running in nearer to the Sicilian shore, the straits narrow into the semblance of an elongated lake, the grand range of the Taurus (Neptunian) mountains, topped by Monte Venere over Taormina, heaped pile upon pile, shuts out the outline of Etna, and nearer heights, jagged, peaked, and indented, press forward to take their place. I can just make out the faint blue line of Cape Schiso, the southern extremity of what once was ancient Naxos, the first Greek settlement in Sicily, and that must be Portus Ulyssis under Aci, but there is such a confusion of beautiful headlands and promontories that I know nothing surely.

"Shall we ever get to Reggio?" I ask the question of a swarthy guard. He does not answer me.

The train is lingering at one of those endless little stations, for no purpose, apparently, but to allow this individual to fondle a dog, evidently alive to the dangers of his position as a dog upon the rail.

The guard is trying his best to tempt him forward on the line, but no coaxing will induce the animal to stir an inch beyond a certain limit of self-imposed boundary, he, in his canine wisdom, has proposed to himself—a very sage among dogs!

He is old and ugly, but '*cute*, and with a beseeching eye turned upon passengers, as for a chance crumb, which not getting, he retreats to the platform with the extremest care, always on the prescribed line, crest-fallen though affectionate.

Now without seeing a single house, we creak into a bare, dusty barn.

This is the station of Reggio. I look at my watch. I have been in the train for forty hours, starting from Rome to Caserta the night before last.

It is ordained that travellers bound for Foggia, Bari, and the southern line to Reggio, need not touch at Naples; so we were turned off in the middle of the night at the Caserta Junction, one hour from Naples. As it was raining a deluge, I should have blessed the railroad authorities for even a tilt to protect me, but in their wisdom they saw it otherwise, and I commenced my journey with a wetting.

CHAPTER II.

Beautiful Messina.—Gods and Heroes.—The Straits.—Ancient Rhegium and Modern Reggio.

YES, there is Messina, Portæ Siciliæ, across the Fretum Siculum!

Not straight across, after all, the ancient Zancle, but just a little to the right of Reggio, towards the other end of the channel at Faro (Pelorus). And there, too, puffing away beside the Reggian mole, is Florio's tiny steamer, which is to ferry us four miles across.

If I say that Messina is a jewel worthy of its setting, and that I find it capable of giving that last touch of human interest to the vague delight of those bewildering mountains which have maddened me with their beauty since early morning, will you understand me?

Throned against a perpendicular background of many-tinted heights, Messina sits like a queen, her white robes sweeping to the sea. Never was a city so exquisitely poised between earth and sky!

On a narrow strait between two great seas, her lines of endless quays, bordered by snowy palaces, her sickle-shaped harbour, with its far-stretching arm and castle of defence (the sun bringing out every detail, as though it prized each particular stone), the exquisite vista down the straits; on one side the shelving terraces of the Calabrian mountains, melting off into harmonious waves of cape and bay; the Castle of Scylla, on the summit of a rugged bluff; the sandy point of Faro, and its lighthouse, midway in the straits (both point and lighthouse seem to touch the mainland and to landlock the straits, but in reality the channel there is two miles across); on the other side, low-lying Charybdis and a range of purple mountains—all make a picture so perfect, so exquisite in itself, I sigh to think that Sicily has a history!

And such a history! Gods and demi-gods, heroes and nymphs, Nereids and Cyclopes, Sicanians, Siculians, Phenicians, and Greeks, invaders from every land, conquerors from every shore—in all ages, since all time—a weight felt as of useless knowledge while gazing on these enchanting shores!

How delicious it would be to have nothing to chronicle but the land itself! To paint the play of sunshine on palmetto-clothed heights, the beds of sea-pinks fluttering to the light, the foam of white sea-surf dashing against lava-cliffs, the warm shadows slanting across vine pergolas, the deep blue tinting in the bosom of the hills, and ever-varying mountain lines wandering heavenwards!

These are my thoughts, standing on the quay at Reggio, while my maid, surnamed the Furiosa, from certain marked peculiarities of temper, marshals the luggage into a tossing boat which is to convey passengers aboard Florio's steamer, tossing at anchor.

The warm air beating on my face, the straits sparkling and glittering with white-tipped waves, the bulging lateen sails of the fishing-boats flying by, the merchant vessels and large steamers from Naples, Malta, and Taranto rolling in the trough of the waves, the yachts that toss and plunge like water-fowl, the murmur of the water lapping against the quay, the hoarse cries of the boatmen, the snatch of a tune whistled by a boy, the

2*

voices of the passengers—some in, some out of the boat
—all come to me with a triumphant sense that Sicily is
no longer a myth, a shadow; that it lies before me there,
my *own*, my *very own*—Beautiful, Unknown, Perilous,
Enticing!

Of Reggio, ancient Rhegium, I can tell you but little.
I had no eyes for anything but Sicily. It was first
colonized from mother Greece, then from Zancle (Messina),
just as Messina was colonized from Grecian Naxos (these
colonial Greeks soon understood the advantage of quiet
neighbours of their own flesh and blood).

From all time, Zancle and Rhegium have stared at
each other across the straits, dissevered in history, in
epochs, in feeling. Rhegium was, as it were, the portal
of Sicily; races and nations entered there, but passed on
as I do, which takes all permanent interest from it.

Modern Reggio is a flat, uninteresting, dirty little
town, without a vestige of its great antiquity. One long,
rattling street begins at the straits, and ends vaguely in
the prospect of a bare-flanked mountain. The dust is
intolerable, the people are half-naked, insolent and ugly.

What we went through, Furiosa and I, in our passage
to the steamer, with the ancient mariners of Reggio, how
they cursed and bellowed at us, and dived wildly among
our boxes, how Furiosa, developing her characteristic
gifts, got all on end like bristles, gave it them back
again, rescued the boxes, screamed in Teutonic Italian,
and finally prevailed in paying what she chose—their
hungry, brown fingers almost tearing the paper money
from her hand; how the bargain once made, the ancient
mariners quieted down, and conversed with us quite
affably, as they dug their awkward oars into the waves,
and how we finally landed on the deck of the tiny
steamer—I shall not further say.

St. Paul did quite right "to fetch a compass and sail from Rhegium." I follow his example. As a great historic centre, where the annals of Greece, Rome, Byzantium, Arragon and Naples meet, clash, and separate, I must often refer to it; otherwise, I personally wipe out Reggio altogether, as the earthquakes have done so often.

I had a letter for the Prefect in my pocket, but I would not have delivered it or done anything to lengthen my stay, for the world; so with my face steadily fixed on Sicily, I go forward.

CHAPTER III.

Queen Messina.—The Sickle Harbour.—Earthly Birth.—Perfidious City.—Dionysius, Timoleon, and Agathocles.—The Sons of Mars.—Hiero and Rome.—Saracens and Normans.—Cœur de Lion.—Charles of Anjou.—Where are your Lovers now?—Peter of Arragon.—Wrinkles on your Brow.—The Grand Monarque. —Garibaldi.

FLORIO's little steamer rocks and heaves. These straits are a miniature edition of our Channel, the same strong currents, the same rocky bottom, the same massed-up ocean at either end, struggling to get free. A cat does not hate the sight of water more than I; nevertheless, on this occasion, I waive my antipathy, and stay on deck, for there, before me, is Messina.

Majestic avenues of white palaces rise above the waves, and long lines of snowy quays, broken by wide flights of steps, now detach themselves from the mass. There are noble arcades and broad spanning arches, fountains and statues and balustrades. Gay villas and dainty pavilions peep out like gaudy flowers among the hills, and a world of blackening masts bristle within the spacious harbour, bounded by the low green banks of the sickle barrier—arsenal, lazaretto, and citadel are within this curve, of which the castle of San Salvador guards the narrow entrance. I seem to touch it with my finger!

Etna is there—to my right, towering high amid a magnificent panorama of mountain. To my left, low down lies Faro, and the Point of Pelorus, the narrow-mouth of the Straits; the boundless ocean beyond, and a world of ruddy cliffs, and hills, gorges and valleys on the Calabrian Apennines behind.

Very beautiful you are, Messina, looking out over the sea, with that fair white face; the poetic lines of your mountains draping around you; the azure straits gliding past you in homage, and bringing the world's treasures to your feet; very beautiful, but false and fickle, and cowardly in all the phases of your history, a ready victim to every invader, a facile prey, ever siding with the strongest!

When Kronos, father of Demeter, ruled in Sicily, he dropped his sickle upon the waters, from his home on the crown of the Pelorian mountains, and named you Zancle!

Straightway your harbour took the curved form it bears.

Later on, came Orion, a mighty hunter imported from the east—gigantic, bold, a kind of Phenician Nimrod, dwelling like Kronos on mountain tops, Orion, architect as well as hunter, built and strengthened your walls, and fortified your sickle-harbour.

Such is your mythic origin, Queenly Messina.

The history of your earthly birth is not so clear as that of your neighbours, Catania, Leontini or Syracuse. It is said that the Chalcydian Greeks from Eubœa, in the Archipelago, settled on the gold-rimmed bay of Naxos, near Taormina, sent out a colony to people you. Strabo calls you "an off-shoot from Naxos," though you have lost every vestige of classic origin, except the soft Greek name you bear. Others say that Greeks from Ionia and Samos were your god-fathers; but call you by whatever name you please,—Zancle, Messina or Messana, —you never knew what freedom meant, nor honour.

Greek as you were you betrayed your Grecian brethren in the great struggle between Athens and Syracuse, when Rhegium was faithful. And then again, your servile temper showed itself with the Carthaginians, when, spite of Orion's strong walls and dykes, and your noble harbour of defence, you permitted Himilcon to win you without a struggle.

Next comes the turn of Dionysius, the Syracusan tyrant, who drove out Himilcon and saved Sicily. For this service you, Messana, unable to defend yourself, owe to Dionysius — not otherwise a humane character — a second birth.

But after Dionysius, you again fell, pusillanimous Beauty, and became the prey of other Carthaginians; until Timoleon, the Corinthian, drove them out, as he drove them out at Syracuse.

And yet again another conqueror enters the sickle-harbour—Agathocles, fresh from his African conquests. A very different man he, to the "just Timoleon," beginning his strange career as a potter's son at Thermæ, and ending it as a king! We shall meet with Agathocles again at Syracuse. So he too comes, one of so many, to pass the yoke of conquest round your neck, Messana, fairest of cities!

Next in order arrive those sons of Mars, the Mamertines (from Mamertium, the present Oppido in the Gulf of Gioia, beyond the Cape of Faro, mercenaries and robbers called into Sicily by the endless wars.

These Mamertines visit Messina on their return to the mainland as *friends;* as *friends* they plunder what Agathocles had left; as *friends* they murder the men, and dishonour their wives and daughters.

A very woman in submission, Messina bows her head and bears it; nay, so deep is her degradation, that without striking a blow in her own defence, she allows these ignoble pirates to blot out even her very name, and, as she changed from Zancle to Grecian Messanà, now she becomes Mamertina!

But not for long. Beauty such as yours, Messina, commands protectors!

Sailing round the Cape of Pachyrus (Passaro), under Etna's shadow, comes help from Syracuse, in the person of Hiero!

For a brief space, Hiero fills the oft-changing foreground of your many-hued shore, defeats the Mamertines, who call out wildly, some on Rome, some on Carthage, for help, then disappear from the historic scene, they, and the new name they gave you.

Again, you are Grecian Messana, surnamed the Beautiful!

Now this Hiero who drives out the Mamertines, is both virtuous and merciful, according to the standard of that day. He rules you, Messina, justly but sternly, knowing your fickle mind.

Was ever such a helpless, changeful city! Tired of Hiero, she calls Imperial Rome to Sicily.

Rome answers to the call without inquiry into motives, all too willingly. Generals, and consuls, and prætors, with train of triremes, and legions, quinqueremes, and transports come bustling across the straits.

If Grecian Helen was accursed by gods and men for causing the fall of Troy, what do you merit, selfish Messina, for this bringing in of Rome? By the Punic wars you caused more sieges, massacres, invasions and carnage than fifty Grecian Helens.

Timoleon, Agathocles, Dionysius, the ignoble Mamertines, Hiero of Syracuse, Carthage, or Rome, it is all the same to you, Messina.

The great Pompey passed by in the civil wars with Cæsar and admired you; and Octavianus, and Pompey's son, Sextus Pompeius, caressed you. But there is little more to tell worthy of record, except that you kept your lovely person intact, by submitting in turn to every master!

Again you bend your fair neck, in the ninth century, to the Saracens; sovereigns at Palermo and Syracuse, careering, like their progenitors the Carthaginians, unchecked over the Tyrrhenian seas, now that the Empire of Rome and Eastern Rome (Byzantium) have ceased to rule the West.

The Saracens are strong enough, to hold you firmly and long—too long, indeed, to suit your disposition. Tired of Saracen, Arab, and Moor (all notes of the same chord), again you raise your white head over the mountain-tops, and this time call upon a new nation, the Normans, to come in.

The Normans are a romantic fashion of men, chestnut-haired, fair-skinned, and blue-eyed; very brave and bold, robbers and buccaneers to a man, if truth be told, yet with a fine sense of justice, honour, and mercy; altogether a band of light-handed, easy-going young knights, with no great sense of the distinction of *meum* and *tuum*, but carrying a clear certificate of good work done: first, as pirates in France, then as robbers in Apulia; later, mercenaries at Salerno, Capua, and Naples; and now, after incredible luck, rulers in the two Calabrias and the Abruzzi.

After all, Messina, you were monstrously ungrateful. You were very well treated by the Saracens, a much more civilized race than the Normans, with laws, science, and arts—poetic in speech, graceful in manners, refined in habits. It was but a dirty trick to call in secretly those wild-riding young Northmen—marauders all; but with a romantic halo round their Gallic name of Hauteville, felt in all history.

Che vuole? It is Messina's way to be treacherous. She welcomes with rapture a new master—a master and a lover; for Roger declares, when he has won the city, that he loves it, and will hold it to the end—he and his race for ever!

There is a little episode at Messina, about this time, worthy of note. Richard Cœur de Lion pauses here on his way to the Crusades, and marries within her walls Berengaria of Navarre, who has arrived chaperoned by his mother, haughty, wicked Queen Eleanor. The marriage festivals light up the face of the splendid quays, the torches flare across the face of palaces, and the English fleet, gathered in Orion's sickle-harbour, blazes with *feux-de-joie.* Then Richard sails to Palestine.

As time progresses, the Normans go the way of all flesh—Roberts and Williams, and Frederic II., and last of all, Manfred, at the fatal bridge of Benevento.

Instead of their handsome, fair faces, flowing hair, and ready arms for every deed of knightly valour, Charles of Anjou comes from Provence, dark, thin, and hollow-cheeked. Charles is brother of Saint Louis, King of France; no saint, indeed, himself, but a man of steel, with heart of bronze; avaricious, revengeful, cruel, blast-

ing, as with a curse, each land he touches. How Charles
tramples on Sicily with iron heel, and especially tramples
on you, voluptuous Queen, throned on your golden shore,
is too long for me to tell.

No one now to aid you, bewitching Messina! Nothing
but fierce fighting between Sicilians and French, and the
hard reality of the Sicilian Vespers; and patriotic John
of Procida massacring all Charles's troops and swaggering
officers; and Charles vowing vengeance for the French
blood shed at Palermo, falling in headlong fury on your
painted shores!

Alas! where are your friends and lovers now, palace-
lined Queen? Of what avail your wiles and enchant-
ments, your tricks and your coquetries? Lonely you sit
on your purple hills, and gather your white skirts within
your walls manned by your bravest citizens!

Once, and once only, you defend yourself. It is
against this terrible enemy, Charles of Anjou; and it
must be confessed you do it well; your very women
mount the walls and fight!

But, Charles repulsed, you soon fall back into your
luxurious beauty-airs, under the southern sun, which
makes his home with you, and prepare to receive a
Spanish master, Peter of Arragon.

Messina—Lady! as I see you now from the deck of
Florio's steamer, you are as fair as ever. The lapse of
ages has not withered your grand face, nor perpetual
servitude soiled the enchanting colours that mark you
Beautiful among cities. Yet there are signs of conquest
on your broad, white brow, wrinkles, one may say, upon
the surface of your walls (a mosaic, of Phenician, Carthaginian, Roman, Saracen, and Norman, rising black
upon your hills). The Emperor Charles V., one of your
many masters, riveted and strengthened them. Those

round towers, too, Rocca Guelfonia, for instance, half
Carthaginian, half Roman (we will call it a mole upon
your blooming cheek), catch my eye as I near the
harbour. The Bastione Vittoria, too, a huge excrescence,
projecting forward on a red-tinted rock, marks an ugly
scar upon your marble-tinted throat, inflicted during the
siege of your bitter enemy, Charles of Anjou; and half
a mile distant, through orange orchards and hanging
vineyards, I can see the bastion of Don Blasco, some
Spanish governor, who died and left his mark.

Monte Griffone, another fortress, calls Richard Cœur
de Lion father. Castle Gonzaga, on a wooded peak, is
a Spanish souvenir of possession, like a link upon a chain.
Spanish too, the Citadel of San Salvatore, down in the
harbour—a fell device of sternest rock and stone, to
hold you captive, fairest of vassals!

For, be it known, seductive Queen, your wiles and
arts for alluring men and nations continued down to a
late period!

Your last victim was pompous, bewigged, old Louis XIV.
How you fascinated him in his old age, who can tell?

Spite of earthquakes and pestilence—(the earthquakes
must have maintained you in perpetual youth, for you
have renewed yourself each time they have destroyed
you)—you call the "Grand Monarque" to your shores,
to aid you against Naples, and trim your palace-homes,
and don your sweetest smiles to meet them. But either
Louis' hands are full of Spanish Successions, or Edicts
of Nantes, or Jesuits, or Madame de Maintenon, or he is
ashamed, at his age, to figure side-by-side with venal,
tempting Messina!—and he does not come!

So you have to put up with Neapolitan tyrants, in
the shape of governors, who are rude and coarse, and
gag and bind you with sharp-cutting cords and chains,

and score your royal form with walls and towers, until your cowardly heart is well-nigh broken.

Last of all in the list of your conquerors comes Don Quixote Garibaldi, with his red shirt, stepping down over the Pelorian mountains, from Calatafimi and Marsala, in the west.

Garibaldi, a grave man, unfit to dally with a Syren such as you, unites you in lawful marriage with Victor Emanuel, first King of United Italy. On the marriage ring is marked—"Liberty." Let us hope you will keep it unbroken!

CHAPTER IV.

Land Pirates.—Fight for Luggage.—Walls of Golden Sunshine.— Furiosa and the Facchini.—Myself a Prisoner.—Gallant Rescue.

In the time of the Renaissance, a strong-minded woman, "such as men honour," was called a virago. Now, unless you feel within you the makings of a virago —take my advice—do not venture alone to Sicily.

Hunger, ignorance, swarthy skins, volubility, savage familiarity, a minimum of clothes, and a maximum of gesture, dirt, noise, and fleas, announce the sunny south, all the world over.

But on arriving at Messina I found all this exaggerated. For a moment I thought Florio's little steamer was boarded by a band of pirates. Over the sides came ragged men, clustering as thick as bees, large-eyed, shock-headed, fierce, casting their brown limbs about, like branches swept by storms.

In an instant we are engaged in a free fight: Furiosa charging valiantly in front, over our boxes (the average is four men to each box), I in the rear, defending the shawls and the bags.

Screams, oaths, threats from the passengers, grappling hands, and menaces, from the pirates!

Not a Guardia pubblica in sight. They never are. They might be "compromised," so prudently retire.

We make a gallant defence, Furiosa and I, but are ignominiously defeated, and behold our luggage, hoisted pell-mell on the shoulders of our invaders, disappear down the side of the steamer.

How every thing in the struggle did not go over into the water, and we after it, I cannot understand. By some miracle, in a wild chorus of yells and howls, I find myself in the same boat with my excited maid and our luggage, in company with two dark grinning boatmen, triumphantly swaying to and fro on their naked feet, as they row us rapidly towards the quay. Arrived before what, in the hurry and the dazzle of the moment, seemed to me walls of golden sunshine, I find a fresh crowd, gesticulating, naked and audacious, stretching out broad arms to receive us. These again fall upon the luggage by right of custom—they are facchini. The pirates offer no resistance. When we left the steamer we belonged to them. Now we are the lawful prey of the land-sharks.

I should mention that the distance from the steamer to the quay, might occupy in time two minutes. The hotel, I learn, is one of the marble palaces, dazzling my eyes across the road.

Now is it that Furiosa merits her name and covers herself with glory.

On the summit of the broad marble steps she stands, a thin diminutive figure, with colourless face and imperceptible hair, midway between two opposing forces—the pirates behind in the boat, the facchini in front, on the steps, swooping down over our two modest little boxes. The pirates roar for pay, leaning over the boat side; the facchini, a dozen hands at least, recruited by some sepia-coloured boys, and a tall classic-nosed woman, with a coloured cloth folded upon her head, raise the boxes in the air, and clamour for pay also. Quite unmoved, Furiosa unclasps the money-bag she wears round her waist, and presents the pirates with fourpence. Shrieks, howls and groans!

"Not a centesimo more," cries Furiosa, shutting up her thin lips and the clasp of the money-bag like a vice; "and as for you," she continues, with the most perfect calm, addressing the dozen facchini who have managed to lade themselves with our two boxes, "I choose two;" here she touches a sort of Ethiop with no hair, and an eager-eyed creature, who looks as if he had not tasted food for a week. "Now *avanti.* Take up those two boxes, and follow me."

This *coup-de-main* carries us on to the quay. I perceive already a good deal of bounce about these ferocious islanders; also an abject surrender to any show of authority, and as I see Furiosa disappear in a pell-mell of sailors, porters and swarthy boys, in the direction of the hotel, I conceive a contempt for Sicilian bravura, that time and experience only strengthen.

Being on the subject, let me note that, arrived in our apartment, I underwent a formal siege on the part of the two facchini. Naturally, as they bore the boxes on their backs into the room, they effected that which is most important in all sieges—an entrance. This advantage they preserved doggedly. To look at, they were two as disgusting facchini as I ever beheld; on their naked feet they took up their position.

Nothing would move them. Furiosa would have died rather than have given them one farthing more than the tariff due for crossing the road. They on their part showed every inclination to starve us out, if they did not get more. And I was so hungry!

I implored Furiosa to give them what they wanted. "No," and she tossed her flaxen curls in derision. "No, Never," she repeated, eyeing the two men with scorn.

I appealed to a fat girl acting as chamber-maid, who blesses me at intervals during the day (*Dio ti benedica*), to a waiter in a suspicious coat and greasy neck-tie. Both made as though they did not hear me. The waiter disappeared. The fat girl whispers into my ear, in a Sicilian brogue I could scarcely understand, affecting to be diligently dusting a looking-glass all the while, "They would follow me at night, and——" here a significant pantomime at the same time cut her phrase and her throat!

"How much do these facchini want, Marie?" (Marie was her real name, Furiosa a nickname.) The facchini had never ceased a jabber of *patois*. They displayed their brawny arms, thrust forward their naked feet, shook their black rags, pointed to their open mouths like young birds gaping for food, then to the modest boxes, still corded and travel-stained, lying helpless on the floor.

"Four francs," screamed Furiosa, in her strongest German accent; "four francs for crossing the road."

"In your interests, Madame, I cannot give it. Madame has not travelled in Sicily. If you once let yourself be *mangiata* (eaten) one tells another, and you will spend a fortune."

"But, Marie, we must get rid of these men. We must dine." At this point the Ethiop facchino resolutely seated himself on one of the boxes, and fumbled in his pocket for his pipe.

"Look here," cried Furiosa, squaring herself before him; "here are two francs, double what you have a right to—*Bestia!*" (This word introduced as a *fioritura*, or agreeable figure of speech, very effective.) "If you do not clear out instantly, I will go to the Questura."

Before she had done speaking, both the facchini were out of the room, we had locked the door, and were uncording our boxes, quicker than I can write.

CHAPTER V.

Our Hotels.—Distracting Prospects.—The Cry of the Beggars.— Teutons at the Table d'hôte.—Good Wine.

I HAVE said that our hotel forms one of that line of dazzling palaces seen from the straits. The grand simplicity of this sea façade stamps Messina as a great capital before you master a single detail. Some columns divide the lofty windows, and a sculptured cornice supports the upper floor. The Palazzetta, as it is called, has quite a history. Overthrown by the great earthquake of 1783, it was rebuilt in 1848. In many parts it has not been carried up to its original height, hence a slight architectural incongruity.

The ground floors are chiefly shops, or rather holes, generally not paved, incredibly foul and stinking, where a low lazzarone population cluster. Besides the Hotel Vittoria along the line, are the Palazzo della Città, the Custom house, health office, banks, cafés, and restaurants —palaces alike, and alike majestic.

The Vittoria, the only tolerable hotel in Messina, and

that is not saying much—is entered from the rear,
through one of the nineteen side streets which cut the
Palazzetta, under sculptured archways.

And how grandly do these marble barriers frame
the view! On one side, the noble harbour, teeming with
life and colour; the sickle curve (Zancle) of the breast-
work of San Ranieri, as green as fresh grass can make
it (Orion, who formed it, being among the stars, it has a
Saint now as Patron); the blue, uneasy straits boiling
and bubbling towards Cape Faro, the broad Calabrian
mountains catching the passing colours of the clouds,
and Reggio like a white jewel shining at their base.

But to return to our hotel. I keep forgetting everything but the view, I cannot keep my eyes off it! There
are but two stories—the first and the third; the second
is quite unattached, a private apartment in fact, into which
penetrating by mistake, I frightened an old lady in bed
almost into fits.

Between these two stories the household of the hotel
slide up and down, holding perilously by the banisters.
A chamber-maid, with a cock in her eye, suggesting
language, the harum-scarum girl, she who blesses me,
and chatters in a *patois* quite incomprehensible; a scared
waiter, with hair on end, always flying, as under the influence of a propelling wind; and a fat man, the *Generalis-
simo*, or *maître d'hôtel*, who tells me when I hurry him,
"That I may eat my food raw if I like, it is all the
same to him; only, if *it is to be cooked*, I must wait!"

To these, add hangers-on, boatmen, vetturini, facchini,
boxes, barrels, casks, old carriages, horses, mules, carts,
and omnibuses—all crammed together down in the
cortile, or under arches—and *Beggars!*

Ah! the beggars! I have not been in Sicily half an
hour before I am brought to a personal understanding

of this curse. "Give, give!" say indescribable crispa-
tions of claw-like fingers (you must go there to understand it). "Give, give!" from fever-stricken wretches
clustering in festering corners. "Give, give!" from the
old—and oh! how horrible in old age!—How reeking!
How offensive! "Give, give!" from halt, and maim, and
blind, motionless by reason of their infirmities, but all
the readier to clutch, and reach, and sign—pointing to
sightless eyes and withered limbs. "Give!" from young
children, beady-eyed, yellow-skinned, and bony children,
who have never been young, and are now old and
stricken in want and vice. "Give!" from despairing
mothers, grasping infants so frail and white, one expects
to see the spark of life die out then and there while one
is looking on. "Give!"—But I have done. It is too
horrible!

Broadly speaking, there is no charity in Sicily. Even
at Palermo, the capital, they who should know tell me
the sick are constantly brought in by their friends to the
hospital in carts, and sent back again, twenty or thirty
miles distant, jolted over mountain roads, to die, because
there is no room for them. Yet, no Prince, or Duke, or
Baron—and there are so many at Palermo and elsewhere
—proposes to enlarge the hospital, to build others, or to
do anything whatever!

At dinner we are thirty, all men except myself, and
all Germans. The overwhelming Teutonic element in
Sicily must have come in as long ago as the Hohenstaufen marriage of Norman Constance with the son of
Barbarossa, and never since gone out.

We gaze at each other through pyramids of mandarin
oranges, dates, roses, figs, and cactus-fruit. Germans
they are certainly, and bagmen mostly, I believe; fat
and oily, twanging out their "*R*'s" and "*Z*'s" emphatically.

3*

Each man wears a napkin tucked under his capacious
chin, like an overgrown baby, and is ravenous for his
food.

The individual opposite me sent his plate away before touching it, because, as he explains to the company
generally, "he requires more soup to start with." Another
forcibly retains his from the hands of the waiter because
there is still enough left to swear by. My right-hand
neighbour barricades himself with a rampart of bread
and butter, which he consumes diligently between the
courses. Some solemnly remonstrate with the waiters as
to supposed slights in the order of handing the dishes;
others crack jokes at them over their shoulders—an in-
discretion, I am bound to say, the Sicilians meet with
silence.

All fall upon the fish—friends passing the word
round as to the goodness of the sauce. (We had first
been stuffed with salame and maccaroni, to clog the
edge of healthy appetite.)

The gravity of everyone, the importance, as of a
religious function, is delightful. Eager eyes follow the
waiters, as the dispensers of good things; frowns for the
offer of a fowl leg or the last cut of a fillet; smiles, and
even exclamations of delight, at the chicken's wing.
One stern-faced old Teuton dissects his quail with an
eye-glass; another gloats over his glass of Veuve Cliquot
with his spectacles. My friend of the bread and butter
—a traveller, as he informs me, in Chinese Tartary, and
who has seen the Great Wall, and knows Syria and
India like his home—is hurt and offended at the sweet
dish (*dolce*), a kind of cake, which he qualifies, reproachfully, as "dry." In return, I suggest "Marsala," a
hint he joyfully accepts, shouts for the dish again (the
bottle is beside him), and devours it on the spot.

I cannot say much for the cuisine, nor for the waiting; but the wine is first-rate. A bad dinner, often no dinner at all—not even eggs—is frequently the fate of the traveller in Sicily; but the vilest, filthiest village invariably offers you a god-like vintage.

Each city has its wine as well as its history. Grecian Syracuse is great in sweet wines; Lilybœum (Marsala) tells its own tale; Girgenti has an excellent red wine; and so on.

At our table-d'hôte, a light Marsala is included in the dinner at four francs. Marsala is the "vin ordinaire" of Sicily. Why it should give the generic name to all white wines I cannot say, for the white grape is cultivated all over the island.

CHAPTER VI.

An Outburst.—Street Pictures.—Amazing Medley.—Gate of the Promised Land.

AH! the South, it is here! What a swing, and freedom in the life! What busy swarming streets! What laughing, chattering, ogling, intriguing! Naples is nothing to it! More like a scene from "Gil Blas," or the "Barber of Seville," than a flesh and blood town.

These heavy-browed thin-faced men, intense-eyed, dark, slow in movement, and dignified in carriage—are Spanish, not Italian.

The low-storied houses (even in the Corso they are low) have in every window a suggestive balcony, projecting over the street on carved corbels, just the height for Susanna to twirl her fan at Figaro, and for Rosina to

coquette with Count Almaviva, and show herself gracious
as to the "Serenade."

The veil, or shawl thrown over the women's head,
not of choice point indeed, but of knitted worsted, is
Spanish too; also, the broad-hatted priests, so sleek and
indecorous, lingering in the street-corners with dark-eyed
beauties (positively I am told the priests' morals are
shocking, but as men they are very picturesque); the
writing-tables set up under archways, or beside a crowded
thoroughfare, at the risk of being whisked bodily off by
some passing cart-wheel; an old scribe seated at one,
his pen touching his nose, his head on one side to match
his perpendiculars, beside him a sad-faced matron, her
head concealed by a shawl, pouring words into his ear,
which he slowly engrosses. A young man is the writer
at the next table close by—the tables generally work in
pairs; I have seen as many as eight pairs, side by side,
in a convenient portico, all fully occupied—a Contadina
giving out the subject of her letter, in a loud discordant
voice, which the young man writes down glibly, without
aid from his nose.

The lovely tropical shrubs and flowers in the squares,
topsy-turvying the seasons (I do not know the name of
half of them, but they send me wild with joy), the
abundant fountains, second only to those of Rome; the
swagger of the handsome Messinese youths, audacious
and picturesque under their mountains; the water-carriers
with classic urns and vases poised on one shoulder like
statues; the ragged idlers, the shopmen, even the younger
beggars, tripping along as if they loved their life under
that glowing vault of heaven; the brilliant market-stalls;
the cries of street-sellers, the shouts of boatmen, the
crash of merchandise, the architectural vistas, blazing

mountains on one side and the blueness of the straits on the other. What a scene!

The painted carts rattle by every instant. The cart, a box upon very high wheels, coloured all over in fresco —a crucifixion on the plash-board, Romulus and Remus on the sides, a ballet girl cutting capers behind, and the wheels running over with angels and cherubim, is the glory of the Sicilian: he will spend half his income to adorn it. The harness, red velvet set in filagree and brass, clinking with bells, and pyramids, and turrets, absolutely obliterating the pretty well-cared-for Sicilian cob, which draws the shafts.

The vivid contrasts of colour—black and yellow, red and blue, green and crimson, dancing along the streets, a remnant of the East, and of the Arab conquest. The glorious sun, oppressive and dazzling, at midday (we are within two days of November); the wondrous mountains looking over into the streets; the laughing Marina, three miles long; the crowd of street passengers; the hurrying to and fro on the quays; the shrill cries of the drivers, the roar of droves of buffaloes; the creaking of the ox-waggons and mule carts (sometimes with the mule, a cow is placed on the off side of the pole, quite sympathetic); the hollow roll of drays, trolleys and vans, piled with vegetables, salt-fish, oil-barrels, sulphur cut into squares, and oranges and almonds; the bewildering light upon the pavement and the walls radiating back like fire; the roar at the port, made up of oaths, engine whistles, and hissing steamers sweeping in and out of the harbour, fleets of fishing-boats, the crews singing choruses as they pass the bar by San Salvador, merchant ships unlading timber and coal.

The dusky groups of Phrygian-capped sailors, hanging about on marble stairs, or bearing incredible burdens on their backs, dancing, quarrelling, lounging, eating, smoking. A wooden theatre, with two day representations of "Pulcinello," announced by a trumpet, an harmonium, and a cow-horn; detachments of Bersaglieri tramping along the thoroughfare, their black cock's plumes waving behind their glazed hats, like storm-clouds; how can I paint it?

Nothing I have seen in Europe can compare with the Marina of Messina. It is longer, more elegant, and more architectural than the Chiaia at Naples; lustier, healthier, rougher, and more pictorial than the mincing refinements of the "Promenade" at Nice, toned down to English fastidiousness; larger, nobler, more motley than the quays at Marseilles; and gayer, friendlier, vaster, than that melancholy sea-walk at Palermo, with its rows of skeleton trees, scathed by innumerable tempests.

Yet Messina is but the gate of the promised land, the threshold, as it were, of bliss!

CHAPTER VII.

Cape Pelorus.—Poseidon, King of Sicily.—"Brothers, Ride Hard!" —Paradise and Peace.—Arrived at Faro.—The Little Horse.

A LOVELY morning tinting everything with the pure rainbow colours of Sicily!

Before I visit anything in Messina, I must drive out to Faro. Ever since I came it sends me sunny greetings across the straits. What spot in all Sicily is more historical than Faro? History and mythology positively weigh it down.

Out of a numerous stand on the Corso I select a little Victoria (a Milord they call it here) with a swift

pony and a civil driver, who agrees to take me to Faro
and back, a good fourteen miles, for ten francs.

How we dashed down the broad Marina, by the
characteristic palaces, and under the shadow of those
nineteen archways that break the façades into nineteen
streets, each with its background of mountains—on to
the great fountain of Neptune, with its balustraded terrace, making a noble curve over the water. (Great Poseidon is the real king of Sicily, whoever nominally
governs.)

Here he is very imposing, sea-weedy and dripping;
grasping his trident apparently to chastise Scylla and
Charybdis bound at his feet. Out at the same pace by
the gate of Campo Basso, and so on, to the wide Corniche
road bordering the dazzling straits.

To talk of the beauty of any other Corniche road
besides this one running from Faro to Catania, is an ab-
surdity. The glory of it is matchless.

The lower line of hills is a paradise of frescoed villas,
coloured pavilions, green vine pergolas, casinos, and
marble terraces, set in glistening groves. The soft sandy
beach is sprinkled with dwarf palms, tamarisk and orange
trees; melons, and parti-coloured gourds sprawl like
aquatic monsters on the red earth, and the pink cactus
fruit hangs flower-like on bristly spikes.

Now we dash down into the dip of a fiumara.

What is that? I hear a voice asking.

A fiumara in summer is a dried up water-course
paved for the convenience of the public, a *cosa di Sicilia*,
of which you will have enough as you progress on your
travels. When rain pours and torrents dash from mountain tops every five minutes, you cannot expect a bridge.
Such an idea is utterly preposterous; besides, in bad
weather you can pass neither road, nor bridge, nor rail.

Poseidon is not king of Sicily for nothing. Roads in his
island are constructed for fine weather; in bad weather
you must stay at home. Above all, don't complain. You
are in a mediæval country and must submit.

A fiumara, or paved water-course, is the legitimate
outlet of a gorge to the sea-shore, ripping up, as it were,
scenes of unknown and unutterable beauty. If the fiumara
were not there, you could not enjoy these peeps into
ideal regions! Be thankful, therefore, and, I repeat, do
not complain.

The church and convent of San Salvadore dei Greci,
a huge modern building, where Charles III. took up his
residence, as Charles V. did at Yuste, is the next object.

But San Salvadore has a higher interest than Spanish
kings. On this spot Norman Roger raised a votive chapel.
Galloping in the early morning from Faro, with his little
band of knights and squires, to surprise the Saracen
hosts, Roger turns his eyes upon this cape of land, so
conspicuous from the road, and beholds the bodies of
twelve Christians crucified on twelve tall poles.

"By St. Michael," cries Roger, reddening with fury
at the sight, "these martyrs shall be avenged! If I take
Messina, as I know I shall, I vow to build a shrine to
their memory. And now, brothers all, ride hard for
Messina; we must catch these Moorish infidels before
they are awake."

The Norman Rollos, and Drogos, and Williams, galloping beside him, echo his words. There is no time
to tarry and bury these twelve Christians then. They
are riding towards Messina for life and death; riding on
golden sands, among acanthus and myrtles, and over
carpets of passiaflora, to raise no echoes. With Roger
are two hundred and seventy armed men. They are to
surprise a walled and fortified city, manned by skilful

Saracens. It is done, and within a year a Gothic Saracenic chapel looks out over the straits.

No sooner did the Normans conquer Sicily, than an
architectural mania seized them: they built churches,
castles, bridges and towers without end. As they came
from the mainland a mere handful of men, never at any
time numbering an army except with aid of mercenaries,
and wholly without artificers and engineers, they gladly
availed themselves of the facile-handed Saracens, who
accept fate, and their new masters, as best they can. Hence
the strange medley of Saracenic-Gothic architecture one
sees constantly in Sicily. Saracenic in all, but Gothic
uses; the outline Moorish, the interior Christian.

Now I am driving on a well-kept road, free from the
obstructive suburbs. The scent of nespole and mimosa
is in the air; and palmettos and cacti, prickly pears, and
aloes, breaking out everywhere. A hill covered with
prickly pear and cactus, thick enough and tall enough
to conceal and overshadow houses, is a weird sight; the
bristly, water-padded leaves and twisted branches flinging themselves about, as if in agony.

Village succeeds village along the yellow strand;
always of stone, a little architectural and Barocco, and
with balconied windows, however low and small. One
village is called "Paradise," another "Peace."

In Paradise a mother is beating a half-naked child,
and a ragged boy, sitting beside a goat, tethered on a
bank of grass, is sobbing bitterly.

The squalid walls of Peace resound to a dog-fight,
extemporized within a ruined hovel. Some kind of
canine *mêlée* is going on, too, outside; two white mastiffs
against three terriers, tearing at each other's throats.

The only happy people are the fishermen, as brown
and sepia-coloured as their boats, drawn up high and

dry upon the strand, under tents of fishing-nets stretched out to dry.

To-day it is blowing too hard to venture out. A warm, moist sirocco has churned up the straits into a kind of fury; huge rollers break upon the beach, and, breaking, boom like a cannon among the rocks.

Oh that I could paint the colours of the shadows and the wild sea mist! One moment land and water all veiled, the next, a flood of white light calling up every detail into fields of brightness; a point of red rock, the mossy greenness of a mountain-side, the foaming trough of a blue wave, a glistening sail, the point of a cape, or a wall, mapped out for an instant, then gone for ever — all to the accompaniment of the cheery tinkling of the little horse's bells, his pattering hoofs marking a sympathetic rhythm.

As I advance nearer the point of Faro, the bowery heights, under which I have hitherto driven, shade off into low, sandy hillocks, running out sea-ward towards Cape Pelorus. By-and-bye the lighthouse at Faro and the straits themselves suddenly vanish, and give place to a succession of ugly salt lakes (Platani) through which runs a high causeway.

The sirocco blows fiercer than before; the clouds gather darker; the sun grows pale. The crown of the day is past; its glories are faded. My spirits sink with the sunlight.

The little horse, too, feels the evil influence. His head droops. He slackens his pace. Alas! He trips! Oh! how the driver lashes him, and what Sicilian oaths he launches at him! How his little legs break into a wild gallop to make up for his fault, and how we tear along on the dangerous causeway!

At the village of Faro, a collection of dirty hovels

half-buried in sand-hills, I am invited by the driver to descend. The brave little horse is fairly winded. His sides are dripping, and he is panting for bare life. A generous little beast, he needs no lashing of sharp whips to make him do his best.

"I always do my best," says his keen, obedient eye, turned reproachfully on his driver. "Will no one understand me?" (The driver is making a new thong to his whip, with which to punish him.)

If the little horse could understand me, I would explain to him that we are all victims of an adverse fate, four-footed creatures and otherwise.

It seems to me, I also have been cruelly beaten in my time, when I did not deserve it.

My heart bleeds for you, unhappy little horse, but I cannot aid you, nor can I even remonstrate. Sicilian drivers are very brutal. I am alone, and perhaps the new thong might be tried on my back instead of yours; so I say nothing!

CHAPTER VIII.

Scylla and Charybdis.—Legend *versus* Reality.—The Strong Current.
—Hannibal and his Pilot.—Orion's Temple.—Hercules crosses
from Rhegium.—Dædalus.—Ulysses and Æneas Pass.

I AM standing due east, on the sandy point of a sandy shore, under the Tower of Faro—a machicolated round tower and lighthouse above; a fortress below. From Messina, Faro appears rising from the waves; here I find it upon a long, low bank, stretching out into the middle of the straits.

On the opposite shore I see the rock of Scylla, two

miles across, backed by the bare face of tawny Calabrian mountains. Homer says the rock of Scylla is "a peak of boundless height, ever hidden in dense clouds, the smooth, polished sides inaccessible to man." "High up, beyond flight of arrow, opens the awful cave, out of which Scylla, with six hideous heads, barks from six dire mouths with triple rows of teeth; serpent-necked; ready to seize six sailors at a gulp." That Scylla is such a monster is the work of spiteful Circe.

Now, in reality, Scylla is a low, dark cliff, overhanging the sea, crowned by a mediæval castle, a gay little town clustering round its base, and giving a title to Prince Scilla of Naples; a winding road, quite friendly and natural, leading up to it from the beach.

The famous caves—for there are many—are low down on the face of the rock. I can see the dark apertures, like hollow galleries, level with the waves, into which they thunder with terrific howls.

Beyond, on a beautiful sea-line, marked by white breakers, come town after town, fitfully revealed in the sirocco mist—Bagnara, Seminara, Palmi, Gioia, with its spacious gulf; and Nicotera, bathing on the water's edge; until all melt into sea and cloud at the extremity of Cape Vaticano.

Between Cape Vaticano and Cape Pelorus (Faro), at the opening of the straits, I ought to see the outline of the Lipari Islands, and the volcano of Stromboli, but I do not.

Already, at my back, I hear the implacable roar of Charybdis, circling round upon low sunken reefs. At the sandy edge of the "Platani" I can see the vortex of the blue water, and the white spray flung upwards, as of a baffled element turned to bay.

"Three times a day Charybdis swallows up the dark

billows, and three times spouts them out," says Vergil, in the "Æneid." Once within the sea-nymph's grasp, not Neptune himself could save a vessel!

To the undecked triremes of the Greeks, Locrians, and Rhegians, Charybdis must have been a most real danger. "Even a seventy-four-gun ship," says Admiral Smith, "may be whirled round in its vortex." "Better is it" (I am again quoting "Vergil"), "with delay, to coast round the extremities of Sicilian Pachynus (Cape Passaro, under Etna), than once to behold the misshapen Scylla and the green sea-dogs of Charybdis!"

The real secret of these classic horrors is the extraordinary force of the many contrary currents running through the straits. It causes one of the most violent whirlpools in the world.

The colours of the ocean, as I stand on Faro, are marvellous. Blue of every tint, from cobalt to azure, running into reds and browns, buff, cream, and yellow— sheets of foam, curtained by the wind, great fields of whiteness, ridges of sea-green walls, bright patches, mirror-like reflecting scurrying clouds!

A Norwegian barque comes riding on, every sail set to the wind. A pilot puts off from Faro to steer her down the straits, just as the pilot in Homer put off to bring Ulysses in, or the unlucky Pelorus, to guide Hannibal's fleet towards Africa. Do you know the tale?

Scipio's successes in Africa calling Hannibal home, he found himself carried out of his sea-track to the entrance of these straits. Seeing the double line of mountains melting together before him, he became alarmed.

"Where am I?" he asked the pilot. (Hannibal is smarting under the loss of some of his veteran troops, and is in no humour to be trifled with.) "Where is the passage? What is the name of those mountains rising before me?"

The pilot answers, "The mountains are in the island of Sicania."

This does not satisfy Hannibal.

"Is it a lake? Am I land-locked—betrayed—sold to Rome?"

Before the pilot can explain, he is beheaded. Then, as the vessel sails on, the mountains divide themselves right and left, the straits are visible, and all is clear.

Hannibal did not understand the western formation of Sicily, nor its nearness to the mainland. The passage of troops between Africa and Italy, and the great naval battles, were all on the eastern and southern side. The Straits of Pelorus had an evil name, as haunted by savage Nereids, roaring sea-dogs, and strife of Poseidon's stormy brood. Nothing would tempt the ancients (always timid sailors) to take that course. Not only the Carthaginian fleets, during the Punic wars, avoided this passage, but even the Romans, when they came to conquer Sicily, never trusted themselves there. Except Messina and Naxos, no Greek cities lay within their narrow limits; nor did these, in importance, compare to Syracuse, Catania, or Acragas.

As I gaze, the lighthouse of Faro fades out, and in its stead a stately temple rises* on a palmetto-covered steep, well dyked with solid walls. A place half sea, half land, where mariners may land and offer sacrifice to Neptune.

The peristyle and portico stand on a lofty stylobate, the cella is rich within, and long lines of granite pillars

---

* Hesiod and Diodorus mention a temple at Faro dedicated by Orion to Neptune.

rise to meet the skies. Earth never bore a nobler pile nor one more suited to a god.

Between sea and sky it stands, firm on a narrow neck of sand, yet poised, as it were, on air.

Vainly does Thetis dash and fling her strong arms around it; and Boreas with white wings and streaming hair rage and roar, bringing inclement blasts from the hyperborean north; and Æolus, king of storms and winds, howl and menace around its lines; for within, upraised on a crystal altar, begirt with smooth-necked shells, sea-weed, and coral, sits the god, looking out eastward towards the morning sun.

Around the temple stretch the wide dykes strong as the walls. No human hands gathered the stones that form them, nor fashioned the links that bind them together so firmly. We must scale the skies to find the architect. It is Neptune's son, the shaggy giant, the wondrous hunter—Orion.

Next to Orion, in the mystic procession of the past, comes Hercules; he swims across the straits from Rhegium, holding on by the horn of his strongest ox, and lands under Orion's temple.

There, as he takes his repose, Charybdis, a Sicilian sea-nymph who with Fauns, Centaurs, and Satyrs, haunts the reedy marshes near the salt lakes, dashes down, and, aided by her friends, steals one of the sacred steers.

For this crime Jupiter changes her into a rock, doomed ever to watch the rising of the tide as she watched Hercules. As a rock she howls and cries, lamenting her hard fate. The waves wash over her from ebb to flow.

Dædalus comes next, a cunning engineer flying from Crete, with a second pair of wings, like those he gave to his son Icarus. Taking a humbler course nearer the earth, Apollo's wrath is not kindled against him, and he arrives safely on Cape Pelorus, from whence he wings his way to Eryx.

From the Ægean Sea, Minos, the Cretan King, the shadowy judge of souls, arrives at Faro in hot pursuit of Dædalus. The Phenicians, we know, had mercantile relations with the Sikels.

Vague, all this, and shadowy, as the passing sea-mist sweeping over waves, outlines of pale, nascent forms that glide by first in the dim procession I am tracing through all time.

With Ulysses as a navigator, I feel on a certain base of solid history. It is so easy to call his venerable figure up and trace his wanderings on the modern map.

Homer makes the most of Ulysses' perils in the straits, getting two adventures out of them, much in defiance of geography. But neither Homer nor his audience knew much of the three-cornered Trinacria but as a vague legend.

Ulysses, towards the end of his career, enters the straits at Faro; the first time unscathed, with his full ship's company, thanks to the enchantress Circe.

She sitting in Colchis, wrapped in her many-coloured robe, an Eastern turban on her head, and dogs and swine around her, metamorphized from men, instructs him. Ulysses is neither to give ear to the Syrens' singing on the Salernian Seas, nor fall into Scylla's jaws, nor be ingulfed by whirling Charybdis.

Ulysses does not even see Scylla, her head is wrapped in clouds, Charybdis is silent, and all goes well.

Not so the second time.

Then as a waif he tosses through the straits, bound to a drifting raft, sucked down by the spiteful Nereid, and only escapes death by clinging, bat-like, to the branches of a wild fig-tree, until the reflux of the waters disgorges the raft, and he drops deftly into it.

(It is worthy of remark, that Admiral Smith, in speaking of Charybdis, verifies the truth of this myth in his account of the tide, which runs six hours each way in the straits, an interval of from fifty to sixty minutes occurring between the changes.)

So Ulysses floats on his raft to an unknown island where Calypso harbours him. Others say he landed at Mylæ (Milazzo), and to this day they show you a hole in a granite rock, and tell you that Ulysses dug it out.

From Ulysses to Æneas is an easy stride. Æneas passes Cape Pelorus and Father Anchises with him. But he tarries not. Æneas is bound to the mythologic coast beyond Aci, where the Cyclops dwell, and thence to the Eastern shores at Eryx, where he is to found a temple in honour of his mother Venus.

CHAPTER IX.

The Normans.—How they Spread.—Raymond at Aversa.—Bras de Fer and General George Maniace.—Robert Guiscard, the Great Count.—"Take All You See."—Roger beholds Messina across the Strait.—Messina's Won.

IF all the romance of Cervantes and Ariosto, the daring of Cortez, the Black Prince, and Napoleon, the courage of young David, the endurance of Xenophon, the parsimony of Crassus, the appropriating appetites of Verres, and the wisdom of Cato, were fused into a whole, the result would be the Norman knight as we behold him about the year of grace 1040.

At Faro, he stares me in the face wherever I turn.

4*

The Norman is as much a part and parcel of Cape Pelorus, as Orion or Hercules.

The name of Norman is first heard of in Southern Italy about the year 1003.

A certain hesitation and dimness clouds the precise reason of their first appearance. Some landed on their way home from pilgrimages or in the fulfilment of a vow to the Holy Shrine. Later occurred the Crusades. They came by twos and threes, now here, now there, mere individuals; only recalled to memory afterwards as the pioneers of that amazing band destined to achieve such conquests.

The first solid basis the Normans attain in Italy is when the Prince of Capua confers on them the township of Aversa, now a railway station on the Neapolitan line. Aversa, built by the Normans, is their starting-point in Southern Italy. To this gift the Prince of Capua was induced by self-interest or generosity to add a good slice of his newly-acquired territory of Monte Cassino, which the swords of the Normans had valiantly helped him to win.

The Duke of Naples not to be outdone by his neighbour prince, went further, and gave his daughter in marriage to the Norman leader Raymond, creating him titular "Count of Aversa."

No sooner did this great news reach the north than scores of needy Northmen made their appearance, intending also "to match with the daughters of kings."

At Aversa the Normans live a free, marauding life— the life of soldiers acknowledging only military rule. There were two bands, or regiments, in Aversa—the *Veterans,* who had themselves come from Normandy, and the *Young Men*, ready to tempt fortune on every battle-field.

Thus the Normans continue for nearly twenty years

comparatively unknown, until the second regiment of *Young Men* elect for their leader William, son of Tancred de Hauteville.

It was to this William, surnamed "Bras de Fer," General George Maniace, commanding for the Emperor of Constantinople in Southern Italy, addresses himself to join in his expedition against the Saracens in Sicily, the terms to be half the booty and half the towns. (Mark the entrance of General George upon the historic scene! Although generally unknown I shall have much to say of him before I end.)

The offer is accepted.

Seeing that the young de Hautevilles had not won for themselves as yet a separate kingdom, nor married a Lombard Princess, as such handsome youths naturally expected to do, after the example of Raymond, how can they do better?

No portent, comet, or meteor is recorded as marking the birth of the De Hautevilles—yet neither the Scipios, the Camilli, nor the African race of Barca came into the world more perfect warriors.

At home, they passed their boyhood in sailing within the bounds of that barren coast under Coutance and St. Michael's Mount, in hunting, and in tilting. The Christianity of monks formed their creed; the code of camps, their morals.

What induced these warlike lads to select Italy as their apprentice-ground, no record tells.

The three eldest sons of Tancred—Humphrey, William, and Drogo—were already fighting in Puglia when William accepted General George Maniace's offer.

Bravest among the brave, courteous, sagacious, flanked on the battle-field by his two valiant brothers (counts also and captains riding beside him) who can resist William, Bras de Fer?

General George is successful in his Sicilian expedition, but General George, like many others, ignores the means which made him so. No booty is awarded to the youthful Normans, nor is a single Sicilian town placed in their hands.

William and his brothers retire to Italy, silent, but indignant. Like wise young men they bide their time, and that time comes speedily.

More de Hautevilles come riding through Europe from Normandy—younger sons of Tancred by his second wife, Fredigonda; Robert, *surnamed Guiscard*, the Cunning, and *Roger, "the Great Count."*

Robert Guiscard, with a mere handful of men, spared to him from Melfi by Brother Drogo, gravely sets about conquering the kingdom of the two Calabrias. He cuts down timber, chestnut and oak, from the forest of La Stela, in the Calabrian mountains over Scylla, and erects a rough hill-fort opposite the sea, which he christens *Rocca San Martino.*

Robert tells the young knights, his followers, "To take all they see."

Daring leader and crafty statesman as he came to be, Robert is an ingrained robber.

. He steals cattle, sacks towns, and captures rich proprietors for ransom in the most approved style of brigandage.

What else can a young De Hauteville do, alone in Calabria?

The last of the twelve sons of Tancred de Hauteville is Roger. He arrives in Italy about A.D. 1056, just twenty-three years after his elder brother William.

Happy for Roger that the Norman rule is already

established. He could never be a robber, like the rest. Tall and broad-shouldered, and powerful as a young David, his long flaxen curls hang down upon his Damascene corselet, and a beaming pair of eyes look out from under the brim of his circular helmet, worn low on the neck, and shaded by a plume of crimson feathers.

With an easy stride he mounts his war-horse, of which nothing is seen but the head and tail for the encasing armour, his glittering battle-axe lies beside the saddle-bow, his lance is in his hand; altogether a splendid youth, a very Lohengrin, or God-born knight.

No De Hauteville can compare with Roger. Easy of access, eloquent in speech, facile, gay, ambitious, as is the fashion of his house, greedy of victory, and turbulent for action, liberal, humane, without Robert's sordid vices, Roger the Great Count, as he came to be called, stands out a grand figure in the procession at Faro, challenging even Hercules himself.

How Roger came here was in this wise.

No sooner had he reached the city of Melfi, than, like brother Robert before him, he was sent down to fight in Calabria with seventy other knights. These De Hauteville brethren can no more rest side by side than young lions in the same den. Each must have a kingdom to stretch himself in; if he does not find it ready made he must conquer it for himself.

Roger's orders are:—to complete Robert Guiscard's conquests in the south, to annihilate all enemies, be they Byzantine or Saracen, to plant the Norman flag on every peak and tower, and to encamp upon the capes and promontories of the shore.

Capo delle Armi, between Cape Spartivento and Reggio, is Roger's goal.

Hither he drives his knights before him, much in the same fashion as Hercules drove the cattle of Geryon. The Norman flag waves from the nearest height.

Before his young eyes expands that sun-lit gulf towards Catania, just as I saw it in the early morning. His outstretched hand seems to touch the fair Sicilian shore and Etna's snowy dome, glorious in changing hues. Those long lines of serried mountains, and those entrancing little bays and smiling capes, wave him a welcome!

Nothing but the straits—a span, a ditch—between Roger and a new kingdom; and he just arrived from pale, dull Normandy, with mists and clouds, damp woods, and barren downs, and all the economies of his father's house and narrow shifts of country life, full in his memory.

Conceive the turmoil of his ardent soul, gazing upon the island of the gods!

Then came that tempting offer from treacherous Messina. Across the straits, three men sail secretly to meet Roger at Reggio, while the luxurious Saracens, their masters, suspecting nothing of, and caring less for, Norman Roberts and Rogers, if they can but enjoy their parks and gardens, streams and flowers, singing-birds, dancing-girls, and sultanas—are shut up in their harems, keeping the feast of Ramazan.

"If Roger will only come," the three men say, "Messina shall be his."

Could any young hero, thirsting for conquest, desire more?

That Roger did not dash across the straits, and charge into Messina then and there, without waiting for brother Robert, now Duke of Apulia and Calabria, says much for his loyalty and prudence.

With that enchanting city opposite, dallying in the
sunshine, how he longed to attempt the enterprise!

The months of March and April pass by expecting
Robert, busy with Pope and Kaiser, and great designs
of a southern empire, to bind the West and Byzantium
together.

Meanwhile, the Saracens at Messina, seeing that the
Normans tarry so long at Reggio, grow suspicious, col-
lect their ships, and anchor off the coast to observe the
strangers.

Little by little it seems to Roger's ardent soul that
the prize is slipping from his grasp. He will seize it
while he may; alone, without waiting for Robert.

He chooses a little band from among the knights
who are with him at Reggio, leaves the remainder and
the small fleet under the care of his brother Godfrey,
and rides down the coast to Scylla.

He arrives at break of day; the weather is fair, the
passage smooth; neither of the spiteful nymphs Scylla
nor Charybdis stirring; the fishermen's boats still drawn
up high and dry upon the sand, under the jutting rock
bearing the mediæval castle. The boats he seizes, and
embarks with his followers. There is no room for the
horses, so they drag them after them by the bridle,
through the waves.

Midway across, Roger hears the cocks crow on Faro,
and his heart is light, for the cock-crow is the omen of
possession!

Silently he lands on this long Faro point, where the
lighthouse stands, he and his men and horses. The first
streaks of daylight are low upon the horizon, the rosy
tints of morning touch the waves, harbingers of a new
day—a day of victory.

Who can paint Roger's joy? He dare not speak, neither he nor his companions. Saracens may be abroad, hear them, see them, and surprise them!

Under the cover of those sandy hills that overhang the shore, and with the deep shadow of Monti Denna-mare and Scuderi upon them, their feet upon leaves and sea-weed to deaden all sound, they saddle their horses, and ride forth upon the flowing river to Messina.

He is safe! Robert may win the world, form empires in the East and West, sack Rome, browbeat France, invade his Norman cousins in England—what matter?

Roger asks no other portion than Sicily!

Messina surprised, submits without a struggle, as is her wont.

The Saracens, struck with a sudden panic, fly; some to their galleys in the sickle harbour; others to the heights behind the city; or along the shore; into the forests; on the mountain-tops—anywhere, from the Normans!

Like a young god, Roger has come and conquered. The keys of Messina are sent to Robert, and he is invited to come across and take possession; which he does.

CHAPTER X.

How they live in Messina.—The Cathedral.—Bullying a Priest.—
Packed for the Next World.—The Virgin's Letter.

THE earthquakes have left nothing standing in Messina but the cathedral. How this has escaped is marvellous. There are no ancient palaces, nor churches, nor monuments. A long list of names looks imposing in a guide book, but "there is nothing in it," as Lord Dundreary says. All the churches seem to have risen simultaneously, like Aladdin's palace, in one night, and that night, the dreariest and most commonplace period of architecture.

The gods have done their best for Messina. No city can appropriate everything. As long as mountain and sea, sun and sky hold together, she will be absolutely beautiful. There is an atmosphere of loveliness one can recognize in a city, as in a woman. Messina has it. She is affable, too, and civilized beyond any other spot in the island. Her commerce and her shipping make her cosmopolitan.

Messina has no amor patria. She does not hate, and rob, kidnap and stab foreigners, who would spend their wealth within her walls. On the contrary, she caresses and encourages them. Very different in this to Palermo, where mercantile settlers are certain to be driven out by terror.

This is amor patria! Sicily for the Sicilians; on the same principle as "Ireland for the Irish," both starving, and both too idle or too proud to work.

"Amor patria," leads Sicily to many strange deeds, best omitted. The Mafia, for instance, and ransoms for human life. At Messina there is no Mafia. It is contrary to the genius of the place. Public security is on a par with any Northern Italian city.

The Messinese are courteous and friendly. "God be with you," is the popular salutation. You see no beetle-browed threatening villains, picturesque in stinking rags; brigands in all but the power to rob and murder. The beggars are noisy and numerous, but they neither clutch you by the shoulder nor bar your road savagely.

Here I can choose my fiacre without fear, and make my bargain with a "*safe*" driver, who will not select the loneliest part of the road, to extort more money—with a pair of ferocious eyes, roaming round in search of possible accomplices.

Seeing what Messina is, I cannot account for the absence of any decent hotels. "The Vittoria" is dark, uncomfortable, and noisy; a real caravanserai. Come to-day, gone to-morrow, is written on the face of everything. You cannot stay there.

Not even the bronzed-face master who sits solemnly, fur cap on head, in a dark den, and doles out to you your bill, as if he were a wizard, and the bill your fate —expects it. There is no other hotel; lodgings they tell me are impossible except to yearly tenants; so, short of a yacht or a balloon; you cannot stay at Messina.

One comes at the antiquity of the cathedral begun by Count Roger, and completed by his son King Roger, 1298—by observing the alternate courses of red and white marble, and the pointed style of architecture which recalls Pisa. There are three pointed doors, which, says Dennis, show the influence of the later Anjouvine dynasty; also the flat wall carvings.

The central arch is very lofty, and finely worked in elongated spirals, mounting to an upper string course of

trefoil arches, each arch enclosing a female head. The
three doors are really a fine study of mediæval work,
distinctly Norman, and Gothic in character, a very striking combination when seen for the first time.

Observe, however, that these remarks apply only to
the lower half of the façade. The hideous moderness
of the upper portion is not to be described. The two
towers in the rear introduce me to Sicilian coloured
tiles, blue, yellow, red and purple—small and trefoil-
shaped, placed thickly upon each other in pattern. The
glare and blaze of these coloured tiles, the whitewash
on the walls, the lack of any little softening veil of moss
or lichen (those harmonizers of the North, rarely found
in these latitudes) is distressing to the eyes.

Inside, one forgets the dirt and the whitewash in the
splendour of the coup-d'œil. How welcome is the gloom
of those twenty-six, deep-brown granite columns, brought,
it is said, from Orion's temple at Faro. You must accept
them and their gilt bases as you must accept Orion
himself, in all faith. The roof is very noble, full of
gold and colour; the gigantic rafters dating back to the
time of Saracenic Manfred and the Hohenstaufens.

Here my admiration ends.

Later, I find myself anathematising the flaunting
frescoes and the obtrusive plaster. The dirt is really
offensive, so is the irreverence.

The facchini, that plague of Sicily, attack you; the
beggars dog your steps with want and hunger in their
eyes. Everybody is familiar, even the priest who is
saying mass in a conversational way at the altar. This
Sicilian *laissez-aller* has its good and bad side. In the
cathedral it is at its worst.

Two men are screaming on the steps of a side-altar
where the service has just ended, the incense fumes still

hanging about it. How these two men do not come to blows I cannot understand. One is a cowed-looking, pinched-up, old priest, the other a stout young citizen, livid in the face.

What the old priest has done, or why the young citizen should swear at him and shake his fist in his face, I cannot explain, as I am ignorant of the Sicilian dialect.

At length a climax is reached. The young man raises his arm as if to strike the old priest prostrate on the floor!

Nothing of the kind! The old fellow limps away without answering a word.

No one interferes, no one looks on. I conclude, therefore, that such scenes are common. I admire the swing, and abandon, and picturesque familiarity of the streets; I can forgive the chatty priests, with ribald eyes, lolling in street corners; I can pardon the beggars—but, in a church! license has limits!

I like the high altar, the central apse covered with bold Saracenic mosaics, like those I came to see at Cefalù and Monreale. (At Monreale the Saviour is an Arab and wears a dark blue turban.) The sides lined with red velvet trunks, let into niches; imperial coffins, ready packed, so to say, for the long last voyage.

Within his own red velvet trunk, ready for heaven or hell, lies Count Conrad, son of that philosophic and intellectual pagan, Frederic II.; Alfonso the Magnificent, King of Naples and Sicily, of the Norman line, and a royal lady, also lend themselves to be so briefly dealt with as to lie buried in a box. The lady's name is Antonia of Arragon. Here they all rest, as passengers in a free berth, on a smooth sea!

Under them sit the purple-robed canons, within the

richly-carved stalls of the choir, chanting matins, mass, and evensong. The archbishop blesses them, the fragrant incense embalms them.

Peace be to their bones! It is very snug lying, after all, especially so near the Virgin's letter. For be it known, the Virgin Mary wrote a letter with her own hand to the citizens of Messina, and that letter is here at the back of the high altar framed in gilt and bronze. I beg pardon, a copy, I should say, for the original, unfortunately, is lost.

The copy is in Latin, translated by Constantine Lascaris, and mentions "that the Virgin takes Messina under her special protection." Dennis says a register is kept of the miraculous cures wrought by it, especially in "*driving out devils.*"

I feel the obligation of faith in Sicily. If I accept the personality of Ulysses and Orion, I cannot dispute the authenticity of the Virgin's letter; only, it appears to me, if the Virgin had disposed herself to write at all she would not have expressed herself in mere scholastic phrases, with such an odour of dog-Latin and the cloister.

As each Greek city in Sicily had its Mimes, or pagan drama, put into action, so each Christian city has its "Mystery," or Festival, only the Greeks had protecting Goddesses, and we, in modern times, have female Saints.

The Virgin is the patroness of Messina. On the day of her assumption, the Festa-della-Barra, there are strange doings—giants, representing Zanchus and Rhea, as fabulous founders of Messina, are dragged through the streets, a huge stuffed camel fixed on a board, attended by a Saracen squire, symbolizing Roger's first entrance into Messina mounted on that animal; a gilded galley, commemorating a miraculous arrival of corn in a time of famine; and the Barra itself, representing the Virgin's tomb, surrounded by the twelve apostles (aged from twelve to five), a revolving circle of infant angels above, sun, moon, and cherubim revolving also, an azure globe floating in tinsel skies; and over all, the Almighty in a rich brocaded robe, carrying upon his arm the Virgin's soul, prefigured by a lovely child, in a white maille, figured in golden stars.

CHAPTER XI.

A Paradise of Flowers.—Campo Santo.—Tombs to Let and No Tenants.—Preparing the Dead.—Painted Carts.—A Substitute for School Boards.—What they Teach.

THE dreamy beauty of the "Flora" haunts me.

Wandering down the Corso I find myself suddenly overwhelmed by the perfume of pompadour cloves, mignonette, and nespole. Rose leaves floating about, and rose blossoms lighting up large parterres invite me to enter a tall iron gateway, and I find myself within "The Flora."

What a delicious name for a garden. And what delicious roses! Waxy, firm, and full of colour, roses evidently proud of themselves as having survived the waste of storm and autumn.

The timber, to put it finely, is various. Light foliaged pepper trees, the jagged leaves as if cut out by a stamp; magnolias, with here and there a luscious flower left sleeping on the bough; broad, woolly-leaved paulonias; tassel-headed thickets of bamboo, sixty feet high, rustling with pensive moans, as if invoking kindred streams; the india-rubber plant, the finest glazed foliage in the world; arbutus, seringa, and fernandia, every member of the distorted race of cacti, casting abroad bristling members as against invisible assailants; the whole aloe tribe, variegated and plain; yuccas and echeverias, a family group in which deformity is hereditary—indeed, the aspect of these fleshy plants is so various, and they partake so much of a tortured individuality, that to me they appear positively human.

After these come the palm genus, with those magnificent fronds formed to wave on battle fields as symbols of victory. Yet after all, if you come to look into the matter calmly as I did, standing in the warm sunshine, the palm divested of the extraordinary dignity of its foliage, is nothing but a magnified pineapple!

Palmettos and dwarf fan-palms assert themselves as stiff as the pattern on a Japanese vase; euphorbias, gay with scarlet tassels; hibiscus, glowing with sanguine flowers; mimosa, a floral sea-weed, one mass of yellowness and sweetness; pomegranates, and carobias, and Judas-trees so glorious in the spring. Banks of mesembryanthemums, pink and yellow, and ivy, run round beds of scarlet geraniums, and blue mimulus, and carnations and tree jessamines still linger as though unwilling to depart while other flowers hold their own.

The tuberoses are very valorous, and open their snowy bosoms to the December breeze, and a lovely wistaria, forgetting it is winter, tosses forth purple ringlets.

A little lake is tufted with papyrus and lilies, flag flowers and reeds. In a moist corner I see that exquisite freak of nature, a tree-fern. Then I seat myself upon a marble bench, to note the ripening dates yellowing in the sun.

A French horn sounds from the open window of a white-washed barn, presenting itself as a *palace* in the surrounding piazza.

An Idle Woman in Sicily.   5

The long-drawn notes come to me as the articulate voice of the rich nature around. I can see the purple mountains rising over the house-tops in a golden haze to which sapphires are pale!

Since the time of Proserpine Sicily has been the home of flowers. We are told that the virgin goddesses, Proserpine, Minerva, and Diana, weaved with their own hands a variegated flower garment for Father Jupiter. "A mythological 'coat of many colours' like Hebrew Joseph's."

No wonder the gods loved Sicily!

I have had enough of *"Messina l'Allegra,"* and its hundred thousand inhabitants disporting themselves in the noise and glare of the Marina. I cannot get away from Figaro nor from Count Almaviva, always meeting Rosina carrying a *billet-doux!* (by chance, of course), and twirling fans at street corners; Don Bartolos, fat and imbecile, leering at youthful beauty out of cafés and trattorie; Don Basilios, by scores, smoking and guzzling; and aged Don Marcellinas, remembering the days of their youth, leaning out over balconies, with knitted shawls upon their heads.

The Teuton may do his best to plant himself in hotels as Baron or Count, but generally as *commis voyageur,* the element is Spanish, Spanish to the backbone.

It is good that this often destroyed city should have some character of its own.

To-day I drive out through a long suburb, degrading in filth, mud, and squalor.

The moment you leave the streets you plunge into the depths of the most hideous poverty—hovels, green with mouldiness, falling walls, villas in ruins, and a population stolid and brutish. At the distance of a mile I leave this wretched humanity behind, and mount to a modern Grecian temple, grandly conspicuous on a natural platform.

This is the Campo Santo, smiling through colonnades of marble pillars over the blue straits. There is Reggio opposite; every house-roof twinkling to the sun; laughing little villages dotting the shore; bays, capes, and promontories, dark forests on the Calabrian heights, and, above all, the stern outlines of Aspromonte. Such a scene as this should rob death of its terrors!

How wondrous is the beauty of this earth when we know where to seek it!

A custode tormented me for pence; he deeply regretted the healthiness of Messina.

"Alas! Signora," he said, as he led me up flight after flight of magnificently balustraded marble stairs, "the Campo Santo will never be finished if things go on like this. Imagine, to yourself, my wages never paid, and but a quarter of the best vaults sold! *Che vuole?* With such a debt it is a *desperazione!* This Campo Santo is much too grand and too large for such a city as Messina. If it were Naples now, or Rome, *alla buon ora!* There are fevers *there*.

"But *here*, Chè, nothing! Municipalities like to have their names published, as beginning national monuments; but they do not finish them. Ah, dear Signora! believe me, a great many people must die to make up the debt; die quietly in their beds.

"A pestilence like the cholera does us more harm than good. We throw the dead into holes, rich and poor alike, and seal them up and leave them. Nobody makes a monument for cholera, or buys a vault."

Here the custode cast his eyes around at the nobly-terraced gardens and funereal groves, clothing the "walks of state," at the rear of the temple.

5*

"They forgot what a healthy place Messina is, when they started this Campo Santo," he added reflectively.

He showed me the apertures for the burial of the poor (one opened every day at sunset, then sealed up for a year, with a stone, as at Naples), within an open, pillared court, in the interior of the building. The contempt the custode felt for the *poor* dead, was undisguised. Afterwards he led me to an enclosed space, covered with graves bristling with little black crosses.

"Here, Signora," said he, pointing to the graves, "we *prepare* the bodies for one year of the rich, those who can pay for it; then we place them in the vaults within the temple." (A Greek notion this, Christianized into something filthy!)

I have mentioned the painted carts. They are passing me every instant. *"Give in the eye,"* as the Italians say, everywhere, not only in crowded thoroughfares, but under the shadow of Doric temples, in the black lava country, among marshy lakes, and upon lonely mountain sides.

The painted carts bear the riches of the land; sulphur, fruit, oil, wine, wheat, meadow-hay, and saffron. If I were asked, I should say they were an Arab invention.

They are mounted on high wheels, and the spokes and panels are so carved and ornamented, one wonders in so poor a country, how the money is forthcoming. A first-class cart costs from £100 to £120 sterling. There are various degrees of merit in the build and the decoration, to say nothing of the harness. A rich farmer's cart flashes along the roads, bright as an eastern tent in action. The red velvet housings of the harness is a splendour! the vast pyramids of tinkling bells, a wonder! I will venture to say there is not a cart in all Sicily, however old and shabby, that is not painted. A bare cart is an indecency!

An incalculable advantage too, attends these carts. Without books, they teach all history. History read in reds and blues, and yellow ochre, crude, it is true, and positive, but effective, and not without a certain "go" and spirit of its own.

No need for school-boards and village dames in Sicily. You have only to study a series of painted carts, to know everything. And so tolerant too! On the same cart your eyes glance from a Holy Family in front, to Hercules and Alexander hob-nobbing on the sides; Napoleon at Sedan jogs in company with Bismarck at the back, and Amorini and Cherubs circle round irrespective of politics.

Tasso's Rinaldo is a great card. I saw him yesterday seated in a boat in green armour, contemplating a shore furnished with an obligato of reeds and shells, on which stands Armida, dishevelled, and naked to the waist, surrounded by nymphs. One figure is veiled—this is the modest, though war-like, Clorinda.

"*Flight of Rinaldo*" (I noticed this cart later, but put it here for sequence). Rinaldo with a parrot nose, blank-faced, his hand upon his hip, staring at vacancy.

"What shall Rinaldo do?" asks the Text. I forgot to say, you are aided by a printed Text—stage instructions as it were—in capital letters.

"Leave the wicked, but enamoured Armida to her fate?" No, replies the Text, with general good feeling, "His sensibility forbids it! His sensibility! His passion!" (Text continues): "Yet duty and religion urge him on. He must go." Rinaldo still wearing green armour listens to "Religion and Duty," and departs. His light bark divides the cobalt waves. His eyes are riveted on Armida. Spite of her attractive knees and outstretched arms, the shore recedes, and, the Text informs us, "Calm returns to the bosom of the hero."

Calm represented by a yellow dash on the green surface of his armour, near the heart.

This particular cart I saw close to the mysterious elephant, in the Piazza at Catania. The horse, a bay, was refreshing himself at the fountain, while the driver was lading it with mandarin oranges.

Rinaldo again (naughty boy), "Knows no duty, but to his lady-love Armida." (Text) His knees are bare (this in Sicilian carts is a sign of passion). Armida, in the violence of her feelings, streaked blue and red—wears a coronet. Rinaldo is reposing on a leopard skin beside her. A tree with unknown fruit waves over his head; while a cupid snug on a leaden cloud draws his bow and grins.

"Where is Clorinda now?" sternly demands the Text; to which question Rinaldo pays no heed whatever.

Your Sicilian enjoys all history, sacred and profane, poetic, biographic, and anecdotal—this last as culled from Gallic memoirs; but a conspiracy recommends itself to the most ordinary intelligence.

A group of olive-skinned boys were crowding round a cart, drawn up on the Marina, one spelling out the Text to the rest, who seemed greatly to relish it. Cinq Mars on the large panel in front—(a dismal spectacle in Louis Treize costume, and perfectly idiotic. The artist in this is true to history—Cinq Mars was a superlative idiot), is in the act of stretching out his naked sword over a round table, Marion de l'Orme striking an attitude at his back. Other swords of other conspirators are crossing each other over his.

The Text exclaims, "Death to Richelieu."

The motto of "Death to anyone" pleases your Sicilian orderer of the cart, and chooser of the picture. "Death" is always a gain to some one, he reasons. Cinq Mars may be obscure to him as a personage, but naked swords tell their own tale. "As many naked swords as possible and men to draw them," is the Sicilian order, answering to the "oranges" of Farmer Flamboro' in the "Vicar of Wakefield."

"Perillus, by command of Phalaris, Tyrant of Girgenti —burning within a brass bull, devised by himself," also appears to appeal to the popular imagination. This was one of the first carts I noticed, on arriving at Messina. The bull, a very notable beast, rubbed on in blue, with a green cavity in his back, good for slipping in Perillus; naked slaves are stirring up the furnace with long poles, and Phalaris sits aloft, grinning complacently.

Then my recollection wanders off to a brau-new cart I saw afterwards at Palermo, in the "artist's" shop— Constantine, with an unmoved countenance, swimming in a yellow bath, unscrewing brass taps to let in more water; while a giant behind, in blue and pink, hits him a sounding blow on the head with a classic water-jug, whether with murderous intent, or from a want of perspective on the part of the "artist," the Text does not specify. At all events, this painting has its value. It instructs your native (already a proficient) in a new form of murder. These Greek-shaped jars come handy. Water, in the country, is always carried in them. Some one will suffer for this. Look out, Mr. Questor! "Robbery with violence and death by a Greek jar!" This cart will not flash along the roads for nothing.

I see the "Prodigal Son" displaying himself often, up and down the roads, heavily laden with sulphur; he is in white pants, a blue coatee with tails, "frac," as the Italians call it, with a chimney-pot hat; one hand clasped in his father's (yellow), the other in his mother's (pink). A dog also present, full of human intelligence, and evidently anticipating the consequences of this sad history.

The next scene I remember on a cart at Taormina, waiting for Mr. Rainforth, who was drinking tea with me. The "Prodigal" has dwindled down into a small boy in blue, with a billycock hat; pigs, sheep, and goats, much taller than himself, group round him; behind is a pastoral expanse, with a volcano in the back-ground; a party of ladies and gentlemen on horseback—riding directly into the crater.

On another occasion, I met "the Prodigal" in green. He has returned; his hair is close cropped, and he is attired in a flowered dressing-gown; his father in a wig, and his mother still in pink, not having changed her dress after so many years—receive him. Valises and trunks, such as a swineherd would require in travelling, pile up the back-ground.

CHAPTER XII.

From Messina to Taormina.—Beppo and Luigi.—Ruins! Ruins!— Scarletta Beggars.—Waiting for the Train.—Hellenic Foot- marks.—The Town of Ali.—Etna.—The Foundation of Naxos —Roman, Punic, and Norman-Saracenic Remains.—Naxos and the Tyrants.

THINKING of what I saw on the rail from Messina to Taormina, makes me sad! How can I describe perfect beauty? In man or woman it is difficult, how much more so in the larger, broader features of nature? I gazed on it with rapture, I think of it with pain. Once it has been given me to behold this enchanting land. Shall I ever return?

From the handsome railway station at Messina you shoot out, as it were, to sea, along shining sands fringing the straits. Such portions of the mountains as are visible (and that is but little, they rise so abruptly from the shore) are mantled in massive foliage; chestnuts and oaks above, citrons, apricots, almonds, and knotted fig-trees below. There are vines trained on arched trel-lises, supported by colonnades; vines clambering wild among the rocks; country-houses, like coy nymphs, blush-ing out of scented woods (some, alas! in palpable ruin; others resplendent with bright frescoes; every gate and aperture a delight of flowers and flowering-shrubs), slopes of emerald grass dotted by fan-palms, fields of cacti, walls hanging over with slender veils of mimosa; here a tuft of snowy nespole, there a dark group of cypress; a grotto curtained with red-leaved creepers; limestone rocks and grey-tinted marble; fantastic bluffs and pinnacles, cropping out into marigolds and lupins; great water-courses (fiumari); pebbly wastes, leading to deep, smiling dells; cornfields carved out upon the heights; flax, saffron, and sainfoin on the plain, and olives everywhere.

Everything but level ground! Of that there is none; no level, except the belt of beautiful shore, the margin of the fiumari, and the course of the streams fading away among the hills.

As we advance, rounding capes and promontories, blue waves break against low rocks, then swarming up-wards in sheets of curling foam, mark the outline of delicate little bays.

Here is the rare charm of a double coast-line; not pressed into one picture, as at Faro, but far enough asunder for each shore to display a character of its own. The Calabrian mountains are twelve or thirteen miles across, and the sparkling straits are widening every moment.

How lively is the channel with passing ships! A man-of-war, with royalty on board, all sails set for Taormina; flotillas of lateen-sailed smacks; Florio's steamers plying from town to town, and innumerable brown fishing-boats tossing in the waves.

And this Messinian shore is as peaceful as it is lovely. A fisherman population, as the rows of boats show, drawn up high and dry in the rounding bays. No fear of brigand or buccaneer here. Beppo or Luigi, with his Phrygian cap, who scrapes the fertile earth when the wind blows too fiercely to go to sea, is as harmless as our English Jacks or Bobs, ploughing the northern fields. The cactus-fruit he gathers at his door, the fish he takes when the rollers, thundering in at either end of the straits, kindly permit him—feed himself and his numerous family. Beppo or Luigi, who have a boat and a little corn-patch, a lemon-garden, or a vineyard, are well-to-do; the rest are destitute.

Now we are passing beside a small town nestling by the sea. In the distance it looks beautiful as an enchanted castle, but, on near approach, turns out to be nothing but a mass of unclean hovels in a confusion of ruined walls.

What a dismal tale of other days these towns and villages tell! Suburban luxury that has been, when Messina was the Neapolitan Viceroy's capital, and ruin that is, under United Italy!

At Scarletta, the first station from Messina, another castle, but in ruins, commands what was once the high road to Catania. (Heaven help those who travel on it now, the ruts are up to the axles of the painted carts.) A feudal fortress peeps out of a cypress wood, and the

whole population seems to gyrate round it. The arrival
of the train is the event of the day, the solitary chance
of pocketing a stray coin. Many miserable faces flatten
themselves against the wooden paling that encloses the
platform; many beseeching children hold out dirty fingers,
and the agitation of the drivers of broken-down fiacres
is painful to behold. They spring up on their seats,
scream, whistle, and crack their whips. In vain! No
one gets out!

From the point of Faro to Catania, is the home of
classic mythology; mythology, embodied and vivified in
the burning tints of southern life. Where stand those
desolate half-ruined towns was the home of gods and
heroes. Every river, headland, and sandy baylet had
its legend, every cave and rock its myth, as sung by the
native bards, Theocritus, Dafne, Stesichorus, and Empedocles.

Wherever the Greek set his foot, temples and statues
to the gods blossomed out upon the shore. He lived in
the open. Earth and sea were sacred to him, not a
river or a stream but was the haunt of deity. The great
volcano of Etna, the earthly seat of Jove, was as a new
faith; its expression, a simple niche to Pan, set up in a
grass field, a sculptured group of fauns in a village
market-place, a frieze upon a rustic temple, or the chisel-
ling of a new altar. The Greek gods were everywhere
—and with the gods came poetry. Now poetry may
haunt great cities, but here she was at home, the hem
of her robe touched everything!

There is nothing of this symbolism on the northern
coast where the Phenicians and Carthaginians colonized
Sicily. Nothing at all like it except on that limited
portion of the western shore from Eryx to Trapani (Drepanum), the second sickle-shaped harbour, rival of

Messina. Eryx is seven miles distant from Trapani. A rocky cliff of yellow limestone, on the level expanse of a pastoral plain is the legendary site of the temple of Aphrodite, founded by Æneas and strengthened by Dædalus (a personification of the erratic energy of the artist, flying from place to place, and creating everywhere). Below, by the sea, Æneas buried his father, Anchises. The very rock is pointed out where the "God-born" reposed on fresh, fair skins to witness the funeral games, and pour libations on the tomb.

From Trapani (Drepanum) Hellenic tradition leads on southward to the ruined temples of Mœgarian Selinus, to Segeste, with its dim legends of Æneas and Sicanian Alybus, which may mean Elymus, or a people said most persistently to be of Trojan origin, to Acragas (Girgenti), second only to Syracuse, Rhodian Gela, Camarina, and Helorus, and to "the city of cities" itself.

The station of Ali rises gleeful out of bowery woods of almond and peach. Its warm mineral springs were dedicated to Hercules by the careful nymphs who attended him on his journey through Sicily. Capo D'Ali and a Norman round tower jutting out to sea, mark the nominal entrance into the Pelorian Straits, opposite Capo delle Armi, the Leucopetia of the ancients on the mainland.

We pass the stations of Alessio and Letojanni—mountains, mountains, nothing but mountains, with fiumari rending them apart.

At Giardini I quit the rail for Taormina, six miles off, among the clouds. I leave Furiosa to fight with the facchini (I see her disappear like a limp rag, among horses, drivers, beggars, and general rapscallionism) and look round.

A bare little station, Giardini, in the curve of a

well-marked bay, jammed in under walls of frowning cliffs, apparently inaccessible. The friendly hint, however, of a white road zig-zagging up to the right relieves my mind, balanced between the appalling aspect of the cliffs and the keen desire I have to scale them.

To the left the heights fall back, and the majestic form of Etna rises. The great giant comes upon me in his summer mood; snow-crowned, indeed, but green, subdued and gentle. Forests wreathe his flattened cone, and indenting lines of a circle of lesser craters sit like a crown of dusky jewels on his brow.

An enormous stretch of ascending country, broken in surface and lava-streaked, rises from Giardini. The brilliant verdure mocks the blackness of the lava boulders tossed on the surface of inky streams, stiffened into black death as they flowed from the crater.

The sight of Etna is to me as a discord—death among life, the very mouth of Tartarus opening in Hesperian fields.

A sombre promontory juts out, forming one horn of the bay. This bay, so lovely in colour, for the rocks are deep red, the water intense blue, and this promontory—a green bank sloping to the sea, where stands a solitary house, half farm, half convent, with a belfry at one end—is very notable as the threshold of Grecian history in Sicily. It is the site of Naxos, the parent colony founded by Chalcydians and by Ionians from Bacchi Naxos, B.C. 735. Here they remained some years stationary, fearing to go further south on account of Etna.

It was in Grecian Naxos that Bacchus wooed forsaken Ariadne, sleeping on the rocks from weariness of grief at loss of Theseus—so, at this second Naxos, Bacchus had his altar. But the great shrine was to

Apollo Archagatas, and the original statue was extant
as late as the time of Augustus, B.C. 36.   If one could
only know on what spot this altar stood!   Or where the
Greeks lept on shore!   Did Apollo stand on the site of
that lonely convent, about which a few tormented olive-
trees cluster?   Or was he placed nearer the point of
Cape Schiso?   *Chi lo sa?*

As we moderns hoist a Union Jack, or a star-
spangled banner, the Greeks (after the sanction of an
oracle had been sought for and obtained) reared an
altar upon which sacred fire burned, as a signal of possession.

In the mythic times an altar to Neptune rose on
the point of Faro, and a shrine to Venus on the rock of
Eryx: thus the god's blessing followed navigators across
the seas, and the people prospered.   There is a battered statue of San Pancrazio on a pedestal, close to
the road at the station of Giardini, which was pointed
out to me by at least a dozen urchins as *"una cosa di
gran devozione."*

Now does San Pancrazio mark the site of the ancient
shrine of Apollo to which all mariners repaired to sacrifice and pour libations before leaving Sicily, as a *sacro-
santo* spot, consecrated by the presence of their first
ancestors?

With the foundation of this Greek colony begins
the real history of Sicily; just as the history of the Norman Conquest begins the real history of England, or the
Capetian race that of France.

No other invasion, conquest, or colony stands out
with a like interest.   The Greeks brought in polished
manners, the knowledge of cultivation and trading, the
splendour of architecture, the worship of the beautiful

in art and nature, intellectual refinement, and the philosophy of the schools.

Rome has left little, considering the length of her rule, and that not of her best—mere journeyman-work, tinkering up Greek walls and monuments.

Indeed, what did Rome ever *create* anywhere?

The Punic remains in Sicily are but few and far between. I only know of some fragments on the site of Motya on the island of San Pantaleo, near Marsala, and two strange monumental statues of a man and woman, like huge fish with human heads, in the Museum of Palermo—Phenician, rather than Punic, and probably the oldest monumental sculptures in the world.

It was in destruction that Carthage left her mark, not in creation. Carthage wrought that mighty ruin at Selinus, turned Minervian Himera into a corn-field, and tore down the temples at Girgenti.

The Norman-Saracenic remains, however poetic and attractive, are but an expression of the bastard union of two styles, as widely different as the two nations which produced them.

Sicily is Greek, Doric Greek. Such we see it even in ruin, and in that grandest monument of architectural art, no ruin, but a complete and perfect structure as it stands, roofless, in which no stone is missing, no morsel of cement wanting—the great Temple of Segeste.

For two hundred years things went merrily at Naxos. So rich was the city, spreading out fan-like upon the lower spurs of Etna, that, if left at peace, it would have ended by colonizing all Sicily.

But a jealous Nemesis called up a tyrant of her own blood to smite her, in Hippocrates of Gela. Gela, now Terranuova, between Syracuse and Girgenti. Hippocrates, obviously provoked by the prosperous Ionian colonies of Catania and Leontini approaching him too nearly, smites not only Naxos but Zancle also.

The next foe who comes to Naxos is Hiero of Syracuse; Syracuse as a Dorian colony being always bitterly hostile to the Ionians wherever they are to be found. Hiero turns the Ionian Greeks out of Naxos with cruel slaughter, and sends them bodily to Leontini; the shrines of Apollo and Bacchus are stained with blood, and the shores left desolate until a band of Peloponnesian colonists appear. Not for long, however. At Hiero's death the Ionians are back again, and the streets of laughing Naxos are once more motley and crowded.

When Alcibiades is sailing about the straits between Messina and Rhegium to pick up allies for the great Athenian expedition against Syracuse, he anchors in the Bay of Naxos, and receives welcome and promise of aid from the Naxians. As Ionians they are thoroughly with the Athenians; who, they hope, may tear down detested Syracuse, and sow its site with salt.

But by so doing Naxos is unconsciously preparing her own doom.

Twelve years pass in peace and plenty after the failure of the Athenian expedition, but Dionysius, the bloody tyrant of Syracuse, is only biding his time.

Now he swoops down in revenge on Naxos, and without a blow the smiling white city by the Ionian Sea falls an easy prey about B.C. 403.

Those of the inhabitants he does not slay Dionysius sells as slaves. The buildings are swept away, and the site of Naxos given back to the native Siculians. They never returned. For twenty-two centuries no man has dwelt there.

CHAPTER XIII.

The Fortunes of Ducetius.—Palicia, an Infernal Lake.—Ducetius at Syracuse.—Shall He Live or Die?—The Beautiful Shore.—The Last of Ducetius.

AND whom did the stranger Greeks find when they landed in this Naxian bay?

On whose footsteps were they treading? The native Sicanians and the later Siculi, who were they? This question will be best answered by telling the story of Ducetius, king or chief of the united tribes of Siculi and Sicani, who, like Garibaldi, absorbed all discordant nationalities into a whole, knitted together by amor patria.

But before entering on the history of Ducetius, it is but respectful to pose him well among his subjects, else he may escape us altogether as a wandering myth, like Orion or Hercules, an undertaking not easy to accomplish among barbarian tribes and in such remote antiquity.

Whoever the Sicani may have been—and their origin is involved in mystery—they were not in good odour among their contemporaries. Homer in the Odyssey twice mentions them, each time in connection with traffic in slaves.

Telemachus is described, as advised by his mother's suitors, "To embark all troublesome strangers from Ithaca (among these is his own father Ulysses, disguised) and to send them across the sea to the Sicanians, "who will give a good price for them."

Whether the native seat of the Sicanian rule was at Acragas (Girgenti) or at an extinct city called Koka-

los, on a mountain-top not far distant, or at Kaltabel-
lotta, now a mediæval castle, planted on a cliff over a
modern town, swept by a river, and embosomed in cork-
woods near Sciacca, or on Monte Platanella on the
Mascoli, "a river flowing through a wild glen backed by
bare mountains," near Girgenti, or at Omphake, an
ancient Sicanian centre, is hard to say.

Speaking largely, one would place the aboriginal
Sicanians in the south, from about Acragas (Girgenti)
into the centre of the island at Enna (Castro Giovanni),
now a station on the line from Catania to Palermo.

In Faziello's time, huge ruins marked an ancient
hill-fort at Leonforte under Enna. (Leonforte another
railway station on the same line.) Enna (Umbilicus
Siciliæ), with its huge, flat, mountain platform, forming a
natural altar dedicated to Demeter, seems planted where
it is as the boundary between two races.

For beside the Sicani dwelt the more powerful Siculi,
who preserved a certain independence on the summit of
steep heights, in the strife of Greek against Greek.
Something, too, they gained from the Hellenes, learning
their language, and acquiring some of their skill in the
arts of war.

But as a nation they were both servile and disunited. Like the Scotch, whom they so much resemble,
union as a principle of strength was unknown; there was
the old heart-burning of clan against clan, the local
jealousies, the small ambitions.

Yet, oppressed and disunited as they were, the Sicels
often made themselves felt as a power at Syracuse; "perhaps," says Holm, "they might even have struck a blow
against Thrasybulus and Hiero, had any chieftain risen
up to lead them."

At length a chieftain did appear in the person of Ducetius, B.C. 461—460.

Within a few years Ducetius had not only reconciled rival tribes, but he had woven every native town, with the exception of Megara-Hybla, into a national league, of which he was the head.

His first recorded act was the siege of Catania; his next, the consolidation of a national capital at Menœ, now Minéo, on a lofty range of hills, between Palagonia and Cattagirone in the great plain of Catania.

This was as much a master-piece of policy, as was the selection of Rome for a Capital among the divided cities of Italy. Menœ, like Rome, was accepted by the united tribes as the *one spot* where jealousies and feuds vanished before the awe inspired by the ancient sanctuary of their faith.

On the great Catanian plain (the only land answering to a plain in the east of Sicily), two miles below modern Minéo, the tranquil waters of the mystic lake of the Palici still sleep in the sunshine.

The Lago Naftia, as it is now called, is of circular form, and of no great depth. Sometimes, indeed, in rainless weather it dries up altogether. To this day, its waters are green, turbid, and bituminous, as in the time of Ducetius, and three distinct sulphureous craters boil within its marshy margin.

Overlooking this lake, arose, according to Æschylus, the dark portico of the temple of the Palician Deities, very terrible in their dealings with man.

Not even the great oath to Demeter was more binding than that taken to the Dii Palici.

Woe to him who broke it!

From Catania, Ducetius turned his arms towards the West and Acragas, and vainly opposed by Syracusans

6*

and Acragentians, captures Motyum, an unknown locality
between Syracuse and Acragas. Thus he has gained a
sure footing in the Grecian colonies.

This is more than Hellenic pride can brook!

An army yet more numerous than before marches out
of Syracuse against him. The two forces encounter each
other at Monai—another unknown locality in those broad
and beautiful shores between Syracuse and Girgenti.

After a hot struggle the Greeks prevail, and Motyum
is retaken. Poor, noble-hearted Ducetius! now is his
position desperate.

An armed force behind him—a combined army in
front; around him but a few native soldiers, and these
not to be relied on.

Should he die by his own sword? No; for with him,
will die all hope for the Siculi; that dastard race for
whom he has sacrificed so much. Should he throw himself into a strong town and fight? Menœ, for instance?
Or within the walls of the Palician temple?

Perhaps Menœ would not receive him. Neither gods
nor men seemed certain to the broken-spirited Ducetius.
Death awaits him on all sides. Yet he will not die, for
with him will die Siculia!

In the darkening shades of evening—(it was in the
early spring when Motyum was taken, and the days were
short)—Ducetius throws himself upon a horse, and does
not draw rein until he reaches Syracuse.

When morning breaks, and the citizens and the slaves
gather about the market-place, before Minerva's temple
in Ortygia, to greet each other and buy the provisions of
the day a tall, gaunt, ill-clad stranger is seen clinging to
the sanctuary of the altar.

He addresses those who approach him, stretching
forth his hands as a suppliant.

"It is I, O Syracusans! Ducetius, whom you have vanquished! Ducetius, but yesterday king of Siculia, now a fugitive and your prisoner. I have fought you loyally. I have defended my native land. I would have driven you out, O Grecian Strangers—I do not deny it, by no treason or treachery, but in the open field. My Siculians have melted before your arms. My ambition has died within me. Now I am but Ducetius of Menœ—a free-born man, your subject. I deliver myself into your hands. I place Siculia at your feet. Have mercy on her! Spare my people!"

As he speaks, the morning light strikes upon the king's bare head, and illumines the wondrous beauty of the shrine, the sculptured doors of gold, ivory and ebony, the gilded roof, on which an enormous brazen shield flings back the dazzling sun-rays, the temple walls, glowing with paintings of Syracusan artists, and exploits of Syracuse by land and sea: Hiero in his galleys defeating the Etruscans off Cumae, the landing of the first Greeks at Naxos, the coming of Archias to Syracuse, the founding of the cities of Messina and Catania and Leontini.

With a sigh Ducetius hides his head in his mantle, as his eyes travel over these pictorial records, witnesses of his country's servitude. Alas! Will not his own defeat at Motyum offer the next subject to tempt the artist's skill?

Meanwhile a crowd of priests, magistrates and citizens, assemble before the Portico of Minerva, talk loudly and move to and fro, within the limits of the same market-place, which has come down to us to this day, open to the soft sea-breezes and honeyed scents from Hybla.

The space fills to overflowing. The word passes round that the Siculian king is captured. Every one presses to look at him.

"What is to be done with him?"

"Is he to live or die?"

"Let him die," cried the young men, "as he caused ours to die." Others shout, "To the galleys with him!" "Drown him!"

But the older men, who have known too much bloodshedding under Hiero, say, "Spare him! He has come to us of his own will; he has freely taken refuge within our city walls. Remember what is due to the honour of Syracuse. He has appealed to the gods. If the gods, on their altar, give no sign, let their sanctuary be respected."

There is a great stir among the people. The arcaded market-place sways to and fro with a doubtful multitude. There is some skirmishing, and swords even are drawn.

At last the counsels of mercy prevail. The young men are hustled outside, into the side streets; the remainder, the older and wiser citizens, call out with one voice, "Let him live!"

Yet it was clear that Ducetius could not remain in Syracuse; he would be a constant focus of rebellion. The fugitive Siculians in the mountains, the disaffected among the citizens and the demos (and where were there not disaffected in Syracuse?), would all endeavour to make use of his name.

Of course, Ducetius swore the terrible oath by the Dii Palici, as much feared by the Greeks as by the Sicels, "never to return to his people without the leave of Syracuse." But what is an oath? Not even an oath to the infernal gods could bind a patriot like Ducetius. So he was shipped off to Corinth.

How it came about is not clear. But in a short time Ducetius was back again, ranging the Siculian mountains with his bands.

Had he broken his pledge? I cannot say. History answers no such question.

Ducetius himself declared that he returned to Sicily in obedience to an oracle, which decreed that he was to found a colony on the "beautiful shore."

If fraud there were, and a false oracle, both Corinthians and Syracusans were a party to it; nor would they have helped an enemy to return, had they not expected advantage from it.

The new colony is founded B.C. 446, on the "beautiful shore," as it was called in the oracle. It was called Kalatto. Now, all the coasts of Sicily are beautiful, but no shore is lovelier than that northern coast, backed by the wondrous range of the Madornian mountains; the rock of Cefalù, the point of Zaffarana, the Semitic ruin of Solunto, and the graceful lines of countless curves and bays, points and promontories, that break the azure seaboard.

I dare not stop to think of that "beautiful shore" as I saw it from Solunto, one soft spring evening, fair as a dream, and delicate with unearthly tintings!

I must hasten on to relate that Kalatto (now Calacte) lies inland from Cefalù, at Caronia. There is still the "Marina di Caronia," a golden stretch of sand down by the sea, backed by groves of tamarisk and cistus; the village of Caronia; and behind "the Bosco," cork, and oak, and pine—the biggest forest of Sicily. It is old Diodorus who speaks of this same forest at Kalatto, under another name. You may see the place now; build up Kalatto in your own imagination, and invoke the shade of Ducetius—Ducetius, a hero without arms, a patriot without a nation!

You will find antique remains to help your fancy—

clay fragments, principally about the village of Caronia;
and legends come down from a remote antiquity.

The town of Menœ on the hills, over the sombre
lake of the Palici has vanished, even as a site; but
Kalatto, "the beautiful coast," still lives in Caronia.

I will by no means answer for your safety in going
there; the Madornian mountains and their lofty spurs
and off-shoots, forest-covered glens, and deep gorges, torn
by rushing torrents, have always been an impregnable
haunt of banditti.

Nevertheless, Calacte, as the Italians name it, is there;
rich, fertile, beautiful. The sea is full of fish; the forests
alive with game; and flocks and herds feed upon the
hills as in the early time.

Many years Ducetius ruled in Kalatto. He tried
once more to form a national league, whether as a conspiracy against the friendly Syracusans, or permitted by
them to serve as a fighting nucleus against hostile Greek
cities, Acragas, and others is not clear.

In vain! While forming the league he died, smitten
by a sudden illness. Was this the vengeance of the Dii
Palici upon one who had broken an oath sworn on their
crater? Or was it poison?

All that remains of him is an heroic memory, a
beacon in the darkness of Siculian night, fading back
into barbarism.

Faziello tells us he saw the Arabic castle which
replaced the Siculian stronghold of Ducetius.

So now, without apology for this long digression (so
well does it fit in with the story of the land) I return to
where I am standing at Giardini station, overlooking the
lonely bay of Naxos.

CHAPTER XIV.

The Ascent to Taormina.—The Mad Peaks.—Modern Taormina.—
The Hotel.—A Polyglot Crew.—The Theatre.—Saracen and
Norman at Taormina.

A GREAT many people got out of the train at Giardini.
Every traveller to Sicily must visit Taormina. They had
all gone on before I addressed myself to the ascent. I
had been standing on the shore, studying Naxos. Then
I mount a perpendicular steep, by a zigzag road, my
boxes tied on to the back of a most rickety carriage.

The scenery is grand in the extreme, but I do not
enjoy it. Furiosa insists on wrangling with the driver
about the fare, to the delight of a light squadron of
nasty little boys accompanying us (*obligato*) from the
station.

Furiosa is a good woman, but Germanic, and absolutely
impracticable. She does her duty in her own way, and
defies remonstrance.

Once I have seen her in a passion, and I hope never
to do so again.

On that occasion she flung everything available, including my own clothes, at my head, and herself out of
the room as a finale.

We are winding up among the great, dusky rocks of
Taurus, hanging out over the sea in a black confusion.
On one side the bay of Catania, with that long, harmonious line of Cape Passaro and the bays of Giarre, Mascoli,
and Aci, bright as autumn flowers.

On the other, the Messinian side, the whole mountain-
bound coast rears itself up in magnificent cliffs and headlands; broad-breasted Calabria lies opposite, and the

blue straits between—a wondrous panorama, painted as
with clear pastel colours, so clear and delicate it is!

As we turn acute angles up the hill (indeed we turn
so often that I come at last not to know my right hand
from my left) how majestic are those buttresses of rock!
Those black ravines and sharp-cut rifts! Those piled up
mountains melting into clouds! What a heaven! What
an earth!

Now I am gazing down upon the calm surface of an
azure-tinted cove, shut in by tawny rocks. A wide yawning cave-mouth opens at one side upon banks of golden
sand, where tiny wavelets break; a splintered mass of
sun-dried limestone fills up the centre, and around lie
shells and seaweed, a place altogether for Ariadne, Dido,
Nausica, or some ethereal presence of the earliest time,
to be sung by Theocritus, or Dafne.

Nearer the town of Taormina, some four miles distant from Giardini, the wildness of the scenery is somewhat tamed. I pass stone balustrades projecting into
space, with seats to rest the traveller by the prospect of
that transcendant landscape. Mouldering Roman tombs
lie buried in a rank growth of sea-pinks, acanthus and
spurge, and crumbling ruins rise out of fields of purple
flag flowers. A large convent towers above, nobly seated
on a cliff, in a maze of almond, pepper, and magnolia
trees, set in a groundwork of blooming parterres. This
beautiful convent is appropriated as a dwelling by Mr.
Rainforth; but nature is so enthralling that nothing arti-
ficial, ancient, modern, or mediæval, has a chance of
notice.

Now we are on a level isthmus-ledge joining the two
rocky cliffs on which stands modern Taormina—altogether,
as it were in air; smaller indeed than the ancient city,
but still faithfully poised on the same foundations.

Siculian first, next Greek, Siculian once more, Greek again under Andromachus, with fugitives from Naxos, then Roman, Byzantine, Greek, and later Norman—what tales those walls could tell!

Behind, wildly flinging themselves upwards, rise three tall peaks, as of mountains altogether gone mad and raving.

In the changeful mistiness of an autumn evening, I fancy these are clouds. Not a bit of it. Well ascertained acclivities with the vestige of a little path upon the lowest, mounting, as it were, the skies.

The nearest peak of a yellow-grey, splintered and cleft like a lump of spar, and so upright, that it becomes a question how it supports itself, is divided into two heads: one thrusting itself forward headlong over the town, and crowned with the battlements of a ruined Saracenic Norman castle; the other in the rear, carrying the outline of a little church, and the vague vestige of a house or two; Saracenic Norman castle and church (Madonna della Rocca), both so precisely the tint of the rock, that it requires time and patience to disentangle each, and not to put the whole down as a further evidence of mountain insanity.

But for a few far-off tufts of spurge and wind-torn aloes clinging in distant crevices, I might be looking at an outline in Tartarus, so hard and vitrified is its surface.

Upon this rock was the acropolis of ancient Naxos. Behind the double peak rises a third eccentricity, altogether apart and aerial. This is Mola, the old Siculian seat, whence the barbarians looked down contemptuously on the fastidious Greeks, buzzing like bees in their acropolis below.

I consider these three rocks dominating Taormina as

a group of monsters. Nothing can familiarise me with their repulsive presence.

Naturally Mola brings me to Dionysius the Elder. If anything can render that rock more terrible, it is a vision of that awful tyrant creeping up through the snow, like a wild beast in search of prey, one winter's night, to enjoy the pastime of butchering the garrison, B.C. 394.

Dionysius had levelled fair Naxos to the sand. He had sold the inhabitants as slaves, and given back the Grecian site to the native Siculi. These had wisely refused the gift, and stuck to their impregnable fortress at Mola.

Now the fickle tyrant, having, for some reason, quarrelled with the Siculi also, determines, impossible as it appears, to lay siege to their strong place of Mola. Looking at it with modern eyes it would seem pretty much like laying siege to the moon!

Diodorus, in his confused way, describes Dionysius besieging "Naxos." He does not distinguish, though a Sicilian, between the Greek city on the shore and the Siculian fortress on the rock. But the Siculi well understood the difference. They knew that since the arrival of the Greek the coast was lost to them, and they had re-entered into their ancient seat, resolved to defend it to the death.

While the fortress of Mola frowned down, inaccessible and grim, "the winter solstice arrived," says Diodorus, and Dionysius remarking that the Siculi were careless in mounting guard, took advantage of one dark and stormy night to climb that perpendicular track; the same which still leads up to the miserable little hamlet of Mola. (I am repeating from Diodorus.)

A path over acute precipices, and a snow-storm beating in front, were as nothing to him. He reaches the

summit and forces open the gate, but the Siculi in despair, mass themselves together, and drive him and his
troops down headlong ——, Dionysius himself carried
along by the pressure and floored by a blow on his cuirass
narrowly escaping being made prisoner.   The Siculi on
the heights killed six hundred Syracusans.

Thus says honest Diodorus, user of no ornamental
adjectives, or picturesque phrases.

Still further back rise lofty mountain-chains, cleft by
yawning ravines and precipices; their distorted summits
thrusting themselves into the sky.

I was called on to distinguish the highest point as
Monte Venere, and am told that misguided tourists from
Taormina often reach it.

I am quite satisfied with the marvels of the road.
As an "Idle woman," these mountains on the whole
rather overwhelm me.   I hate climbing, and I prefer the
beautiful to the terrible in nature.

Now, the scenery about Taormina is the acme of the
terrible.

The long street of Taormina is filthy, depressing and
ruinous.   The numerous family groups of all nations,
picking their way in the mud, is not attractive, spite of
the façades of Norman-Gothic palaces, mediæval churches,
and many a quaint "bit" of delicate sculpture.

To its extremest length, from the Giardini Gate to
the Porta Tocca, under the mad peaks—this street follows the edge of a rocky precipice, from which you
might drop a plummet line to the shore at Giardini.   At
the further end is the principal inn facing the south.

I pass under an archway into a weedy court-yard
bounded by a low wall.   Straight before me, in all its
length and breadth, rises Etna.   Nothing lies between.

Snow has fallen and lies thick in the clefts of the

wooded region round the cone, and white clouds heavy
with storms gather about the crater.

This is a new phase of the great mountain; less
varied but more imposing. On all sides, except behind,
where the precipices of Mola and the range of Monte
Venere shut up the horizon, Etna fills the eye.

Mounting a flight of steps into the hotel, I am con-
firmed in my opinion that the merits of Taormina are
confined altogether to the outside.

A more wretched, ill-smelling, ill-furnished, cold, and
draughty caravanserai, I never entered.

As I saw it, it was crammed to overflowing with
tourists of all nations. French shrieking in the passages,
Germans smoking on the stairs, English and Norwegians
returning from mountain excursions, dripping with mud
and snow, Russians arriving, swearing, in broken-down
landaus, with luggage enough to furnish a house, escorted
by a troop of expectant boys. The hotel is full of boys
of all ages, and in all degrees of squalor, ugliness, and
dirt.

Now an English party, bags in hand, bar the corridor.
They are quarrelling over the bill.

"Ma, padrone, non pago questo chose."

"Si, si, lo pagherete!" shouts the landlord in a rage;
"altro che lo pagherete!"

"No, monsieur; va console Inglese a Messina."

"Al diavolo!" roars the landlord, throwing his arms
in the air; "Messina! We are at Taormina. Consuls to
the Inferno, me lo pagherete."

And so on, da capo.

I am lodged in a cell downstairs, with one window,
as high as the ceiling. I accept it joyfully, for it is
warm and quiet. The snow on Etna has made the air
piercing, and in the better rooms above neither doors

nor windows close properly, and the walls are so thin that I am informed one unhappy *poitrinaire*, who certainly must die, keeps an entire floor awake all night with coughing.

The extortionate landlord rushes about in a vain attempt to keep order, and grows insolent if you remonstrate.

"You see how full we are," he remarks to me with a grim smile, and a wave of his hand as if to take in all his abominable accommodation. "I have turned away two English families to-day; two English milords, you un-understand? Taormina is full of hotels, Signora. You can accommodate yourself elsewhere if mine does not suit you. Do you, or do you not, intend to keep your room at the price I demand? Two gentlemen are now waiting on the stairs for your answer to engage it."

The greasy Sicilian waiters are as unaccommodating as their master, and the hideous boys who grin about the door, are on the look out to rob you. I am continually facing those boys. My room being on the basement, I have to take an airy turn down a corridor, and up a flight of open stairs *(al fresco)* with Etna grey and freezing opposite, to reach the *table d'hôte*.

Table d'hôte! Good heavens! The cuisine is on a par with the rest of the establishment.

The company is, like the cuisine, execrable! We fight for the dishes, and warm our fingers on the plates. It includes a savage-looking, long-haired Norwegian, the proprietor of the cough, which cough, by the way, only seems to sharpen his appetite (a fact naturally provoking to those he keeps awake, but he certainly will die, if that is any consolation to them); a spinster looking out for a matrimonial niche, pities him, otherwise I can detect nothing but looks of indignation passing round the table, when he heaps cutlets on his plate; a vulgar German artist and his wife, very prominent at meal-times (he is engaged in manufacturing pictures out of "Rococo" bits); and a promiscuous crowd of English, French, and Germans.

Fortunately I have the resource of Mr. Rainforth and his poetic convent on the cliff, embosomed in flowery groves; so, after breakfast, in the teeth of a cutting wind straight from the snow-flanks of Etna, I pass out of the Saracenic walls of Taormina, touched up by Charles V. (one continually finds oneself *vis-à-vis* to Charles V. in Sicily) and drink countless cups of good warm tea in my friend's excellent company.

I find I am expected to admire various architectural "bits" in ragged palaces, a grim cathedral spotted with damp and mildew, and several other churches in the long straggling street, all "Rococo," or Sicilian Gothic, as Mr. Denis calls it, as well as many foliated capitals, slender-clustered shafts, ogee arches, and dog-tooth mouldings.

I am also tormented to look at a Naumachia at the top of a precipice, which, as being an obvious discrepancy, I altogether refuse to do. Indeed, Taormina is so ruinous and mangy, and the "bits" are so few and far between, and I myself so angry, that I decline to go anywhere.

Even the palace of the Duca di San Stefano with "bits" all over, fails to excite me. I can only see the slush and the mud before it, naked children and pigs wallowing in the puddles, and Herr——, the obnoxious German artist, with flying hair, sitting at his easel, perfectly unmoved, walled in by a solid mass of street-humanity, fingering him all over and staring.

It is true that there are other *soi-disant* hotels, but they are much worse. Taormina exists on the principle

of a rotten borough. Everybody *must* come, and everybody *must* put up with what he finds. A really comfortable hotel would make any man's fortune. Will no
one try?

Along the thin edge of an olive-wooded precipice,
looking down over cactus-scrub and palmetto sprouting
out of holes and crevices, tiny patches of green corn, and
sheets of flowering almonds—all clinging on to the rocks,
so as not to fall down into the sea, I make my way to
the far-famed theatre.

To reach it I must grope through abominable alleys,
paved with the roughest of stones, mount flights of earthy,
breakneck steps, or rather fragments of steps, and pick
my way through nastiness unutterable!

At last I reach a wooden gate in a dark corner. I
know I am right, for I am accosted by a custode in
official livery. The custode after opening the gate, has
the amazing discretion to conceal himself. Jewel of a
man! Would I could immortalize him!

Before me is the theatre, belted by a circuit of arti-
ficially-scooped-out rocks.

The first glance disappoints me. A unique position,
I say to myself, but unpoetic.

Roman red bricks, showing off against white marble
pillars, amidst a grey loneliness, hung up between earth
and sky! *Bricks* in the same island with the amber-tinted
blocks of Segeste, creamy-pillared Girgenti, and sun-dyed
Solunto! The Romans themselves are so modern in Sicily,
their bricks are but a detail. But nothing can poetize
bricks! From first to last I cannot abide *them!*

Nor do I forgive this present theatre for replacing
the Greek original. It is so stiff and common-place.
Guide-books tell me that the stage is the best preserved
in Europe—this concerns me but little. The colours and

the architecture are neither harmonious nor imposing, and Taormina is a spot where Nature is so lavishly prodigal. Man must follow suit.

Behind the proscenium are three arches divided by clustered marble pillars. The central arch, or royal gate, as it is called, much loftier than the side ones, is broken in the midst.

Between the yawning columns appears the glorious sea, the mountains, and Etna.

The walls are stripped of all ornament. The mouth of a channel, or passage running beneath the stage, has been laid bare; also another passage crossing this one at right angles, called the bronterium, from the brass vessels filled with stones, to imitate the thunder, which were kept here.

Of the proscenium, or stage itself, probably of wood, ninety-seven feet long and thirty-eight feet deep, the brick foundations alone remain.

On either hand are the huge fragments of two vaulted halls, or temples, or, as some say, "green-rooms" for the actors.

In front is the semi-circular amphitheatre, with ranges of seats for four thousand spectators. Few of these, cut in the limestone rock, are entire.

The stucco still clings to the walls of the scena, and white pillars supporting the central arches cutting sharp against the deep red of the bricks, may lend themselves to *painting* but are fatal to prose. How can I make "*bricks*" interesting?

It is only when I arrive at what was once the upper seats, into which the ruined mouths of ten vomitories open, that the ill-humour which has possessed me ever since I came to Taormina vanishes.

I stand amidst a universe of blue—blue over heaven

and sea, and such a blue sea—with dashes of orange, lilac, and purple, as the light falls from passing clouds on mighty breakers rolling in southward, from Greece.

To the right, Etna, in all the majesty of its eleven thousand feet of altitude, cuts the blue sky as sharp as steel, without an intervening cloud and fills up the picture. What a world! What memories! Jove's throne, Vulcan's workshop, the Titans' prison, the Cyclops' home, Demeter's torch, the fiery dungeon of Enceladus, the tomb of Empedocles!

The broad white flanks sweep down into a fertile plain dashed with green and veined with blackened lava-streams; towers, towns, villages, convents, churches on every height, gleaming white in the transparent atmosphere.

Full in this glorious prospect sat the Greek, and after him the Roman, to nourish himself at Nature's banquet, and drink in the verse of Sophocles or Euripides, with a fiery crater for a background! Here, he could tell himself that the whole universe could offer nothing fairer or more awful.

Now one last look, and then adieu for ever to sunny capes kissing the sapphire waves, to graceful bays basking in loveliness, to the rich harmony of yellow strands and tawny rocks, to weird, wild heights, and that grey old town crowning the cliffs, cold and hard against a lemon-tinted sky.

Adieu to the thick, rich turf bordering the ruins, to the beds of peas and marigolds, mole-wort and sea-pink, homely buttercups and trailing convolvulus that paint the ground! Adieu to the sheltering arches under which my foot sinks deep into acanthus and vine leaves, ivy and moss. Where the very stones are beautiful, clothed with

7*

golden lichens; and spurge and rush, caper and fern, aloes and fennel wreath the ancient tombs!

Adieu! Adieu!

As the scene fades before me my thought passes on to later times, and dwells on two episodes in the changing history of Taormina.

Greek has been succeeded by Roman, Roman by Byzantine, and now rocky Taormina is the last stronghold in Sicily, with the exception of Castro Giovanni (Enna), which holds out against the Saracens.

Ibrahim, the Saracen Emir, is on the road from Palermo to conquer it; and Byzantine Leo, called the Philosopher, far away on a remote throne at Constantinople, instead of sending an army to oppose him, is building churches and monasteries on the Bosphorus.

Leo can think of nothing better than to despatch a certain Eastern bishop to Taormina, called St. Elia, eighty years old, and certainly childish, to defend it by his prayers.

St. Elia prays, kneeling in the middle of the narrow street, bound in chains, and attired in his drawers. He does not exhort the soldiers to fight, but to cleanse themselves from sin; nevertheless, he evokes the memory of Grecian Epaminondas and of Roman Scipio, and prophesies destruction to every one.

"See," cries this episcopal Cassandra, "what rivers of blood flow through these streets! Behold the corpses of the Greeks upon these stones! The infidel is on the road! He is coming. He is here."

But no attention is paid to St. Elia by the Byzantine garrison, and after a vain defence, impregnable Taormina is taken by Ibrahim's soldiery to the fierce shout of "Ak bar Allah."

"'This," says Amari, "happened on a Sunday, the 1st of August, A.D. 910."

But even as the Mussulman had robbed Sicily whole and entire from the Goth, so in turn they were to yield it whole and entire to another foe.

When the victorious banner of Count Roger de Hauteville waved over the rocks of Taormina, and the Norman knights and squires assembled in thanksgiving within the Gothic cathedral of San Niccolo, Sicily was Norman!

CHAPTER XV.

Where is Antonio?—Round Etna.—The Black Country.—Towns and People.—The Ascent.—Desolation.—A Feudal Castle.—The Descent.—An Awful Road.—Welcome to Maniace.

I WAS to be met at Piedimonte, one station on from Giardini, by a vetturino to take me to Maniace.

Now, to start fair with my readers, I must explain that Maniace is a house, and not the Byzantine General historically renowned in the eleventh century. Maniace, the house, lies immediately under the further side of Etna, eight miles from Bronté. The site has retained the name from a neighbouring town founded in honour of General George, patron of the Normans, and commander of the Byzantine armies after Belisarius and Narses.

From Maniace, General, the site after eighteen centuries passed to Nelson, Admiral; in gift from the king of the Two Sicilies. Now, it is possessed, together with the title of Duke of Bronté, by his lineal descendant Viscount Bridport—

To arrive in time at Piedimonte I rise at three a.m.

Hours are early in Sicily; the express train generally starts about four, more or less punctually.

When I descended on the Piedimonte platform, I looked round. There was the usual allowance of tumble-down fiacres, and one decent-looking landau. Into this I was lightly stepping, when a voice from the box arrested me.

"Signora," the voice cried, "this is the carriage of Signor Gregorio, I am waiting for him. You cannot use it."

"Are you not Antonio, who is to take me to Maniace?" I asked.

"No, I am not Antonio," very sulky this time the voice. "I do not know him. I am Signor Gregorio's coachman. No one shall take liberties with my master's carriage."

I turned round aghast to the porter carrying my bags, and beheld Furiosa's eyes flashing and her mouth wide open, preparing for a fight with the coachman of Signor Gregorio.

"Be silent, Maria, and look after the luggage," I said. "Where is Antonio, porter?"

"I do not know, Signora."

"Where does he live?"

"Up in Piedimonte;" and the porter pointed vaguely to a dark crown of buildings somewhere among the clouds.

"How am I to get to Maniace if Antonio is not here?" I asked, feeling plainly I was to be pitied.

The porter, a good-natured man, and sorry for me, suggested calling the *impiegato*. The station-master, or *impiegato*, leaving his desk, came, and with most humane eyes sympathized.

"How can I find Antonio? I am going to stay with

the Signor Duca at Maniace.   Here are my boxes, what
am I to do?"

The *impiegato* suggested *patience* and the waiting-
room.

"Yes," said I, "but patience will not get me to
Maniace, forty miles on the other side of Etna, before
night.   Antonio was to be here when the train arrived
at eleven.   It is now twelve and he is not come."

"I will do anything for you that I can," said the
polite official.   "I am very sorry the Signora is disap-
pointed.   It is a long journey to Maniace, all uphill for
at least thirty miles round the back of Etna; and the
road is freshly mended with lava.   The weather, too, is
cold and stormy."

I had always dreaded this expedition to Maniace.
Etna looked so grey and deathlike from Taormina; three
parts covered with snow, the rest as black as ink.   And
there was a chance, at any moment, of another storm
coming on, and the road being blocked up.

But the Duchess had sent three telegrams.   In the
last she had said that "Antonio would be in waiting for
me at Piedimonte at eleven o'clock on that day, Thurs-
day."   Now, who Antonio was I did not know, only that
he was to take me to Maniace.

"I am very sorry for you, Signora," repeated the
polite *impiegato*, reflectively.   "Come into my room, there
is a fire."

Just 'as I was turning my back on the road, the
jingling of harness and of horse hoofs was heard coming
in haste through an olive wood lying between the station
and the shore.

"That is Antonio's young man," said the *impiegato*,
brightening up most sympathetically, and pointing to a

half-naked figure astride a bare-backed horse, with a gigantic bridle.

Antonio's young man, a boy, arrives breathless, leaps down, hitches up his falling trousers, sailor fashion (by this time all the *personnel* of the station is collected round me and Furiosa), and thus delivers himself:—

"Sor' Antonio is coming up with the carriage directly. He makes excuses to the Excellency for being late."

The boy is panting, the thin bony horse panting also.

"Why is Antonio not here?" I ask indignantly, forgetting that in Sicily no one ever is where he ought to be, or ever answers a question except with a lie.

"I do not know," says the boy, too young to be inventive.

It is well past twelve o'clock before a rattling of wheels is heard coming very fast through the same olive wood.

"Antonio is certainly on the road now," says the kind *impiegato*, who still hovers about me benevolently. Meanwhile, he has had my modest trunk removed within the rails of the platform, away from the beggars who, at intervals all through this scene, have been rushing at me as much as they dare.

A travel-worn landau now appears, dashing up to the gates, and Antonio announces himself by throwing down the reins and springing from the box. He is not in the least affected by all the trouble he has given, and, whip in hand, smiles at me serenely.

"Why were you not here at eleven?" I ask, as the modest trunk is being lashed on behind. "The Duchess telegraphed 'eleven precisely.'"

"Signora," says Antonio, taking off his hat, "I was slightly incommoded, and one of my horses went lame. But we have plenty of time."

All this I knew to be lies; but, *cui bono?* When a whole population lies, one cannot reproach an individual.

"At what hour shall we arrive?"

"About nightfall." (Now, as we are in the month of March this may mean anything.)

"Is it safe?" I ask next.

"Perfectly, Signora. I drove the Signor Duca down last week without an escort. But the roads are newly mended with lava, and are very heavy, we must go generally at a walking pace. The Signora must be prepared for this. Pray let us start."

"We should have been half way up Etna by this time but for you," puts in Furiosa, with the air of a war-horse scenting battle. "All very fine to talk of 'starting,' when the Signora has been waiting for you more than an hour."

This reproach Antonio affects not to hear. With a masterful roll of his dark eyes, and the mere shadow of a smile on his lips, he hands me into the carriage, Furiosa grumbling in her native tongue, and the bags follow.

There are three horses: one in front, tandem-fashion, inclined, throughout the journey to be discursive, and to peep over precipices; the others immoveably steady. The ragged boy is, I find, to accompany us, stationed behind on my box. I may mention, *en passant*, that that boy utterly ruins it, reducing the surface to a pulpy substance with the stamping of his naked feet. When we go up-hill he runs beside us; when we go down, he stamps on the lid.

His eyes wait on the Padrone; he is continually fiddling with the harness, adjusting the bits, or smoothing the reins. When he lags behind, Antonio whistles to him; and when he is beside him discourses in the Sicilian dialect with an air of benignant superiority.

Up the slopes of Etna we labour by a zigzag route to the town of Piedimonte. As at Taormina, the station is on the shore, quite irrespective of the town. The day is grey, misty, and squally. Now and then the wind sweeps off the clouds in the valleys, and a dash of lurid light illumines mountain bases along a rocky river bed; but our general out-look is murky. Taormina to the right, and Etna to the left, are hopelessly veiled.

I hear the Fiume Freddo dashing down as we labour up-hill. The river Cantara and its bridge we leave to our right. The Cantara and the Fiume Freddo are the two principal outlets of the snows of Etna on this side. The Cantara debouches at Giardini; the Fiume Freddo runs down to the sea at Piedimonte station. Its icy waters are said to be poisonous. At any rate, the trout and eels do not think so, as I came to know at Maniace.

We fly across the high arches of an old bridge (the Ponte della Disgraziata), over the parapet of which our tandem horse, dangerously reflective, gazes into the foaming waters. Antonio, an admirable driver, suitably admonishes now, and on every other occasion, this misplaced curiosity. The Fiume Freddo is one of the mountain streams said to have sprung from the blood of Acis. In its whirling current down Etna's side we picture the beautiful shepherd ever fleeing from terrible Polyphemus.

Now we pass altogether into a black lava world. The road is black as the country, and so continues all day. The stones piled up to mend it are black also. The vineyards are terraced in rich black earth. The rocks are black; ravines, cliffs, valleys, boulders, precipices, black also. A few orange-grounds and olive-woods, and those omnipresent cacti, bursting through stony limits, dash the sombre earth for a little way with colour; then these also vanish.

Terraced vineyards are everywhere—above, below, at hand. The lava earth is precious for good wine. The sun darts down upon the metallic soil, giving the grapes that much-approved burnt flavour.

Every foot of ground is utilized. On the most inaccessible rocks, under the very snows of Etna, on the edge of Tartarean lava-streams, invading the bounds of mighty chestnut and oak forests, I can spy out vineyards.

The industry is marvellous. The cleanness of the ground, the healthiness of the plants, show this. No *dolce far niente* for the poor peasant here as in the sunny gardens of the sea-shore. Hard work and patient labour are needful to draw wine from this lava-smitten soil.

Piedimonte, built of lava, is a wretched, poverty-stricken town of one-storied houses; the roofs strapped down, as it were, ready for avalanches of snow or of fire.

We pass through the single street at full gallop, Antonio lashing the tandem horse into a flying madness. The beggars have no chance. Outside, we mount again at a foot's pace.

Quite a different population this from the seaboard; thin, hard-featured, leather-skinned peasants, quite Scotch in their ugliness. A sad-eyed child, her head bound by a thick red cloth (any scrap of available clothing is always piled on the head) looks up at me with pitiful eyes, as she trails along upon her naked feet, dragging a heavy axe behind her. Does she want a penny, that little maid? Or is her pathetic gaze but the sadness of poverty? A father, in knee-breeches and blue stockings and a ragged coat, with a wallet at his back, followed by

two pinched, hungry-faced boys, trudge painfully, bare-
footed, through sharp stones. Where is that father bound
for? Infinite space is before us; the terrible crater at
one side; boulders of lava as big as houses on the other.

Always ascending, we reach a second squalid-looking
town, Linguagrossa, built also of lava. Linguagrossa (so
named from its ugly dialect) is seventeen hundred feet
above the sea!

Linguagrossa, backed by the dark line of forests, is
bad; but it is better than Piedimonte.* There are
carved balconies to the windows, bringing with them just
a suspicion of rustic Rosinas, guitars, castanets, and
moonlit nights; and the one long, wide street is full of
people staring. Whether it is a *festa*, I know not.

I find melancholy children not incidental, but in-
digenous. Blue and black eyes of every shade are turned
upon me imploringly.

Mr. Antonio, however, flies along whenever he can,
profiting by every inch of level ground to push on his
horses. He is saluting friends with his whip all the way.
When he meets an acquaintance, the ragged boy, hanging on behind, performs, as I discover to my cost, acro-
batic feats on the lid of my box. These raise a languid
smile upon the sad faces of the peasants.

More barren and more wintry grow the acclivities of
Etna.

As we mount upwards, we penetrate into shifting
mist clouds almost palpable; lava ridges break out of
the snow, the woods over our heads are white and hoary,
and small cones and extinct craters upheave beside us.

Beyond Linguagrossa even the lava vineyards little
by little fall away, and are succeeded by small hazel-

---

* Since the last eruption, Linguagrossa will not look so well.

woods as green and nutty-looking as Berkshire copses.
Like these, they are cut for burning, leaving the tufted
roots mossy and verdant. Not only hazel-woods, but
silver birch, and the grass sprinkled with familiar prim-
roses and milk-wort. The sight of these May flowers
and the quaint copses, along with the cloudiness, the
greyness, and the keen damp air beating in my face,
comes to me like a vision of home and of England!

We are always mounting, always at a foot's pace,
and always on the surface of a black road newly laid
with lava; a very disagreeable process, I can declare from
experience.

You must love your friends very much to reach them,
forty miles over a lava-bed.

The erratic boy is the only bright object in the
ghastly landscape. He vaults up and down like a monkey,
laughs to himself, sings, whistles, runs and leaps beside
the horses, chatters incessantly to Antonio, and turns
wheels at the corners of the road.

As the scene grows more and more desolate and
involved with accumulating lava, the boy becomes more
and more discursive, and Antonio increasingly condescending. Towards me he maintains a civil, but rigid,
demeanour. On every subject except the "Duca" I find
him impenetrable.

As to talking with Furiosa, I never dream of it. She
regards the whole journey with jaundiced eyes, and herself as a victim to circumstances.

If I speak, I know she will complain, so I hold my
peace.

We are rising painfully round the flanks of the
mighty volcano crater, of which we can see nothing but
an impenetrable wall of mist.

Above us, piercing through the snow, the lower spurs

of the wooded region of Etna follow us. I can see the skeletons of huge trees lining the sides of sombre cliffs and snow-clad gorges.

The clouds sweep across even this limited view, and now and then we are favoured by a violent snow-storm. In spite of the upraised hood, it beats coldly in our faces. Furiosa, with indignant glances, heaps shawls upon her head. I draw my sealskin closer round me.

Still mounting! Antonio will give no certain information. It is about three o'clock now; he always says we shall be at the summit in an "oretta." (They will go out of their way here to invent a lie rather than answer a question.)

How cold it is! Snow patches beside the road, and lying about in the little English copses. I do not put my wraps on my head like the Furiosa—fortunately she has dozed off to sleep—but I am glad to cover myself as with bed-clothes.

Now and then the clouds lift a little to our right, and I can espy a deep, deep valley, mapped out on the further side by purple mountains.

This is the upper valley of the Cantara, cleaving asunder lava beds, as it thunders downward to the sea at Piedimonte.

On the further side of Etna, the Simeto, rending apart green downs and tossed-up hillocks, cuts deep into the mountains-flanks, and flows drowsily into the sea through the great plain of Catania.

On every side mountains rise over our heads—grave, sombre, repulsive.

They might be of cast-iron but for scaly patches here and there, of coarse grass and brown moss: a scene such as Dante dreamed for his "Inferno"—where the dead earth is bound in a black winding-sheet!

The sight of Randazzo, a small mediæval town, is a great relief, the houses massed upon a conical hill, like a background of Masaccio or Ghirlandajio.

You enter it through a wall and a gate—quite refreshing, I assure you, after a sea of lava waves.

Yonder are the ruins of a feudal castle, perched on a rock; and there are human beings in the narrow streets and shops—a living world in fact, the existence of which I began to doubt, as we crawled up the naked sides of Etna.

Randazzo anywhere would be an interesting little place, how much more here, amid the weariness induced by lava.

In the time of Count Roger, it was a great centre of Norman-Saracenic annals. The encircling walls, and towers, the Castle and sculptured house-fronts, with pointed doors and ogee windows, announce the period.

The Emperor, Frederick II., born of a Norman mother, and through her, King of Sicily, christened Randazzo "Ætnea"—not the first city so named, as I shall have to tell hereafter. The Great Crater is only twelve miles distant.

For a little space, the earth laughs back at us, in gardens and fruit grounds. There are vineyards and fig-trees, and prickly pear and aloes make hedges for tiny fields, which men are tilling.

Deep below rises ridge upon ridge of mountains (I can count seven), opening into as many valleys, towards the centre of the island. But all so dim and shadowy, that these mountains might be grey clouds, or the grey clouds mountains!

Nothing is positive but that black mystery over our heads, and the black road before us.

Antonio, now grown into a mass of overcoats and

capes, is dull and silent. I would not insinuate that he is dozing, but if not, his immobility is amazing.

The tandem horse, resigned now, and incurious as an ancient wheeler, scents the keen air with upturned ears, and goes on his way subdued and patient. The boy still runs beside the wheel when the road allows it, but runs as one whose legs are weary!

Whenever I have interrogated Antonio as to the distance, he has two answers, which he uses turn about. "The Excellence will arrive after night-fall"; or, "In an *orella.*" Can anything be more vague?

Looking, as from a balloon, I make out a town, deep down over a precipice—a tawny-walled, desolate town of massed-up houses gathered round a castle. I am told that this is Maletto. The broad valley of the Cantara yawns beneath.

Before us, a dolomitic rock shoots up—straight on end—against a pale saffron-tinted sky. In the twilight it might be a Cyclops, barring our path.

Heavens! how our road circled round that rock for miles and miles in a kind of serpentine conglomeration of zigzags!

Now we have advanced so far that Etna is drawing off, out of sight, behind. Yet, though unseen, its awful presence is felt—in the famine-stricken land; in the empty river-beds, dried up by lava; the precipices up-hurled; the rocks shivered!

I have much of the resignation of the old traveller about me—I bow to the inevitable. But as the cold wind whirls across the rocks and screams among the crannies, I feel I have had enough.

What sustains me is the unmoved aspect of Antonio's back. As I view it from the inside of the carriage, whether he is waking or sleeping, it is full of confidence;

also the cock of his hat eminently re-assuring. If he did this road last week, with the Signor Duca, I can, and ought to do it now, though I am not a Duca.

At this point, driving apparently into Chaos, we take a sudden turn and descend a road so steep that the carriage is almost lifted to the horses' flanks, as they cautiously feel their way. The tandem horse, specially careful, smells the road like a dog.

A roaring torrent announces its presence by our side. In the gloom I can just see the steely blue waters pouring over stones.

The declivity, the torrent, and the vague outlines of greenish-tinted downs, shut us in on every side.

The skill of Antonio is admirable; but it is an awful road.

"Down, down, among the Dead Men!" I am humming to myself, to an accompaniment of roaring waters and sighing night winds!

There is but a stone or two between our wheels and the brink. Then a violent surging downwards, and an equally violent heaving upwards, and another water-course—bound for heaven knows where—rushes across the road.

Still down, down, down, as if to Tartarus!

Turning an acute angle, with a perilous jerk, a sudden light strikes across my face.

Furiosa screams, Antonio draws up. Before a word is spoken, I cry out, "I know it is Alec, come out to meet me with his lantern!"

"Yes, it is Alec," answers a pleasant voice, "Welcome to Maniace."

CHAPTER XVI.

"My Diary at Maniace."—A Mediæval Monastery.—A Ducal Family.
—Home Life.—Etna, the Godlike.—General George Maniace.

THERE is the house;—one long line of windows, all
alight.

Under the archway we dash into a blaze of torches
and lamps and candles, hastily caught up, and flaring
in the wind.

In the cortile stand the Signor Duca and the Signora
Duchessa, as in a picture, backed by campieri (rural
guards), in a sort of Tyrolese uniform, and servants,
male and female, a score.

Coming out of the cold black night, I am fairly dazed.
Kind words of welcome mix themselves up in my brain
with the windy shouts of Etna and the rush of many
waters. My knees barely support me as, on the Duca's
arm, I mount the stairs to the "piano nobile."

What luxury and warmth! A large room (the old
refectory), square, and full of colour, half hall, half
parlour, filled with the scent of flowers. Great logs are
blazing on the hearth; a piano, pictures over consoles,
vases of spring daffodils and wood hyacinths, hats and
gloves ranged in a table against the wall, a letter-box,
sofas with dogs asleep on them, dogs also wandering
about inclined to bite, a long vista of convent corridors
lighted by ranges of lamps, leading to bedrooms—all is
so strangely English, yet so foreign—a comfortable man-
sion, evolved out of a mediæval monastery, with that
mountain desolation outside.

Specially noticeable is the ducal family in the foreground. Alec, without his lantern, resplendent in evening

dress; the Duca, tall and aristocratic; the young ladies, lovely; the Duchessa, in a pink dress, all arrayed for dinner. The whole party are so smart and trim, I am suddenly overcome with shame at my own appearance— my wind-scorched face, my old torn dress, my battered hat, with the feathers all on end, and that indescribable all-pervading "crumpledness" consequent on a long journey.

How dreadful! "Come in here and be quiet," says her Grace, moving about the room like a bright domestic bee. (I am so giddy with the light and the heat, and the sound of many voices, that I can hardly stand.) In her own hearty way, which has so agreeably affected me ever since we were girls together, she drags me off into the drawing-room, presenting itself to me at that moment as the most gorgeous apartment I ever beheld, and shuts the door. I still, however, hear the voices of the party I have left in the saloon.

"Do leave Gru alone!" says A——, "he's so comfortable under a shawl."

"No, no," cries dark-eyed R——, apparently in the act of depriving Gru of his shawl, for sundry low growls reach my ear; "it is a bad habit. Go away, Gru! Downstairs, sir."

"Did the crushing-machine work well, sir?" asks Alec, my friend of the lantern, of his father, shut out of his own drawing-room by the abrupt kindness of the Duchess.

"Capitally," replies the Signor Duca; "it went uphill in splendid form."

"And the stones, papa?" asks a fresh young voice, I know is charming R——'s. "How many stones did you break with your own hands?"

"You may judge by my gloves; they are all in

holes. Mend them for me, my dear!" A general laugh
follows.

All this time I am telling the Duchess, who has gradually peeled me of my wraps, like an apple of its rind,
all about my journey. She is afraid of nothing. The
deluge would not alarm her. She would simply put on
her waterproof and goloshes, and go out and look for
the ark.

I thought the going round Etna in mist and hail
and snow, in an open carriage, a great feat, but she
laughs at it.

"Gracious! we shall soon teach you not to mind
that! at Maniace."

"But it was quite dark! and torrents, too, over the
road; why, the wheels quite hissed through them!"

At this she only laughs the more.

Alec, from behind the door, and R——, "If you do
that again, I'll——!"

A scuffle in the next room, peals of laughter, the
door opens, and the Duke walks in.

"I wanted to look after those new pigs, but I can't.
It is nearly dinner-time. Look at me."

"Yes," says the Duchess, "and not dressed."

I jump up. Dinner time, and dress! Good heavens!
Dress—after forty miles' jolting over lava! Can I
do it?

"Come along, my dear," says her lively Grace;
"unpack your boxes and make yourself respectable."
This said with a glance at my head.

"Yes," I say vaguely. "Yes, respectable for dinner,"
and I follow her down the monastic gallery to my room,
thinking how on earth I shall get Furiosa to do it, or
whether I can do it myself.

Of course I must. How can I present myself with

my head in its present condition at dinner, before the
Duke and Duchess, the young ladies, and all the
servants?

Well, I shut my door, and shovel off my clothes.
What does one not do in desperation?

I drag everything out of the box. I strew the floor.

Furiosa, frozen with cold, and with many shawls
gathered upon her head, stands by stony. She is incapable of help, and inclined to wrath. But just arrived
in a "casa ducale," she restrains herself.

Finally, I am turned out, as *from a bag*—well shaken
up and dusted. But my hair is impossible. I twist it,
I coax it. No use!

One cannot sleep *en coiffure*, yet up at three a.m.,
travel in wind and rain from that hour until eight p.m.,
and then expect one's hair to arrange itself! This
affair of my hair depresses me, also the redness of my
nose.

I hear the Duke and Duchess in the next room
laughing heartily. Are they laughing at *me?* At my
hair? my old black dress? Why else should they
laugh?

What a fool self-consciousness makes one! Is it
likely that the Duke and Duchess, the most good-
natured people in the world, should laugh at a guest
they have invited to their mountain home?

What a donkey I am! What a donkey any one is
who fancies other people trouble their heads about
them! Everybody has so much to do, so many subjects
of interest; there are so many highways and byways in
individuals, in families, in societies; such a narrow
circle round each entity, that the moment you are out
of sight you are as clean forgotten as though you never
existed!

All I remember of the evening is, that, though painfully sleepy, I contrive to listen to what Alec is saying
to the Duke about a murderer who rents a farm near
the house, and who went away in the morning, after
much litigation.

No one seems to care at all about the murderer,
not even R——.

The Duchess, who evidently sees a vista of repent-
ance and conversion, is, I think, sorry, that he is dis-
possessed. The Signor Duca only asks Alec "If he has
paid his rent?"

Now I must mention that Alec (I cannot tell you
how nice he is) is his father's *alter ego*, and permanent
agent at Maniace. The Duke and Duchess and lovely
young ladies being here only on a chance visit.

It is Sunday. While morning service is going on in
the saloon, read out by the Duke to the family, including the English servants, and the courier, Mr. Curzon,
a very important personage, and much more imposing
than the Signor Duca, I will note my impressions.

At Maniace, Etna towers over everything. It dominates us like a Deity. Its presence forms a part and
parcel of our daily life, as much as food, or sleep, or
motion.

The lines, too few and simple for absolute beauty,
are utterly overwhelming. A dazzling cone, perfectly
shadowless, pinnacles against a cold, blue sky. Beneath
the cone, close at hand, one dark horizontal line of
bank cuts across it. This bank is the "*Balzo*," an
accumulation of ancient lava beds, rent with crevices
and grottoes, and sprinkled with a sober verdure. That
is all.

What a mystery between those lines — the white
crater and the dark Balzo! What treasures of sighing

waters, dancing cascades, verdant glens, sombre pine
woods, fair lawns thick sown with Alpine flowers, moss,
ferns, basaltic backgrounds, yawning gulfs, and mountain
paths exquisite in lonely beauty, covering, as with a
slight glaze, a hidden world of subterranean fire! And
such a world! Grim, Satanic, awe-struck, terrible with
the crashing of earth's pillars, and black with the
reflex of extinct flames; a world of thunder-roar, earthquake, whirlwind, and avalanche; birth of a thousand
deaths, germ of an infinite variety of life, cut off and
annihilated!

But one day ago I had passed through that mysterious region—looked down into those bottomless chasms,
and lingered on the ledge of volcanoes; and now where
are they?——

I have seen Etna all round—on the eastern side
from Calabria, on the south from Catania and its plain,
and from Syracuse like a monstrous cloud, but nowhere
is it so stupendous as at Maniace.

That Etna should therefore, like King Charles's
head in Dickens' story, mix itself up with our daily
life, is not astonishing.

If we have a nightmare, it is Etna!

If, at dinner-time, it is announced that the cone is
visible, we all rush from the table, fling open the windows, and stare at it with eyes and opera-glasses. If
the moon shines clear on it at night, still greater excitement! Conducted by the courier, Mr. Curzon—dress-
coat, watch and chain, and quite the gentleman, who
also, like Etna, mixes himself up in all our life and
doings, and escorted by a bevy of dogs, we all tumble
over each other downstairs, and precipitate ourselves
outside. If Etna condescends to show itself continuously

for many hours, we seize on chairs and benches under the tuft of trees in front of the house, and sit gazing.

If it veils its head in cloud and mist, as is too often the case, we are miserable. Her Grace goes to a certain window in the dining-room every five minutes to report progress. Mr. Curzon fidgets in and out incessantly, always closing the door with a bang, while Alec and the Signor Duca discuss the chances of lifting clouds and currents of wind.

At Maniace life is a blank without Etna. One March day, after much bad weather and consequent disappearance of the Presiding Deity, when the sun did come out, turning the cone into marvellous crystallization of a seraphic whiteness, we saluted each other in a burst of ecstasy.

As in the East, at break of day, the word is passed round, "Rejoice; it is Easter!" so we pass round the word—A—— to K——, Mr. Curzon to the Signor Duca, for once caught napping over the *Times*, Alec generally, and the servants to each other, "Rejoice, behold Etna!"

Even in continuous snow and hail, rain and fog, the fact of its sublime presence cannot be overlooked. There it is, like destiny, dominating the storm-clouds.

The long, low, many-windowed house, with a fine old Norman church and Norman outbuildings attached, lies chill and grey, under the shadow of green downs, and rushing waters, dashing over mossy stones, sing everlasting melodies to the moated walls.

Behind there is the old convent-garden, where tulips and hyacinths, violets and daffodils, snowdrops and Turk's-head, crowd into beds of antique patterns. The trees, mulberry and walnut, with big bare limbs, are much exercised by the wind. A donkey is tethered under one of them, on a bit of grass, hee-hawing agreeably.

Gru's kennel is attached to another tree, and Gru is solacing himself with barking.

In the centre there is a worm-eaten quadrant, rising out of lavender and herbs; four little fountains are trickling at the four corners, very chary of water, and lilacs and guelder roses shut in the whole. Behind there are a bake-house, a wash-house, and a wood-house, to all of which I am conducted by her active Grace.

Maniace is at the confluence of many rivers. One of them is the Simeto, on which lies Centorbi, a Siculian centre of Ducetius.

Each river opens out chains of green rounded heights, and each height divides itself into long lines of green valleys, sad and silent as the grave. Through these I walk with the Signor Duca, among weeds and stones and mossy grass. Aloft, on the summits, are ancient oak-forests, dimly visible, and, here and there, a dolomitic crag uprises, as if in mockery of the plain.

What scenes of idyllic loveliness these untrodden valleys hold, who can say? Only Etna, looking over into the heart of the earth's secrets, knows!

To me it all comes as a wilderness of primeval beauty—a sort of "no man's land," exquisitely attractive.

In one of my many walks among the valleys, the Signor Duca points out to me a dark isolated rock beside a river-bank.

"That," says he, "is called the 'Saracen's Rock;' and there was gained a famous victory. We take our name from that spot, the site of a Byzantine city."

The mention of a city brings me to General George Maniace.

On this very spot, eight miles from Bronté, where stands that huge splintered rock beside the river, about a mile from the house proper, General George beat the Saracens, and founded a city, named after himself.

It was in the eleventh century, Leo the Philosopher, and, later, Michael Palæologus, reigning at Constantinople; and Sicily become a Byzantine province.

Belisarius had been fighting here, and afterwards Narses—both trying their hand against the omnipotent Goths.

Now it is the Saracens. General George was a very famous soldier, although the British public know nothing more of him than as a street and castle at Syracuse, and a house appendage to an English peerage.

To me he is interesting, as the first commander who seriously appreciated the nascent qualities of the Normans.

CHAPTER XVII.

The Duchess and Bino of the Lion Head.—"Baleno."—"Too Comfortable."—Walk to the Boschetto.

THE murderer is back in his farm. Alec has sent for the Guardia pubblica (police) from Bronté. We can see him—not Alec—but the murderer: a dark figure, going in and out of his door, on a tract of moorland under the shadow of the Balzo. He shares our attention all the morning with Etna. We have been studying both at intervals with opera-glasses, out of the dining-room window.

It is very cold to-day; everything sparkling like sugar crystals, under a steely sun. Furiosa is in her tempers —shut up in her room with a large brazier of charcoal. After calling to her many times to come and dress me, and indeed running down the long corridor in a dishevelled condition to batter at her door, she emerges at last, prepared for battle.

I can do nothing all the morning but watch the Duchess in the garden, in her waterproof. Now she is thrashing Gru for killing a drake. Bino of the lion head —Alec's pet—meanwhile attacks the tethered donkey, and is mauling him in style. In an instant her Grace turns on Bino, while R——, with her large black eyes and upturned face, her graceful coaxing ways, and womanly form, is pleading for both the dogs.

But R—— pleads in vain.

The Duchess is inexorable as fate. Condign punishment is administered by herself on Bino, assisted by Mr. Curzon, metamorphosed for the time being into a Sicilian peasant, in attendance on the Duke, just arrived from the carpenter's shed.

I am invited by the young ladies to drive. But on the appearance of a black horse, called Baleno (Lightning), harnessed to a basket-carriage, I vehemently declare that "I prefer walking." It is quite true. I prefer walking at all times—and now!

Fancy the hippogriff, on whose back Rinaldo rode to the moon, in harness, and you have Baleno!

He inaugurates his appearance by rising on his hind legs, and pawing in the air; then he kicks, bounds, and plunges.

A campiere in uniform, who drives him from the stable, winks at me, and whispers, "*Capriccioso, ma buono.*" I reply, without the wink, "*Demonio!*"

The Duchess, in her waterproof, looks on quite composedly. The sweet young ladies prepare to get into the carriage, during a partial cessation of kicks and bounds. A——, I see, is to drive; R—— to sit beside

her; the campiere to perch behind and intervene in case
of danger.

"Good God! Duchess, do you mean to say the girls
are going out with that fearful animal!"

I feel that a look of horror is on my face. The
Duchess bursts into her merry laugh, echoed by A——
and R——. (A—— is now oscillating on the seat; the
other sister holding on, and not yet able to put her foot
on the step.) Imaginary flies seem at this moment to
drive Baleno mad. He is tossing his head wildly from
side to side, and switching his tail. Very imaginary
flies indeed! It is so cold that I am clapping my hands
together to keep them warm, while I stand staring. I
never do anything else at Maniace but stare.

Now A—— has the reins in hand. Brave girl;
R——, her petticoats a mass of mud, is beside her;
both are quite unmoved and smiling at me. The
Duchess, surrounded by dogs, smiles also. The campiere vaults into his seat behind, like an acrobat. A
rear, a bound, a dash, and they rattle through the portone, and fly, rather than gallop, up the only road to the
Balzo.

"How can you?" I ask, gazing reproachfully at the
Duchess, then at the fading prospective of the girls, already quite small in the distance.

"Good Heavens, my dear! What a fool you are!
We drive out with Baleno every day. I have stayed at
home for you. Don't talk nonsense!"

"Nonsense! Hum! If I hear,"—etc. etc.

Exeunt into the garden. Duchess laughing, surrounded by dogs barking, myself wearing a serious
visage.

Scene changes. The garden.

The Signor Duca—very tall, upright, and handsome

—striding up and down among the flower-borders, in company with his son Alec, discoursing eloquently about the stone-crusher—a machine newly imported from England.

Scene closes.

Night approaches. Dinner (and what a good one!) —and to bed. Scene opens.

Etna throned in amazing majesty. Much snow has fallen; and the flanks are blazing white down to the Balzo. Nothing to distract the eye—nothing to confuse the brain, nothing to hinder infinite contemplation! There are some dark far-off stains near the crater, as if Typhon had escaped, and these were his footmarks——

We all spend the entire morning under the dazzling splendour of "The Presence."

In the house it is dark and chill, spite of huge wood fires, and pretty graceful R—— hovering about; and Alec occasionally refreshing us with the sight of his slim legs and neat knickerbockers.

I feel I eat too much, and I resolve to reform; but every time I sit down I break my resolution. The cuisine is so good, and I am so hungry!

It is a well-furnished board. The Signor Duca does the honours gracefully; the Duchess picks like a bird, and laughs and talks. The young ladies, as sweet as flowers in May, have delicate appetites; and Alec—well, I cannot put down in print all I think of Alec.

The only discord is Alec's French wine grower, or sub-factor, who, through the kindness of her Grace, is admitted. This man is coarse, contradictory, and ill-dressed. The ducal pair, perfect in the simplicity of their high breeding, inspire him with no respect whatever. They are too good-hearted to assert themselves, especially with inferiors.

"Signor X——," says charming R——, twisting her piquant mouth into a *moue*, and pointing to the tall, obnoxious figure retreating through the hall. "Signor X—— is Signor X——. Fortunately no one is, or can be, like him. He is utterly without tact."

"Utterly," I reply; "and very impertinent."

"You think so," joins in Alec. "But he has his good qualities all the same. In the office I keep him in order. When alone with me Signor X—— is as well drilled as Bino."

(I may add, *en passant*, "that Bino is anything but well drilled," spite of the Duchess's flagellations.)

"Goodness! don't talk so loud," whispers R——, "X—— is on the stairs. He may hear you."

"Why does not the Duke snub him?" I inquire.

"My father likes a quiet life," returns Alec. "Soldiers always do at home, you know. And my mother is too amiable."

At this moment the obnoxious individual becomes visible from the window, amongst the masses of purple violets, red tulips, and sceptres of pink and white hyacinths, scurrying up and down the trim, box-edged walks, a cigar in his mouth, like a spirit in torture. Straightway the flowers hang their dewy heads as though oppressed; the birds fly low, over his billy-cock hat, chirping and twittering to peck at him if they can; and the donkey, chained on a grass-plot, under the great mulberry tree in the midst, lifts up his head and brays!

After lunch we take a long walk to the Boschetto; the Duke mounted on a very small donkey, his feet touching the ground; Alec brandishing my shawl like a star-spangled banner in the breeze; R—— showing her well-turned ankles in the neatest of walking-boots; and I—I tear a flounce early in the entertainment, and have to hold it up, also my dress, and a pair of goloshes which hurt me, *I* am laden like a pack-horse, and *wretched!*

The great smooth green mountains lie around. In their midst the grey old Monastery and the venerable Norman church. The roar of many waters is in our ears; and Etna—no, I will *not* say one word more about Etna!

We leap across streamlets, vault over puddles from stone to stone, run up and down rotten banks, and slide upon black mud, the Signor Duca riding on serenely in front, attended by two campieri, and followed by Mr. Curzon, in a mixed theatrical costume of a highland character.

Conversation under these circumstances is circumscribed, especially as Bino (of the lion head) occupies the entire attention of the gentlemen.

With the utmost difficulty they prevent the sudden massacre of two donkeys, a red cow, and a most innocent calf, reposing on the grass; likewise of a neighbouring dog, of a peculiarly humble and retiring turn of mind.

This kind of tournament continues, until I come to look on Bino as a criminal of the most sanguinary type.

At last we reach the gate of the Boschetto—an open wood of scathed, wind-tormented oaks.

Here we come upon one of the Duke's new roads (this winter alone he has made four miles of new roads to open up the mountains), a mass of sharp piled-up stones, along which we pass in a series of gymnastics.

We drop the Duke at the stone-breakers—six old men in a row, all rap, rap, rapping.

He, dismounting from his donkey, takes off his coat

and joins them. Mr. Curzon at the same instant dis-
encumbering himself of an elegant black velvet jacket.

As an "Idle Woman" I have seen many strange
sights, but never so strange a one as a courier breaking
stones!

That *is* a rarity! A Duke will do a great deal on
his own land—especially an enthusiastic road-maker and
farmer—but a courier!

Anyhow, Curzon hit away with a will. We left them
all at it, assisted by three boys, with skins like Red
Indians, carrying three baskets; the Duke's small donkey
reposing meekly on the grass, knowing that he is in for
it, and willing to take it easy—as to his battered legs.

On we go, following Alec over the abominable stones,
by the venerable oaks of the Boschetto. Etna (no, I
won't—only really it is lovely) glistening behind us in
the paleness of a spring sunset; on, until I thought the
Boschetto had miraculously extended itself like the
widow's cruse of oil.

Alec and R—— are used to new-laid roads; so, apparently, is Bino, rampaging about among perpetual
donkeys, only escaping death by a vigorous application
of Alec's stick; and pigs who scud off with Bino's fangs
at their throat—Alec, on his long legs, giving chase,
until the scene forms quite a tableau—donkeys, pigs,
and Bino, with Alec in the centre, triumphing like St.
Michael, and laying all his opponents in the dust!

CHAPTER XVIII.

A Picnic.—The Start.—Scenery.—A Courier Equestrian.—A Rural
Tragedy and Superstition.— Otaheite.— The Summit.—Back
again with the Dogs.—Mr. Curzon everywhere.

A PICNIC got up in my honour!

Dramatis personæ present at the start:—

Etna, four mules, and several stray donkeys; a campiere, armed to the teeth; a basket of provisions; another
French vine-grower, introduced by Alec—friend of Signor
X——; Madame, j'ai l'honneur de, etc., etc.; cocks, hens,
dogs; a crowd of mules ready saddled and bridled; Alec
in knickerbockers; two strange men with whom he is
bargaining about timber (one with a fur cap and tartan
shawl, the other dirty and ragged. Loud talking indicates that Alec is disgusted and angry); the English
carpenter; Mr. Hodder, newly imported with engines
from England; (Hodder's wife "wishes she were a fairy,"
and could fly to Maniace! If you could only see the
sodden, matter-of-fact face and figure of Hodder, you
might realize what sort of "fairy" Mrs. Hodder would be
likely to make); two painted carts, gorgeous in colour; a
glorious sunshine; the Signor Duca shouldering an opera-
glass; his own particular small donkey. (Let the Duke
break stones, or ride a small donkey as much as he
likes, he is always *the* Duke—the finished gentleman,
the polished courtier; and so Mr. Curzon thinks, as he
comes out of the portone behind him, imitating him in
fancy clothes.) To these, Enter the Duchess in a rather
Meg Merrilees hat, with red poppies (Her Grace lends
herself rather better to the occasion than her consort
with his aristocratic clothes, and perfect boots and

An Idle Woman in Sicily.   9

gaiters); Charming R——, as fresh as fresh can be, in a black hat and feathers; A——ditto; myself a blank, but satisfied with my appearance; Retainers, Campieri, Servants, several Ladiesmaids, chastely elegant, grouped about in attitudes; Furiosa, two shawls on her head, looking askance, out of a window; a Cook, all in white, like a ghost; a ragged Colt, and several Beggars.

Amid the roar of waters, the braying of mules, the cackling of fowls, the screech of peahens, and the barking of dogs, we are off, a long cavalcade, riding singly —Indian file, on mules. Over one boiling river, crossed by a wooden bridge; then turn to the right across another, and, further on, a third river, white with foam.

The round green mountains we are to scale rise before us. The air is calm. There is a great silence. The colour as of a desolate nature all around. Not trimmed and dressed, but primeval, archaic—nature as it got itself out of the ark, purified by the waters.

The crown of the mountains before us are fringed with dark lines of wood. Those are the oak forests—as old perhaps as the Saracens—Druid-like trees, to cut down which is the scope of the Duke's road on which we are travelling.

For are not the aged trees spoiling? And are not the wide valleys which stretch upwards, each watered by its foaming river, to be garlanded by luxurious grapes?—the grapes which, by the energy of Alec and the rude Frenchman, are to make the good Bronté wine?

All this is clearer to me; and I admire the blank loveliness and green solitudes of the intertwining heights the more, because my back is to Etna. No one can do justice to a scene with Etna dazzling the eyes, as from Maniace.

Our road, like that of the Boschetto, all stones,—it

grows rougher and rougher as we ascend (the stone-
crusher can only do its work by degrees). We can come
to no harm, for the bridle of each mule is held by an
armed campiere, and Alec, with his blue eyes everywhere, is walking.

To the Signor Duca the road is much more beautiful
than the mountains. It is his own work, four miles long,
and it will bring down riches from the summits.

When the Duke came to Maniace there was no road
but that perilous one which brought me there. Now
they are winding all about. No wonder that to him
roads are beautiful, and that he is proud of them!

On strides Alec up-hill, and we follow silently.

Alec is so young, and merry, and boyish, yet so wise
and kind withal, and with such a talent for taking care
of every one, he always takes the lead!

Bino bounds on the green turf, ready to commit any
number of crimes *en route*. Bino and Martino, an ugly
terrier, and little Gru, the soul of mischief, both conscious that the Duchess cannot admonish them.

Mr. Curzon, in blue spectacles (that touch of refinement is perfect) rides a very lively roan cob, which carracoles among the stones, and gives him a world of
trouble.

Even when that roan is quiet, he rounds his neck
and champs his bit like a war-horse. In a general way
he kicks and rears, and occasionally bolts, carrying Mr.
Curzon and his blue spectacles into such remote distances
that he becomes a mere silhouette against the sky.
Sometimes the roan stands stock still, like the marble
horse of the Commendatore in "Don Giovanni," or sways
himself up and down as does a rocking-horse, until poor
Curzon is purple in the face.

The roan and his rider are the success of the day.

9*

The Duke and Alec follow them ceaselessly with their eyes, making signs to each other. The Duchess, less cautious, laughs outright, especially at the rocking-horse business, which does put poor blue-spectacled Curzon, well defined on the edge of a cliff, *an dernier· ridicule.*

Alec, biting his lips vigorously, not to explode before the men, whispers to me:—"That Curzon gave himself out as being very horsey, and begged for 'an animal with some go in him, you know, Mr. Alec—something lively.'"

(At this moment the roan [not Mr. Curzon, for he has no command of him], after one of his mountain excursions, pounds down recklessly upon the young ladies, causing A—— to scream, the Duke to utter something like an oath, and Alec to rush into the *mêlée.*)

"And the beggar don't ride three parts badly," says Alec, returning to my side after restoring order. "That roan is a stiff one out on the hills, let me tell you. I gave it to him on purpose, and he sticks to his saddle like a man!"

We rise and rise by the long zigzags of the new road. We look back on the crests of the hills, descending in long lines to the lonely valleys, and we gaze down into their silent bosoms (a sort of sacrilege in that majestic solitude). We behold the five rivers that meet and foam about the monastery of Maniace, and raise our eyes to ancient oak-forests fringing the heights.

We are in another world up here, quite near the sky —a fair, clear world, in which the light is born. The swallows dart hither and thither, low on the downs, affrighted at our presence. The crows wheel round in circles overhead, cawing loudly. The delicate green of the young wheat on the cultivated patches, and the fine sprouts of the grass, seem trembling with life. Dew shines on the leaves of every delicate way-side plant; spurge and fennel, acanthus and thistles, mere weeds, are sparkling in the sunshine; the hills cast long shadows into the valleys; and the white flowers of the beans scent the fresh breeze.

A sense of immensity overwhelms me. Etna behind, encircled by its white crown of satellite volcanoes, quivering in fields of light. But Etna, beside the sweetness of idyllic nature, wakes no sympathetic chord. In that pastoral paradise it comes like the blanched image of death, dominating a green and teeming life.

Naturally the new road does not grow smoother as we advance.˙ New things always are best at first; witness marriage, houses, bargains, and friendships.

We cross mountain torrents, over which Gru has to be carried on the Duchess' saddlebow, and landslips, over which Bino bolts and Alec sighs, for it is all fresh toil and trouble to the dear fellow.

Then we arrive at a steep incline, where the mountain-tops and oak forests are at hand-shaking distance; next, to a clayey bank, where a sudden chill seizes us.

Beside this bank, embedded in a heap of fresh-cut stones, stands a disabled stone-crusher, with one wheel missing.

A silence falls on all. Alec and R——, who have been chaffing become suddenly mute.

Checco, the guard in uniform, riding on in front with provisions for our picnic, who has been throwing stones for Bino to crack (failing any living game, a stone suits Bino), suddenly bows his head, uncovers, and crosses himself.

The Signor Duca raises his hat also, and Alec's pleasant eyes cloud with tears.

All the men in passing reverently uncover and cross themselves. A horrible gloom seems to float in between us and the disabled engine, as the shadow of that clayey bank falls.

I turn to Alec for an explanation.

"Ah, it was a sad business!" says Alec, with a sigh, pseaking low.

"My father was so pleased, and we were getting on so nicely with the road. The engine was first-rate. I drove it myself up Etna side here, from Piedimonte, forty miles, and a tough job I had! Three days on the road, and little time to sleep, and less to eat. And I was proud of it, and proud of the work I had done to show my father, when last week, while Beppo and the boy were filling, and Salvatore stood behind spreading the stones half of the iron tyre of one wheel flew off, and struck him dead.

"Poor Salvatore! he was a first-rate workman; I suppose it was a flaw in the iron.

"I attended the funeral as chief mourner.

"But the Sicilians will never work at that stone-crusher again. Nothing will persuade them that it was a simple accident; '*they see further*,' they say. What can you do? Heigh-ho! So we must finish this new road by hand, and a fine time we shall have of it."

After this nothing but Bino's antics can raise our spirits. In the absence of donkeys he is careering after crows, in the young wheat, a harmless occupation.

A—— is found to be seated on her horse's tail, and has to descend and have her saddle adjusted; and Mr. Curzon, with his blue spectacles, is discovered at a distant point, his fiery roan upright on her hind legs, over the brink of a precipice.

The Duchess is silent, and keeps well ahead. The poppies in her hat bob up and down. My mule, Giulia, and the campiere in a new suit of embroidered cloth, who leads her, are both so steady that I cannot get up the ghost of a fear.

We draw rein at a brick hut called "Otaheite," because the men from Maletto, who work there, live in round, mud wigwams, with smoke pouring out of the doors.

We exchange compliments with the swarthy men of Maletto: "How goes it?"   "What's doing?"

Then with each other: "Are you cold? Tired? Hungry? How grand it is! Superb! What a brick Curzon is!" (He has returned to us now, with the air of a conqueror, his roan reeking.)

The general result of inquiries is, that we are all, including the men from Maletto, crowding round our mules and staring their black eyes out of their heads, well and hearty; also red in the face with the chill mountain air blowing off Etna. Only we are dying of hunger. But no one dares to say so, because, even on mountain-tops and amid virgin forests and upon overhanging precipices, we are creatures of convention; and in company with dukes and duchesses, however condescending, one must not betray vulgar appetites.

The Signor Duca is building a large engine-house up here, and making a deep well, and doing all kinds of tiresome things. So we have to dismount, and wade through liquid mud and slush to admire them.

I use superlatives to get over it the faster. R——— pouts her pretty red lips and flashes her eyes. (R———

has the effect to me as of a maiden goddess bidden to a feast with no young god to meet her.)

What are stone-crushers, and engine-houses, and Etna, Mr. Curzon in blue spectacles, five rivers thundering to the sea, and picnics on mountain-tops, to a brilliant London belle?

Yet she bears it cheerfully, does R——, and smiles like an angel.

Alec strides about, explaining everything to the Signor Duca and to his mother. The workmen, covered with red mud, crowd round and kiss hands; then stand back, their rough caps off, and their shaggy manes of hair blowing in the wind, until the Duke, touching his hat with that true instinct of good breeding which made Louis XIV. bow to his housemaid, begs of them to "be covered." Upon which the excellent dark-skinned creatures, all teeth, eyes, and broad grins, murmur, "Benedica Eccellenza," and retire.

How they work, these Sicilians, with the eyes of the Duke upon them, rolling Cyclopean rocks up and down, thumping the sides of stolid oxen, and drawing wooden cradles, laden with stones, through the mud!

In the meanwhile, "we others" are wending our way on foot to further altitudes, towards a plot of fresh green turf, under the riven face of a stone quarry. An agreeable prospect occupies the foreground.

Mr. Curzon, on his knees, without his blue spectacles (though the wind is blinding, and wrenches us about as if it resented our invasion of its legitimate domain on the mountain-tops)—Mr. Curzon, I say, on his knees upon a white tablecloth, his head immersed in hampers and baskets, sandwich-papers flying about him like kite-signals, and an army of black bottles around, portentous to behold, is arranging our lunch! Blessed sight!

The campieri, in uniform, are rolling down great blocks of stone to serve as seats.

Seats! What, here? On a bleak mountain-side! By Heaven! I had pictured to myself a sheltered nook within friendly walls, knit together by ivy, vine, and oleander—a nook tipped with golden lichen and dainty parasites of echeveria and stonecrop—a nook, a cave perhaps, deep in the shelter of the oakforest! And here! Three thousand feet over Maniace, not a coign of shelter, with Etna for a background, and all the winds· of Æolus for neighbours!

I am trembling with cold inside and out. I say nothing, not even to A——, who, blue in the face, I am sure, feels much as I do.

If I *must* sit and eat in a hurricane, well: it is all in the day's work; but I don't *prefer* a sore throat, or a lumbago, or perhaps a fever.

I cannot join in heartily when the Duchess, with her cheery laugh, says: "It is glorious to lunch in face of such a prospect!" and the Signor Duca, rubbing his hands, echoes her.

Then they both seat themselves on two flat stones, and instantly become helpless victims to a tornado.

Meanwhile, Mr. Curzon's incantations (including kicks all round to the dogs, and muttered oaths at the campieri) have produced no end of good things—cold jellied beef, out of a case, juicy and trembling, hams, fowls, pâtés, cakes, and wine.

When I cannot help it, I sit down too. When I have my plate full I can bear the wind and cold better.

The Duke, brandishing his silver horn full of rich Maniace wine, rises, and is about to drink a *brindisi* to the new road, when the thoughtful Alec stops him.

"Salvatore was only killed last week, father," he whispers, "and the widow and the little children——"

"Right, my boy," says the Signor Duca, tossing off his horn in silence, "I forgot——"

How we eat! I don't think I ever enjoyed a meal so much in my life. My back turned to the keen wind, and to A—— and R——, who kindly forgive me.

Between the courses the mules and Mr. Curzon's roan, tethered to the outstanding oaks, neigh and prance, the Duke's donkey hee-haws, and the men, six in number, with long muskets—everybody is armed, and always goes about armed; for although this is the province of Messina, and considered safe, yet Sicily is a land of brigands—are stretched on the ground full length, waiting for their turn to eat, and singing choruses in a sad minor key—the wind bearing off the notes, in a wild, random way, God knows where; perhaps to Vulcan or Enceladus.

In these strange latitudes, who can tell what becomes of stray voices? Only let us hope Enceladus may not hear them, and turn upon his side, for that would mean an earthquake!

We eat and we eat; the wind blows and it blows. Bino, raising his lion head, barks, and feeling inaction fanciful, attacks the heels of Mr. Curzon's roan, causing the downfall of piles of plates and the overturning of cruets.

The Duke grumbles to Alec about that "confounded beast" (I am not sure the Duke did not use a stronger word), and Alec answers, "Bino is no worse than the others—only bigger and stronger. Martino is just as spiteful; and Gru a little devil."

A family dispute ensues. The Signor Duca says, "Bino must be muzzled." Alec replies, "It is cruel." And so on.

Then we all settle down again to our plates. Mr. Curzon, like the Genius of Plenty, dispensing more food out of more flying papers of cakes and sandwiches.

Will the picnic ever end? A question.

The sun comes out; and what with Bordeaux and Maniace wine, I am as warm as a toast, and I can now turn round on my stone seat and look at R——, always a pleasant object for eyes to fall on; only it is a Barmacide feast to her, poor girl, as I tell her, and she smiles acquiescence.

At last Mr. Curzon, when the frenzy for serving us has abated (he has let no one else touch anything, but done it all with his own hands), replaces his spectacles.

He can persuade us to eat no more!

"One leetle slice more, your Grace. Now, Lady R——, just dees one tart." (For I have forgotten to say that for reasons of his own, Curzon—as honest a Briton as ever wore shoe leather—affects a German accent.) "Zee! look—zo good—zee be di laast. Mr. Alec, von coop more vines."

"No—no—no, Curzon," a chorus runs all round. "Nothing more."

We rise; leaving the scraps to the excellent Curzon, and to the Sicilians; who, as far as I can see, do nothing but drink out of a barrel. Let us hope it is from a spring!

As we have nothing to do, we stroll vaguely about in the cold sunshine, among the fine old oaks; slipping up and down rocks, and stepping inopportunely into holes, when we scream and jump—sometimes on thornbushes, when we scream again.

As to the view, we have long ago said everything possible about it.

So, by common consent, the view is tabooed. Not even her Grace expatiates on it any more.

I distinctly declare that I do not relish mountains. The ascent, the picnic over, all my old prejudices return. The wind cannot be said to have returned, as it has never been away; only while I was eating I did not heed it.

Now, it becomes to me a violent and pertinacious enemy, getting very much the better of me.

In an incredibly short time Mr. Curzon has eaten, repacked everything in hampers, and mounted the ladies. When he himself succeeds in vaulting into the saddle, his lively roan strikes out so fiercely on all sides, that everyone avoids him.

I am to walk down with the Duke and Alec. We begin by the road; but, like the dogs, soon take to short cuts, very rough, and moist with landslips.

The rest file down solemnly, one by one showing dark and gaunt against a grey sky.

Bino varies the monotony by unearthing a pig. Martino goes at the pig first, then Bino follows. Then the pig—audacious creature!—faces Bino, who, in face of this provocation, flies upon it tooth and nail.

Oh! the squeaking and the howling; the cries, the curses, and the kicks!

The Duke rushes upon Bino. Alec belabours him with a stick; the campiere kicks him. In vain! Bino—his red and black mane all afloat—his eyes glaring like fire-coals, sticks to the pig.

What a scene in the high wind!

At last Bino is beaten off, and stoned ignominiously down hill. The Signor Duca declaring, and this time with a frown, "That that beast must have a muzzle or be shot."

"Yes, father," answers Alec, meekly.

Meanwhile escaped piggie rushes up a bank, squeaking dismally, into the shelter of some hole, known to himself, and is seen no more.

Nor is Bino; nor is Mr. Curzon, save in the very far distance, combating with his horse—a silhouette as before.

So, at last, down we are again, at the river, which crosses the new road. And Maniace is close by; with its long lines of convent roof; its Norman-Gothic church, dark and imposing; its outbuildings, and its almond-trees, white with blossom.

At the Sambuco ford, Martino, who dashes in, is carried away by the current. As his tan head and glassy eyes float past, there is a cry, and a "Save him—save the poor dog!" from everybody. Upon which, Mr. Curzon, coming from no one knows where, like fate, dashes off his horse, seizes the reins, rushes into the river—the horse after him and—pulls Martino out.

Setting the frightened animal on his legs upon the further bank, Mr. Curzon, his face flushed with the ardour of victory, turns round for applause. Alas! he does not obtain it.

The Duchess remarks coldly that Martino had much better have been left to his fate. He is a cur. No one wants him, and he is always getting Bino into scrapes. At which Mr. Curzon, much crestfallen, touches his hat, remounts his roan, and gallops on.

Here we are, back again on the wooden bridge, whence we had started in the morning, only with a difference. We are covered with Sicilian mud, and we have seen the mountains.

Close at home we find the English carpenter, Mr. Hodder, working on a beam with his chisel; and the idiot, Sanzio (who takes care of the poultry, and kills all the young chickens), beside him, astride on a newly-cut tree.

Sanzio lost his mother yesterday; and when the melancholy fact, with much caution, was announced to him, replied "*Tanto meglio.*" So not even the good-natured Duchess can make anything of him, though she does knit him a pair of red muffetees.

All the cocks and hens; the ducks and the pea-fowl; the campieri; the cook, in his snow-white cap, standing like a ghost in the portone; Furiosa, her head covered with shawls, leaning out of the window, are just as we left them. To see them, one could fancy our picnic was a dream!

So now indoors to have a cup of tea and rest before dinner.

CHAPTER XIX.

Aci Castello.—The Seven Rocks.—Polyphemus and Ulysses.—Aci Reale.—Acis and Galatea.

THERE are two railway stations on the coast between Messina and Catania, named after the shepherd-boy Acis, Aci Reale, and Aci Castello. His spirit is also embodied in at least two streams, running down *terrified* to the sea.

Aci Castello is but a poor, brown-looking town on the shoulder of a hill; a ruined Norman round tower in the midst. Here nature sings no pæans of delight, as at Ali and Scaletta. That lava death which sets in after Piedimonte reigns supreme. A pall lies over the earth.

Nothing but dreary skeletons of rocks, and streams as of basalt.

It is best to overlook the mean little town altogether, the red brick, sloping roofed station, at which we pause to take in water for the engine (perhaps from Acqua Grande, one of Acis' streams), and to turn to the left towards the slumbering waters of the bay.

Is it not lovely? The rolling depths of a watery world, smooth as orient pearls and clear as chrysoprase; a world in which distance is not, nor proportion, only colour!

And that fragrant line of perfect shore singing to the harmonies of the sea! What tints! What masses of colour! Acres of blue and white lupins, fields of marigolds, rosy sea-pinks clothing the rocks, delicious yellowness of citron and mimosa; fierce-eyed genista peeping out of rocks, brilliant young grass. A carpet fresh from nature's loom, sown with oxalis, bee-orchis, gentian, pimpernel, and moon-daisies, mixed up with the blackness of lava-streams!

On one side of Aci, seven basalt rocks rise out of the calm blue sea, following each other in a regular irregularity. These are the Scopuli Cyclopum which blinded Polyphemus hurled after Ulysses as he was putting off to sea.

The first rock, a short distance from the beach, called Isola d'Aci, is flat and wreathed with a few brown vine leaves, an olive or two, and plants of spurge and fennel. A cave on one side, reached by some steps cut in the rock, is called the *Grotta dei Ciclopi.* But this dreary hole does not at all correspond with Homer's cheerful description of Polyphemus' cavern, shrouded by groves and woods.

The six other rocks rise bare and pointed from the

sea; diminishing in size as they recede; the last, but a little one, an after-thought, as it were, of spiteful Polyphemus.

Polyphemus and the Cyclops must not be confounded with the Titans—heaven-born warriors, sons of earth and sky and own brothers to Saturn, who, for their rebellion against Jupiter, are bound within the fiery caves of Etna from the dawn of time.

The Cyclops neither fought, nor ploughed, nor sowed, nor, although Neptune's sons, were they seafaring, or possessed of any craft. Simply they lived apart, dispersed in caves and holes on Etna's side, tenders of sheep, milkers of herds, and makers of cheese; yet, not objecting to a meal of human flesh when it fell handy.

Impious they are like the Titans, mockers of gods and scoffers of Jupiter, whose thunder, forged at hand in Vulcan's workshop, they thoroughly despise.

Polyphemus is their king, of bulk so great, that his head towers above them all, as Etna's cone towers over its clustered crown of lesser craters. His one eye is but the poetic necessity of the one volcanic blaze.

His roars, the rumble of the earthquake; his heavy footsteps, the crushing of the storm; his uplifted arm, the thunderbolt that falls. Whether Polyphemus be made for Etna, or Etna for Polyphemus, who can tell?

At least, each theory harmonizes with the other; they are poetically one.

Familiar as it is, one loves to recall Ulysses' adventures with the Cyclops.

One can imagine the wrath of Polyphemus, returning to find his cave occupied by the Trojan chief and his luckless crew, who had taken shelter there awhile, on their voyage from the land of the Lotophagi. And one pictures their dismay, when for all answer to the specious words of Ulysses, the monster seizes on two of the sailors, the plumpest and the reddest, and cracking all their bones within his jaws, bolts them outright.

But Ulysses reflects; he has plenty of time for reflection, for he and his comrades are shut up all day while the Cyclops is away pasturing his flocks; only to return, however, and sup luxuriously on two or three more plump sailors.

"Cyclops," cries Ulysses, who has reflected to some purpose, "as human flesh seems so pleasant to you, let me offer you a draught of human wine to wash it down."

As the liquor gurgles down his throat, the delighted monster grunts with savage glee.

"This is no mortal juice," he cries; "but nectar stolen from heaven; give me more!"

Then, turning to Ulysses, "I promise you, Trojan stranger, that for this good wine I will devour you last of all."

When Ulysses once forms his plans, the issue is seldom doubtful.

One can almost anticipate what follows; how, while the giant sleeps, overcome by the fumes of the wine, Ulysses bores out his one eye with the stake he has so carefully made red-hot beforehand.

And how the yells of the blinded wretch echo uselessly round the cave, as he gropes about trying to clutch Ulysses.

And lastly, how, standing mournfully at the mouth of his cave to let his flock out, but keep the strangers in, he misses his prey after all.

For Ulysses and his crew have passed out, under his hands, bound by withy bands beneath the bodies of those very sheep!

Of little avail is it that Polyphemus rushes after them and hurls rock after rock into the sea, whence comes the voice of Ulysses, taunting him from the ship.

It is too late! Ulysses sails away unscathed, and the seven rocks forming the strange line before me settle into their places amid the waves.

This throwing about of rocks by the Cyclops has a double moral. Polyphemus, apart from his personal adventures with Galatea and Ulysses, prefigures the earthquakes that upheave Etna's sides.

The rocks flung at Acis and Ulysses are but a combustion of nature on this volcanic shore.

The Greek myths are always faithful to local tradition.

Looking, as I do now, at this heaped-up coast of lava barriers, loose stones and gigantic boulders, all black as Erebus, I feel this instinctively without any process of reasoning.

Similar in its meaning of fabled detail is the myth of Enceladus—a Titan, or Typhon, brother of Jupiter, bound under his earthly throne on Etna.

The roars of the mountain are Typhon's groans; the flames and smoke his breath; and when he turns upon his fiery bed, earthquakes shake the world.

Prometheus, lying bound outside Caucasus, was delivered by Hercules, but the torment of Enceladus, in the throes of the volcano, knows no rest nor end.

With Vulcan, God of Fire, who plies his hammer within the crater to forge the bolts of Jove, we have the thunders of the mountain.

It is curious to note how all the myths of Etna group themselves round Jupiter. In the mythologic division of Trinacria, Himera on the north was Minerva's portion; Diana possessed Ortygia in the south; Demeter and

Proserpine, the plains of Catania and the mountain of Enna; and Zeus, the great fire-dome, dominating all.

Either as prison or work-shop, flame-crowned throne or forest wilderness, loved by the maiden goddesses, his daughters, Etna is altogether Jove's.

Next to the station of Aci Castello is the pretty town of Aci Reale.

Here we are well out of the lava-death. Lava, indeed, does crop up all along this coast; but here, the wealth of vegetation enshrouds it like flowers upon a bier.

Aci lies gleefully mapped out upon a smiling hillside, decorated with white churches and campanili, barocco palaces, and galleried houses, belted in mazes of oranges and blue-leaved olives.

Down at the station, level with the road, in the midst of fiacres, beggars, dust, railway whistles, and rumbling of trains, a native millionaire has built a magnificent hotel. The long rows of cheerful windows, cool behind their green shutters, look out on fig and fruit orchards nodding over high walls.

The hotel is, I believe, commodious, clean, and cheap.

Why did the native millionaire, with all that dazzling coast to choose from, select a site where there is nothing but walls to gaze on?

Here Acis was crushed by the rocks hurled on him by jealous Polyphemus, enamoured of the yellow-haired Nereid whom he loved; and here he was turned into a stream, as a merciful escape from death.

But the stream called Acqua Grande is not at all the Fiume Freddo I had passed on my way to Maniace, so here we have a direct divergence of poetic origins.

As there are many Aci, so there are many streams,
all born among the lava borders of Etna, and all running
down *terrified* to the sea.

Galatea was a sea-nymph of that golden strand. A
creature of flowing locks, entwined with tangling sea-
weed, shells, and coral-spray; bathing her amber head
and round white limbs amid the foamy waters of the
sandy bay.

"The loves" of Acis and Galatea were just below the
modern town, spread out upon the hills, over lava caves
and grottoes.

Loves of the woods and fields, pastoral and out-of-
doors, under the canopy of the blue heavens or on the
glittering sands.

The giant Polyphemus loved Galatea too; but she
disdained his surly gambols and his leering eye, disdained him, and fled from him.

He, straying about the lava crests in search of her,
looks down into a dell, and, oh! horror! beholds her
and Acis together!

With a hideous roar he rends the solid rocks and
flings them down on Acis.

This time he is not blind, and his hand is sure.
Acis is crushed.

Changed into a stream, he flies in rapid bounds
down to the sea.

Galatea dissolves into a fountain, lamenting in ever
murmuring sighs and tears of watery spray, for Acis'
loss.

CHAPTER XX.

Catania, Classic and Mediæval.—Chiarissima or Ætnea?—Catania and the Athenian Expedition.—The Theatre. — Alcibiades' Oration.—The Campanians.—The Carthaginians at Catania.—Roman Catania.—Saracens and Normans.—The Hohenstaufens.

A SERIES of tunnels engulfs us after Aci Reale. I am dazed by the rush and the darkness. The sweet air grows damp and chill. Deeper and deeper spreads the lava-death around, marked by bare scoriæ barriers (iron waves heaped up by rushing fires), miles of basalt walls, as through Phlegethonian fields; then with a screech, a trumpet-call and a whistle, we rush into the station of Catania.

From the moment I enter Catania and behold black houses, black roads, black flag-stones, black dust, black earth, a black harbour, and a black lava shore, I hate it. And the much-vaunted climate!

Already I have caught a cold from the damp air. How can it be otherwise? Close under Etna (the great crater is but twenty miles distant, straight up, the rise begins, one may say, in the very streets of Catania) the most violent transitions are inevitable.

Whether the wind blows, or does *not* blow off the snowy dome of Etna, except for one month in the year, under normal circumstances, it is capped with snow—makes summer or winter. And then what fighting with Boreas and Æolus, and windy Harpies let loose through miles of straight, broad streets—Etna at one end, and the lava-bound seaboard at the other!

Lava and Etna! You can no more get away from either here than at Maniace. Etna, very bare and very

ugly on this southern side, dominates Catania like a
demon! No shelter! No escape! Freezing or grill-
ing, as the ill-conditioned temper of the volcano may
decree.

Freeman calls Catania "the iron-bound child of Ionic
Naxos, created to do battle with Doric Syracuse;" and
he wonders how it has ever survived the blows of Syracuse, on one hand, and the fire-deluge of Etna at the
other. (The hostile states were very near each other.
From the Grand Hotel of Catania I can see the heights
over the Bay of Agosta, flowing on towards the ridge of
Hybla.)

What induced Hohenstaufen Frederic to christen
Catania "Chiarissima" is quite beyond me.

Was it the glamour of her soft Greek name? I am
not sure that that did not attract me also.

Yet who can predicate by what crack-jaw syllables
Catania was known in the Sikel dialect before the
Greeks came with their musical terminations, just as the
Italians euphonise rough-sounding surnames and cities.

An excellent idea of Syracusan Hiero's to call Grecian
Katane Ætnea. Cause and effect are not more indis-
solubly joined together than are the city and the mountain; but it was a strange freak to call himself Ætneas,
and claim heroic honours, as though he were the veritable
founder.

The whole thing was but a mere outburst of family
vanity. Gelon, his elder brother, accepted heroic honours
as founder of Syracuse, to which he had no right; and
Hiero, not to be behind-hand, became Ætneas, accepting
heroic honours also.

Hiero could boast that Attic Katane became under
him a Doric city. An easy process, achieved neither by
the sword nor conquest, but simply by forcibly ejecting

the Attic Greeks, and calling in Doric Greeks from Syracuse and Peloponnesus to take their place.

But with Hiero's death the exiles returned with Ducetius—and Catania, says Pindar, became as powerful a city as Carthage, and so Attic in temper that it entered into the Athenian war against Syracuse with a fury of partizanship which cost it dear.

Into the details of that great struggle, recorded by Thucydides, I cannot enter here, save as it touched Catania; at Catania it was that the first war-note was sounded.

In fact, but the flimsiest pretexts were needed to fan Athenian ambition in regard to Sicily. Insults by Dorians had been offered at Segeste and Leontini; and how could Ionic Athens, in the heyday of her power, refuse to interfere when solemnly called upon to do so?

And would Syracuse ever rest until it had subdued the whole island and the parent state also—Syracuse representing on fresh soil the eternal feud between Chalcydian Greeks and Dorians?

Besides, Athens longed passionately for Sicily—the seat of Jove, the home of her gods and demi-gods, the legend-land of her heroes, sung by her poets, chronicled by her historians, and knit to her by alliances many and close.

So Alcibiades, with Nicias and Lamachus, comes sailing with his Athenian fleet into Sicilian waters, and with great longing looks upon the sea-walls and splendid harbour of Catania!

But Catania, worked upon by a remnant of Doric partizans, mans her walls, shuts up her harbour, and refuses to receive him!

"However," say the Catanians, to sweeten the refusal, "although we cannot admit the Athenians into our harbour, we will not refuse Alcibiades and the other generals an audience in our theatre, hear what they may have to say."

This is in B.C. 415.

Imagine a black and very dingy stair, leading down to a still blacker and dingier hole, and you have before your eyes the ruins of the theatre at Catania, buried under ages of lava.

I went down as into eternal night. Certainly there was a torch carried by a "guardiano," but that only served to make darkness visible. The walls that open out at the bottom of the stairs, smutty in themselves, appear especially so, coming from the brilliant daylight outside.

There are eight flights of steps to descend, and thirty-three tiers of seats in the theatre, but all so mangled and built over by foundations, that my conceptions are utterly confounded.

One portion, near what remains of the proscenium, I did distinctly understand—some square-cut recesses, lined with marble in the thickness of the wall, once serving as seats of honour.

Here I was called upon by the "guardiano" to observe that upon these square-cut seats, once lined with marble, sat Nicias and Lamachus; and that on that proscenium Alcibiades made his celebrated oration to the Catanians while the Athenian troops were treacherously possessing themselves of their city and harbour.

If I could only believe in that rugged bit of dark stage, how interesting it would be! But I cannot.

The stage on which Alcibiades trod has never survived so many earthquakes. The theatre was too lofty to be spared. Count Roger, also, despoiled it. We know that one pillar was stolen for a statue of St. Agatha, set up in a piazza, and what he took as materials for his new cathedral, it is impossible to say.

These are the ruins of a Roman theatre, erected pro-bably on Grecian lines, but not in themselves Grecian.

While the Catanians dwelt upon the honeyed phrases of the "curled darling's" lisping speech (we are told that in Alcibiades *a lisp* had an *especial charm*, and set off his eloquence), marked the charm of his splendid person, and statue-like purity of feature, his scented locks lying heavy on his brow; his gold-embroidered chlamyde, the badge of the old country sweeping behind him; breathing, as it were, that fragrance of poetic at-mosphere which surrounds him even to this day, the Athenian hoplites were quietly pulling down a little gate of a very sorry structure, and swarming within the walls; "which undertaking being completed," says Thucydides, with a caustic sense of humour, "Alcibiades ends his oration, and the Athenian fleet finds at Catania a proper anchorage for ships and men, in the war against Syracuse."

Could Catania but have foreseen! Had she but re-flected! Hiero had loved her, but Dionysius hated her, and now, in revenge for the part she has taken against Syracuse he smites her as he smote Naxos. Though he is himself Greek, he gives Catania, bound hand and foot, to the Campanians, nor is she ever Greek again, except nominally under the Eastern emperors.

Once again was Catania and her harbour an object of eager envy, in that contest which almost gave Sicily to the fierce Carthaginian. Terrible was the naval battle in which Leptines, brother of Dionysius, was defeated with twenty thousand men before the onset of the Car-thaginian admiral, Magon.

And all the while Etna, in full eruption overhead,

barring the way of Himilcon, coming by land to support
Magon!

This is the historical eruption of B.C. 396.

The very course of the lava is still to be seen in a
blackened ridge above Giarre, one station from Aci
Reale, and twenty-four miles distant from the crater.
The spot is called Bosco d'Aci.

But in spite of this brilliant victory, Catania would
not yield. The Carthaginians perished miserably on the
promontory of Plemmyrium, Himilcon fled, and Dionysius
remained more powerful than ever.

The romantic figure of Pyrrhus appears for a moment, like a passing meteor, at Catania, to be followed
by greater Rome. Catania was one of her earliest ac-
quisitions after Syracuse had fallen to Marcellus.

One can judge of what Roman Catania was by her
monuments; to be groped for, indeed, now underground
and in darkness (the lava has taken care of that), but
still existing.

The Roman Amphitheatre of the age of Augustus is
under the street of Stesichoros; from its fragments it
appears to have been but a little smaller than the
Coliseum. The Roman building engrafted on the Greek
theatre of Alcibiades and Stesichoros (I forgot to recall
that Stesichoros figures on the proscenium as the intro-
ducer of lyric music) is very vast; and had its aqueducts
for Naumachiæ, as the Greek theatre at Syracuse has
its Nymphæum and water-course.

The Roman Forum is under the Cortile San Pan-
taleone.

A gymnasium near Frederic the Second's lava castle;
the basement of a Roman arch in the Corso; and vague
remains of aqueducts, baths, and vaults, lie under the
modern houses.

These are but names.

Believe me, the theatre is the only monument worth visiting in the dark; the Odeion, situated near it, is interesting only to archæologists.

Much that the lava and earthquakes had spared, was torn down by Theodoric to make his walls, and unhappily Count Roger followed his bad example, for his cathedral.

But whether it be Greek or Carthaginian, Pyrrhus or Rome, Goth or Saracen, throughout all the changeful conditions of Sicily, Catania, from her position, plays an important part. Sheltered by a great promontory, between two vast seas, and with that wonderfully fertile plain and spacious harbour (before the lava destroyed it), her history is the history of the world!

After Sicily had been overswept by Goth and Visigoth, rushing in on the ruins of Rome, and Belisarius, with easy victory, made the island Byzantine, only to fall, after an interval, into Saracen hands,—we have daylight with the Normans, and Catania falls before Robert Guiscard.

"No one," says Freeman, in his valuable chapters, "could have dealt worse with Catania than the first Hohenstaufen, Henry VI. of Germany, when he came to claim the Sicilian crown in right of his Norman wife, Constance.

"Neither age, nor sex, nor calling," says he, quoting Freising's "Chronicle," "neither house nor church was spared in the slaughter, the burning, the carrying into bondage." Not only Henry ill-used Sicily, but his successor, Frederic II., born of a Norman mother, a son of the soil, and professing to love it with as passionate a devotion as the great Count himself. I will say nothing of that dark ruffian, Charles of Anjou, and the Arragonese under Peter.

Yet when the legitimate branch of Norman princes ended abruptly by the execution of Conradin, grandson of Frederic II., by Charles of Anjou at Naples, so well were they beloved, that the illegitimate branch came in, with another Constance, daughter of Manfred, Frederic's natural son, and Sicily fell as a fief to her husband, Peter of Arragon.

.

CHAPTER XXI.

Catania at the present day.—The Grand Hotel.—Sicilian Cookery.—
Stesichoros —Charondas and Empedocles.

THE Grand Hotel is a stone's throw from the station; you reach it by an omnibus, as in any other city.

In form it is like a huge white box, pierced by windows; in fashion, altogether Teuton, evidenced by its greasy cuisine, saurkraut, and bacon.

Now, this is too bad, for Sicily is the land of good eating. I will venture to say there is no country in the universe where you can get a better dinner, and better cooked. The Palermitan "chefs" are especially famous for their repertoire of mediæval dishes, excellent in themselves and historical to boot. I take it, that every conquering race in Sicily has left, so to say, its culinary mark.

Of the Benedictine monks at Catania, so renowned for their table, I shall have to speak. At least the tradition of good living should have been respected.

Otherwise, I have nothing to say against the Grand Hotel. I mention this, because good hotels in Sicily are altogether the exception. It is reasonable too; and the landlord, as gigantic in size as his hotel, an excellent fellow.

Here, for a mere trifle, you may enjoy the comfortable assurance that you are lodged in the island of the blest, in the enjoyment of all the advantages of a Sanatorium, announced by the presence of invalids from many lands, lounging in the sun within a very desolate garden, where the bougainvillias blossom upon open walls, and Etna towers opposite,—without being charged for it in the bill.

And this brings me once more to Etna. You cannot open a chink of the window without its thrusting itself forward as an actual intruder upon your peace of mind. Entering so immediately into practical life, shorn of the majestic beauty I admired so much at Maniace, Etna becomes oppressive and vulgar.

Still it fascinates. I cannot take my eyes off its broad flanks, dotted with white villas, screened by evergreens, nor from "the wooded region," a verdant cincture, six or seven miles broad. As to the "desert or volcanic region," ashen and death-like, it is absolutely hideous!

What poor Charles Kean styled "local favourites" are Stesichoros, Charondas, and Empedocles. Stesichoros, called the Sicilian Homer, and blind, like the father of poetry, dealt with classic themes,—Medea, Hercules, Atalanta, and the siege of Troy. Horace's little hint about him indicates high praise. But what can we tell about a writer whose collected works amounted to twenty-six books, or divisions, when not three consecutive lines remain?

He composed, too, philosophical fables like La Fontaine, and excelled in depicting the power of love.

In one of his poems, Stesichoros dared to slander
Helen of Troy, for which crime he is said to have lost
his sight.

But promptly writing a recantation, in which he declared that only a *phantom* of Helen went to Troy, he
saw again as plainly as before.

We are in the dimmest antiquity about Stesichoros,
as also about Charondas, only we conclude that "his
laws" must have been written in verse, as they were
sung at Athenian wine-parties.

Diodorus is very rich about Charondas—a quaint
kind of primitive Solon, who forbade a man who gave
his children a step-mother, to legislate in the state, and
decreed that whoever proposed a change in the existing
laws, should do so standing before the people with a
halter round his neck, ready to be hanged if his motion
were not carried.

Aristotle celebrates Charondas as the first man who
made false witness indictable; a logical conclusion, for,
without truth, justice would be impossible.

Charondas' death was as eccentric as his laws.

Going one day into the country near Catania, armed
with a knife, to defend himself, says Diodorus, with much
naïveté, against "brigands" (brigandage in Sicily is of all
time), Charondas, on his return into the city, hearing a
tumult, runs into the public place to find out what it was,
forgetting the knife which he carries.

Now Charondas had made a law forbidding any man
to go armed within the city upon pain of death.

"Look at our Charondas," calls out one man to another, from the crowd. "A fine fellow indeed; carrying
a knife! He is breaking his own laws!"

"No, by Jupiter! Nothing of the kind," answers

Charondas. "I die to maintain them!" and with that he plunges the knife into his own breast.

In those early days, five centuries before Christ, lived Empedocles, philanthropist, poet (he wrote a poem called "Nature," in *two thousand verses*), naturalist, physician, and philosopher.

Philosophers of that day united in themselves the knowledge of many arts and many sciences, which we, in our narrow, modern views, deem incompatible.

Empedocles came from Acragas, where he is re-membered in the name of the new port, at the termina-tion of the railway (Porto Empedocles).

He cut through the hills at the back of the city, to let in a current of fresh air, and drained the marsh after-wards called of Tiberius as a cure for fever.

His figure, on Etna's side, wandering among the oaks and beeches, clothed in a purple robe, and bearing in his hand a Delphic crown, is as familiar to us as that of Acis or Polyphemus.

As a god, he communed with earth and earth's mysteries—his iron sandals clanking as he trod. Those treacherous sandals! It was on Etna's side, amongst the scented pine woods, that his ear first caught the sound of Kalliches, the boy-harper of Catania, and found him lying on a bank flower-crowned.

Empedocles has no chronicler like Apollonius of Tyana to raise him to the skies, barring which distinction he celebrates himself in his own verses, as a saviour, to whom the sick and dying came for help.

What were his claims to divine honours is not clear; but in the twilight of the world there was a constant tendency to deify everything beneficent.

At any rate Empedocles was worshipped as a god by

the Selinuntians, and his friend Pausanias raised an altar
to him.

Whether scientific curiosity about the flames of Etna
led Empedocles too near the brink, and he toppled over
into the crater, or whether he deliberately flung himself
in, as it is said, to sham immortality, and was betrayed
by the casting forth of his iron sandal—who can say?

The belief implied in the disappearance of Empedocles
is found in many lands. Elijah was whirled away, like
Pluto, in a fiery chariot; Apollonius of Tyana was not;
and Lycurgus, to preserve his laws, mysteriously vanished.

CHAPTER XXII.

Public Buildings and Gardens.—Eruptions of Etna.—Irrepressible
Catania.

A MORE hopelessly modern city and more monotonous,
I never beheld!

I feel it a personal wrong that "the eldest daughter
of Grecian Naxos" should look so white and new. I
specify *"white"* as applying to the principal thoroughfares; the cross alleys and narrower streets are of lava,
and as black as pitch.

Yet, apart from classic associations, Catania is spacious
and imposing, with its two miles of "Strada Stesicorea"
(the upper portion where the flanks of Etna rise from the
pavement called "Strada Etna," after the fashion set by
Hiero) crossed by the Corso, twin-brother to Stesicorea,
and each parallel to the four points of the compass.

Handsome ranges of palaces border these streets, very
new and very vast; specially notable, the Biscari Palace,
containing a fine collection of relics dug out of the lava:

Greek sarcophagi, bronzes, sculpture, vases, and terra cottas. Church domes, pinnacles, and towers rise behind; Catania possesses a hundred churches, there is a glittering cathedral as a vista to the Strada Stesicorea, also several theatres; one so large that, like the Campo Santo at Messina, it will never be finished.

There are showy shops full of nothing, the finest harbour in the world destroyed by lava, a population of ninety thousand souls, and the smallest newspaper I ever beheld, quite a curiosity, published twice a week, and with a notice on the front sheet, that "if subscribers do not pay punctually, their names will be posted up." Why, a backwood settlement three months old would beat this!

What is called the "Marina," is a filthy garden under railway arches.

When I visited it, I found a frightful stench and a very feeble band playing; stench and band accepted with equal favour by the company.

But *en revanche* the new Bellini Garden (Bellini is the modern god of Catania, his native city) at the other end of the town under Etna, is charming; the prettiest thing in all Catania, which I always liken in my own mind to a stiff white pattern traced on a black sampler.

All this is Etna's fault. Catania is what Etna permits it to be. You may calculate the period of the last eruption from the aspect of the streets, just as in Paris you can fix the date of the last Revolution by the girth of the trees on the Boulevards.

I do not know whether Etna is also responsible for the immorality. At Genoa, it is said—

"Sea without fish,
Mountains without trees,
Women without shame,
And men without honour."

The first traditional eruption of Etna dates from before the Trojan war, when the Sicani are said to have
retired from the neighbourhood of Naxos, and the Siculi
took their place. The first historical eruption occurred
in the time of Pythagoras, six centuries before Christ.
Then we have the legend of the Pii Frates, Amphinomos
and Anapios, who by turns bore their father out of
danger, as Æneas bore Anchises out of Troy.

Pausanius saw the Pii Frates drawn at Delphi by
Polygnôtos. They are recorded by Strabo, says Freeman,
furnished Claudian with an idyll, Pindar with a poem,
Apollonius of Tyana with the materials for a long sermon,
and Æschylus with a play—the Ætneia.

That Æschylus and Pindar should celebrate Etna,
town and mountain—Pindar speaking of the mountain as
that "snowy pillar vomiting forth purest fountains of un-
approachable fire—" is but natural. Both poets were
living at Hiero's (Ætnæus') court but a few years after
an eruption.

It was the eruption of 1669 which destroyed Catania.
The morning of the 18th of March, broke, says Dennis,
as though the sun were eclipsed. A furious whirlwind
shook the island, and earthquakes upheaved the soil.

At Nicosia, half-way up Etna, people could not stand
upon their feet. Everything rolled as on ship-board. In
an hour or two, Nicosia itself lay a heap of ruins; then
amid the din of labouring nature, eight fresh craters
opened beneath the cone, pouring forth lava, sand, and
stones to the height of twelve hundred feet.

From these eight new craters a stream two miles wide
poured down the mountain, dividing itself mid-way into
two currents: one running west towards Palermo and the
plain of Simeto, the other precipitating itself over Catania

into the sea. Hissing, roaring, seething, the two rival elements meet, clash, and battle.

Neptune, as is meet he should in the tripart island of Sicily, conquers! The waves arrest the fiery element. A lava wall, forty feet high, fills up the port, and a new black promontory runs out half a mile to sea, in advance of the old coast-line.

For *four* months Catania lay besieged by a sea of lava; a city of Dita, such as Dante paints in the "Inferno."

Over and above the lava, there is an earthquake, which, without waiting for Etna's slower proceedings, lays the whole city in ruins, and kills eighteen hundred people.

Two years after, in opening out the lava, flames burst forth. Eight years later hot mists rise from it after rain.

The fears of the first Greek settlers at Naxos were fully justified. "They dared not go further south," says Diodorus, "on account of volcanoes."

They were right.

It is an ill wind which blows no one any good.

> "Se Catania averse Porto,
> Palermo surei morto,"

says the proverb.

Strange to say, after the awful experience of 1669, and so many other awful experiences ever since the time of Pythagoras and the sixth century B.C., the Catanians persist in rebuilding the city on precisely the same lines! We have a Catania of the time of the Trojan war, of Alcibiades and the Athenians, of Himilcon the Carthaginian, whose advance was checked by the lava, as far down as Naxos; a Catania of the civil wars of Cæsar and Pompey, of the Emperor Caligula, whom the roar of Etna, as far off as at Messina, frightened away from Sicily; a

11*

Catania of the time of Titus, and also of Decius, when people were Christians, and the merits of St. Agatha's veil were tested in an eruption; a Catania of the time of Frederic II. and of Charles of Anjou; and, lastly, a Catania of William the Good, 1169 (William, third in succession from the great Count Roger), when, in a single instant, Catania became a heap of ruins, including the Norman Cathedral, the bishop, and his congregation!

Yes! Hiero's Ætnea is a city of fire, according to its name—was, is, and ever will be. God help the people!

And the insolence and the caprices of the lava!

In a quarter of the city called the Gambayita, where the city walls are thirty feet high and very thick, a spring of water was embedded. A century later, the want of this particular spring being felt, search was made for it, and the lava hewn out, when the living waters were discovered, cool and abundant as ever!

The mediæval castle, too, a grimy-looking edifice, by turns the Hohenstaufen Palace, Arragonese Parliament, and general city fortress, built by Frederic II. from the wreck of the city walls, close to the harbour, now stands high and dry in the middle of the town.

The Saracens styled Etna Mongibello, and "dreaded it exceedingly." To them it was a fetish or devil, to be exorcised and worshipped like the Palician gods.

CHAPTER XXIII.

Military Friends.—Catanian Bluebeards.—A Mysterious Elephant.—
The Cathedral.—St. Agatha.

To-DAY I have had three telegrams from General de
Sonnaz, commander-in-chief of the army of Italy in Sicily.
"If you come while I am there," said this most
fascinating of men and bravest of soldiers, "I will take
care of you."
"Brigands! No, not with me. Nonsense; you shall
have a regiment of Bersaglieri to escort you, if you like."
"No," say I, "not a regiment."
"Well, then, half a regiment. Understand me, I
guarantee your safety. You shall go everywhere, see
everything. Trust me."
When this was said a year ago, we were walking,
General de Sonnaz and I, up and down the Pancaldi
Baths at Leghorn.
And he has kept his word!
Three telegrams from Palermo this very day, telling
me what to do and where to go. I am waited on everywhere by the authorities like royalty. At Messina I had
an invitation to stay in the house of the Prefect.
The Prefect there, and the General here, the latter
in uniform, presented themselves on my arrival. (Now,
I am quite come to despise simple generals, as I have
commanders-in-chief and generals of division awaiting
my pleasure.)
Marchese X——commands at Catania. He has just
called with his two aides-de-camp, in the whitest of
gloves and with the politest of manners. And he is such
a nice, fat, fatherly general, Marchese X——, so anxious

to please the friend of de Sonnaz, there is nothing he
will not do for me; even going into the question of my
luggage with the patience of a benevolent courier! (You
are only allowed to travel with a certain amount of kilos.
in Sicily.)

Nothing would do but that Marchese X—— must return in the evening in his open carriage, to show me the
effect of the gas in the long lines, Strada Stesicorea and
the Corso ditto, a blaze in the Elephant Square, and the
cafés more brilliant than Paris boulevards.

A most agreeable man, Marchese X——, and full of
pleasant gossip.

Catanian husbands, according to him, are real tigers.
One is known to lock his wife into her carriage when he
cannot accompany her in her drive up and down the
Corso; another reads his wife's letters first, even those
from her mother.

"We Piedmontese despise such espionnage," says
General X——, who has a remarkably handsome Mar-
chesa: "if our wives are honest, *bene;* if not, we cannot
force them into virtue! These Catanian nobles are full
of Arab blood, only half civilized.

"No lady here is seen walking [this I had noticed
myself] after a certain early hour, say, two o'clock, then
only in the side streets, avoiding the cafés and the
thoroughfares. If she meets a gentleman of her acquaintance, and the gentleman accosts her, her reputa-
tion is 'gone for ever!'"

At this, General, Marchese, X—— laughs, thinking
of the civilized freedom of Turin; his two aides-de-camp,
Captains Cavalotti and Franchetti, laugh also, and both
opine that Sicily is a barbarous country, a thousand years
behind Northern Italy.

At the bottom of the Strada Stesicorea I find a

thoroughly Italian square, large, white, and uniform. On one side is the Cathedral, in the centre "the Elephant."

Now "the Elephant" is a mysterious quadruped, bearing on its back the name of a certain "Heliodorus," Diodorus, or "Diotro." It is carved in lava smaller than life, and accommodated with tusks and a houdah of white marble, on the top of which is an obelisk covered with hieroglyphics.

Whence the elephant came from, and who Heliodorus, Diodorus, or Diotro is—Byzantine, Greek, Bishop, Jew, or Magician, is not known.

Did Agathocles' Egyptian wife, asks Freeman, bring him in her pocket? Or the Crusaders? I ask. Was he imported under Maniace? Or was he a Meta in a Roman circus?—or an idol?

As to the Cathedral, when I saw it bristling with barocco ornamentation — Tritons, Nereids, Centaurs, foliage, gargoyles, capped by a frieze from the Greek theatre, had I followed my inclination I should have turned and fled!

Barocco has a "*faux air*" of the cinquecento, deformed and exaggerated into burlesque. Such as might be the graceful carracoles of a racehorse, compared to the ungainly antics of a mule.

People tell me Barocco is picturesque; so is a red brick wall, or a cupola, scaled with coloured tiles.

I hate shams.

Now Barocco is the apotheosis of shams, invented by artists who, without power to create themselves, ape and distort the creations of genius.

Not even the fact that the Cathedral was founded by my favourite, Count Roger, can reconcile me to it. Its real date is 1757, when the sham style was rampant in Sicily. Some blackened arches at the east end, and

a lancet window or two, are all that remain of the
original structure, destroyed in the reign of William the
Good by an eruption.

If the outside is overcharged, the interior is singularly
cold and nude. St. Agatha is the presiding goddess, as
one may say—as is Santa Lucia at Syracuse, and Santa
Rosalia at Palermo. St. Agatha doubles her part with
that of a virgin goddess.

Her chapel, where she stands, a female St. Michael,
with a dragon at her feet, blazes out on one side of the
bare walls. A silver chest contains her relics, and the
wonder-working veil, which so distinctly drove back the
lava from Catania, A.D. 254.

Until then, the Virgin ruled in Catania, as in Messina.
But after showing herself so thoroughly incompetent on
that occasion, she was publicly dethroned and repudiated,
and the maid Agatha installed in her place.

It is in the year A.D. 251, and Decius is Emperor.

St. Paul has long ago landed at Syracuse, on his way
to Rome, and Vesuvius, not to be behindhand with Etna,
overwhelmed the cities . of Pompeii and Herculaneum,
A.D. 79.

As Sicily has been a Roman province some forty
years, all these events come to affect Catania more or
less, especially the landing of St. Paul, for now the city
has a Christian bishop and a Christian Church, like
Syracuse, and all Sicily might have been converted, only
with Decius have come cruel days, when to be a "Na-
zarene" is death.

At this time the young Roman Prætor, Quintianus,
loved a Catanian maid, named Agatha. But Agatha,
consecrated to God from her earliest youth, would not
listen to his suit.

As a Christian, Agatha was absolutely in his power. Had she returned his love, the young Prætor would have little cared whether she worshipped Jupiter or Christ; but, as it was, he became a red-hot persecutor.

Will Agatha yield or not? (He gives her a last chance.) "No." Will she die the death of a martyr and a slave? Yes, a thousand times, Yes!

Despised love often turns to bitterest hate; so it was with Quintianus.

The fair Catanian, tall and comely, her golden hair abroad upon her shoulders; her large blue eyes full of sweetness, as pictured at her altar, by Bernardius Græcus, 1588, is dragged by the lictors, naked, to the judgment-seat of her lover.

The rounded apse of the Basilica is filled with soldiers, hard, wolfish-eyed, and sensual.

In front, between the fasces, on his curule chair, sits Quintianus, wrapped in a purple toga, hemmed with gold: the golden eagles and wreaths of victory behind.

Agatha gives Quintianus no time to address her.

"Take me, Lord Christ," she cries, clasping her hands, and raising her eyes to heaven. "I am Thine. Do with me as Thou wilt. Like Agnes, I am Thy lamb; lead me to the sacrifice."

She weeps, she cries; not for sorrow, but for shame.

Quintianus, maddened by the sight of all that grace and beauty, condemns her, not to death, but to infamy. But the Catanian maid comes pure out of the ordeal.

After another month, Agatha is again summoned before the Prætor. Whatever mercy was in his heart, fanned by the hope that degradation and shame might conquer her, has fled.

She stands before him a common culprit. In answer

to his interrogations, she has but one reply, "I am a Christian."

This time Agatha is led to prison.

We know where that is. The Santo Carcere, as it is called, in memory of the saint, is near the Via Stesicorea, underground, not far from the remains of the vast circle of the Roman Amphitheatre.

Above the spot is a modern church, pilastered, white-washed, and frescoed, like the rest; only there is a rare Norman portal, which has survived perils of earthquakes and lava, from the time of William the Good.

The little cell, where Agatha lay, is built into the city walls. Within, on a block of lava, is the impress of two dainty feet: her footmarks, as is devoutly believed by the Catanese, when she was flung into the prison.

A third time Agatha is summoned before Quintianus. A third time she cries out, "I am Christ's!" This is too much for the outraged lover. The valiant Agatha is stretched upon the rack, and her fair body wrenched and torn with red-hot hooks and pincers. Her courage is immense.

"Lord, take me!" she cries, as long as she can speak. "I am Thine!"

It is a horrible struggle between brute force and woman's fortitude.

Still she lives, and still she cries.

"Silence that woman's voice by agony!" shouts Quintianus, a very Herod in his vengeance.

Her virgin breast is to be cut off, Quintianus says it.

"Monster!" shrieks Agatha, writhing on the rack, in the hands of the Roman lictors. "Are you not ashamed —you, who have sucked the paps of a woman's breast yourself?"

Carried back to her cell, Agatha is comforted by the presence of an angel, who dresses her wounds.

Then she makes this prayer: "Lord, my Creator, Thou hast protected me from my cradle. Receive my soul."

And so she sweetly dies.

Her relics, carried to Constantinople by our friend General George Maniace, were brought back to Catania, in the reign of Roger, son of the Great Count.

Saint Agatha La Vetere, on the site of Count Roger's original cathedral, is the spot where Agatha suffered torture. There is her tomb.

But it is in the Barocco Cathedral you must look for her remains.

Twice a year the silver chest is taken from the altar and placed upon a car, to be carried in triumph through the city.

The Catanian citizens, prostrate on the stones, line the streets by thousands, to see her pass.

Hymns are sung in her honour, bands play, trumpets sound, and tall tapers glisten!

CHAPTER XXIV.

San Benedetto.—The House of San Niccolò on Etna.—Adventures of an Austrian Prince.—A Benedictine General.—The Supper. —The Sleep and the Awakening.

I AM just returned from a drive, escorted by a hoary rascal of a cicerone, with a swollen face, and a grizzly beard. Beware of him!

We started vaguely in a one-horse shay, to look after a temple of Ceres.

Such a thing does not exist in Catania. He knew it, the wretch! It was only an excuse to jolt me miles over dangerous lava-roads, at so much an hour.

The horse, like his driver, trained to idleness, drawled on hopelessly until we landed in a vast piazza, before the Church of St. Benedict.

St. Benedict is the great modern sight of Catania. A glaring, semicircular building of enormous size spread out upon a rise. Of course it is Barocco, the only architecture permitted by the lava.

The façade is imposing, but essentially commonplace. Through what seemed to me miles of corridors, and pillared galleries, and countless courts, I was led by a monk, robed in white flannel, to a gaudy church, 550 feet in length—a kind of court ball-room, glittering with chandeliers.

"No one lights them now," says the monk, with a sigh, as he sees my eyes travelling round the desert of variegated marble, agate, jasper, mosaics, silver-gilt reliefs, stalls of carved walnut-wood, and glaring wall frescoes.

"The King of Naples used to have his rooms in the Abbots' quarter. Then we had masses sung every day, at all the altars. An orchestra came from the opera-house of San Carlo at Naples, to play for us. And candles, ah! myriads of wax-candles. No one looked to the cost when the King and Queen were here. Humbert and his Consorte came once—*ma chè*" (a gesture of supreme contempt occurs here). "They stayed two days, and spent nothing. *Diamine!* We are fallen on evil days!"

In the church is the finest organ in the world; Dennis says finer than at Haarlem or Lucerne. Now at Lucerne, I can personally answer that the thunder and earthquake stops are the most appalling combination of sound human ear ever listened to.

If the Benedictine convent is the great sight of Catania, "the garden of the miracle" is the great sight of the convent, matching in miraculousness the Pii Frates and the veil of St. Agatha.

It is clear that our monk thinks so. With a species of ecstasy he points to a black lava pile, close upon a flowery grove of paulonias and pepper trees, and explains that here the fiery flood of 1669 turned aside of its own accord, out of respect to the house of St. Benedict.

Before this palatial establishment was built in Catania, the Benedictine monks, lovers of mountain-summits and free-air, had, as early as the sixth century, settled themselves on the slopes of Etna, within "the wooded zone," near Nicosia. But after enduring the havoc of three separate eruptions, they deserted the treacherous volcano, and came down here.

Anent this change of locality, a curious tale is told. (N.B. It is not my invention.)

A certain Austrian, Prince Wrede, started from Prague on his travels southward. Being at Rome, he went on to Naples, and from thence sailed to Messina and Catania.

Now the Prince's object in visiting Sicily must not be misunderstood. He was not a savant; he was actuated by no religious zeal in what he was about to do. He was simply a hard-headed, somewhat eccentric Austrian, fond of good eating, and an amateur of ancient monasteries, especially those of the Benedictine order.

Also he had been told that the finest quails in the world were shot on Etna in their passage from Africa, and that the Benedictine church and hospice of San

Niccolò, near Nicosia, was one of the most ancient monastic establishments in the south of Europe.

At Rome he had provided himself with a letter from Cardinal Orsini to the Benedictine superior.

There is now a good road from Catania to Nicosia, zig-zagging twelve miles up the side of Etna; I can see it from the Hotel, but a hundred years ago this was nothing but a mule track.

At Nicosia you enter into what is called La Boschiva, consisting of oak, beech, and chestnut forests. For miles and miles there are nothing but trees, lava boulders, extinct craters, and broom. A fine turf grows between into which the foot sinks like a carpet.

Near Nicosia are the "Tre Castagne," mere tree-shells of unknown antiquity, and standing beneath them you have a bird's-eye view over the plains of Catania and the sea.

If the trees were bigger, La Boschiva would be like an English park, but as the woods are all wind-tossed, scorched, and stunted, it is a very desolate place indeed, especially to be avoided in those days, as infested by banditti and *mal viventi* of all descriptions.

Prince Wrede had been told at Rome to go to the Convent of San Niccolò on Etna. He knew of no other convent or monastic establishment bearing the same name in the city; when, however, he went out to engage a mule for the ascent, the muleteer seemed greatly surprised and quite puzzled him by his questions.

Was he *sure* where he wanted to go? "Was it to the Convent of San Niccolò or to the Hospice of San Niccolò?"

The Prince not understanding the Sicilian dialect, explained as well as he could that he desired to visit the Benedictine establishment on Etna, but still the muleteer hesitated to comply. *"Pago bene,"* repeated Prince Wrede to all the muleteer's objections, which he did not in the least understand. *"Pago bene."*

These words, spoken in a loud voice and in an imperious manner, seemed to decide the muleteer. "Try to talk Italian, instead of that infernal gibberish," added the Prince, availing himself of the good impression his 'repeated offers of money had made, at which the Sicilian bowed low and kissed his hand.

But when a little later he saw the Prince's boxes spread out on the ground, his astonishment again returned.

"Does your Excellency really intend carrying all that with you?" (As the muleteer now spoke in Italian, he and the Prince could understand each other perfectly.)

"Certainly," was the reply; "every article."

"Your Excellency has friends up there," and he pointed to Etna.

"I have a letter for the General?"

"For the Captain, your Excellency?"

"No. For the General, I say. Now don't stand here talking and losing time. I know it is a long climb; but, *Pago bene!* you understand."

"I don't doubt that," answered the Sicilian, greatly exercised in his mind; "or that your Excellency intends to keep his word, but as we are both here safe at the present time, would you mind giving me the money beforehand? I should prefer it in case of accidents."

"What accidents?" asked the Prince, sharply.

"Well," and the muleteer looked up Etna, then rubbed his nose, and last of all winked, a familiarity the Prince showed he resented, "Accidents do happen on Etna. Before we get up it will be midnight. I should like to come back at once. If the Excellency pleases it will be better to pay me now."

"Do they sup as late as midnight?" asked the Prince, thinking of the quails at San Niccolò.

"Oh! certainly, at midnight. Much more likely to find them eating by night than day."

"Capital!" cried the Prince, rubbing his hands and looking quite condescending. "How cool it will be!* The very time for a good supper! Here is your money, muleteer."

"Mille grazie," said the honest fellow, taking off his scarlet cap. "Now I can start off back as soon as you arrive, and run down the mountain to Nicosia in no time."

The first part of the ascent was made in silence. The orange-groves and olive-grounds, and all those innumerable little white houses dotted about Catania, were soon left far below; then their path lay over the lava till they came to the little town of Nicosia.

As they made a short halt here, all the peasants turned out to stare at them, and one old woman said: "Many people go to San Niccolò by force, but you are the first I ever knew go there of their own accord! *Dio vi benedica.*"—At which observation the muleteer shook his head, but Prince Wrede was thinking too earnestly about the quails to heed her.

The little town of Nicosia, looking from Catania like a white rag°hung up on a peg, now consists of two rows of black huts, built very near the ground. It has suffered so fearfully from whirlwinds and earthquakes, that the Nicosians build as low as possible, for safety. There is a magnificent view. You can see all the indentations of the beautiful straits on both sides, down to Aci, Giarre, and Mascoli on one side, Capes Spartivento and

Delle Armi, Reggio and Scilla on the other; the peaks of the Taurus Mountains over Taormina, the great blanched city of Catania spread out upon the plain, the Point and Bay of Agosta, the Bay of Thapsus, and so on, to the heights of Hybla.

Before the Prince had left Nicosia night had come on. There was no moon, and but little light on the horizon; but as the muleteer and the mules appeared to know their way, this did not matter. About a quarter of a mile distant, they made a sharp turn to the right, into what seemed to be a dry torrent-bed. Here the path ended. After scrambling for some time among the stones, a black mass barred their progress.

"Behold the Convent of San Niccolò," said the muleteer, speaking under his breath, and crossing himself.

"What a dismal place!" exclaimed the Prince; "it is like a prison."

"We can still return to Nicosia, if the Excellency likes," whispered the Sicilian, eagerly. "No one is about; no one has heard us. It will be much better to sleep at Nicosia, believe me."

"I have given you my orders," answered the Prince, stiffly. "Go on; I am hungry."

At this, the muleteer gave his mule a savage cut on the back, and, with a little more climbing, they stood before the door. Near at hand the building looked to the Prince more like a fortress than a monastery. It was partly in ruins; and every eruption, since the time of the great Count Roger, seemed to have left its mark upon the walls.

"Knock," said the Prince to the muleteer; "what are you staring at?"

The sound of the iron knocker rang out hollow in

the night. A little bell, a long way off, was heard to
ring, then there was a sound of footsteps. A window,
low in the wall, opened, the barrel of a musket was
directed full upon the Prince, who was close to the entrance, and a rough voice asked, "Who are you?"

"A friend," answered Prince Wrede, calmly putting
aside the musket-barrel with one hand, and raising his
hat with the other. "You are quite right," he added,
"to be cautious in such a solitude, and not to admit
strangers. I do not blame you. I should do the same
in your place; but you need not be afraid of me, I have
a letter from Cardinal Orsini to your General."

"For our Captain?"

"No, no; for your General."

"Ah! that is the same thing, General or Captain.
Are you alone?"

"I am," answered the Prince.

"Wait then, and I will come and unbar the door."

Meanwhile the muleteer had quietly disappeared.

"What a delicious smell," exclaimed Prince Wrede,
as the door opened.

"I am glad you like it," said the owner of the rough
voice, in a very sulky tone, still holding his musket
dangerously near the Prince. "You smell our Captain's
supper; he will be back directly. By the way, do you
know him?"

"Here is a letter addressed to the Most Reverend
the General of the Benedictines, at the Convent of San
Niccolò at Catania."

"Ah! now I understand," cried the monk, a broad
grin parting his thick lips. "Capisco! Si! Si! He! He!"
and, quite condescendingly, he laughed until his sides
shook.

Unobservant as was the Prince, the interior of the

convent did strike him as very strange. Oak-trees were
growing up inside the ruined walls; grass was everywhere; not a cross, crucifix, or altar to be seen.

The monk, observing how he stared round, explained
that it was only their country convent, their *villeggiatura*.
"Besides the Hospice," he added, "we have a splendid
establishment down at Catania."

"Ah!" exclaimed the Prince, considerably annoyed,
"no one told me that; perhaps I was mistaken in coming here; but, at all events, here I am, and here I must
spend the night. Meantime," a bright thought struck
him, "would you allow me to go down to the kitchen
and see what there is for supper?"

"Upon my word, I see no objection," replied the
monk, his lips once more parted with a broad grin. "I
will show you the way; but tell me, first, how much
money have you in your purse?"

"Three thousand five hundred lire."

"Ah! then," muttered the man, half aloud, "I'm sure
the Captain will be glad to see you!"

In the kitchen Prince Wrede found a cook, dressed
in white, double his own size, busy before the fire.

He was just about to ask this giant how he cooked
his quails, when an exclamation from the latter caused
him to turn his head. A tall, dark man, dressed in the
full Benedictine habit, was standing immovable behind
him.

"Ah! The General! General," said the Prince,
tearing himself from the contemplation of the quails, "I
am delighted to see you? You have an excellent cook,
he has got quails for supper!"

"Are you Prince Wrede?" asked the General, fixing
upon him a pair of eyes glistening like coals.

"Yes, General, at your service. I am a student of

history, especially of the history of Benedictine convents. I know all about this place better, perhaps, than you do," added the Prince with a smile.

A smile passed over the General's face also, but it was not a pleasant smile.

"These Sicilian monks are queer fellows," thought the Prince; "they all seem alike, sulky and silent; nothing at all of the amenity of the Churchman about them. I suppose it is the wild life and Etna."

When the General and the Prince reached the top of the stairs, the whole community had assembled. There were about thirty, not one pleasant to look at. They all wore their white cowls drawn over their heads, except the superior, who, uncovered, led the way into a well-lit refectory, where a long table was laid for supper.

The Prince, who had all his wits about him, was astounded at the splendour of the plate and the fineness of the linen. The refectory itself had evidently been the ancient church. An open hearth filled the place of the altar, and the niches for saints were ornamented with firearms.

"The most self-denying Benedictines, I ever knew," thought the Prince to himself, "and who best carry out the precepts of their great founder."

"Prince!" said the General, seeing the admiration depicted on his countenance as he gazed around, "I really must apologize for a very bad supper, but you gave me no notice. I am afraid, too, our country habits will surprise you. Every brother eats with a pair of pistols beside his plate, and there is a sentinel at the door as a precaution. Pray excuse us if we do not alter our custom even in the presence of so illustrious a guest!"

"I should be shocked to disarrange you in any way," was the Prince's courteous answer.

Upon this the General threw open his robe, took a superb pair of inlaid pistols from his belt, and laid them upon the table.

"Excellent!" cried the Prince, watching him; "I like the idea vastly! Pistols are the traveller's best friends. I have a pair also; I will put them beside my plate, if one of your obliging monks will be kind enough to fetch them."

"Another day, another day," said the superior, taking his place. "Sit opposite to me, Prince! Can you say a 'Benedicite?"

"I could formerly, but I am afraid I have forgotten it."

"What a pity," returned the General. "I reckoned upon you; I fear we neglect it, and to-day the chaplain is absent. So if you cannot help me, with your permission we will omit Grace altogether!"

Prince Wrede ate both his supper and his quails with the appetite of a long-fasting man, helping himself at the same time to copious draughts of Marsala, a wine to which he was now introduced for the first time. So delicious did he find it, that he paid no attention to the repeated warnings of the General, that it was a very heady liquor. To this and to his ignorance of the Sicilian dialect may be attributed the fact that he listened but carelessly to the talk of the monks. Yet they told the strangest stories—about brigands, convents sacked, ransoms paid, and gens d'armes shot.

After the Marsala, came Isola and Muscat; the Prince drank of all these until he fell into a half sleep.

Was it true or was it a dream? Did the monks throw off their robes and transform themselves into brigands, with pointed hats, knee-breeches, embroidered jackets, and endless poniards and pistols stuck into their belts?

Did the General rap the table with a naked dagger, throw over the lamp, and order a door to be opened, upon which three prisoners appeared, at whom he took deliberate aim, standing in his place, their blood flowing down the refectory in a crimson stream?

At length the Prince's eyes closed in heavy slumber; nor could he open them, nor had he the power to sit upright. His last recollection was an effort to rise and free himself from the horrible blood which had collected in pools about his feet. But his legs failed him, and he fell heavily, dead drunk, upon the floor.

When he awoke it was broad daylight. He was lying under an oak, at the edge of the Boschiva, or wooded region, the flat roofs of Nicosia peeping out beneath. Beside him, on the grass, lay all his luggage, untouched, even to his pipe; and in the valise his purse containing the exact sum he had placed in it on leaving Catania!

Within was a letter, which he eagerly opened; it was addressed:—

"To his Excellency the Prince Wrede.

"I have a thousand excuses to make you for the suddenness of my departure, but important affairs call me to Cefalù. I hope you will not forget that the hospitality you received from the monks of San Niccolò, was, however unworthy of your acceptance, the best they could offer. When you write to Cardinal Orsini, I beg you to recommend us to his prayers.

"You will find all your luggage, except your pistols; these, I trust, you will permit me to retain as a souvenir of your visit.

"GASPARONE.

"General of the Monastery of San Niccolò upon Etna."

The Prince turned homewards, a wiser and a sadder man. Years after, he saw in a newspaper that the "famous brigand chief, Gasparone, had been captured by the Neapolitan troops, after a desperate resistance, to the great joy of Nicosia, Catania, and the whole of the two Calabrias."

CHAPTER XXV.

Catania to Syracuse.—General X——.—The Doctor.—Plain of
Catania.—Lentini.—The Unlucky Sicilian Sculpture.

How I have come to dread that word "trasborgo" (break-down), applied to Sicilian railroads! They are so badly engineered all through the island, that they are always breaking. When you start on a journey, it is as necessary to ask if there is "trasborgo?" as to inquire the price of your ticket.

I had heard of "trasborgo" on the rail from Catania to Palermo. Now General Marchese X——, accompanied by his aide-de-camp, Captain Cavallotti, has just been here to inform me that there is also "trasborgo" between Catania and Syracuse!

That best and most sympathetic of generals did all he could to dissuade me from going; and Captain Cavallotti, in resplendent uniform, supported him.

"Was there any fear of brigands?" I asked.

A loud laugh from the General, and a suppressed one from the Captain, as of an inferior officer obliterating himself, even in mirth, before his chief.

"Ah, madame! you are like all the forestieri! You conjure up a brigand behind every rock. Believe me, the east coast, from Messina to Syracuse, is much quieter

and safer than—well, say—than the neighbourhood of
Rome, for instance." (Piedmontese have, and will long
retain, a certain spite against Rome, as robbing their
beloved Turin of the privileges of a capital.) "About
here the people are pretty much like sheep; you may
drive them where you like. That is not the question.
But you may have to walk miles through the mud, in
open fields; you may be drenched by the rain—Sicilian
rain! Your baggage may be left behind, for want of
some one to carry it, and then——"

(A vague motion here of the General's fingers, in-
dicative of total disappearance into infinite space.)

"This time it will be boats," added the Marquis.
"A bridge near Lentini is broken—a river is out. Will
milady like a boat? Two boats perhaps? For I believe
there is a double trasborgo; and the country so inundated
that the line may break anywhere—at any time. It is
really hazardous."

Now, although I am the most arrant coward breathing, I was not in a mood to be stopped by anything
short of an earthquake. I had also learned not to believe one half of what was told me, even in official
quarters. I was dying to see Syracuse. My vision by
day, my dream by night; and I had fallen upon two
friends in precisely the same condition as myself.

I will call one Physic—he was a Scotch doctor of
high position; the other S——, in delicate health, and
going to try the climate of Syracuse—only S—— joined
us later.

The doctor had travelled all over the known world—
Chinese Tartary and Cambodia were as nothing to him.
He had walked over such parts of the Himalayas as are
walkable, and had lived with Hindoos, Persians and
Arabians—emerging into civilized life as the politest of

gentlemen and the pleasantest of companions that chance ever threw in the path of an Idle Woman.

One fine afternoon Physic and I booked ourselves for Syracuse—*secretly*. If the fact of my departure from Catania had oozed out, I should have had the General-Marquis, and his état-major in white gloves, and the Prefect and Sub-prefect, waiting on the platform to take leave of me.

From the moment you pass the last house in Catania you emerge into another world—flat, dull, swampy, treeless; altogether so different from the other side, that but for Etna dominating, grey and majestic, over pale, receding heights, you might fancy yourself in another planet.

These are the Catanian Plains, the Campi Leontini, or Campi Læstrygoni—as you like—once the granary of the world. It was the fertility of these plains, and the security of her harbour, which made "daughter Catania" so much greater than "mother Naxos," sunk in her quiet little bay, under Taormina.

Here Ceres, the Greek Demeter, sowed the first wheat with her own goddess hands, and taught men how to cultivate the soil; and here she sought her lost daughter, Proserpine, to the sound of drums and trumpets.

Here, too, lived the Læstrygonian giants, own cousins to the Cyclops.

In our day, the Pianura di Catania is a dreary swamp, bordering the coast, traversed by the river Simeto (Symœthus) which, in its time, has seen strange sights, running beside those mysterious towns without a name, at the back of Etna.

Cicero celebrates this plain as unsurpassed for fruitfulness. The soil, a stiff, alluvial clay, mixed with driftings of volcanic rocks, is as fertile as ever; but what modern Ceres will teach the thriftless Sicilian to till it? Where are the golden wheat-ears of Proserpine? The ruddy glow of classic harvests? What river-god will order Simeto back into his bed? What national chief, like Ducetius, breathe energy and ardour into his coun trymen?

"A trasborgo here would be awkward," I remark to Physic, who is sitting serene and silent in his comparti- mento, with his head buried in a newspaper.

(I cannot make Physic out. At Catania he spoke with enthusiasm of his desire to see Syracuse. "I am too old a traveller," said he, "not to notice everything. I love to see not only a place, but its surroundings. Syracuse is an historical record of all time; as such, the very way to it is sacred. Every step from Catania is classic ground."

Now, I declare he has fallen into such a fit of dis- traction, that ever since we have been in the train he has never once raised his head.)

"If you are afraid, don't look out," he answers curtly, lifting his eyes for a moment. "When an accident is likely to happen, I take a book and read."

This is not re-assuring, nor is the alarmed silence of a French dignitary, in a purple soutane and red stock- ings, who sits next to him. The dignitary and his priestly secretary are hanging on to each other with that sym- pathy which common danger breeds.

Still on the Catanian Plains!

The soil is oozing out water as our heavy train puffs slowly over it. A broad belt of black mud runs, wide- spread, to the sea. Streams form themselves into rivers among the swamps, and splash and gurgle maliciously as we pass.

Like the water from the soil, my courage also is

oozing out. I recall with a sigh the General's warnings. In absolute terror I watch, minute by minute, our slow advance.

Further and further recedes the white-capped dome of Etna; further and further the cold blue hills vanish into space; and the valleys purple off vaguely into soft hazy clouds.

Among those hills lies Mineo (the Siculian chief place Menœ) near Caltagirone and Palagonia, looking down upon the mystic lake of the Palici, where sulphurous mists veiled the presence of the demons. The Menœ of Ducetius was one of the towns taken by the Saracens, when they penetrated into these Catanian plains as far as Palagonia.

We passed one miserable little station, then another; wooden arks upon the surface of the waters, with just room for the guards to turn round, as on a pivot.

Then into a region of stone-bound breezy downs, broken by rare clumps of scanty olive trees. The aspect as of old battlefields, flattened by the iron heel of the great hosts which in all ages have trodden here, hurrying to Syracuse; a land blasted and woe-stricken, grown silent with despair!

Nothing living breaks the long lines of the grass-grown rocks. I see a solitary house (a kind of shanty) in the bosom of grey cliffs, an orange-tree or two, clustering together, a bunch of cactus, or an aloe. That is all; then, on again, into the vague greenness of the hills!

Thus, it seems to me, dead Syracuse should be approached. With the death of Syracuse the land died too; died, and lies at rest.

At the station of Lentini (Leontini) I get a peep at the historic lake, a very dead sea, with sad, lone shores, the largest lake in all Sicily, and excellent for wild fowl. Look at it while you may!

I nudge Physic (now, I grieve to say, fast˙ asleep). He smiles faintly, looks up at me, turns himself round, then sleeps again.

The French dignitary and his clerical young man are in the same condition.

We are now half-way to Syracuse. The light is waning. In that hollow lies what was once ancient Leontini, the ally of Athens, the foe of Syracuse, and as old a colony as Naxos or Catania. Not a stone remains.

Cities, like individuals, are born to misfortune. So it was with Leontini; made captive by Hiero, crushed by Dionysius, or ground down by its own tyrants, the only passing gleam of prosperity came to it when Timoleon, in his crusade against Sicilian tyrants, drove out Icetas.

In our own day Leontini is still a most unlucky little town, smitten by malaria and earthquakes, and poor, beyond the power of words to describe.

Once it must have been prosperous, spite of its acknowledged pauperism in the Athenian war.

Pausanias tells us "that the men of Leontini dedicated from their private means a statue of Jupiter seven feet high at Olympia, as well as the Eagles and the Thunderbolt, in accordance with the Poets." (One would like to know how the native artist *put in* the Thunderbolt!) Another statue, of Hera, ten cubits high, at the harbourmouth, is recorded.

Pausanias makes various mention of statues by Sicilian artists, not only in Sicily, but in Southern Italy, meaning Tarentum, Crotona, and Rhegium, as well as Syracuse.

Various plaster offerings representing chariots and

charioteers, and single or double horses, were cast in Sicily and sent to Olympia by the Dinomenes, Gelon and Hiero, to celebrate their various victories, all more or less rudimental, for as Pliny says of a Rhegium sculptor, "he was the first to express veins and sinews, and to treat the hair more naturally."

The realism of art at that time is indicated by the story of the famous cow of Myron, to which the bulls were attracted by its likeness to nature.

Now, Myron was the master of Phidias. At this moment the French dignitary woke up, read the name of the station "Lentini," and expressed unfeigned surprise. He possessed, or desired to assume, classical proclivities. When not asleep he ostentatiously handled Thucydides as well as a notebook and pencil, announcing his intention of recording his "*impressions de voyage*," but the dismal aspect of Leontini seemed to drive all idea of this kind out of his head.

After a lengthened conversation with his secretary, and many amazed glances at the station, he put back his pencil and books into his pocket with the air of an ill-used man, and relapsed into slumber.

What he expected I do not know.

Perhaps, like the American who opined "that Rome would be a very nice place if the public buildings were in better repair," the Frenchman expected to see a brannew Boulevard by the lonely lake!

CHAPTER XXVI.

The dreaded Trasborgo.—Megara, Hybla.—Epicharmus.—Glorious
Night.—Arrival at Syracuse.—The Doctor and his Valise.—The
Hotel.—Tableau!

As night approached, we suddenly drew up at a
platform.

Is it a station? No. An accident? No. Yet everyone is getting out. The platform is crowded with passengers; there are guards, boys, old women, dogs, a
monkey in a cage, and an old man on crutches.

I wake up Physic. He, bounding out of sleep, wakes
the priest and his secretary. It is getting dark. What
is it?

"*Bisogna scendere*," says the gruff voice of a guard,
as he flings open the door. "*È trasborgo!*"

We get out.

I cling on to Physic, Physic clings on to me; Furiosa,
the maid, hangs on to both. I have a settled conviction
that our loose bags and luggage will be stolen. I am
not afraid for my box, I have a ticket in my pocket for
that. But the bags!

We try to carry them, but are unmercifully jostled by
the crowd. A light brigade of eager boys bear down
upon us. We are the last of a long line proceeding on-
wards down the platform.

The boys, infant brigands doubtless, almost naked,
as brown as nuts and as nimble as squirrels, insist upon
carrying the bags—a bag for each boy, and the railway
wrappers between two, which is confusing. I scream,
Physic swears, and Furiosa gives chase, at which the
boys laugh and outstrip her. (Furiosa is a thin, spare,

little woman, of uncertain age.) Physic's broad, good-humoured face inspires no fear. So the boys chatter in an incomprehensible gibberish, still keeping fast hold of the bags.

Seeing, however, that all the other travellers confide their belongings to other boys (they are like a flight of crows), we make no more resistance, only we keep them well in front under our eye.

Not an easy thing to do, for with those naked feet of theirs, they can run, while we are embarrassed by civilization and shoes.

Down a slippery flight of wooden steps we go, lighted by pine-torches held by peasants in knee-breeches, like ragged Irishmen (torches everywhere throwing an infernal glare upon the scene); then down again to a lower platform, where we are pulled up short by a deep chasm, between cloven banks—a chasm through which dark waters are rushing with a thundering roar. This would be utterly overwhelming, but for the sight of a raft, nearly as broad as the chasm, waiting to ferry us across.

This, then, is the broken bridge of which the General spoke. In the red torch glare we can see its gaping arches wide apart over our heads.

On the other side, another flight of steps—another avenue of torches (torches—an obligato—one may say, in a "Sinfonia" of darkness), and the light brigade of boys running.

"If this is trasborgo, I rather like him!" I remark, laughing, to Physic, as he hands me up the second flight of steps out of the raft, where the tenderest care has been taken of us by half-clad natives in knee-breeches, on, into another train waiting to receive us on the opposite side; the little boys keeping close to us all the while, and looking up at us with such bright beseeching

eyes, as each deposits his bag on the seat, as well as the
two who bear the railway wrappers like a mummy between
them, that we shower down coppers upon them, *ad libitum*.

In the carriage we laugh again at trasborgo, and the
two French ecclesiastics join in, and we all agree, some
in very bad French, others in worse Italian, "that we
never will believe anything we hear in Sicily again."

Now, as to the constant breaking of the rails, I do
not question the fact, it is too notorious. But I do
dispute that the traveller is not well cared for. I have
since met my friend "trasborgo" in many localities, and
always accompanied by an amount of preparation and
attention, almost incredible in the wild solitudes through
which Sicilian railways carry you.

Again we are steaming through the night among the
desolate, formless hills leading to Syracuse—on, for long
miles, until, gently descending, we dip towards the sea,
round what seems the basin of a spacious bay.

The waves lap upon the beech—the revolving lamp
of a distant lighthouse sheds a scattered glare. Without
knowing it, we have passed the site of ancient Megara
upon the rise—part of the great ridge of Hybla over
Syracuse. The waves are in the Bay of Thapsus.

Megara, named like colonial Naxos, from the parent-
city in Greece, was an outpost against the Athenians in
the siege of Syracuse. It was afterwards besieged and
taken by Marcellus, whose fleet long hung about the Bay
of Thapsus, under Hybla, until he found means to enter
the great harbour, just as the Athenians, under Nicias,
had done before him.

We do not want Strabo's authority to remind us of
"honey from Hybla"; it is a household word.   ·

One celebrated name comes to us from Megara (it is
the doctor who recalls it).

Epicharmus, philosopher and dramatist, who first adapted the ancient Mimes into regular dialogue, and shaped a central plot, round which the various characters gyrated to a conclusion.

"Something, I take it," said Physic, "as dull as Walter Landor's 'Imaginary Conversations,' worked up with a spice of Archaic coarseness to suit the rude Dorian taste. Epicharmus ridiculed the gods too.   In this there was a touch of Socratian humour. We know something of what this ridicule was, from the paintings on ancient vases. But Epicharmus was wiser than Alcibiades, he let alone 'the mysteries.'"

Epicharmus was a Pythagorean speculator and thinker. Wandering about, like many another Greek poet and philosopher of that day, he came from Cos to Megara, then to Syracuse.

Epicharmus happened to be in Megara when Gelon took it. This led to his going with him to Syracuse, where he was patronized by the whole family of the Dinomenes. As a dramatic creator, Epicharmus is re-markable.

From the rudimental mass of mythologic myth, he moulded something tangible.

The revolving lighthouse that I see, is on the Point of Agosta, at the further horn of the Bay of Thapsus.

While I gaze, star after star peeps out of the deep vault above.   Anon the whole heavens are aglow.

How glorious!   Not one, but millions of stars blaze out. The Pleiades twinkle in sisterly unison. The mighty track of that aerial highway, the Via Lactea, trails like a huge serpent in the sky; and the prosaic moon, with her bleared, chequered face, repeats herself upon the waves.

Then the doctor, who is also learned in the stars, looks out for the Great Bear ("to see," as he says, "how his old friend looks in these unfamiliar latitudes"), and just catches sight of his tail.

There is Venus sublimely bright—"the power of love epitomized, and visible to the naked eye" (Physic's own words). Orion sprawling across the sky, in all the ease of masculine power and size; his three belt stars conspicuous; and Cassiopeia, the mother of boastful Andromeda, glittering in her starry chair.

And so, under star-sown skies, and along dark, inarticulate strands, we whistle into Syracuse.

No sooner had I—much elbowed and shoved by modern Syracusans, impatient for their homes—passed a wicket gate, leading to the entrance of the station, than I was seized upon by a Smart young man, who informed me "I was an English Princess," and "that he had been directed by the Prefect to escort me to the hotel in his own carriage, which was waiting outside."

Nor was this Smart young man to be reasoned with. If I had not been a Princess, but a gorilla, he could not have kept firmer hold of me, until he placed me in a high cabriolet from which it would have been impossible to escape, repeating continually, "that he acted by the Prefect's orders."

And he would have driven off with me then and there, had I not vehemently remonstrated; representing to him that I was not alone, but had a companion whom I could not leave.

Nor had I long to wait; for, high above the din of departing citizens, I hear the voice of Physic, uplifted in tones of rage. His voice speedily followed by his bulky person, shouldering, right and left, indignant Syracusans.

"Never, No, never!" he cries, "shall I see my beloved valise again. All I have in the world is in it—
all—all. The valise which has travelled with me in
Chinese Tartary, to the Himalayas, and Timbuctoo!
Never, Never more! Why did I come to Syracuse?"

While he asks me this question, impossible to answer,
he is precipitated into the cabriolet by the Smart young
man, who by some official legerdemain, has already
possessed himself of my maid, also my solitary box, and
all my bags, and who now seizes on the Doctor as a
detail in the Princess's luggage.

In the moments he can spare from me, the Smart
young man assures Physic "that his valise is safe; that
he will find it at the hotel; that he will answer for it."

"What is that impudent puppy saying? What does
he mean with his jargon?" asks the indignant Physic,
purple in the face. "What the devil has he to do with
me and my valise? I have a great mind to kick him."

Then his mood changes, and a look of perfect indifference comes over the broad disc of his ruddy countenance.

"Don't mention it, I beg," he replies gravely, in answer to my consolatory phrases. "It is of no consequence.
I am resigned and happy. I shall have reason to remember Syracuse."

Then in another tone with a sly wink at me—

"This is what comes of travelling with a Princess!
Let the valise go to the deuce!"—Here he flings up his
arms in mock despair. "I do not complain!"

I never laughed so much in my life. The Doctor
ended by laughing too; even the grim visage of Furiosa
relaxed into a smile. I think the Smart young man
must have thought us all mad.

And so we drive a long, long way in darkness, until

we cross the three drawbridges, the three moats, and
under the three portcullises with which Charles V. chose
to adorn what was left of the island of Inner Syracuse;
then through dark and narrow streets, dimly lighted by
the dingiest of oil lamps, we rattle up to an hotel.

The Smart young man hurls himself from the box
to assist me in getting out. The better to reach me he
drags poor Physic out first.

"How dare you, young man?" the Doctor is exclaim-
ing in a loud voice, when suddenly he stops short; a
look of beatitude comes over his face, his eyes glisten.
There, in the doorway, lies his beloved valise!

TABLEAU.

Physic, mounting a flight of very dark and dirty
stairs, hugging his valise; the Smart young man rushing
after him, under the impression that he has stolen part
of the Princess's luggage!

CHAPTER XXVII.

"Cicero upon Verres."—Ancient Syracuse.—Ortygia the Outer City.
—What to Know.—Bad Inns.—Good Wines.

"You have often heard," says Cicero, speaking upon
Verres, "that Syracuse is the largest of Greek cities, and
the most beautiful.

"And so it is in truth, as reported. For it is both
strong of natural position, and striking to behold from
whichever side it is approached, whether by land or sea.
The ports are almost enclosed by buildings, and form
part of every view. They have separate entrances, but
communicate at the opposite extremity. At their junc-

tion, that part called the island (Ortygia) is separated from the mainland by a narrow strait, and reunited by a bridge. So vast is Syracuse that it may be said to consist of four very large cities." (Cicero did not include the suburbs, Temenitis, or Epipolœ.) "One of these is the island mentioned, Ortygia, which is enclosed by two ports, and projects towards the mouth and entrance of each. In it is the palace which was formerly that of King Hiero (II.), but is now the residence of our Prætor. Also there are several sacred edifices; two of them far superior to the rest: one a temple of Minerva, the other of Diana, which before the arrival of the man Verres" (against whom Cicero is pleading) "was most richly adorned.

"At the extremity of the island is the fountain of Arethusa, of incredible size, and abounding with fish. It would be entirely covered by the sea were it not protected by a massive wall.

"Another of the city quarters of Syracuse is called Achradina, in which are a Forum of very large size, most beautiful Porticoes, a richly-ornamented Prytaneium, a spacious Curia, and a magnificent temple to Jupiter Olympus. The other parts of the city are occupied by private buildings, laid out in one continuous wide street, with many cross ones.

"The third city is called Tyche, from an ancient temple of Fortune which it contains. In it is a spacious Gymnasium, with many other temples, and it is the part of the town most densely inhabited.

"The fourth city is called Neapolis. At its upper end is a Grecian theatre of very great size, besides two splendid temples of Ceres and Libera, and a statue of Apollo, called Temenitis, of very great beauty and colossal size."

A city consisting of four or five cities and suburbs, each with its own name, history, and monuments, further subdivided into two parts, *Outer* Syracuse on the mainland, and *Inner* Syracuse on the island, is difficult to grasp.

But when even the ruins of these five cities (all but one, Ortygia on the island) have utterly disappeared, the difficulty increases tenfold.

Such is Syracuse.

Inner Syracuse on the island, the modern town, occupies the site of the original Corinthian colony, founded by Archias, B.C. 724.

Ortygia, misnamed "the Acropolis," for it is lower than the rest, is separated from the mainland by a narrow channel, connecting the Greater and the Lesser Harbours. It is this channel, or *fosse*, for it is now little more, which is crossed by the three bridges we passed last night, built by Charles V. of Spain. Cicero mentions *a bridge* in the Roman days, as connecting Ortygia with the mainland. Naturally, in all ages, there would be a bridge; now there are three.

The island of Ortygia lies in the open sea. On the east side is the Great Harbour; the southern, or furthest point seaward, marked by the mediæval castle of General Maniace (on the site of the temple of Juno), opposite the Cape and Promontory of Plemmyrium, about half a mile across. Cape and Castle form the harbour-mouth.

On the mainland, bordering the Lesser Harbour, across the bridges, lay Outer Syracuse, terracing upwards on the surface of rocky hills.

Outer Syracuse consisted, as Cicero says, "of Achradina on the low slip of shore, immediately opposite Ortygia; of Neapolis, or New Town, on the rising ground to the left; and of Tyche and Temenitis on the face of

the rise; Epipolœ, "the furthest off of all," and the
highest of all the cities, extended over an elevated table-
land, six miles distant.

Temenitis and Epipolœ are spoken of, and were considered as suburbs. Indeed, the whole of Outer Syracuse may be considered as a congeries of suburbs, only
the suburbs were five times bigger than the parent-city
of Ortygia, on the island.

Even on the spot it is hard enough to distinguish
what is, from what is not; to paint the wondrous history
of the past on the bare foreground of the present, to
imagine a city fourteen miles round, shrunk up into a
little island; just as Freeman says, "As if London were
reduced to the Tower and Tower Hill, or Paris to the
island of the Seine"; but, to understand Syracuse this
must be done.

Also, you must be ready to fall back into the full
current of Greek and Roman history, and accept its
details as though actual and present.

Broadly speaking, there is no history of Syracuse
since the days of the Greek tyrants—Gelon, the two
Hieros, Dionysius the Elder, his son the Younger,
Agathocles, and Timoleon and Dion the Deliverers.

Every rustic artist represents one or the other on
the cart he is painting, when not induced to make forays
into French history. The Republicans prefer "the
Deliverers," as democrats; the Conservatives, and they
are few, select the Tyrants. The Syracusan children
are called by Greek names, even the dogs. Our dirty
waiter is "Themistocles," and our padrone is very proud
of a mongrel hound answering to the name of "Pericles."

Greek names are written at the corners of the streets;
bays, caves, rocks, and quarries bear them also; and

right or wrong, Greek history is flung about with a pro-
digality that would astonish an Oxford professor.

As to the Smart young man, our cicerone, he tosses
classic names to and fro as if they were marbles and
he were playing with them.

Not the names only, but the lives of the home-bred
Tyrants and the Deliverers must be mastered familiarly,
also the minutest details of the Athenian siege, the in-
terminable Punic wars, from Gelon to Agathocles, the
coming in of the Romans under Marcellus, the Norman
and Saracenic sieges, all appertaining to Belisarius and
the Goths, and Maniace with the Saracens,—otherwise a
visit to Syracuse will be a pain rather than a pleasure.

And here I am in this same famous city of Syracuse,
utterly discomfited and disheartened by reason of the
badness of the inns!

The Smart young man has taken me to two—the
Aquila d'Oro and the Sole. Impossible to say which is
the worst! Only I give my vote for the Sole, because
there *is* the sun, lighting up the squalid, barrack-like
walls, and playing antic-tricks upon the stone floors;
moreover, by craning my neck very much and standing
on tiptoe, I can just look down over the blue expanse of
the Great Harbour, and on the tree-tops of the Marina,
terracing its shore.

But oh! the desolation! The food, the cooking, the
waiting! Heavens! It is life reduced to its most primitive conditions! In a land teeming with flesh, fruit, and
game, with an ocean lapping the shores, stored with the
choicest fish, there is nothing to eat, and no one to cook!

The night wind rattles through every cranny and
under every door; the windows tremble, a smell of musty
apples pervades the rooms, opening one into the other

like a Chinese puzzle, and a waiter not washed, and stinking of garlic, hovers about!

Thus do we, myself, the Doctor, and S——, whom we find at the Sole Hotel, discuss such supper as is vouchsafed to us. Even in my borrowed plumes of an English Princess, I encounter the common lot of mortals.

But do not misunderstand me. The food is bad and scanty, and the beds are coarse and hard, but both table and beds are clean; and the wine! Ah! I am no drinker, but I wish I were, to appreciate their excellency.

Physic, a moderate man, helped himself to glass after glass of Albanello, and then finished off with Amareno (this last with a cherry flavour); and S——, whom we found in very delicate health, and much fatigued, woke up to declare that "Isola" was the nuttiest, richest sherry that ever moistened the lip of mortal. So thus we go comforted to our hard beds!

CHAPTER XXVIII.

Spanish Defences.—A Poverty-stricken City.—Loved by the Goddesses.—The Long, Broad Street.—What Hosts have Passed?

THE morning broke with the threat of a visit from the Prefect; to escape him I wandered out as soon as I had breakfasted, and seated myself upon a rampart close to our hotel.

The day is lovely; a December sun tempered by a sea-breeze, soft and creamy, calling forth bright, delicate lights, and transparent shadows; nothing hard or positive, all neutral tints, dear to the eye, and suggestive of the mysterious and the unknown!

Yet my first impression of Syracuse is bewilderment;

a maze of dirty, mediæval streets, beginning and ending
in fortifications, with here and there a Gothic church, or
a low-fronted barocco palace, with stone balconies, ogee
arches, dog-tooth mouldings, and pointed doorways, all
woe-begone and dreary; the aspect as of a Spanish town
run to seed, with here and there the pillared ruins of a
Grecian temple.

In modern Syracuse the Spaniard has set his mark
as plainly as the Grecian did of old.

The arms of Charles V., surmounted by a fat, imperial crown, announce themselves too often and in too
conspicuous a position for any one to forget him or his
inheritance.

You may, or you may not, remember, that Gonsalvo
di Cordova conquered Sicily for his masters, Ferdinand
and Isabella, and that their grandson, Charles V., built
the city walls and the three bridges on the foundations
of Hiero's palace, at the weakest point of Inner Syracuse,
because nearest to the mainland.

One can see the huge, uncemented Greek blocks
worked into the Spanish masonry, a strange link between
the Classic Tyrants who trod out political liberty in Sicily,
and the mediæval Tyrant, who failed to tread it out in
Flanders!

The inhabitants of this once great city—the rival of
Athens and the mistress of Sicily—are now reduced to
a miserable twenty thousand souls.

Such as I see them in passing they look polite and
smiling, the men with the long, red Phrygian cap hanging down on the shoulder, and the women with black veils.

But the poverty! It is apparent at a glance. Open
doors disclose hovels with earthen floors, no better than
pig-styes, and rags, sunken features, and the dull, dreary
look of suffering, everywhere.

A group of keen-eyed, hungry-faced old crones, huddled together in a filthy corner spinning, recall to me the lines of Theocritus about the Sicilian distaffs. But I confess, I find the Syracusan old women much like any others of the South. Hairless, foul, and horrible; oftener asleep or begging than at work. The young men have a handsome air, with low foreheads and classic profiles, without that murderous caste of countenance so repulsive at Palermo and elsewhere in the west, where the Arab blood prevails.

By daylight I can see how small is modern Syracuse; just the little island of Ortygia, which Corinthian Archias filched from the Sikels.

Before selecting Ortygia as the Doric capital of Sicily, Archias consulted the Delphic oracle.

"Which will you have?" asked the High priest; "wealth with an unhealthy soil, or poverty and fine air?"

Archias chose wealth and fever, and was straightway directed to the island of Ortygia situated on a swamp. Thus we have the highest authority for considering Syracuse unhealthy.

Here, too, one notes the love of the Corinthians for an isthmus and a double harbour. Primitive Syracuse in Ortygia, dividing a great sea lake into two unequal portions, the Greater and the Lesser Harbour, is Corinth in miniature. Peloponnesus answers to Ortygia, and the isthmus of Corinth to those three irrepressible bridges of Charles V., connecting it with the mainland.

The stately buildings that came to line the "Island" —Dionysius' Castle, or Acropolis, as Plutarch calls it (though, indeed, there never was an acropolis at Syracuse); his palace, gardens, mint, prison, arsenal, and magazine of arms for seventy thousand men; his mausoleum, erected by his son, Dionysius the Younger (to be

seen by all who entered Syracuse); the Pentapylæ, or
five-gated fortress, to guard the entrance of the island;
the famous sun-dial, looking eastward (surrounded by a
portico and bazaars), where Dion mounted on a rostrum
to harangue the people; the Decasteria, or courts of justice,
erected by Timoleon when Dionysius' palace was razed
to the ground; the Hexacontaclinus (or house of sixty
beds) of Agathocles (a Sicilian Tower of Babel, over-
topping all the Ortygian temples, destroyed by the gods,
who struck it by lightning); the public granaries; the
Temple of Juno, on the present site of the mediæval
castle of Maniace, at the harbour-mouth, within which
stood the famous statue of Gelon, which alone was spared,
when all the others in Syracuse were judged and executed
like living men; the great Doric temple of Minerva, where
Ducetius took refuge, now the cathedral; and the Temple
and Grove of Diana—have all either disappeared altogether, or been absorbed into ugly walls and sea-worn
ramparts.

When we hear of the "Seat of Artemis," and the
"Sanctuary of the virgin goddesses," it means Ortygia.
All the early pagan associations are with "the Island."
Diana, the "Protectress," was as great at Syracuse as at
Ephesus, and Minerva, the "Guardian," as much honoured
as at Athens.

Hither came Diana's nymphs—Arethusa, of Elis, flying
before Alpheus to hide herself as a fountain in the darkness of the goddess' grove; and Cyane, changed into a
pool by Pluto for attempting to stay him in his flight
with Proserpine.

Beyond, upon the mainland to the right, I see the
long, sad lines of what once was Outer Syracuse.

When the inner city on the island grew too small,

in the time of Gelon, it spread itself out on the mainland of Achradina and the adjacent heights.

The eastward extremity of Outer Syracuse melts into the sea at the Capuchin Convent. The Creek of San Panagia and the Bay of Trogilus lie behind.

To my left, a little upon the heights, and partly upon the flats, marked by the road to Florida, extends what once was New Town. Above were the suburbs of Tyche and Temenitis, each clustering round a tutelary temple. These temples—in Tyche, to Fortune; in Temenitis, to Apollo—are mentioned as early as B.C. 466, in the outbreak under Thrasybulus, brother and successor of Hiero the First. They were coeval with Ducetius.

In Tyche were also the temples of Ceres (Demeter) and Proserpine, built by Gelon, B.C. 500.

Ceres was peculiarly a Sicilian goddess. She was invoked as "the great mother," and her anger was as terrible as that of the Palician gods.

When Timoleon sailed from Corinth to drive out the Tyrants, he was accompanied, says Plutarch, by Ceres and Proserpine, a galley being specially fitted out, called the "galley of the goddesses," which "led the fleet, shedding a divine light all through the night."

The carrying off the brass image of the most "venerable" Demeter from the great temple of Enna was the darkest crime charged upon Verres by Cicero.

The mass of the outer city, as I see it from the Spanish ramparts, must have laid in the hollow of the hills between Achradina and Neapolis.

Here stretched up that long broad street, the Via Lata, mentioned by Cicero, leading to the great temples, theatre, and amphitheatre, the Latomiæ, and Street of Tombs, and on to Epipolœ. Among white paths and high garden walls, I can see the track of a dusty road

losing itself on a gentle rise; a reproduction, possibly, of
that storied way.

(Not an inch of that hill-side before me but is eloquent in classic history.

Aloft on Tyche Marcellus wept over Syracuse, and near
at hand lived Archimedes, who defended it so bravely.)

By this broad street passed Pompey and Augustus, and
the deliverers, Timoleon and Dion, and Hiero in triumph
from Catanian and Etruscan victories.

Here, too, Dionysius hurried up and down to speed
the rising of his famous walls, and here the Roman
prætors—among them the "man Verres" came and went.

Down here passed Cicero, on his way to seek, among
the ruins and brushwood, for the tomb of Archimedes
near the Agrarian Gate; and, long before him, Pindar
and Æschylus, and solemn Plato, come from Greece to
Syracuse to teach wisdom by academic rule to a royal
profligate; and its stones must have echoed—oh, strange
contrast!—to the steps of another great teacher, St. Paul,
going from the harbour to preach where now stands the
Christian church of San Marziano, in Achradina.

Those dark cavities of black, against the white sky-
line of limestone hills, are the famous Latomiæ, prisons,
quarries, and Nymphæum, all in one.

On that hill-side in Neapolis the people crowded to
see the play, and such Athenians as escaped from the
massacre of the Asinarius begged along the pavements,
chanting Euripides, in the hot summer air.

What hosts have passed by! What carnage! From
every quarter of the globe enemies have come to Syracuse, always and in all ages the land-mark for invasion.

The heart was taken out of her by the Romans.
From the time that Marcellus pitched his camp in Tyche,

Syracuse drooped and languished. The flesh was torn from her bones by Vandals and Saracens.

To Byzantine, Greek, Goth, Saracen, Norman, Teuton, and Spaniard, she fell an easy prey.

The city hills look on the Great Harbour, and the Great Harbour looks to the bright sky, the Spanish walls of Ortygia glitter in the sunlight, and Charles's portcullises rise where the Pentapylœ once stood, the rocky outline of Epipolœ catches the first rays of morning as of yore, and Hybla and distant Etna still throne in the clear air; but it is but a *fetch* or shadow, Syracuse is dead. The nations have buried her!

CHAPTER XXIX.

The Village Green. —National Monuments. —Disappointment. —Party to Epipolœ. — The "Smart Young Man." — "Brook of the Washerwomen."—Timoleon's Villa.—Pagan Landscape.

ONCE disentangled from the tortuous streets and the portcullises and drawbridges of modern Syracuse, you emerge upon an open space along the shore—the Village Green, as one may say, upon the mainland.

Here young men and maidens pass and repass, on festa days, to the churches of San Giovanni, San Marziano, and Santa Lucia; and old men smoke and doze, and beggars and human waifs generally, huddle under the bare white trunks of what once was an avenue of mulberry and elm-trees, reduced by age and sea-storms to mere poles; and there are little stalls, with mandarin oranges, plums, and dried figs threaded upon sticks; and bits of paper fly about, and children tumble upon their heads, or play *morra* in the shade; and lame horses graze.

Yet it is scarcely green at all; muddy if wet, and dusty if dry: the most uncanny Village Green I ever saw —hoar with age, and crossed and recrossed (as with deep wrinkles) by ragged little paths, threading along under whitening orchard walls.

This Green was the ancient Forum. One melancholy, weather-beaten column of red-veined marble, bereft of its capital, is there to witness it.

The Forum lay beside the open sea and the Lesser Harbour; around rose those stately porticoes, so bravely set with statues, and lined with marble slabs and pillars —lauded by Cicero—and the richly-ornamented Prytaneium, with its statue of Sappho, "stolen by the man Verres." (There is nothing Cicero, in his orations against Verres, deplores so much as the loss of that statue of Sappho, the *chef d'œuvre* of Silamon, and according to him, "the most inimitable work of art ever beheld.")

Here, too, lay the Curia, the statue of Marcellus in front, where senate and priests assembled within walls dignified by historic sculptures: the Timoleonteium (Timoleon's tomb), with porticoes, gardens, and a palestra, in which games where held in his honour; and the great Temple of Jupiter Olympus, built by Hiero II. (not to be confounded with that one on the Olympeium, dedicated to Jupiter Urios), containing the statue of the god; also noted by Cicero as having been carried off to Rome by Verres. (There were but three other statues of Jupiter in the world to compare to it for beauty.)

All this strip of level shore, indeed, about the Forum, was devoted in the Grecian time to national monuments, religious processions, the burial of the dead, triumphs after victory, games, and ceremonies.

Here Gelon was proclaimed king, after his victory
over the Carthaginians at Himera; Timoleon received
the thanks of the grateful city he had saved; and
Agathocles sounded those fatal trumpets, the signal of
massacre and pillage.

Standing within the Curia, or under the shelter of
the elegant colonnades of the Prytaneium, the Syracusan
citizen could admire the effect of the setting sun on the
painted walls of the Pentapylœ, observe the working of
Archimedes' bronze rams over one of its five gates (by a
mechanical contrivance the rams turned on a pivot and
bleated, to indicate the direction of the wind), watch the
shadow on the historic sun-dial, or pass the time in
counting the triremes and quinqueremes constructing in
the arsenals of the Lesser Harbour—much as we now,
on the same spot, contemplate (I, for my part, much
against my will) those distracting three portcullises and
three drawbridges of Charles II., which pursue me everywhere.

Outside the circuit of the Village Green, from which
opens up that broad, dusty road, I presume to be the
Via Lata in the hollow of the hills, follows a labyrinth
of rocks and orchard walls. (I can see no pear-trees,
from the snowy blossoms of which, "white Achradina"
was christened), also three Norman churches, very much
alike, and the front of the Capuchin Convent.

Such is Achradina as I see it.

Of these three Norman churches upon the shore, I
know not which is the ugliest—Santa Lucia, with its
Catherine wheel window, like a monstrous eye, mocking
the pagan ruins; the meagre arches of San Giovanni
and Santa Maria di Gesù; or the uniform buff-coloured
front of the Capuchin Convent beyond, on the furthest

point of Achradina, where the waves come booming in from hollow caverns filled with bones.

As I gaze upon the whitened wilderness, depression seizes me. I ask myself: "What interest can I draw out of these stony heights? What history? What poetry? These blank, nude shores, and desolate garden walls and vineyards, what do they say? A very city-skeleton, yet wanting that form which even skeletons retain!"

"Churches and Convents! Santa Lucia and Capuchins at pagan Syracuse!" I exclaim, looking round. What a mockery!

I am addressing myself to the Doctor, seated stolidly beside me, grasping a tall stick, prepared, as it would seem, for any emergency, by his resolute look, and to S—— opposite, who, if all things fail me at Syracuse, will never, I know, fail me in kindness.

(I am wofully disenchanted, I confess it. After Messina and Catania the bareness of Syracuse is crushing. When I come to disentangle its confusing localities, and to frame them duly with their history, I get to like the place and its angular, unpicturesque aspect well. Now, I am in the neophyte or moonstruck stage, overwhelmed with the unfitness of things in general, and groping about to comprehend them.)

It strikes me all at once that I have not explained that the Doctor S——, and I, are seated in a rickety fiacre, bound for the Castle of Euryalus, on Epipolœ, six miles off, and that the "Smart young man," who positively refuses to leave the English Princess, is seated on the box, offering explanations, to which Physic refuses to listen. Also, that two mounted carabineers in uniform, with cocked hats and little brass fusees going off all over them, are stationed behind us; the carabineers, a delicate attention on the part of the Prefect towards the friend of General de Sonnaz, such as a bouquet or a bonbonnière would be in more civilized latitudes.

Our long halt on the Village Green, over which these warriors trot every day of their life, evidently puzzles them greatly. They stare, pull their moustaches, whisper to each other, snuff, smoke and finally give themselves up to slumber; their quiet horses, as much as the flies will allow them, dozing also.

Why we, Physic, S——— and I, should have come so far to Syracuse, and turned our backs on the maiden goddesses, Diana and Minerva, in their island city of Ortygia; on Arethusa bubbling in her fountain; and Cyane clear and beautiful under her sheltering canopy of papyrus—is more than I can say. It was one of those freaks inexplicable to one's self—sheer contradiction perhaps; or the wondrous splendour of the day, or chance. *Chi lo sa?* Anyhow, we four are seated in a carriage, bound for Epipolœ, a good six English miles away.

On a paved road blanched with dust, we gaze over desolate flats, pressing up to the edge of the limestone rock, on which stood Outer Syracuse.

Before us is the Great Harbour, vast as an inland lake; strangely unaltered since the old Greek days. Sadly blue its tideless waters lie, as if nothing more warlike than Florio's steamers had ever ploughed their tranquil bosom. The low shore is shut in by the sombre rise of Plemmyrium, running on to the harbour-mouth, where the sparkling sea-surf rolls in, in banks of foam.

If you inquired of a modern Syracusan where Plemmyrium was, he would stare and inform you that no such

14*

place existed; that the low rocks running out to sea are
called Isola, and that it is famous for its wine.

So much for history.

To the left the quays of the modern town blaze out
in the sunshine, belted by ramparts—a formless mass of
flat-roofed, white-walled houses, set in the brilliancy of
an azure sea.

In some damp-looking gardens close upon our road,
our cicerone points out a slimy ditch, which he informs
us is the "Brook of the Washerwomen."

He speaks under difficulty; every time he opens his
mouth the Doctor interrupts him, with a menacing
motion of his stick.

"Young man," he says, at last, his face flushing
ominously; "we have got George Dennis' 'Guide to Syracuse,' and George Dennis ought to know if any man
does. Perhaps I can tell *you* that the 'Brook of the
Washerwomen,' fed by the overflow of the broken
aqueducts in Epipolœ and Tyche, marks the division
between the suburbs of Achradina and Neapolis. You
see," he adds, turning to me; "it is all marsh down
there along the edge of the harbour on to Anapus and
the Olympeium, on which you know the Temple of
Jupiter Urios once stood. This particular marsh was
called in Siculian *Syraco*, from which, it is imagined, the
city took its name. Don't believe that fellow! He
knows nothing. A sorry imbecile!"

Between the two, I make out that the "Brook of the
Washerwomen" (true to its name, a snowy display of
white linen lay upon its margin) marks the extreme
points of the Athenian camp, after Nicias was driven
from the high land of Epipolœ, and his fortresses on
Plemmyrium, by Gylippus. Observe, that before I have
been in Syracuse two days, I have traced out with my

own eyes the localities of three of the greatest wars in Grecian story—that of the Athenians, in the siege of Syracuse, under Nicias and Demosthenes, at Epipolœ and the Great Harbour; of the Carthaginians, under Himilicon, upon Plemmyrium; and of the Romans, under Marcellus, upon the heights of the Outer city.

I can also understand the pestilent miasma, predicted by the Delphic oracle, which contaminates Syracuse on the land side, and ruins it as a permanent residence, spite of its lovely climate.

In all times, an enemy encamped on the low land bordering the harbour was doomed. The Syracusans might fold their hands and sit idle; death did their work for them, and did it quickly. Readers of Thucydides, Plutarch, and Diodorus, know this for themselves. Those who are not readers, I inform that the shores of the Great Harbour, except on the rise of Plemmyrium, where the sun never seems to shine, are altogether swampy water-meadows and salt works.

That Plemmyrium is not much healthier than the plain, is proved by the plague which smote the Carthaginians there, 395 B.C.

That particular plague might have been imported from Africa; but no invading force has, in any age, escaped some poisonous infection. That the Romans under Marcellus fared better, was due to the elevated position of their camp upon the hills, and the superiority of their sanitary laws.

We all feel this realism to be sad; but no one as much as I. To me it seems as if Syracuse had fallen back into the primitive sea-marsh from which the genius of Gelon and Dionysius called it forth to reign.

We drive dreamily on under the lee of the rocky

ridge upon which once was New Town, now Old indeed,
and seamed with rents, fragments of caves, and tombs.
Breaks in the low cliffs lead up to ancient foundations—
the Temple of Fortune, perhaps, or Grecian gate-ways;
the Hexapylum, the Scala Greca, or towers of defence.

This rocky ridge, open to the plain, was lined with
walls and ramparts.   Now there is neither form nor
colour even in the landscape—a dull sage-green, verging
into brown, with distant blue-grey Hybla far beyond,
and the pale dome of Etna outlined among the clouds.

By and by we come upon patches of young barley
at the Podere di Mira; castor-oil plants wave over broken
walls, and fluttering pepper-trees and oleanders cast faint
shadows.

"Principessa!" cries the Smart young man, suddenly
from the box, with the consciousness of having something to say too good to keep.—We are passing a flat-
roofed villa, shaped like a chest, close by the road in a
little clump of magnolias.

"Principessa, if it be permitted"—his eye is on
Physic's stick, very freely used to illustrate discourse.
Now, Physic, since the episode of the lost valise, has
conceived such an antipathy to him, and shows it so un-
mistakably, that the Smart young man is in bodily fear
of him—"That is the Villa Tremiglia, three miles from
Syracuse, the site of Timoleon's house, where he lived
on his estate, Eccellenza, after he was blind, and retired
from public business."

"Hold your tongue!" cries the Doctor, exasperated
at this long speech.   "Do you imagine we don't know
all about it?"

"The Eccellenza must know a great deal, then,"
replies the Smart young man, pushed beyond endurance.
"The position of Timoleon's country house is much dis-

puted. There is Timoleon's tomb, too, above in Neapolis."

"You are a blockhead!" shouts the Doctor, at the
top of his voice. "What you say shows it. Everybody
knows Timoleon's tomb was in Achradina, near the
Forum. Plutarch says so. Do you dare to gainsay history? What a hole!" he continues, turning to contemplate the villa; "not at all like the elegant and agreeable retreat Plutarch talks of, where Timoleon was visited
by illustrious strangers. Of course, he had his town-
house in the city as well. We don't want that fellow of
a cicerone at all," he bursts out savagely again; "an
empty, pig-headed puppy! Why did you bring him,
Mrs. E——? He annoys me exceedingly!"

The Doctor had lost his temper, and, notwithstand-
ing his assumed indifference, could not find it again.
Fortunately, the sight of some outstanding olive-trees of
great beauty, breaking an expanse of emerald grass,
dotted with the loveliest lilac-coloured lilies I ever saw,
restored him to his usual serenity.

"Observe," says he, elevating that eternal stick of
his, which emphasized all his discourses, "that group of
hollow olives. Did you ever see anything finer? Why,
old Pluto, crown, sceptre, chariot, and all, might hide in
one of them. It is wonderful! There's an uncommonly
pagan look about all this landscape. I should not be a
bit surprised to see Ceres or Proserpine walking about
in yellow robes, crowned with wheat-ears and poppies;
or Hercules himself, with his club and lion's skin, start
up. A group of gods or goddesses would just fit in with
the background!"

Thus Physic rambles on, on all subjects, until inter-
rupted by a loud fit of coughing from S——. Then, in
a moment, he is professionally interested. Armed with

various curative lozenges, concealed in his many coat-pockets, he asks all sorts of questions which, poor S——, evidently desirous of being left alone, fences with as best he can.

So the "Smart young man," thanks to Timoleon and the gods, and S——'s cough, gets off this time with a whole skin. But, seeing the effect he produces on the Doctor's nerves, I resolve never to take them out together again.

CHAPTER XXX.

Epipolœ.—Castle of Euryalus.—The Doctor's Notions.—Peasants.—
  Who Built the Castle?—The Athenians and their Defences.—
  Gylippus to the Rescue.—Revenons à nos Moutons.—The Walls
  of Dionysius.—Remains of Ancient Walls on Epipolœ.

It has been uphill for some time, and a very rough road.

We are mounting slowly, with steaming horses, what Thucydides is pleased to call the "Pass of Euryalus," whatever that may mean. If anything were wanting to prove that Thucydides never was at Syracuse, it would be this phrase twice repeated. There is no "Pass of Euryalus" at all; only a moderate rise, on a flat, rocky surface.

"Epipolœ is a rocky point of table-land" (I am still quoting from Thucydides, who is nearer the truth this time), "lying just over Syracuse, but sloping downwards, so that everything within the city is visible from it. It is called Epipolœ, because it lieth higher than the rest."

Epipolœ, in general terms, in the early days before

the Castle of Euryalus and the temples of "Fortune" and "Apollo" were built, or the suburbs of Tyche and Temenitis, added to the nomenclature.

By this time we are six miles from "the island," yet it is all Syracuse. Now the rocky uplands we have followed, end abruptly in a low headland or scarp, overlooking the sea. And here let me remark once for all, that "the dangerous rocks and terrific precipices" (I quote from Thucydides) "down which armed men were hurled," which give such dramatic force to his relation of the horrors of the night attack of the Athenians, and also to Plutarch's character-sketches of Nicias and Marcellus, are grossly exaggerated. There is no really high ground at all about Syracuse, except Hybla, and Hybla itself is nothing but a lofty line of hills, imposing from the uniform flatness of the plain. Neither Thucydides nor Plutarch could ever have visited Epipolœ. Why, a harmless cow could descend the rise blindfolded!

One speaks of "going to Epipolœ," because history gives that generic name to the high ground commanding Syracuse; but it is the Grecian castle of Euryalus, we have come to visit.

There it stands, a low, grey-white cairn, upon a rugged, grey-white rock! The castle so like the rock, that one has to face it not to believe it to be a dolomitic diadem planted by Nature on its crest.

Beyond everything extant, this view carries one back to the minutest details of Greek military life. The richly-worked helmet, preserved in the British Museum, which Hiero I. wore when fighting the Etruscans, is curious, doubtless, as a relic of antiquity; but what is a helmet to a whole castle? To touching with your fingers the rows of iron hooks, neatly let into the walls for fastening horses' bridles three hundred years before Christ? To moving the slabs before a range of apertures cut in the rock, through which Grecian arrows flew, and by which Grecian troops were screened? To examining stone supports for drawbridges placed, say, during the siege of Marcellus? To passing up and down steps leading into subterranean passages, where not a stone is missing? To peering down, as into an uncovered mystery, a double line of ditches, or fosses of defence, embrasures, galleries, and magazines, all softened and beautified by folds of passiaflora and clematis? Scrutinizing trap-doors and ladder-rests? And passing out to the ivy-clothed rocks seaward, by cunningly-concealed sally-ports (probably planned by Archimedes), one sally-port high, for a mounted trooper, the other low, for a foot-soldier; and both slanting, so as to deceive the eye from sea or shore? It seems to me that Greek antiquity can go no further.

We get out close to the three stone shafts thrown across the fosse, once supporting the drawbridge of the castle. The carriage draws up in the shade; our gallant carabineers, much incommoded by six miles of continuous bumping under a hot sun, dismount and stretch their legs, as is the manner of horse-soldiers.

One look from the Doctor sends the Smart young man, who is blandly advancing, to the rear. He himself much heated, like the carabineers, and flourishing a handkerchief, is volubly discoursing history to S——, lazily hanging on to the carriage-door, a shawl wrapped round his shoulders, looking morbidly indifferent to all sublunary things.

No drowsiness or absence of mind about Physic since we have arrived at Syracuse, but all to the fore,

with a memory and historical knowledge which is perfectly amazing.

He has *clean* forgotten Timbuctoo and Chinese Tartary, and has never once referred to his walk over the
Himalayas. His lively fancy revels in finding himself
face to face with the old Greeks. To him they are real
flesh and blood, and he discusses them with as much
excitement as he would the last political telegram.

Calm-minded S——, an excellent scholar, and well
read in the classics, is of a more metaphysical turn of
mind, and cares less for facts and localities than our
good Physic; besides, he has all an invalid's rebellion
about being driven when he feels ill and languid.

To-day he is in one of his "dark moods;" and altogether refuses to join in our rattling conversation; wandering away by himself, book in hand, with a melancholy
air.

About us gather some half-dozen peasants, in knee-
breeches and sheepskins, the long wool outside, offering
coins for sale. These the Doctor declares to be spurious.

Whence the peasants rise from is a mystery. All at
once we are surrounded, yet we have not heard a footfall,
nor seen a living creature anywhere for miles. There is
no roof in sight over the broad stretch of plain; no
building, indeed, except a telegraph station, a most discrepant object, perched on the conical top of Belvedere,
another abrupt rise, or tumulus, of Siculian origin, some
half mile or so distant, in the direction of Hybla.

They are very cringing and humble, these peasants.
Seeing we are many; gallant carabineers, too, in the
background, with exploding fusees all over them, invariably strike terror into the Sicilian heart; but only give
them a chance—let them find us alone, straggling in
those subterranean vaults of Euryalus, or away on the

plateau, wandering in search of Dionysius' Wall—we should find our unassuming friends develop rapidly into highwaymen or brigands.

Your peasant in Sicily is a born brigand. It is only the force of circumstances which bridles his national propensities; kind Nature has, I am bound to say, so written the fact on his brow, that he must be a fool indeed who would trust him!

Who built Euryalus is an unanswered question, even to the Doctor. (Now, the Doctor knows, or says he knows, everything.)

There are those who hold, with him, that Euryalus is the fort, or castle, mentioned by Plutarch as conquered by Dion. Others believe that it was one of the principal stone forts, or towers, occurring at certain intervals on the long walls of Dionysius. That Dionysius the Elder should overlook so strong a position as "the crown of Epipolœ" is not likely.

However that may be, all we know for certain is, that the irregular pile of stones before us—with its little adjacent fort, like an attendant squire, called Euryalus, surrounded by its double fosse, or ditch, to which wild mignonette and purple caper-flowers cling—was brought to its present form by Hiero II., the successor of Agathocles, —Hiero's friend, the great Archimedes, giving the master-touches.

Outside the castle looks so small and insignificant, we wonder "what we have come forth for to see;" but, once within the fortification, Euryalus swells into size and importance, with spacious courts for horses, and spacious courts for troops; stations for catapults and magazines, subterranean galleries, and long, walled passages.

Underneath, cut in the virgin rock, all remains ab-

solutely *in situ* from two centuries before Christ. That
the upper portion is somewhat chaotic, is more the fault
of Saracens and of earthquakes than of time or war.
The Carthaginians came by sea; and, as far as the
Roman siege was concerned, Archimedes managed so
well with his war-engines and catapults, that Marcellus
could nowhere approach the walls.

Outer Syracuse was finally entered by a ruse, and
Inner Syracuse by treachery.

In the great Athenian siege, under Nicias, Lamarchus,
and Demosthenes, we know Epipolœ was undefended:
the Syracuse generals, Hermocrates and Heraclinus, being,
in fact, found altogether napping when Nicias made that
first rush from Catania.

Nicias came by night from Catania and Megara, and
at once possessed himself of the high land of Epipolœ.
Having, up to this time, all things his own way, he
pitched his camp here, then sailed into the Great Harbour,
as if it were his own; the Syracusans, with no ships to
oppose to him, looking on with dismay; then running to
hide themselves in "the city," says Thucydides—a vague
expression, if you know the ground, seeing that there
were many walls and many cities.

On Plemmyrium, at the mouth of the harbour, opposite the temple of Juno, now the modern fortress, Nicias
pitched his second camp, and built three forts, besides
the citadel, or fortress he had constructed at Labdalum
on Epipolœ, as a principal magazine or depot, connecting
it by a line of wall with the Great Harbour. Up to
this time all supplies and stores to Epipolœ had to be
brought across by land from Thapsus, a tedious proceeding.

And here occurs another blunder of Thucydides. He
speaks of Labdalum as "on the steepest ridge." The

site is not certain, but from the mode of the attack made
upon it by Gylippus, it could not have been on any
ridge at all.   On Dennis' map, which I have used
throughout, Labdalum is placed near Epipolœ, on the
Colle Buffalaro, some half a mile *below the line of the
summit*, and on the land-side, looking towards Thapsus.
Close beside is marked a quarry, the Latomia del Filosofo, so called afterwards from Philoxenus, imprisoned
there by Dionysius.   This Latomia may have provided
the Athenians with stone for their walls.

Anent all these works it is difficult, standing on the
spot to credit the extent of wall described by Thucydides
as having been completed by the Athenians day by day.
It must be remembered, however, that many of these
so-called walls were often merely palisades formed of
wood, mud, and stones.

Much is said about a wall called "the Circle," covering a space of ground somewhere on the table-land
of Tyche, joining Epipolœ.   From this "Circle" other
walls descended on the seaside to Port Trogilus, near
the Capuchin Convent, and on the land, or Neapolis side,
to the Great Harbour by the Scala Greca.

Yet in spite of all their outworks the Athenians were
driven from Epipolœ.   For Gylippus, ugly Gylippus, sent
by Sparta to aid the Syracusans, quickly takes the bull
by the horns, builds a cross wall in no time, on Epipolœ,
cutting through the Athenian out-works, then, attacking
Labdalum from behind, on the sea-side, takes it with
all its stores, and drives the volatile, over-confident
Athenians down to the Great Harbour.

Alas for the Attic Hellenes!   I have said that no
army ever encamped on any part of the Great Harbour
without paying the penalty.   (Give them time! Give
them time! was the motto.)

I recall all this just as we recalled it, standing in the clear, warm air beating up from the Ionian sea, dashing at our feet. We did not admit the Smart young man to our confidence, although most anxious to offer historical information; so he sulked all alone, behind a shady angle of Euryalus, shooting off small pebbles at the shaggy peasants, still hanging about, offering coins, no opportunity having, as yet, presented itself of stabbing us singly on the hills, or capturing us in the dark vaults below.

"*Revenons à nos moutons!*" cries Physic, at length. It is time! He has been prosing about the Athenians, and the night attack by Demosthenes, with its episodes of men and horses flung down the "awful precipices" of Epipolœ, and about the tricks the moon played them, just eclipsing herself at the critical moment when they might have made good their escape!

Besides talking until he shines all over, the Doctor has led us up and down the underground galleries and passages without mercy.

We have broken our shins on the dark stairs—once ending in wooden ladders, to be instantly drawn up, if necessary; we have fingered iron horse-rings, stared at the cunning escarps and sally-ports, and traced the outer fosse, or ditch, said to extend underground to Labdalum.

Now we are standing breathless at the summit, S—— white as a sheet, Physic red as a poppy, and I who write, with no legs at all to stand upon.

"*Revenons à nos moutons!*" repeats the Doctor; the "*mouton*" in question being Dionysius the Elder, a great favourite with the Doctor, and much connected with Epipolœ; no sheep, indeed, but a sort of human tiger—beginning as a common soldier, developing into a poet, musician, and general, and ending as a tyrant and butcher.

"Why," continues Physic, testily, addressing himself to me, who am far too cautious to commit myself, "Why do you keep on so about these Athenians? There is so much else more interesting to talk about. Besides neither Euryalus nor the walls were built in their day, nor for more than two centuries after."

I do not answer. I had said nothing at all about the Athenians; but it would only vex him to contradict him. And who would willingly vex the Doctor? His very foibles are virtues. He is so eager to impart his great historical knowledge, that he is a little overbearing —that is all.

Dionysius learned a lesson from the Athenian siege. Outer Syracuse could not be properly defended by sea or land without walls of circumvallation, and there was little except that old sea-wall from Santa Panagia, at the point of Achradina to the Great Harbour.

He has a long account to settle with Himilcon, for he remembers Leptines and the great defeat off Catania. Besides, he knows he must fight for life and sovereignty; the strongest wall at Agrigentum had not saved the inhabitants from the ferocity of Himilcon, and now he is marching on Syracuse. Epipolœ must have walls, but not as other cities; Dionysius' Walls must rise like magic.

The stone was quarried from the Latomiæ; the Latomia del Filosofo, near the Colle Buffalaro, giving materials for the further or eastern end, towards Euryalus, and the other Latomia furnishing the rest.

The Athenian walls, and those cross-walls of Gylippus

in connection with Labdalum, would appear to have been more inland. These are nowhere mentioned.

Seventy thousand freedmen work above-ground, and tens upon tens of thousands of ruder hands toil beneath, to cut and prepare the stone. There were six thousand yoke of oxen to cart it to and fro.

You can still plainly see the line of Dionysius' Wall, following on along the table-land of Epipolœ—a line of loose blocks of stone, sometimes almost obliterated, sometimes varying from two to three feet in height.

And here again the question arises, whether these walls were wholly of stone? We know that Dionysius sent armies of workmen to fell timber on Etna. Was this in part for his walls as well as for his navy?

In twenty days the wall was finished. It was thirty stadia long—(over three modern miles)—solidly built and strong; no signs of haste in it, of a suitable height, nine feet across, and guarded with frequent towers of defence; all of uncemented stone, carefully jointed.

For twenty days Dionysius stood on this breezy platform urging on the workers. He promised, he gave, and still he urged with mad impatience. Old Diodorus says he even laboured with his own hands.

Wonderful walls these to read about, and yet how useless! A complete and comprehensive line of circumvallation, such as modern defence requires, was almost unknown to the ancients. Dionysius committed the same mistake as the Athenians, and Himilcon entered Outer Syracuse.

Who built the walls on the southern cliff of Achradina? Achradina had walls before the time of Dionysius. They are still to be traced in fragments roughly tossed about at the back of the Church of San Giovanni, mixed up with orchards and fruit-grounds, on to the site of the ancient sea-gate and little cove called Buon Servizio (from the "good service" Archimedes did his country on that spot).

We know from Plutarch on Marcellus, that Achradina was enclosed by a separate wall.

Many ancient walls intersect Epipolœ. The one still well marked along the summit, passing the ruins of the Hexapylum and Scala Greca, and breaking off at the Torre di Galeaga, is clearly Dionysius' work. Another— (a short one, for the sea is so close)—descends from the Castle of Euryalus to the beach; its course marked by bee-orchis and moon-daisies, with here and there a wind-tossed olive-tree.

Over the farm of Tarcia are also remains of ancient defences. Some hold Tarcia on the slope of Epipolœ seawards, over Thapsus, as the site of Fort Labdalum; but Labdalum, whenever it was, was not where it ought to have been, viz., upon a height.

To Hiero II., and his friend Archimedes, falls the credit of selecting Euryalus as the strategic key of Syracuse, and of specially fortifying the escarped ridge of Epipolœ that Nature had made so strong. Only starvation or treachery could force that lock.

CHAPTER XXXI.

The Two Plains.—The Doctor on his "Hobby-horse."—The Hexapylum and Torre di Galeaga.—Archimedes the Necromancer.—
Marcellus taking Notes.—The Romans in Syracuse.—Tears of
the Victor.—The Suppliant City.

BEFORE long the Doctor insists on our climbing the
lesser fort of Euryalus to see the view. S—— objects
as an invalid, on principle, to all exertion. So I am the
victim. Poising myself on Physic's arm, and Physic
poising himself on his stick, we hold on to tottering
stones with trembling feet.

What long, low, desolate lines! What a vast saddened
plain! Plain, west, towards Lentini and Catania; plain,
north, towards Enna, in the centre of the island; plain,
south, towards Ragusa and Noto; nothing but plain!

Not a fertile vega, dark with mandarin and citron
groves, and broken by palms and magnolias, as at Palermo, but ashen, bare, desolate!

"Oh! for a dash of red, purple, or orange, on the
mountain-sides! A tawny sunset over ilex woods! Or
that pure coral tinge which mantles the northern peaks
when the sun sets!

And the sea!

Just under Epipolœ there is another plain, boundless as the land; only this glitters in azure and opaline,
fading lines, and broad circles breaking its surface.

The sparkle and gaiety of this second plain, with
its harmonious ripple and fresh-breathing airs, shadowed
by great cirrhus clouds that come riding up from the
south, make the monotony of the land all the more
solemn.

15*

On land there are no trees, no houses, except the little heaped-up island-mound in Ortygia far away. There are rocks, ruins, and stones, and the dead, lone look of what was once a great city, trodden out by war and conquest!

But for its history, who would come to Syracuse?

The sun is setting in pale rose tints over the wide channel, across which the Carthaginians came for so many centuries, Himilcon, Hannibal, Hamilcar, and afterwards Saracen Emirs, and Kalifs, in fleets of galleys and triremes, their black painted sides outlined in gold and purple; the African captain at the poop, the dusky rowers rising and falling to the banks of oars, the dusky sails set for victory!

A bright sun-ray strikes on a modern land-mark, the telegraph on Belvidere, so discrepant in these pale solitudes, and leads the eye on to Hybla's long line of lofty headlands.

The Great Harbour lies at our feet, bounded by Plemmyrium, and the Olympeium, sombre, as with a curse. The Lesser Harbour borders what was once Achradina, and the Village Green and the Forum are below!

Dr. P——, map in hand, firmly established on a block of stone on the wall of the little fort of Euryalus —I am seated beside him—is fairly off on his historic hobby-horse.

The gods have not made the Doctor analytical and romantic, like S——, facts are his mania. "Now, why keep on about those Athenians," he is saying (it is no use to argue the point, I let it pass). "I find the Roman siege of Syracuse much more interesting. From here you can see it all. With the Romans you have all the excitement of a double siege, Romans besieging Syracusans, and Carthaginians besieging Romans.

"That Hamilcar had the pluck of the very devil, and Bomilcar, though a traitor, was a very able sailor.

"And Marcellus! What a fine fellow! Those tears of his over Syracuse do him infinite honour. Any brute of a soldier can be cruel. To be merciful in those days showed character."

"Where is S——?" Physic breaks off to ask.

"I cannot tell," I answer, taking a look round.

"Poor chap! Poor chap!" says the Doctor; "it is mind, not body with him. Grief is ruining his health. Now, if he would only let me prescribe for him!"

A momentary gleam from the setting sun again breaks his line of thought.

"Ah yes! Short days, Short days; we must be moving. Marcellus' camp was down there on the shore; you see the place under the hill?"

"Yes," I reply.

"For a long time he could not get within shot of Syracuse. His Romans, who had faced Gauls and Carthaginians gallantly, were fairly posed by the necromancies of Archimedes. He had fortified all the line of Epipolœ, and utilized Dionysius' Wall with its towers running down towards the shore at Tyche and Achradina. You see it yonder"—pointing with the inevitable stick—"in and out on that plateau. If the stones were not so much the same colour as the rock, one could trace it much better."

Then the Doctor turns landward.

"You can distinguish the line along that road to Florida and Lentini, running like a white ribbon across the plain. Thank God! bad as the rail is, it is better than a Sicilian road any day. You see it?"

"Yes."

"The Hexapylum, a six-gated tower, commanded the road inland; at the Scala Greca, doubtless, for the ground sinks, as if there had been an outlet there.

"Further on is the Torre di Galeaga, nearer Achradina and the sea.

"Now, when all these great towers, castles, and forts set their machines and pulleys going, you may fancy the roar!

"Towards the shore there were machines which struck the Roman galleys with such force, that at one blow they yawned open and parted in two; tackles and chains which lifted vessels bodily into the air, whirled them round, and then plunged them into the sea. As for Marcellus' poor little war-machine, called *Sambuca*, which he carried with him on eight galleys, of which he was so proud, Archimedes just struck it with a stone or two, and shattered it to bits.

"This caused Marcellus to reflect.

"'Close to the walls,' he reasoned, 'the war-engines cannot hurt us; they require a wider range.' So daybreak finds the Romans crowding under the walls. By Jupiter! They soon found out their mistake. Archimedes was not caught napping. He had short as well as long beams to his engines. He had even had apertures made in the walls for 'scorpions'—that did not carry far, and could be readily discharged. So the Romans, close under the walls, are saluted with a shower of darts and stones, which crack their skulls as they retire discomfited; while other engines are made to play upon them at other distances; fresh ranges varied to the distance—graduating every step they take with a new aim.

"Then there were his lenses.

"At the little cove of Buon Servizio, Archimedes is supposed to have planted those wonderful reflectors which set the Roman galleys in a blaze.

"'What is the use of trying?' cries Marcellus, laughing heartily, as he sees his engineers and artillerymen flying, and his ships burning on the sea.

"But Marcellus found a way, after all.

"Torre Galeaga is marked here, on Mr. Dennis' map, as just below the little Bay of Trogilus, near Sta. Panagia, beyond that roof down there, by the tuft of olive-trees. You may find plenty of stones and ruins there, as elsewhere; and I daresay that conceited scoundrel, the 'Smart young man,' as you call him, would swear to the site and the measurement, besides showing you the mortar and the materials, though no one knows precisely if that is the spot. Well, it was at Torre Galeaga, where he had occasion to hold a parley with the Syracusan leader Epicydes, that Marcellus cut the Gordian knot of the siege of Syracuse.

"Standing near the wall, and biting his nails at the long harangue to which he was forced to listen, Marcellus, to pass away the time, fell to counting the string-courses of stone from the top to the bottom, and thence to measuring the height with his eye. This particular wall, he saw, was lower than the others, and but slightly guarded; the ascent, also, that led to it was easy to scale.

"Now, George Dennis, who, I agree with you, knows more than any living man about Syracuse, states that you may see the ancient foundations close to the road to Lentini and Catania, near that fall in the hill called the Scala Greca, once probably the approach to an ancient gateway.

"For that I cannot answer.

"Any way Marcellus was set thinking. An assault was impossible; but a surprise . . . .? Two scaling-ladders, for instance, measured to the height of the string-courses, and a dozen Romans, not scared by war-engines and catapults . . . .?

"It is worth trying."

"But," say I, "that story of the wall is told of a Roman soldier."

"Right, my dear friend; Livy says so; but I prefer Plutarch, who, however inaccurate about places, is wonderfully minute about individuals.

" 'The great festival of Diana,' Livy says, 'falling out at that time, was a good opportunity. The country people, shepherds and peasants, flocked into Syracuse with fruit and flowers, dancing and singing before the altars of the gods; and the citizens, exultant over the three years the Romans had been kept waiting, joined in the fun. Diana, as you know, is the protectress of Syracuse, and the Syracusan wines are too good not to be drunk plentifully at festivals, even of virgin goddesses. So freely did the Syracusans drink, that for two days they lay about the streets like pigs.'

" 'On the morning of the third day, they were awoke by the blowing of the Roman trumpets and the whistle of the fifes. Marcellus was inside the tower, and had filled the great six-gated Hexapylum with Roman troops.'

" 'There was no doubt about it. As the sun rose over Epipolœ, all the Roman war-music was sounding at once—drums beating, pæans singing, and Roman short swords and Roman helmets flashing on the ramparts. Epicydes might seek at first to rally the fugitives he met, telling them only to have courage, and he would soon drive out the small band of Romans, who must have got within the walls by accident. Accident indeed! It was all in vain. Syracuse was taken!'

"'Now it was that, looking down over the great and magnificent city lying at his feet'—as its white ruins are lying before us—'Marcellus shed those tears so greatly to his credit.'

"'He thought upon the Athenian fleet sunk in the Great Harbour; of the two vast armies cut off by carnage; of the miserable deaths of the Generals, Nicias, Lamachus, and Demosthenes; of the repeated invasions of Carthage, so gallantly repulsed by Syracuse; of the great men who had dwelt there—Hiero I., Dionysius, Agathocles, Dion, and Timoleon, and especially Hiero II., that staunch Roman ally, who bequeathed Rome's alliance to his grandson; how they had all beautified the city, and loved it, and dwelt in it; and so his soul melted.'

"The speech made to him by the Syracusans is very fine. Do you remember it? The sense of it is this:—

"'Neither we nor the other citizens have been in any way at fault, oh Marcellus, in going to war with Rome. It is Hieronymus, a wicked tyrant, our ruler—young in years but old in crime—who has ruined us by allying himself with Carthage; also Hippocrates and Epicydes, his generals and instruments, who did likewise. We Syracusans are innocent.'

"'Marcellus: the gods have given you the glory of taking the most renowned and most beautiful of all the Grecian capitals! Whatever we have done memorable, by land and sea, will go to swell your triumph! Let it not be said that you have ruined so powerful a city, but rather that you left it entire, as a monument of your greatness.'

"'Alas! Let not the memory of Hieronymus weigh more with you than the memory of Hiero! Hiero was much longer Rome's friend than Hieronymus was her enemy. Yours be it, Marcellus, to reconcile the two— to transmit Syracuse unimpaired to your family, as *your* glory, and the glory of your descendants, the race of the Marcelli!'"

"Do you think I know nothing of all this?" I ask, rather nettled at Physic's complete appropriation of all history.

"I do not know if you do, or not; nor do I care," replies Physic, looking me full in the face, in his quaint way, his eyes just moistened by a tear; "I know I read it up last night for your benefit." Then he rises, and stands a moment, supporting himself upon his stick. (He is a little lame, the good Doctor, though so active.) "Any way, you will know it better now," he adds.

"If I have amused you, so much the better. I have only *recalled* the scenes to you—'*recalled*,' I say, I presume no more." Here he takes a sweeping glance round in search of S——, still on the same spot reading. At this sight the Doctor shakes his head, while I confound myself in excuses for my petulance. "Yes," he continues, with another look round, this time rather irritated, "and as I would have done for S——, too, had he condescended to listen. I take it very much amiss that S—— should prefer that mawkish *In Memoriam*, to my conversation. Why, there is more real life-drama in one Greek siege than in all Tennyson put together! And now the sun is gone down and it is time to return. So, call up the carabineers, Mrs. E——, in your choice Italian, and let us get back to dinner."

———

CHAPTER XXXII.

A Day in Syracuse.—Santa Lucia taking the Air.—Grecian Theatre. —Two Queens. — Hiero - Ætneas. — Æschylus and Pindar. — "Earth and Sea, a Comedy."—Phormis.—The Golden Youth. —Dionysius at the Play.—Anecdotes.—The "Younger" after Dinner.—An Ancient Farce.—Timoleon and the Statues.—The Theatre and Every-day Life.

I HAVE had a wonderful day in Outer Syracuse. The Grecian Theatre and the Street of Tombs, San Giovanni, the Catacombs, the Latomiæ, St. Paul, and the Athenians, are all simmering in my brain. I hope something clear and definite will come out of it; only, if I am very long and very misty, put it down to the way in which I have been see-sawed to-day, over all history, Grecian, Sacred, Roman, and Phenician.

In the morning I began by Santa Lucia. I knew nothing about her, except that she usually carries her eyes in a plate; but, before reaching the drawbridge, I found out a great deal. My rickety little fiacre could not pass for the crowd. Now, as a crowd of any sort, except beggars, is very unusual at Syracuse, I at once inquired the cause.

"It was the festival of Santa Lucia, and the procession would pass *subito* (immediately)," I was informed by many voices; and many pair of dark inquisitive eyes were turned upon me, the *forestiera*, in wonder at my ignorance. As it was burning hot, I drew up in a shady corner under the Spanish walls to see the show. I was just in time.

Santa Lucia, born in Syracuse in A.D. 304. of Christian parents, who suffered martyrdom under Diocletian, takes in all respects, as a virgin saint, the place of the virgin goddess, Diana, in Ortygia.

Wherever there were Hellenic colonies, there was a divine female influence. This influence passed from the elegant Greeks to their unlettered conquerors the Romans, and from the Romans to the early Christians established among them; only, instead of the purely pagan notion of simple physical beauty, intellect came to be added.

Santa Lucia usually resides in an ugly side-chapel in Minerva's temple, now the Cathedral. Twice a year she is taken out for an airing, to visit her country seat in Achradina (one of those abominable Norman-faced churches I find so unsympathetic in outer Syracuse). After a stay of three or four days she returns to her side-chapel in the city.

All the town assembles to escort her to and fro. Every one who has a carriage sits in it; but fiacres, painted carts, and even donkeys are not disdained by the accomodating saint, knowing the poverty of her Syracusan worshippers.

A tremendous crowd on foot, serious and intent, fills the open space where I have drawn up under the walls. Salvoes of artillery and the clang of drums and trumpets announce the Saint. Long before she is visible, every soul is kneeling.

As for Saint Agatha at Catania all the troops in the garrison head the procession; the General, wearing his orders, seated on a carracoling charger; the Prefect, a pleasant-looking gentleman, (whom I have, as yet, happily avoided,) in his uniform, (I really do admire their seriousness,) then the Bishop, mitre on head, in blazing vestments, followed by the whole Cathedral body, down to little acolytes in red, swinging censers.

A sort of master of the ceremonies, in black, bearing

a wand of office, marshals them along, and keeps off the
crowd, ready to precipitate itself forward, as if before
the car of Juggernaut!

Last of all, appears a platform, or car, harnessed by
men, two and two, on which sits the Saint, a huge dusky
idol, larger than life, very pagan and barocco.   Her
flaxen head, thrown back, glitters with many crowns;
her neck is a mass of jewels; her outstretched arms
grandly appealing; her flowing robes, like burnished gold
in the fierce sunshine, falling in great folds over the
edge of the platform.   (To kiss this robe is beatitude,
accorded to few.)   Altogether, a very imposing Saint,
with a fixed vitality in her painted eyes uncomfortable
to scoffers.

Now through the mass of her worshippers she passes
—slowly, solemnly, dispensing, as it seems, silent bless-
ings with those outstretched arms—until she fades into
the shadow of Charles V.'s lofty portcullis.   The carriages,
carts, and donkeys follow; the military music grows
fainter and fainter on the breeze; the piazza gradually
empties, and Syracuse resumes its usual aspect of desolate weediness.

The Grecian Theatre lying on the hillside of New
Town, or Neapolis, about half a mile from Syracuse, is
a graceful and gracious monument, smiling to the island
city, the azure heaven, and the glittering sea.

How useless to describe a ruin!   Yet it is so grand,
the curved lines so harmonious, the symmetry so perfect,
that it fills me with artistic joy.

Thank Heaven! we need not burrow underground, or
go to Cicero or Pausanias to be told about it.   There it
is before us!   The shape a semicircle; the seats like

descending rays collected in front of the proscenium; the colour a delicately warm tint, responsive to the sun. That it is built of limestone, and not of marble, must not lessen it in artistic estimation. Marble is not plentiful in Sicily as in Greece, and the native stone could be worked with great delicacy, and brought up to a brilliant surface, by a fine coat of stucco.

I can count forty-two successive rows of seats in good preservation. Towards the top there are more, but less perfect—room enough to accommodate twenty-four thousand spectators; the fascia, carved in the rock, bearing the names of the different divisions (*cunei*) into which these seats were classed.

Here I can read titles of that day—five hundred years before Christ—the architect assuming that all the world knew them well, without index or glossary.

But alas! after the supreme name of Jupiter Olympus on one *cuneus* supposed to mark the seat of the priests, and that of Hiero on another (Hiero naturally glorified as the founder), we come upon two queens, Philistis and Nereis (the Eugénie and Victoria, as one may say, of that day), of whom, in spite of the confidence of the architect flinging them at us, as it were, from afar, certain to hit—we know nothing.

Dennis, the solver of all Sicilian mysteries, opines that one of them, Nereis (shutting up in herself, one feels, a perfect chronicle of the scandal of the day), was a daughter of Pyrrhus the Epirote, married to Gelon, son of Hiero II., and thus grandmother to Hieronymus.

About Queen Philistis, whose name is graven on the *cuneus* next to that of Nereis, even Dennis himself knows nothing, except as a beautiful head upon a silver coin, called after her "Philistia." "Possibly," he says, "she may have been married to Hiero II., a sort of Dorian

Bluebeard, with so many wives that history refuses to chronicle them."

The streamlet from the Nymphæum, which has done its best to obliterate these ancient names, is in full force now, and gurgles beautifully to the ear, as I stand overlooking the graceful curve of the theatre, before it joins the "Brook of the Washerwomen" below.

Fronting the ranges of seats are two square hewn rocks, the foundations of the stage, or scena, and a pit for the curtain, or siparium, to rise from; the whole theatre, rugged indeed, and chaotic in detail, but as distinct in its principal lines as if built but yesterday.

A great king was the architect—Hiero I. (Ætneas, as he loved to be called), brother of Gelon. (The architect, Democopus, only finished what Hiero had begun.)

A very refined and artistic tyrant, Hiero, and witty and popular withal, but a tyrant all the same, wrathful and suspicious, with countless spies in that elegant and literary court of his, "the very harvest-field," as Pindar calls it, "of the ripened ears of all that is excellent."

Look at him! He is entering the royal door, which bears no name upon it, seeing that Syracuse, like Rome, is a nominal Republic—a tall, grandly-proportioned man, resembling his great brother Gelon,—attired in the short tunic of a warrior, and wearing a regal circlet among his curling locks.

Æschylus and Pindar are with him; and behind him walk the inferior poets, Simonides, Bacchylides, and Epicharmus.

Æschylus has lately come from Athens to live at Hiero's hospitable board; disgusted, as it would seem, by the success of inferior poets, and the coolness with which the Athenian public received his "Eumenides," because, forsooth, ladies in an interesting condition

declared, "they were alarmed at the chorus of t]
Furies."

Others said Æschylus left Athens because he h;
dared to allude to some detail of the Eleusinian Mysteri(
Now, both these were capital offences, as causing a la
of births and a failure in the harvests.

Here the great Poet has no reason to complain. H
famous play of "The Ætnaiai" has so charmed t]
Syracusan audience, that it has been followed by a
other, "The Persians."

We know how much these colonial Hellenes delight(
in dramatic poetry, from their treatment of the Atheni;
captives. Such of them as could sing or recite Euripid
were liberated from the Latomiæ and well treated; t]
rest left to die!

Pindar also has hailed Hiero as Ætneas. He
always writing odes to him. That one celebrating }
victory with colts, beginning, "Oh, mighty-seated Syr
cuse! precinct of war-plumed Ares, breeder of men ar
horses," is the most popular, because it is the most ea
to understand.

At this moment, Pindar, somewhat jealous of t]
attention Hierois paying to Æschylus, leans over to i
quire, "In what measure it will please him to have h
recent victory with a single-horse chariot at the Pythi;
Games recorded? Whether he shall associate the nan
of his brother Gelon with his own, or celebrate him ar
his horse Pheremicus alone?" At last, a happy id(
strikes him: Diana in Ortygia shall hold the reins, whi
Hiero only *seems* to drive the chariot.

While this is discussing, Epicharmus, who finds
dull, turns round to take note of a line of skin-coat(
Siculi, sitting, with open mouths, upon a distant bench

Then silence is proclaimed; the curtain rises; ar

the actors, shouting through echoing masks, claim attention for a poem of Catanian Stesichoros, following upon
a versified fable of Empedocles.

There are not always actors at Syracuse equal to
filling the parts of the great plays of Æschylus or Euripides. You must go to Athens for that. But, as the
Greeks love new things, a constant change of perform-
ance is provided.

So Epicharmus, who knows this, writes such light
pieces as "Earth and Sea," a gastronomic farce, showing
off the Syracusan love of good living (we are always
hearing of Dorian gluttony) a favourite travesty also
called the "Syrens," who, instead of singing melodies
to Odysseus, treat him to a succulent supper of fish and
birds, which take up a dialogue on the gridiron and the
spit, after the fashion of Dr. Kitchener's "Bubble and
Squeak."

Dafnis, like Epicharmus, has hit on a new thing—
Pastorals in dialogue, "Eclogues," as they are called:
the idea taken from the rustic part songs and choruses
sung to Diana by the shepherds coming into town for
her festival; just as the Abruzzi shepherds, in our day,
come into Rome to sing *Novenas* to the Virgin in the
streets.

Phormis, general and dramatist, is also a very amus-
ing fellow, sharing with Epicharmus the distinction of
having substituted comedy for fable, though unfortunately
nothing but the titles of his plays remain. Phormis has
lately insisted on dressing the actors in long robes and
showy draperies, and hanging the proscenium with purple
stuffs, and gilt leather, alterations in accordance with the
gorgeous tastes of Hiero, and much approved by the
audience.

In the pauses between the acts, the "Golden Youths,
flower-wreathed and scented, wearing embroidered chla
myds, and broad coloured fillets bound in their perfume
locks, mount to the upper galleries to drink a bowl c
wine and breathe pure breezes from the sea, passin
over ranges of orange and jessamine gardens.

Others cool themselves in the freshness of the Nym
phæum, just above.

What a glorious view! Island, city, and distant plain
the dark strand of Achradina kissing the Ionian Sea
and that calm expanse of the Great Harbour glitterin
with gaudy triremes and galleys!

Within the Nymphæum are grouped the slaves an
painted Phrynes of the day, a band of Hetairæ scantil
clothed, and curled and painted, as the Greek youth
love, singing to harps and lyres, or lolling on couches c
rose-leaves, beside that self-same streamlet which *sti*
gushes out abundantly from the white rock.

Again the trumpet gives the signal that the curtai
is rising, and all hurry back to take their seats.

Later on, Dionysius the Elder crosses over from Oı
tygia to the theatre, and sits upon the royal seat whe
Hiero is dead.

Dionysius wears armour under his royal vestment
and his beard is burnt, not shaved, for fear of razors!

With him are his two young wives, Doris and Arıs
tomache, married on the same day.

How Dionysius ventures to the theatre at all is
marvel, but he is mad about poetry, and spite of hi
campagns finds time to write verses himself.

When his new piece, the "Bacchanals," which h
had sent to be represented at Athens, met with som
success, it caused him such transports of joy that he ı

popularly said to have died of it. He was not always, however, so successful.

Plutarch tells of the embassy of singers, musicians, and reciters, with gilded chariots and prancing steeds, bearing tents of richest stuffs and jewels of gold, which Dionysius sent to the games of Olympia, as an escort to his verses; and how the chariots were broken, the tents pillaged and spoiled, and, worse than all, his verses hissed, and he, himself, sneered at as a sorry fellow and a tyrant, by the orator Lycias; and how he tried a second time and was again hissed by those critical Greeks, who if they had many faults, possessed, at least, the merit of artistic consciences.

Also, how Dionysius imprisoned his best friend, Philoxenus, in a Latomia, for daring to criticise his poetry; and that when he called him back to liberate him, Philoxenus, firm to his standard, cried out—

"Send me back to prison, Dionysius; kill me if you like, but ask me not to change my opinion. The verses are bad, and I will not praise them."

A many-sided man is Dionysius, his "funny" side coming uppermost in more anecdotes than of almost any other Greek.

It was Dionysius who, like Haroun-al-Raschid, placed a common man, Damocles, on his throne for a day, and hung that famous sword over his head to frighten him.

It was Dionysius who pardoned the old woman who prayed the gods loudly as he passed along the street, "to spare his life, for fear his successors should be more wicked than himself." It was Dionysius who permitted his brother-in-law, Dion, to rebuke him for calling the great Gelon a "laughing-stock," and who could appreciate the devotion of Damon and Pythias, even if he could not tolerate the advice of Plato.

16*

A silent terror-stricken court takes its place at the theatre around Dionysius, opposite the stage.

The play is a severe tragedy, the "Agamemnon." Nothing lewd or gross is patronized in this reign. The manners of the Tyrant are bland in public towards the people he tramples on; his habits frugal, like a soldier as he is; his vices private.

The drunkenness and rough ways of his son, the "Younger," and his hideous revellings, came later.

After all, the Elder was a "soldier before everything," spite of his flirtation with the Muses, and a caustic wit.

The real lover of the drama is his son, the "Younger," as true a Bohemian as ever flourished in the *Quartier Latin.*

A young man who takes his wine as lovingly as mother's milk, is drunk for ninety days together, lives to a good old age, writes in comedy, and teaches, to fill an empty purse, has claims in this respect.

The "Younger," who has dined and already drunk many cups of Muscata, down at the splendid palace of his father in Ortygia, comes up in his chariot, by the long broad street to the theatre, to enjoy himself, and make a row.

Tottering towards the royal bench, he is supported by a fair-haired boy, dressed as Ganymede, who bears a golden amphora.

On one side sits his "Sister-queen," the meek Sophrosyne; on the other Plato, who has ventured back again to Syracuse to teach him virtue; beyond frowns iron-faced Dion.

Now Dionysius, lolling back on his silken cushions, is flinging roses with one hand at the Hetairæ who have collected near him, laughing a deep guttural laugh.

With the other he is clutching stern Dion by the mantle, and grinning in his face.

Is this the fruit of Plato's lessons?

As for the courtiers, they are so obliging, that not only are they all drunk like the king, but, like him, they are all near-sighted. Since Dionysius suffers from his eyes, no man about the Court can see beyond a stone's throw.

At last there is a hush, the king is quieted, and the curtain rises for a light piece of mythological buffoonery, called "The Marriage of Hebe."

Behold the whole circle of Olympus engaged in a debauch! Jupiter licks fried fish off a plate like a dog; Juno consumes a bundle of lettuces, in honour of her child; Minerva plays the flute; Apollo dances a jig; the Nine Muses figure as nine poisonous rivers; while the nuptial rites of Hercules and Hebe are celebrated with every detail, in public.

How the king roars and claps his hands, as Bacchus treads the wine-press, Neptune serves the table, and Hebe plays the prude. And, how the sound is taken up and runs from bench to bench!

The very actors—old men and youths—laugh too, under their masks; and, look, even Plato smiles!

Then kings at the theatre go out of date.

Instead, we have Timoleon the "Deliverer." A law-giver, and a soldier—very practical and republican, with no elegant tastes at all, wearing the severe and awful visage of a man, who, like Rhadamanthus, judges both quick and dead.

Stern Timoleon turns the graceful theatre into a law-court, where not only civil and criminal causes are heard, but all the defunct tyrants of Syracuse, represented by their marble effigies in the Inner and Outer Cities, are brought up and judged like living men.

Gelon's statue is alone judged worthy to remain on its pedestal, and comes to be placed within the Temple of Hera.

Not only effigies of tyrants, but tyrants themselves are judged.

Mamercus, for instance, tyrant of Catania, Timoleon's friend, at his first landing from Corinth, then his foe—because Mamercus allied himself with Carthage—is tried and sentenced to suffer the punishment of thieves and robbers.

Besides condemning tyrants and their effigies, Timoleon condemns the monuments which they raised. The palaces of Dionysius and Hiero in Ortygia, the fortress of the Pentapyle, the historic sun-dial, are all demolished as "*bulwarks of tyranny*."

It is lucky that Timoleon leaves the theatre untouched. But there is a certain respect for the multitude in "Deliverers," as in "Tyrants."

Everyone, old and young, rich and poor, bondsmen and free, goes to the theatre. Not only does the critical Greek hear there the voice of the elder poets sounding the deeper notes of human passion, in such stories as the Pelopidæ, and Œdipus; but it is his forum, domus, debating-club, lecture-room, rostrum, audience-chamber, and exchange.

At the theatre politicians discuss state secrets in the upper galleries, or near the Podium, where no listeners can lurk, courtiers plot assassinations, and generals plan possible expeditions against Messana or Acragas.

As for poets who like to muse, or lovers to bill and coo in solitude, close at hand, level with the Nymphæum, there is the Street of Tombs. There, if so minded, they can stroll among the ashes of their ancestors, lying within the square loculi, or wander beyond, upon the breezy platform, towards Apollo's colossal statue and the sacred groves.

CHAPTER XXXIII.

The Street of Tombs.—Archimedes' Grave.—Cicero's Relation.—
A Misnomer.

I AM now within the vaulted recess of the Nymphæum, over the Theatre, a cool retreat, hewn in the solid rock, festooned with feathering lady-ferns, yellow oxalis, and purple caper-flowers.

The circular seat is worn and splintered; the ancient water-course splashes down, without form or order, from broken apertures of Grecian architecture, moistening the stones; and little gusts of air come swirling down to greet me.

Close by, the dark rocks yawn apart, a heavy shadow falls, and a narrow passage opens.

This is the Street of Tombs, winding upward to the plateau of Temenitis and Tyche.

For a distance of two hundred yards the rock is honeycombed with the dark mouths of open sepulchres running back horizontally into the earth's depths—a dark and solemn Golgotha, rifled of bones!

To make all more real this sepulchral highway is marked and wrinkled with the ruts and roughnesses worn by the wheels of Grecian cars and chariots.

What far-off ghosts sat in these? What footsteps pressed these stones?

Cicero, followed by his Roman proctors, seeking for

the tomb of Archimedes; Scipio Africanus, fresh from the conquest of Carthage, bringing back the precious statues stolen by those irrepressible robbers; Agathocles coming from the Sea Gate with his African veterans; Icetas, to attack the citadel; naked athletes, on prancing horses; heavily-draped Syracusan maidens bearing water-jars; the priests of Demeter, carrying corn-sheaves and oil-jars, and driving before them cattle for sacrifice; Flora's servants, laden with wreaths and flower-baskets for her altar; Apollo's Hierophants, with music of harps and songs; the sacred cow of Hera, led by golden reins; or rude idols of sun-dried clay—mere emblems of divinity, offered by peasants, to hang up on Pan's rustic altar?

That this Street of Tombs opens so close upon the Grecian Theatre, is not by any way of contrast. The Greeks knew nothing of sentimental philosophy, and hated mournful images and the idea of death. The position only indicates its great antiquity.

Here we are brought face to face with a period when Syracuse was but the Island of Ortygia, and the walled suburb of Achradina.

The Street of Tombs, leading probably to the Necropolis Himilcon robbed, near to the Temples of Ceres and Proserpine, was then outside the city, in the open country towards Epipolœ. Later, when Neapolis and Tyche grew into rich and flourishing quarters, the Street of Tombs came within the circuit of the walls, close to the spot on the hillside chosen by Hiero as most appropriate for his theatre.

A little onward, up the hill, the "Smart young man" —whom I have brought for protection, not for company —shows me what he calls "the Tombs of Archimedes and Timoleon." (It is lucky Physic is gone out yacht-ing!)

Archimedes, when dying by the hand of that ignorant Roman soldier, charged his friends to mark his tomb with a sphere and a cylinder. He also dictated his epitaph. A hundred and thirty-seven years later, not only the tomb, but its very existence, was forgotten. Cicero, then Roman Quæstor at Syracuse, sought for it, and found it with the greatest difficulty, near the Agra-gian Gate, in Achradina.

These are Tullius Cicero's own words:—

"I discovered the burying-place of Archimedes—quite unknown to, and even denied by the Syracusans—by certain verses which I heard were inscribed on it; and also because I knew that on the top were placed a sphere and a cylinder. For, as I was scanning all the sepulchres (further, there is a great abundance of them at the Agragian Gate), I remarked a small column rising but slightly above thickets and brambles, bearing the figure of a sphere and cylinder. Turning immediately to the Syracusans who accompanied me, I exclaimed, 'This is the monument I am seeking.' So I sent per-sons in with knives and sickles to clear the trees and open a way, and as soon as this was done, we went in, and there, on the further side of the pedestal, appeared the inscription I was looking for, with half the verses eaten away—

> " 'So Tully paused—amid the wrecks of time—
> On the rude stone, to trace the truth sublime,
> Where, at his feet, in honoured dust disclosed,
> The immortal Sage of Syracuse reposed.' "

What the "Smart young man" calls the "Tomb of Archimedes," is a small square sepulchral chamber, hollowed in the rock, with a recess opposite the entrance, for a body, and some sepulchral niches in the side-walls. The stranger could scarcely pass it by unnoticed among the barren rocks over which he is led along the high ground above the theatre, for it bears a rudely-carved Doric portal, low and small, with sunken pillars at the entrance. But the position by no means tallies with Cicero's description. The Agragian Gate, supposed to be close to the old Sea Gate, is to be sought for in modern Syracuse, beyond the Capuchin Convent, among the cliffs at the headland of Santa Panagia.

The so-called "Tomb of Timoleon," rather higher up on the rocky surface on the Tyche platform, upon which I am standing, is very similar to the other in form, only not in such good preservation. Both are heavy, graceless monuments, much more Roman in style than Grecian.

The names are purely arbitrary. Timoleon was buried, as I have said, on the site of the Roman Forum, where his famous statue stood, as the "Deliverer." (It was afterwards removed into the Temple of Juno.)

The Timoleonteium, with lofty pillars and porticoes, bright gardens and flowery groves, in which stood Palestra, where games were held in his honour, was his mausoleum.

All about here the rocks mould themselves into the semblance of tombs and mortuary chambers; but of whom? Who can say?

More congenial with the neighbouring theatre was the colossal statue of Apollo, rising from sacred woods of laurel, cypress, and elm, on the rocky ridge looking towards Ortygia and the sea. The temples of Ceres and Proserpine were near, but the exact site has never been determined.

CHAPTER XXXIV.

A Delicate Attention.—An Enchanted Region.—A Greek Quarry.—
"Dionysius' Ear."—The Ara.—The Roman Amphitheatre.—
Greek and Roman Architecture.

UP to this moment I was not conscious that the delicate attention of the Prefect, had bestowed upon me the escort of two carabineers.

I suddenly became aware of the fact, by the glitter of military accoutrements, near the Nymphæum, hanging about the door of a little mill, worked by the same classic stream of the broken aqueduct which flows through the theatre.

(All that I have described lies so near together on the hill-side at New Town, one might almost throw a pocket-handkerchief from one point to the other.)

Yes! there they are, two carabineers smiling at me benignantly, in cocked hats and well-brushed uniforms, and along with them a half-naked miller, smiling too, cap in hand, as he leans against his own door-post; a group so suggestive of the Opera Comique that had they broken out into song, I should not have been the least astonished.

Instead, however, of serenading me with an *aria d'en-trata*, or joining in a chorus—the handsomest of the two carabineers, a corporal named Giuliano, and a bachelor, as he takes care afterwards to inform me, having been evidently instructed beforehand, to make himself useful, stands forth, and, with a military salute, opens a wicket-gate, leading down a narrow pathway, bordered by orange-trees, or rather by oranges, so thickly does the fruit hang upon the boughs, to make my first acquaintance with a Grecian Latomia.

I presume that all well-educated persons know that a Latomia is a quarry on a hill-side, worked down to the depth of some eighty or a hundred feet. Naturally a Latomia varies with the level of the land, whence was drawn the stone to build the five great cities that made up Inner and Outer Syracuse. Slaves and prisoners cut the stone from the living rock, and artificers and masons formed those shafts, and blocks, and columns, destined, age after age, to increase and multiply. The whole hill-side is dotted with the dark openings of Latomiæ. In many the mark of the chisel is yet plainly visible.

A Latomia is not only unlike any other quarry, but unlike anything else.

Neither picture, nor photograph can properly represent it; you must see it for yourself.

A solemn labyrinth of whitish yellow lime-stone, sympathetic to the sunshine, it winds along a narrow underground valley, as of a pre-Adamite world, its sides, sheer and perpendicular, breaking into caves, low-mouthed grottoes, and chaotic vaults.

Nowhere is the surface plain or even. When not split or wrenched asunder, it is scooped and ridged into roughnesses and crevices, marking the form of the gigantic blocks cut from it, or the capricious action of rain and storm, libeccio, and sirocco, through long centuries.

In these many-shaped crevices a whole animal life exists. The field-mouse and the swallow build their nests secure; the owl rests peacefully on a rocky ledge; frogs croak below in the dark holes; innumerable lizards run in and out upon the stone; and butterflies and dragon-flies, even at this late season, fly round in circles.

In the still, heavy air, thickets of flowering shrubs

retain their blossoms through the entire year; euphorbia and mimosa fluttering in sweet yellow tresses, pomegranates, jessamine, myrtle, and oranges, all shooting up into unnatural height.

Great clumsy knots of cacti and aloes heave the earth asunder, and the twisting roots of fig, vine, and rose-bush, make for themselves a home, while banks of mesembryanthemum and geraniums join in, with star-like flowers.

A curtain of ivy trellises the rock into ideal lace-work, and spurge, capers, and sea-pinks peep out from the green sward above, bordering the azure sky-line.

In the deep shadows, every plant and weed leaps into wondrous life. Although it is almost winter the moist air is that of a hot-house open to the sky, the colours, neutral and strange save where some blossom, pomegranate or hibiscus, burns into the light. The scent of flowers, especially of the yellow jessamine run up into thin trees, makes me faint with its fragrance.

Passing from essence to essence, a draught of damp air, out of some darkened cave, comes to me as a new life. All is so strange, so exotic, I wander on in speechless wonder, silent myself, amidst subterranean silence.

Nothing is familiar. These huge, white walls shut in an enchanted region, neither earth nor heaven, while both are there resplendent.

It is well for me that I am recalled to myself by the measured cadence of Giuliano's sword clanking against his spurs. He has left his companion on guard at the wicket, along with the dusty miller.

I can see that the handsome carabineer is overwhelmed with shyness. He would not mind facing a brigand or a smuggler, but alone with a lady, a Princess, in a Latomia, is evidently a new experience.

Still in the one case, as in the other, Giuliano's sense

of duty is absolute. Awful as is the lady, unfamiliar as is the spot, she must be addressed.

That he must do so has evidently been made plain to him beforehand. I can read his thoughts on his comely face, crimson with blushes. At last comes the effort. With the military salute of a finger raised to the brim of his cocked hat, and many hum's and ha's, and clearings of his throat, Giuliano produces these words—

"Excellent Princess, I have been instructed to accompany your Highness to this Latomia of the *Paradiso*, and to point out to you the cavern, called the Ear of Dionysius."

I long to ask Giuliano what he knows about Dionysius, and who he was, but I have not the heart to trifle with his feelings. From crimson his cheeks have passed to purple; and after he has spoken, his lips shut themselves up, as if no force could open them.

Dionysius' Ear is the strangest-shaped arch I ever beheld. Long and narrow, and ending in a sharp point, perfectly Saracenic.

If the hands that wrought it had tried, they could not have formed anything more thoroughly Moorish. The point of the arch almost reaches to the grassy margin of the rocks. High up on one side is a small square aperture like an odd-shaped door, within which Dionysius the "Elder" is supposed to have sat, and by cunningly-contrived acoustic galleries, to have collected into a chamber not only the voices of the prisoners and their words, but the very rustling of their garments, as they turned uneasily within their rocky cells.

That these Latomiæ were used as prisons is historical. But this mysterious cave, rounded below like the lobe of an ear, and black within, is certainly nothing but the freak of some unconscious stone-cutters, who having driven their work sharply upwards too near the edge, enlarged it in this manner below to keep it from falling. A veil of ivy hangs over the mouth like a green shroud; and long ferns and grasses float from the sides.

Holm would have us believe, that upon the summit of the Latomia, Dionysius built a palace in which he concealed himself when overcome by those fits of panic-terror to which he was subject. A palace, to which the prisons underneath, cut in the solid rock, served as a foundation and from whence he could also see and hear all that passed upon the stage, in the theatre below, just as Louis XIV. enjoyed the advantage of hearing Mass said, in his antechamber, while the first prince of the blood present, passed the shirt over his naked shoulders.

Holm's idea is ingenious, but upon what it is founded I cannot say.

Further on (I am following Giuliano glancing like a human butterfly along the shady paths; having acquainted himself with the sound of his own voice, he has become a little more communicative) is a garden of pot-herbs, and fruit-trees grown into timber.

Another chasm in the rock—deep, mystic, weird, takes the form of a pillared water-temple, where springs and rain gather into a Styx-like lake.

Within I gaze upon shadowy perspectives of halls and vaulted chambers, of dark galleries, rocky screens, and shapeless barriers. A subterranean world, as form-less and terrible as Eblis.

It is twelve o'clock, and I am still in Neapolis.

A little lower is the Ara, or altar—close upon the up and down lane, by which, in a most antiquated little gig, I reached the Grecian Theatre.

The Ara is a monument of the superb ideas of Hiero II.

On this rough hill-side, so·encumbered by ruins and modern walls, one might mistake it for a line of Cyclopean defence, or the fragments of a spacious temple.

In reality it is a monstrous sacrificial altar, partly cut in the native rock, partly formed of roughly-hewn stones, raised on three steps. It is 640 feet long, and 61 feet broad: a solid square of masonry, and well marked in all its circumference.

An Ara was dedicated to the terrestrial, or inferior deities—an altar to the Celestial gods. (Yet *ara* is the Greek word for both, so this would seem to be a distinction without a difference.)

An altar, with or without a temple, was used for invocations, vows, supplications and prayers. It was wreathed with fruit and flowers, or festooned with spoils and offerings. Upon it perfumes were burnt, libations poured, and sacrifices made. An altar was small, and if not placed in a temple, stood under an arch, or in an Ædiculum. In shape, it was square, oblong, or triangular. There were the domestic altars of the Domus, to the Lares and Penates, and the public altars of the Great Deities for the multitude.

The Ara at Syracuse only laid bare in 1839, was constructed expressly for the burning of hecatombs of victims in honour of the gods. On the Ara before me, 450 oxen were annually sacrificed to Jupiter.

It is divided into three parts, or stages, reached by steps. On the first, or lower stage, the women sat, and the victims were killed by the servitii, or inferior priests. (Upon this stage I can still see some indications of stone runnels to carry off the blood.)

On the second stage, the freedmen and citizens were placed. On the upper one, or summit, the priests, standing before great furnaces of wood, roasted the flesh of the victims, pouring over them oil, wine and spices. An Ara, therefore, of this size, was adapted not only to bear the weight of such amazing sacrifices, but also of the whole assembled city.

The Ara at Syracuse was dedicated to Jupiter, and is the largest recorded, excepting that of Pergamos, in Asia Minor, numbered among the nine wonders of the world.

What magnificent ideas the Romans, under Marcellus, must have formed of Syracusan architecture! How they must have stared at this Brobdignagian altar, so much bigger than anything at Rome, or even in Greece. (The Ara of Olympia was but a square of eighty feet.) Did they attribute its vast size to the excessive piety of the Syracusans? Or were they informed that it was a tardy record of national gratitude to Jupiter for escape from the tyranny of Gelon's weak brother—the tyrant Thrasybulus?

Close by, I find myself in full Roman antiquity, before the amphitheatre or circus, one of the imperial monuments left in Syracuse.

This also is of limestone, mostly excavated from the solid rock, and dates from about the Christian Era, when Augustus established a Roman colony at Syracuse. At all events it did not exist when Cicero was Quæstor.

We know that Rome had no theatre of stone before the reign of Augustus. Is it likely, therefore, that a captive city—however famous in its day—should possess one before the capital?

The change of representation, too, from the theatre to the games of the circus, is all Roman; a proof of the submission of the vanquished Greek.

As long as they were a free people, the refined and humanely-tempered Hellenes, abhorred all sanguinary

shows, hideous images, and suggestions of suffering and
death; nor could their Roman conquerors ever instil into
their minds, any sympathy with their own love for barbarous exhibitions.

How closely they meet upon the same hill-side—the
Roman and the Greek—the Theatre and the Circus.
Yet what divergence of taste and habit!

The Roman, fierce, aggressive, formidable, thirsting
for war, carnage and conquest; the Greek, refined, idle,
voluptuous, ready enough to fight when forced by tyrants
to do so, but accepting war as an accident in a life of
æsthetic ease.

Then from the people pass to the position of the two
monuments.

On the same hill-side in Neapolis, and with the same
outlook as the Grecian Theatre, the Roman circus carefully sunk below the level of the ground, is as striking
for the want of any prospect as is the other for its
glorious view.

Doubtless, the *débris* of the excavation piles up the
ground in front; but the Amphitheatre must always have
lain in a hollow.

In no Roman theatre or circus, except such as are
raised on Grecian lines, as at Taormina, is there apparent any of that abstract love of the beautiful in nature,
which led the Greeks to choose the finest sites—that
epicurean instinct, to absorb, as it were, at the same
moment all that nature and art could offer to enthral
the sense.

The pleasure-loving Greek would have his theatre
like his temples—spacious, airy, elegant, hung up, if possible, between earth and sky on some gay, breezy rock,
on a mighty sea terrace—on the verge of a vast open

plain, or, as here, nestling in the slope of some smiling eminence, open to land and sea.

How unlike the Roman! He came to his games to fire his soul with blood, to revel in slaughter, and to give the signal of death! Closed in with solid walls, there was nothing to distract his eye from the carnage going on in the arena. He could identify himself with it.

Not only the site chosen, but the architecture is equally opposed to the grace and symmetry natural to the Greek.

Man writes his mind on his works. Monuments are but the record of the masses, to be accepted as proofs of a nation's qualities, as much as history of its deeds.

This particular amphitheatre at Syracuse possesses no special charm either of history or of art.

It is of elliptic form, under the level of the soil, and, in itself, neither imposing nor pleasing.

Though larger than the amphitheatres of Verona and Puzzuoli, it is much less perfect. There are the remains of eight gates; some for the audience, others for the gladiators and for the wild beasts.

In the centre, I see traces of large stone cisterns or fountains, communicating with the same aqueduct which gushes out so gracefully from the Nymphæum, and trickles over the stone benches of the theatre (the same aqueduct cut by the Athenians on Epipolœ),—used for turning the arena into a naumachia for sea-fights and water pageants.

There are no subterranean chambers, I am told, under the amphitheatre, so that the wild beasts must have been kept in *vivariæ*.

Between the Ara close by and the circus in Neapolis, the Humanitarians would have had ample scope for reform; only the Greek offered holocausts to his gods, the Romans but gratified a gross appetite for bloodshed.

CHAPTER XXXV.

Achradina.—The Crypt of San Marziano.—The Catacombs.—The Saracenic Siege.—End of Day in Syracuse.

AT two o'clock I am down the hill again upon the shore of Achradina, under the same avenue of ragged mulberries—the only trees, I believe, in modern Syracuse —bordering the "Village Green" (and they are dwarfed, maimed, and deformed), which I passed on my way to Epipolœ.

To the outward eye, this strip of sun-dried beach presents nothing but mediæval churches, utterly out of sympathy with Pagan Syracuse.

The ancient walls, especially the old sea-wall leading to the Sea Gate near Cape San Panagia, behind the Capuchin Convent, far more ancient than those of Dionysius, must be laboriously sought for among the walled-up fruit gardens which cover the site.

The oldest part of this outer city is undoubtedly Achradina, which follows on to the shore and beach of Tyche, on the reverse, or seaward, side of the Epipolœ hill, by which we mounted to Euryalus.

The overflowing of the city took place, it is thought, in the time of Gelon, B.C. 500. (I have said this before, but let that pass.)

Bit by bit, the wild pear-trees of the primitive downs disappeared to make way for buildings. This part of Achradina, Dennis says, "being at first rather a site for national monuments than for the common purposes of life." Houses came later as the population rapidly in-

creased, and Tyche, Temenitis, with temples, and Neapolis, with its theatre, were added on as city quarters.

Such was the process of formation in Outer Syracuse.

The three Norman churches, San Giovanni, Santa
Maria di Gesù and Santa Lucia, almost in a line beneath the undulations of the hill, are all pretty much
alike. About a quarter of a mile off flaunts the staring,
yellow face of the Capuchin Convent at Cape Panagia,
looking out, over massed-up rocks, towards the sea.

How Pagan Syracuse became Christian, is not my
business to explain. St. Paul is said to have found a
Christian community established here.

San Martino was the first bishop, and what meant
the same in those days of imperial persecution, the first
martyr. Agatha of Catania, and Lucia of Syracuse
suffered A.D. 251 and 304.

A very green, mouldy, old church is San Giovanni,
jammed into a shady corner among walls, heaps of stone,
and prickly-pear hedges. A bell and a cross surmount
the front. There are three round arches below, fringed
with weeds, and a sculptured doorway, with twisted
marble columns.

Opposite is a little osteria with the announcement,
"*Quì si vende vino di Siracusa.*"

A girl picking another's hair is seated on a stone
bench under a vine pergola, while a monk, our cicerone
that is to be,—looks on complacently.

A most tumble-down old edifice, with nothing inside
it but a brass eagle and a poor fresco—altogether, but
the vestibule, or ante-room, to the most ancient crypt of
San Marziano below—reached by a dismal stair.

This crypt, which takes the form of a Greek cross, is
supported by low, massive pillars. Behind one the monk
points out "The Episcopal Seat." In another corner is a

broken column, upon which San Marziano was executed, he informs me, and a rude stone altar where *St. Paul said mass!!!*

It is historical that St. Paul touched at Syracuse on his way to Rome. But this is not enough. You are asked to believe that he was accompanied by SS. Peter, Mark, and Luke; and that St. Mark also suffered martyrdom here.

Unfortunately, another legend claims St. Mark for Alexandria. However, you had better not mention this to the monks at Syracuse, if you wish to preserve a whole skin.

Up again, out of the crypt, quite staggered by Christian traditions; and down again, once more under a low arch and another flight of steps into the catacombs, said to be eight miles in extent, if indeed, as some affirm, they do not reach to Catania!

(Much faith is required in this part of my day's work.)

A ray of sunlight,—for these catacombs are by no means sunk deep into the earth, shoots down upon these walls of death, and displays rows of yawning sepulchres, hewn in the rock; not in stages or layers, as in Rome, but in horizontal lines as in the Street of Tombs.

Here whole generations lie on their last beds, side by side, taking their rest together.

Some in carved sarcophagi, stolen, probably, from the Greeks; others in rows of simple rock-pits; and there are small loculi cut in between, like after-thoughts, for the bodies of infants and children.

At intervals, open out large, domed chambers, banqueting-halls for the dead, lighted by shafts, down which the sun pierces through screens of ivy and creepers.

Nowhere have any bones been found. Are these

strange loculi, so unlike any other catacombs, to be ascribed to the early or to the later Greeks, the Romans, Saracens, or Christians?

Various and discordant are the opinions.

Were they like the Latomiæ, used as prisons, in that tyrannous State which needed so many? Dens for wild beasts, quarries, barracks, or refuges?

No one knows.

It is said that they date back to the time of Archias, more than seven hundred years before Christ.

Be it so.   But what interests me is that I stand face to face with the Saracens, who in A.D. 749 fortified themselves here.

We have all the particulars of this Saracenic siege of Syracuse in Amari, as related by a monk called Theodorus, belonging to the metropolitan church.

And a most pitiful account does Theodorus give of that time, when a measure of wheat was sold for fifty byzantines of gold, the flesh of horses and donkeys weighed against silver, and even dead bodies devoured with avidity.

For nine months this dismal state of things continued.

At last a breach was made in the "Great Tower of Defence," and the Saracens entered Ortygia.

Now this "Tower of Defence," "situated on the neck of land extending right-hand from the city," must have been no other than the site of what was Dionysius' Great Fortress of the Pentapylæ, now Charles V.'s gates, and portcullises, and bridges, always the weakest part of Ortygia, as being nearest to the mainland.

For twenty days the "Great Tower" was defended with the greatest constancy against overwhelming odds, but at last the Saracens carried it by assault, and the entire garrison put to the sword.

"This," says Amari, with "Amor patriæ" strong upon him, "was the end of Ancient Syracuse."

The city of Gelon, Dionysius, and the Hieros, which Timoleon and Dion came from Greece to deliver, that Agathocles gloried in ruling, Marcellus wept over, and Cicero and Augustus adored!

For two whole months the Saracens were occupied in beating down temples, statues, palaces, tombs, and monuments—everything that was Grecian.

Hence the labyrinth of ruins that we see.

With the catacombs and the churches ended "my day" in Outer Syracuse.

I was back at the hotel by three o'clock. Both the Doctor and S—— were anxiously expecting me. They are like all other strangers, and insist that Syracuse and every other town swarms with brigands!

CHAPTER XXXVI.

History of Ortygia.—Gelon of Gela.—Dionysius fortifies Ortygia.— Born to be Born.—Uncle Dion turned Enemy.—The Fruit of Plato's Teaching.—The Deliverers.—Timoleon in Syracuse.— The Battle of Crimissus. — Hiero II. — The Last Tyrant of Syracuse.

HEAVEN forfend that I should be dull, but being in Ortygia, I must speak, however slightly, of its history!

Nowhere is Syracuse so various as in "the Island." Here the strange phases of her emotional city-life intensify themselves into episodes of fiercest passion; passion, indeed, without patriotism, for every element of change and disunion was there—ambitious and selfish citizens, a fickle, time-serving Demus, and leaders too often beneath the dignity of the Greek name.

At once slavish and turbulent, the Syracusan Greeks

could only be dominated by the strong rule of autocrats or tyrants.

Of these tyrants, the first was Gelon of Gela, B.C. 485, whose form hovers like a shadow over the nascent glories of Syracuse. He it was who first raised it to such an overwhelming superiority over the other Grecian colonies, broke up the oligarchy of the Gamori, or primitive land-owners, and, by his sagacious scheme of government, united the many discordant elements into a strong whole.

Gelon, too, it was who beat back those new invaders, the Carthaginians, in the decisive victory at Himera, and slaughtered one hundred and fifty thousand prisoners in cold blood!

The extent of his power is also indicated by the fact that the Lacedemonians and Athenians sent an embassy —though to no purpose, to beg his aid against the common enemy, Persia.

Thus at length it came about that Gelon, after a career of complete success, convened that meeting of the citizens in arms upon what is now the "Village Green" in Achradina, clad in simplest raiment, without ornament or weapon, to give an account of his whole life as *Strategus* (general).

No wonder that they hailed him by the names of Benefactor, Saviour, King, and decreed that his statue should be set up before the city, in the mean dress he wore.

Gelon was no lover of art, like his brother Hiero, but Hiero was never so popular.

As for a third brother, the unworthy Thrasybulus, his oppressive rule lasted but a year.

Then came Dionysius the Elder, whose acquaintance we have already partially made, a name associated with the grandest phase of Syracusan history.

Of obscure birth, he is first heard of as a soldier in
the siege of Agrigentum by the Carthaginians. Then, by
skilful intriguing and adroit flattery of the Demus, he
creeps on to a dictatorship, and at the age of twenty-five
becomes *Strategus*.

Now it is that Dionysius decides to fortify Syracuse
by sea and land. Ortygia—the core of the city, the seat
of his power—he surrounds with strong walls, builds a
citadel (the Pentapylæ), with walls and towers, looking
towards the mainland; erects the famous sun-dial, circled
by vast pillared porticoes for repose or exercise; bazaars,
markets, prisons, a palace with hanging gardens, a mint,
magazine for arms, docks, arsenals.

The most skilled artisans flock to Syracuse, workers
in brass and bronze, silver and copper; armourers, potters,
masons, architects, and shipbuilders;—Dionysius accepts
them all.

Always fighting, always in the front, always ready
to put his hand to anything, to run all desperate hazards,
Dionysius grew old in harness. His years may be counted
by his battles.

An oracle declared "that he was to die after a victory
over those superior to himself."

He read the prophecy as of Carthage.

Not at all. It applied to himself. His death followed
upon the acting of his play at Athens.

How he died is doubtful.

Now from the palace in Ortygia, where he had been
shut up during the lifetime of his father, with women
and slaves, Dionysius the Younger comes forth to reign.

Naturally easy-tempered and jovial, he is ruled by
the favourite of the hour. Sometimes it is the courtiers
who get the upper hand, and let no sober person ap-

proach him; then it is Plato, who turns the palace into an academy; or Uncle Dion, laying down an ideal law of liberty impossible to carry out.

Nothing, it seemed, could change the king's love for Plato. Like a wild beast, Plato had tamed and softened him, and with a beast's affection "the Younger" clung to him. Not till Plato, after alternating between Athens and Syracuse, had now visited his royal pupil for the third time, did "the Younger" at last weary of him, and despatch him finally into Greece, under plea of having discovered a second conspiracy against his life.

"I suppose," says the King, as he takes leave of Plato on the beach of the Great Harbour, "when you return to Athens, my sins will often be the subject of your conversation at the Academy?"

"I hope not," was Plato's disdainful answer; "we must indeed be in want of a subject, to be driven to talk of *you*."

Plato gone, the scene quickly changes. "The Younger" is often drunk for months together.

We see him once shut up in the Pentapylæ, offering terms to banished Dion, whom the people have recalled. But Dion is assassinated.

Then later comes Timoleon the Deliverer; and the Younger, after reigning twenty years, finally collapses, and retires to Corinth as a private man.

"What did you gain?" he was once afterwards asked by Philip of Macedon, "by giving up so much of your time to Plato?"

"I learned to bear misfortune," is the melancholy answer.

And now those awful forms pass before us—the Deliverers.

Dion is spoken of as "a physician worse than the disease." Plato says of him, "that though reared in the servile court of Dionysius the Elder, he was no sooner acquainted with the knowledge that leads to virtue than his whole soul responded to it."

But Plato was Dion's ruin. A man sincere of purpose, severe and unbending towards himself, he was possessed with the notion of reforming the Syracusans, as Plato had been of reforming the tyrants; and, like Plato, he failed.

And so, although all the Syracusans flocked out to meet him, and scatter flowers on his path, on that day when the Younger was shut up in Ortygia, they soon tired of him in their fickleness, and he left the ungrateful city to its fate, retiring in disgust to Leontini.

Yet again they call him, and again Dion comes, with infinite magnanimity and a patience worthy of Plato.

But it is still the same story. He will remit nothing of his severity; no, not even though Plato writes to him from Athens entreating him "to be less austere."

And so at last came the inevitable plot, and as inevitable death at the hands of assassins.

When Timoleon came from Corinth to deliver Sicily from tyrants, the city of cities had become a howling wilderness. So many of the inhabitants had fallen in the civil wars between "the Younger" and Dion, and so many had fled, that in Ortygia "a crop of grass was growing in the great square before Minerva's temple, high enough to pasture horses; and in the outer city deer and wild boars roamed up and down at will among the ruins."

A crop of grass, indeed; but what a crop of tyrants! Tyrants everywhere! The wretch Icetas at Leontini; Andromachus at Taormina; Hippo at Messina; Mamercus

at Catania; Leptines at Apollonia on the north coast,
now modern Cefalù; and, worse than all, a Carthaginian
fleet flaunting with black-sailed, brazen-prowed galleys
up and down the Syracusan waters, with Icetas encamped
in Achradina.

How Timoleon defeats Icetas, and evades the Carthaginians, till the moment when, advancing on Syracuse,
he finds the Great Harbour empty, were too long to tell.

After that exhibition of iconoclastic zeal against the
statues of the tyrants which I have spoken of, Timoleon
set forth on his Quixotic expedition to knock off the
heads of living tyrants.

Keen upon his prey, he threatens the Phenician set-
tlements in the north-west, which rouses the Carthaginian
spleen to such an extent that war is again declared.
"This time Syracuse shall fall;" Hamilcar and Hasdrubal
are to strike the blow!

As Timoleon, with his brave twelve thousand Greeks,
marches forth to meet them, he meets some mules laden
with parsley, and, seizing a handful, twists it into a
chaplet, and wears it as a symbol of victory.

It is a long road by the plain to the north-west,
towards Panormus (Palermo), Ragusa, Noto, and the
shore. The river Crimissus, where the Carthaginians
lie encamped, falls into the sea not far from Alcamo, a
modern town upon a hill—still looking down over the
ancient battle-field, with many a Moorish tower and Norman façade within its walls.

The season is summer; the time break of day; the
weather hot and sultry, with clouds heavy with brooding
storms.

From the deep valley, dotted with palms and cistus,
and delicate openings to the sea through lines of parting
hills, where, deep below, the Crimissus tosses over its

rocky bed,—a thick mist rises. Nothing can be seen of the barbarian camp below; only the inarticulate noise and hum of a vast multitude come swelling up the glen.

We who have been there know what Sicilian river-beds are—a tangle of oleanders, wild myrtle, tamarisk and acacia, with here and there a cypress, overshadowing a deep solemn stream.

As the sun rises over the hills, the vapours expand and spread, the mists lift themselves.

Now it is the Syracusans who are veiled while all below in the river-gorge is clear.

The Carthaginians—led by Hasdrubal and Hannibal in person, are at the ford, in the very act of crossing. There are the great Tunisian horses, without manes and ears, shaved to the skin, with silver horns on their foreheads rhinoceros-like, bearing the Carthaginian chiefs, robed in black stuffs, fastened over their armour with clasps of gold, and necklaces and earrings of coloured stones, followed by tame panthers and fierce dogs of the desert, leashed together; elephants with painted ears, caparisoned in bronze, worked into fine scales, with brass towers on their backs; within each, three sable archers, ready with their bows; baggage piled upon dromedaries; the sick and wounded lashed upon mules; war-chariots drawn by camels; chariots covered with brass and shining scythe-blades at the wheels, to sweep the enemies' ranks, grating upon the rocks; war-engines and catapults borne by elephants ploughing through the deep stream; shields inlaid with jewels catching the morning sun; pikes, battle-axes, and spears; a casque of bronze, or a brass bracelet burning in the light; troops of light-riding Libyans, swarthy Numidian horse, fleet with lance and dart; tight-set Iberians, and behind, marching heavily downward, to the sound of trumpets, cymbals, flutes, tympanums and drums, seventy thousand men resplendent in white bucklers—the pick of Hasdrubal's army.

As Timoleon gives the word, the trumpets sound, and the twelve thousand charge after him.

The veteran Carthaginians, armed with breast-plates of iron and bronze, repel the first attack, unexpected as it is. But when Greek and Barbarian stand shoulder to shoulder on the river's edge, and instead of pikes, battle-axes, and javelins, short swords and scimitars are drawn, and art as well as strength is needed, the heavy-armed Carthaginians waver.

At this moment, a sudden darkness overspreads the earth; long forks of lightning sweep across the downs, and awful thunder echoes in the gorge.

. The storm, pent up since morning, is at the back of the Greeks, but full in the face of the Carthaginians; torrents of rain swell Crimissus into a flood; the wind howls in the crannies of the rocks; deafening hail beats into their eyes, and clatters upon their metal armour; horses neigh, camels groan, elephants raise their unearthly shriek; massive chariot-wheels sink in the deep soil; mules and dromedaries flounder, and heavily-armed soldiers lose their footing.

Where they fall they lie. The folds of their tunics fill with water; the red soil clings to their feet.

If the Carthaginians are unwieldy and heavily-armed, the Greeks, light-footed and ready-handed, slaughter them with ease upon the slippery ground.

Four hundred riders in the first rank are instantly cut down; thousands are trampled upon the shiny banks; others fall back into the river, and are carried off by the swollen current; but the mass of the great army flies over the rise, and is pursued and overtaken by the Syracusan horse.

Numbers cannot be counted in such a rout; but when the storm ceases, and the sun shines out again upon the gorge of the Crimissus, the very earth is knee-deep with the bodies of the slain.   And such spoil!

The tent of Timoleon is piled with glittering treasures. Besides the jewelled breast-plates, casques, shields, golden armlets, earrings, bangles, and sandals, there are drinking-cups, sparkling with uncut gems, carvings in ivory, plates of worked bronze, bucklers of graven brass, lances, darts, spears, embroidered silk for tents, purple canopies; red, green, and golden embroideries.

The lowest Dorian hoplite despises the brass and the bronze—only gold, and silver, and jewels are worth the trouble of gathering.

For three whole days the Syracusans were engaged stripping the dead.

When Timoleon returned to Syracuse his work was done.   Not only had he broken the Carthaginian power and restored peace, but all Sicily was freed from tyrants.

So I leave him to be interred in due time and with due honours at the Timoleonteium.

Of Agathocles, the next tyrant, I shall speak in another place.

Hiero II., who followed Agathocles, of obscure birth like Dionysius the Elder, rose from a simple soldier to be general and then king, winning his spurs in the Sicilian wars of Pyrrhus.

A great and enlightened ruler Hiero, whose laws, known as the *Leges Hieronimæ*, were observed all over Sicily, and, as bye-laws, respected even by the Romans. Magnificent in his tastes, he built another great palace in Ortygia, in place of the one demolished by Timoleon. He was also the cousin and patron of Archimedes, who encouraged him to build that monstrous galley called the "Syracusan," with twenty banks of oars from stem to stern; chambers encrusted with ivory and precious stones, mosaic floors of jasper, topaz, and porphyry, representing scenes from the "Iliad" and the "Odyssey," a gymnasium, baths, libraries, an arsenal, fish-ponds, dancing-halls, and an academy for philosophy. Altogether, a galley so enormous that the sea, it is said, "bore it with astonishment." Even the Great Harbour could not float it, and it was finally disposed of in Egypt as a present to King Ptolemy.

By the wise policy of Hiero, Syracuse "looked on" unharmed at the mighty contest between Rome and Carthage, declaring itself as a spectator only,—for the former.

So Hiero dies, at the ripe age of ninety, urging his grandson and successor Hieronymus, with his dying breath, "To keep true to the Roman alliance."

But the new king, a boy of fifteen, knew so much better than his grandsire, that he at once became the ally of Carthage.

Alas for Syracuse! within fifteen months Marcellus was besieging it, and Hieronymus lay dead, assassinated in the streets of Leontini.

As Gelon of Gela was the first, Hieronymus was the last tyrant of Syracuse; a leap as from Augustus to Augustulus!

After him the city of cities sank into a provincial capital——

In this slight outline I have endeavoured to sketch the history of Ortygia.

CHAPTER XXXVII.

Lovely Sea Walk.—Pier and Custom House.—Arethusa's Fountain.—
A "Miasmic Ditch."—Proserpine's Veil.—The Nymph Cyane.—
The Olympeium.—The Necropolis at Polichne.—Gelon's Tomb.

BELOW the Sun Hotel lies the Great Harbour, a blue
world, wonderfully calm and beautiful!
Blue sky! Blue sea! Golden blue lights resting on
the lines of shore, the castle point of Maniace, and the
promontory of Plemmyrium just fringed with wild olives
—brownish-blue on reedy Anapus and the plain, whitish-
blue on the heights of Neapolis and Tyche, and palely,
delicately blue in the mists of the far distance.
Along the harbour stretches a charming sea-walk,
called "the Marina," where marble seats, avenue rows
of pepper-trees with leaves trembling in the breeze,
oleanders shedding their last pink blossoms, and glorious
date-palms expanding their yellow-fruited heart-cones to
the sun.
Behind, a high, sheltering wall or rampart, one mass
of passiaflora and exotic creepers, shuts all in. Upon
the summit range themselves the gayest and prettiest
houses in Syracuse!
All this is so different from the ugliness of the town.
I stand amazed.
Can this have been the site of Dionysius's famous
gardens? I ask S——, who is with me. "And has it
persisted in keeping itself beautiful ever since?"
S—— cannot enlighten me. There is no one else
to ask. An old fisherman is sitting astride on one of
the marble benches, mending his net, and an officer is
spurring a terrified young horse into a wild gallop up

and down. I do not count the beggars, who even here charge at me out of remote corners, like modern catapults.

It is a lonely solitude. No one ever comes here, even on festa days.

Among the bones of dead and buried Syracuse, sunshine and sea breeze, the perfume of flowers and the shade of scented groves are inappropriate.

Alas! how are the mighty fallen!

On the Great Harbour before me, where two Athenian fleets went down in blood, Mr. Bibby's smart new yacht, with sails as white as snow, rides triumphantly at anchor, and happy mortals may espy the two Miss B.'s, attired in brilliant blue costumes, leaning over the side engaged in fishing. (I have, I think, said that the Great Harbour is five miles round, with all the appearance of an inland lake.)

A shabby steamer from Malta, with a tubby keel, promising little for the comfort of passengers during the ten hours of boisterous passage, is getting up steam, and countless brown-sailed fishing-boats are tacking about the quiet waters from shore to shore.

The little pier-head is darkened by a coal-barge unloading. Among the black dust lie, quite uncared for, heaps of lemons, oranges, prickly pears, green almonds, and yellow cakes of sulphur.

Some olive-skinned street-boys, with a pretence of clothes, are in the act of helping themselves to the oranges. One urchin, evidently an economist by nature, is not eating, like the rest, but silently stuffing his pockets for future use.

No one interferes. A group of sailors, seated on a low wall, smoke and listen, more or less drowsily, to an "anziano" (ancient man) reciting Tasso in a falsetto voice, his quivering old hands beating a kind of measure.

To the right, in a curve of the shore, there is another pier—a degraded one, for fishermen only. The smoke from the railway station just behind, in Neapolis, settles over it, and behind there are warehouses, and a tall chimney, also puffing.

It is here that the "Brook of the Washerwomen" falls into the Great Harbour, marking the southern limit of the last camp of the Athenians.

"Why is it," as Doctor P—— says, "that, in the midst of so many great wars, I am always thinking of the Athenians?"

I put this question to S——, who has had a bad night, and has come down to take a *"sun-bath,"* as he says—"I think it is," he answers, "because, as Freeman puts it, the tale is told by Thucydides in the finest prose poem in the world. Carthage fought for many centuries, not only at Syracuse, but all over Sicily and along the coasts of Italy, more bravely and much more desperately than the Athenians during that really small siege, of one Greek state against another. But Carthage had nobody but slipshod old Diodorus to record her valiant deeds, and who cares to read Diodorus?

We pass the Dogana—a stone building, with many doors—in and out of which the doganieri, in a blue kind of uniform, pass, with a feeble effort at having something to do. A flight of marble steps leads to a marble landing-stage, and a marble pillar holds the rope of a freshly-painted six-oared barge, abandoned apparently by all mankind.

This is life at Syracuse.

Around the Dogana, a small grove of Judas trees and pomegranates, so beautiful in the far south, shade the limits of a stiff, box-bordered garden. Beyond, a huge mass of rock, or wall, or both, descends from the ramparts to the shore, and ends the Marina.

Into this rock we plunge, through a long, cavernous passage, to emerge in a blaze of sun at the Fountain of Arethusa. Ye gods and goddesses, was ever anything so hideous!

The Fountain of Arethusa is a semicircular stone bear-pit, lined with fresh masonry, very high on one side, towards the town, and very low on the other; guarded by a neat balustrade, where a custodian stands, rattling his keys, inviting us to descend upon a pavement, reached by steps, through a cast-iron gate.

Such is Arethusa!

Cicero calls the Fountain "sweet water." Truly it is very clear and very deep (twenty feet), and exquisitely pellucid; as beautiful water as heart can desire, if let alone; but having been meddled with, the salt brine has been let in, and it has grown brackish.

The spring gurgles out of an archway in the high portion of the wall, by four openings—just as Strabo described it, so long ago; and it is so abundant that it overleaps the verge, and ripples forward in tiny wavelets to our feet.

Tufts of graceful papyrus wave over the surface, the long reeds shooting boldly up from below, and dragon and butterflies flit among the spikes.

The sacred fish, not to be eaten even in the extremity of famine, are gone; gone, too, the splendours of Diana's Grove, where, under the shade of ilex, cypress, and laurel, the statue of the goddess, adored by pagan maidens and wives, who invoked her help as Catholics do that of the Virgin, mirrored itself in the fountain.

Meanwhile, as S—— says, "we will thankfully accept that solitary carobia;" and he points to a wide-spreading tree, clothing an angle of the wall. "Even *one* tree is precious in such a chaos of stone!"

A solid bastion divides the Fountain from the Great Harbour. Standing where we are, we cannot even *see* the water—as much shut out as if it were an enemy.

Cicero speaks of "*a wall;*" but who built these special walls I do not care to inquire. The Spaniards, I believe.

S——, in a low wail, consigns them and their work to everlasting perdition!

"Alas! this is Arethusa!" he continues, casting a rueful glance around; "Diana's friend and Shelley's heroine! Arethusa, who, beautiful as day,

> " 'arose,
> From her couch of snows
> In the Acroceraunian mountains.' "

"Shelley has done all that the refinement of poetry can do to idealize her, and the Syracusan municipality have certainly banished the washerwomen; but she is hopelessly vulgarized, all the same."

"Surely she need not have fled from Greece to be buried in such a hole!"

"Beautiful Arethusa!" continues S——, sighing, "with her rainbow, and 'footsteps paved with green,' who has been running, running from Alpheus ever since history began—to be so caught at last! Why, this is worse than Cyane buried in her pool, and Acis and Galatea parting lava-beds. The Ionian Sea cannot even look at her now; and as to Diana—well, Diana is turned into Santa Lucia in our time; and Santa Lucia certainly does not care for Arethusa!"

Facing me, on the opposite shore, a small river passes under the staring white arch of a commonplace

bridge (San Guiseppe), and disappears into the Harbour.
—This is the Anapus.

Poor Cyane! She lives a long way off among the
water meadows. The banks of the Anapus, by which
she is reached, are, I regret to say, very muddy; and on
a hot day, unpleasantly odoriferous. The Doctor, indeed,
calls the Anapus, "a miasmic ditch, foul enough to
poison a generation."

Anapus (modern Anapo), is clothed by a rank growth
of papyrus, arundo dorax, acanthus, and water-lilies.
This sounds beautiful on paper, but in reality means
slimy banks of water-reeds, fouled and trodden down by
droves of lean red oxen, with round menacing eyes,
which rush down to stare and stamp at the stranger,
helplessly seated in a flat punt, towed through many
weary windings.

If Proserpine dropped her veil now on the banks of
Anapo, heaven knows in what a condition poor Mother
Demeter would find it!

The Nymph Cyane is hid in a beautiful pool dedicated
to Proserpine—"a dark blue water," as the poet sings.

At the bottom, are many-coloured pebbles, and fish
as brilliant as those "who did their duty" so long ago
in the "Arabian Nights."

Here Pluto dashed in, driving his fiery chariot across
the plain from Enna, with "white armed" Proserpine by
his side. It was the sight of Proserpine by Pluto's side
which broke poor Cyane's heart. Her bubbling tears
have never ceased to flow.

Vainly had Ceres wandered all over Trinacria in
search of Proserpine, and while she wanders, the earth
is stricken with barrenness.

Arethusa had told her, and Apollo also repeated it,

that it was Pluto who had carried her daughter off, and
that she had vanished into the earth with him at the
pool of Cyane. Ceres, too, had found Proserpine's veil
close by, lying on the banks of Anapus. Now she questions Cyane, but the Nymph is silent. Faithful Cyane!

Then it is that, standing on the pool's brink Ceres
calls on Jupiter for vengeance.

"Vengeance on Pluto!" thunders Jove, astride upon a
storm-cloud, "Impossible! My brother Pluto is next to
me in greatness. As I rule space, and Poisedon the
wide seas, so Pluto rules in Hades. He is too mighty
for vengeance, as you are also my sister, most venerable
Ceres!"

But Ceres does not see this at all. Brother or no
brother, still she clamours for vengeance, for her child!

It cannot be! Proserpine has eaten the pomegranate
seeds, and Ascalaphus has seen it. Proserpine is Queen
of the infernal regions, and immortal.

Then that compromise is come to between Jupiter
and Ceres. Fruit-bearing Proserpine is to live six months
on earth, and six months in hell. Again the earth is
fertile; the grass upon the mountain laughs, the vineyards
purple with abundant grapes; the olive boughs are heavy
with fruit; and rich corn crops load the fertile earth.

Standing on the brink of Cyane's pool, I see, a little
to the left, a gentle rise among indian-corn fields and
meadows; so gentle indeed, that looking across from the
Great Harbour it might escape the eye altogether, in
such a world of flats and cloud-shadows.

A great temple crowned the rise dedicated to Zeus
Urios—Lord of the Winds, which indeed meet here from
every quarter—not to be confounded with the Temple
of Jupiter Olympus, on the beach of Achradina.

This ancient shrine of the Olympeium, built by the Gamori, in the dawn of time, and vast and solid as is the Doric temple of Minerva, still left to us in Ortygia,— was approached by broad flights of steps, cut in the green platform, and surrounded by dark woods of planes and laurel. In the shadows stood altars to rustic gods —Hermes and Terminus, Sylvanus and Faunus, and shrines to good old Pan.

The four sides were adorned with pillars—drummed and fluted in the native fashion; and on the pediments stood statues of the gods—coarsely sculptured, it is true —as were the metopes within the peristyle, but venerable from their antiquity.

A massive cornice caught the morning sun, and the flat roof glistened with metal tiles. The statue of Jupiter sat in the cella, clad in that mystic robe of many colours, woven for him by his daughters, the maiden goddesses, Diana, Pallas, and Proserpine, from Sicilian flowers.

Hippocrates of Gela coming to besiege Syracuse, pitched his camp on the rise of the Olympeium; but Gelon, himself a Hierophant, and more pious, dedicated to the god his Carthaginian spoils taken at Himera, in the form of a golden mantle.

"Gold!" cries that arch-cynic, Dionysius, a century later, when tyrant in his turn, "Who ever heard of gold for immortals! Why, I have just cut off the golden beard of Apollo! His father Æsculapius was content with hair. What does Zeus want with a golden mantle? Too hot for summer and too cold for winter! Strip it off. Give him a coat of wool!"

At Polichne was the city Necropolis, close by, on the open plain. Here a little town sprung up connected with the great shrine, where priests and servants lived, and chaplets and wreaths, flowers, offerings, and torches were sold on wooden stalls to worshippers from the town.

Being in the open country, the largest tombs, like that of Cecilia Metella, outside Rome, were fortified, and used as defences against hostile armies. And it was here Gelon lay interred, at the Nine Towers, a castle of great strength belonging to his wife, Demareta, daughter of Theron of Acragas.

On a certain day, five hundred years before Christ, a long pale line, as of a countless multitude, dim in the distance, wended its way along the shore of the Great Harbour to Polichne—a procession without pomp of music or show of statues, trophies, torches, or banners.

To the Nine Towers it came, bearing the honoured corpse of Gelon. Over him the Demus raised a sumptuous monument, and decreed heroic honours.

In due time Demareta, his faithless wife, was laid beside him. He had so willed it, and Gelon's word was law. In her funeral pomp she wore upon her brow the golden crown given her by the Carthaginians in gratitude for her merciful interposition at Himera.

Now Polichne has disappeared; Gelon's monument is gone; the fortress of the Nine Towers has vanished. Agathocles, who could not brook the greatness of Gelon, destroyed the tomb, which the Carthaginians had already sacked.

Two mutilated shafts upon the rise of the Olympeium, the highest staggering earthwards, alone remain—, all that is left of Jupiter's Temple, Polichne, the fortress of the Nine Towers, and Gelon's grave!

CHAPTER XXXVIII.

Visions.—The Great Harbour.—The Athenian Fleet.—"Try them by Sea."—Syracuse Conquers.—The Column at Noto.—At the Ford.—The Latomia del Paradiso.—"Just as the Greeks saw it."

I HAVE described the Great Harbour as it is; but I have said no word of its history.

Now—how can I sit by it, day after day, and not evoke visions of the past?

I will set down my thoughts as they came to me, musing idly, on my favourite seat—a marble bench under a palm—upon the Marina, the high rampart wall behind me, one sheet of purple creepers, scenting the air with aromatic perfume.

I look south towards Plemmyrium, and a new horizon unfolds.

The ragged fringe-line of wild olives melts away, and three Grecian forts mark the sky-line. They are so placed as to command the harbour-mouth and the harbour.

Behind, under the green rise of the Olympeium, the army of Athenian Nicias lies encamped; his fleet rides at anchor close at hand.

The day is just breaking. In answer to the signal of Gylippus, who has said, "Try them by sea," half of the Syracusan fleet is foaming through the water of the Great Harbour, leaving the shelter of the city walls.

The other half, by a preconcerted movement, rounds the southern wall of the city from the lesser port, and passes the rocky point on which stands the Temple of Juno.

The Athenians, imitating these tactics, also divide

their galleys into two divisions. Forty triremes row to meet the Syracusans; the rest remain to guard the beach of Plemmyrium and the camp.

Gallantly the Athenians fight at the harbour's mouth, until they have beaten the Syracusan fleets.

Then they proudly row back to their moorings under the Temple of Hercules, and take up their old position under Plemmyrium.

But if the Athenians have had the best of it by sea, by land Gylippus has clearly conquered.

The three Athenian forts on Plemmyrium are his; money, naval stores, provisions, all.——

It is a great victory. Henceforth the harbour mouth is closed against the Athenians.

I look east. The Athenians are in their last camp on the marshy shore at the extreme end of the harbour, close upon Syracuse.

Only a little brook divides them from the hill-side of Neapolis, where stand the statue of Apollo and his grove.

The marsh of Lysimelia is behind; the river Anapus to their left.

The great plain is dried up; hot mists lie on the low grounds, the pear orchards in Achradina droop from the heat, the very olives flag.

It is autumn. Already the heavy fever-stricken air has done its work. The dead are being carried outside the camp for burial in the marsh; the dying lie about the tents, and those not stricken sit heavy and heartsick, dreaming of their far-off Attic homes, their wives and little ones at peace under the pink and purple tints of setting suns and pearly-dawning morns in native Attica!

So close to the city as they are! Why, the Syracusans are before their very eyes, white-robed matrons watching them from the ramparts; Corinthian guards sharpening their swords on the walls; the savage Sicani letting fly their arrows at them in jest. See! To-day the people are holding a market on the quays to sell meat, fruit, and wine to the sailors.

The flower-girls, fruit-sellers, and watermen are there, and singers shouting ribald songs in ridicule of Athens!

Every moment, full boat-loads are coming in for provisions from the fleet, with just time for the sailors to snatch a hasty morsel and depart.

There is but one thought in the Athenian camp, from Demosthenes, the brave sea-general, down to the lowest slave, and that thought is *Flight!*

Yet Nicias will not listen to Demosthenes and Eurymedon. He would rather face defeat than the indignation of the people at Athens.

Still they urge him. Then the moon is eclipsed—a fresh excuse for delay. Nicias will not stir until three times three days after the eclipse, and when all due sacrifices have been offered to the gods.

On the third day, Gylippus orders his troops on board, and stands out in order of battle.

So low have the puissant Athenians fallen in public esteem, the very shop-lads and street-boys follow in fishing-boats and skiffs "to see them beaten."

One lad, Heraclides, rows in so near them, that an Athenian galley touches his boat's prow. Heraclides will surely be taken, and a great ransom asked! No! Just in time, Uncle Pollichus, a sea-captain, bears down before the wind, charges in with ten Syracusan triremes, and rescues him!

Now comes the extreme moment when the Athenians must conquer or die. Nicias makes his final appeal; he exhorts crews and captains; he entreats them to remember that they have no reserves, no more triremes, that it is their last chance. "Recall," he concludes, "the past glories of Athens; our honoured Penates and the temples of the gods!"

Boldly, too boldly, does the Athenian fleet answer to his word; the Syracusan galleys close round them in a circle.

Now do the Athenian galleys, built light for rapid motion through the water, and to answer readily to every change of helm, feel the want of good sea-room in the narrow limits of the harbour. The Athenian tactics are, to avoid direct attack, to retreat before receiving the shock of an enemy's prow, then to return and strike, by driving their metal beaks into some weak part of the adversary's hull so rapidly, that he cannot retaliate. In all these manœuvres the Athenians are great.

But this requires space. Here the very size of their fleet is an impediment to them.

The Great Harbour is but five miles round, and half of it taken up by the Syracusans! The Athenians are so closely packed, they can neither advance nor retreat, tack nor stand to windward; one vessel drives up against another, and cannot get itself loose. As one captain boards the trireme of an enemy, he is himself grappled by a third.

Such a multitude of vessels never fought in so small a space before!

The crash, the clamour, is overwhelming. The bowmen, slingers, and throwers hurl masses of stones, darts, and missiles; the metal prows thunder against each other, be it friend or foe. It is all confusion. Skill is of no avail. The word of command is inaudible; the officers cannot shout loud enough. Their voices are only heard by a few about them.

"Let none escape! Will you fly before those who are beaten? For Dorian Gods and altars!" shout the Syracusans in reply, steering madly forward.

The Athenian army, and those left in the camp, press down to the water's edge. With heart and soul each man fights with his fellows. They are all so near, so mixed up together, that in the clear southern air they can see each others' faces, hear each others' voices, mark the line of each familiar form, read the ships' names, and recognize the crews and the captains.

"Victory! victory!" shout the Athenian soldiers from the shore, as Demosthenes scores an advantage. "Undone! undone!" is the lament when Menander is driven back by Python.

Then, as the issue of the battle becomes doubtful, shrieks and groans arise from the beach—invocations to the gods, deadly curses of the Erinnys, execrations and prayers. Some stand paralyzed, others' bodies are contorted by terror, limbs become rigid with suspense. There are a wringing of frenzied hands, and wild leaps into the air.

Now it is clear the fortune of the day turns wholly for Syracuse. There is no doubt of it.——Alas! alas! for the great armament! The pick of the golden youth of Attica! The faithful Siculian allies! The brother Naxians, and Catanians and men of Leontini—The honest Generals, rough and ready Demosthenes, and courageous Menander!

The Athenians are in full retreat. Their triremes are driven straight upon the beach, their transports and light boats drifting rudderless.

Nearer and nearer they come, rising on the crest of the waves, the dead and dying cumbering the decks; the flapping sails, the rowers' empty benches, the wounds of the living, the disabled vessels—all ghastly evidences of defeat. They come with the bloody wash of the tide, with the masses of floating corpses, with oars, rudders, figure-heads, and masts, flung upon the shallow shore.

Syracusans pressing behind, friendly arms stretched out in front!

Such as are living leap to land. They rush, they fly to the shelter of the camp.

The army opens its ranks to receive them—opens, but with groans, shrieks, and execrations.

I shift the scene. I am four miles from Noto, on a wooded height, not far from Cape Passaro. Around is an open, undulating country, broken by dwarf palms, carobia-trees, acacias, and orchards. Near me is a flat, low-roofed house, where, at the door, a peasant guide awaits me.

From this house—little better than a hovel, with a stable and some ruined outbuildings—a narrow footpath leads through the verdure of green cornfields to a gentle rise, on which stands a column of uncemented blocks of limestone.

The column, raised on a solid base of steps, and tapering to a point, though broken in the middle, is still lofty. This is La Pizzuta; said to be the veritable trophy erected by the Syracusans after their final victory over the retreating Athenians.

The Fiume di Noto, winding through a deep, rocky defile, runs below. In the Athenian's time it was not called Fiume di Noto, but the River Asinarus. Here the last struggle took place between the Athenians and their pursuers.

It is on the eighth, some say the sixth, day of their
flight, that the Athenians, under Nicias, near the banks
of the Asinarus.

Demosthenes, involved in an inextricable labyrinth
of walls, has already surrendered within an enclosure
known as "the olive-ground of Polyzelus."

Nicias sends out a horseman to ascertain if this is
true.   Alas! no horseman ever returns to tell him yes
or no!

So weak are the Athenians, so overwhelmed by the
agony of thirst, and worn out with perpetual watching
and fighting, that they have come to wander on vaguely
through brushwood and scrub, from hill-top to hill-top,
with no thought but to find water.

No sooner do they behold the stream, than the whole
army as one man rushes down to the river; the heavily-
armed press on the front ranks, the horses on the
hoplites, the hoplites on each other, and the Syracusan
horsemen on all!

What matter enemies' lances and darts, flying javelins
and arrows, if they can only drink!   Drink—drink—for
ever!

In their haste to reach the bank, hundreds upon
hundreds fall down and trample upon each other, piling
up confused heaps upon the rocky edge.

Those who are on the water's brink fling themselves
down full length, or cast themselves upon the shoulders
of others.   Swords are drawn, mortal blows exchanged,
helmets seized for drinking-cups, cuirasses torn off for
scoops, and outstretched hands carrying the trickling
water to the mouth, seized on by those behind.

Many, standing on the bank, are so close together,
they cannot slake their thirst at all; others die, pierced

by their own weapons whilst stooping; hundreds, entangled and helpless, fall into the stream, and are drifted away by the current.

Even those who can drink their fill—and they are but few—are so galled by darts and missiles of the Syracusans on the further banks of the river, that they die; the Peloponnesian light-horse, too, plunge breast high into the stream, and beat down the foremost ranks cruelly. The waters, shallow with the summer heats, soon run blood—blood and turbid foam.

Only to drink!

At last the carcases of the dead fill up the river-bed, and no more water flows.

It is now that Nicias surrenders himself to Gylippus.

This takes place on the twenty-seventh day of the month Carneus, called by the Athenians Metagitnion (the day was celebrated afterwards at Syracuse by a festival named the Asinaria).

It was decreed that the Athenian soldiers should be sold for slaves, and the freedmen imprisoned in the Latomiæ. The two Generals, Nicias and Demosthenes, were condemned to die; but not waiting for the sentence to be carried out, they fell by their own swords.

Would it have consoled them to know that Euripides will write their epitaph?

Again I change the scene. Now it is the Latomia del Paradiso, behind the Capuchin Convent in Achradina.

A smiling peasant girl opens a little wicket-gate, and I am straightway engulfed in flowering thickets of citron, nespole, daphne, bay, spirea, and oleander.

At my feet spreads a carpet of scarlet geraniums, purple cyclamen, yellow oxalis, and the classic acanthus, with its boldly-veined leaves; there are fuchsias, flag-flowers, many-tinted peas, and showers of pale pink roses—all wild and dishevelled as Nature has placed them.

Walls of white cliffs rise sheer out of this exotic glen, sheeted and tapestried with ivy; so near together these walls, no sun can penetrate.

All is as in a delicious twilight, a subdued poetic day—in itself luminous.

The smiling girl, singing to herself as she gaily dances along the path, pulls down snowy branches of orange and nespole, as if they were brambles, scattering the white petals at my feet.

The shrivelled leaves of the fruit-trees are the only indications of the late season. In these evergreen groves there is little change from summer to winter. The cactus, variegated aloes, and prickly pear are of all time, and these, spite of efforts to drive them out, are here also.

On I pass in a great silence. The clouds fly overhead; the birds are mute in the still air; the insects do not hum; the very air mounts to the brain in wafts of intoxicating perfume.

Above, around, rise the limits of this narrow valley, white, inexorable, cut as with a knife straight down—, no issue anywhere.

Here in this most lovely quarry was enacted the last sad scene of the Athenian siege!

Seven thousand soldiers thrust down here after the surrender of Asinarus, as into a living tomb; seven thousand men huddled together, with scarcely standing room, "conscious," as says Thucydides, "that they cannot possibly escape death."

The heat, the glare, the chills of dawn, the dews of

night, the change of season, thirst, starvation, wet, in that uncovered dungeon cause a deadly mortality.

Many die directly of their wounds; others languish slowly. The dead and the living are massed together in sickening heaps. The awful stench rises to poison the outer air.

Thus they lay for seventy days.

The Syracusans, looking down from above over the grassy margin, must have beheld as revolting a scene as ever was enacted in that human tragedy called life!

I wonder, did the wild cactus break the blue sky-line to the longing, hopeless eyes of the captives as I see it now?—cutting hard and fierce, an infernal fringe between rock and cloud?

Did the trailing caper, and wild fig, and the ivy, breaking the whiteness of the mocking cliffs, tempt the dying men to scale the walls and fly? Or has this Elysium of verdure come on, only with the damp still-ness of decay?——

I wander on, stupid with wonder. To this moment the whole scene comes to me like a dream: the hot, breathless air; the dark caves, low mouthed and horrible; the sunmotes slanting down upon a leaf, a petal, or de-fining the delicate lacework of a fern; the blanched cliffs taking fantastic shapes of pinnacles and towers, or cut and hacked as by Cyclopean chisels, into the sem-blance of a huge trireme; a gigantic profile; a tomb, a coiling serpent, a monstrous lion!

"Just as the Greeks saw it!" I keep repeating to myself stupidly. "Not a stone changed, not a line altered since four centuries before Christ. And this subdued light was just so; and so were the clouds; only not the groves, nor the flowers!"

Still I walk on, bewildered. Nor do I well know

where I am, until the smiling maiden closes the wicket-
gate behind me, and I find myself again upon the rocky
stretch of sea-bound Achradina, in the full glory of the
setting sun.

CHAPTER XXXIX.

Carthaginians in the Great Harbour.—Himilcon.—Where is Dionysius?—The Pestilence.—The Attack.—The Harbour on Fire.
—Himilcon Disappears.

A NEW invader fills the Great Harbour.

Instead of Athens we have Carthage.

Magon has just defeated Leptimes, the brother of
Dionysius the Elder, in a naval engagement off Catania,
and sails superbly triumphant into the port.

Two hundred and eight triremes and galleys follow
him, and a close mass of rafts and transports; the line
of shipping stretches across from the southernmost point
of Ortygia to Plemmyrium.

Spacious as is the vast basin, with its many rounding
bays and creeks, there is not room enough for the play
of the long oars and the drifting of the anchors.

Nothing to be seen from Syracuse but sheets of dark
sails, and forests of black masts, a burnished background of gilded poops hung with Grecian spoils, pictures, crowns, vessels of gold and silver, goat-skins,
statues, arms and armour!

The swarthy-skinned captains sit at the bows, richly
clothed, and wreathed with poplar-leaves. Others stand
equipped for battle, round shields of bronze upon their
arms, and head-coverings of pointed caps and casques.

In the transports, stabled upon the decks, are the

elephants, screeching at the smell of land, the dromedaries, mules for baggage, and brazen chariots.

The African rowers rise and fall with the motion of
their oars from raised banks of benches; their bodies
bare and oiled, hung with innumerable strings of coloured
beads, shells, and charms.

Thus they pass, hands upon oars, shoulders bent forward, arms outstretched, waiting the signal of the
trumpet.

It comes, followed by a savage beating of drums and
clashing of cymbals! With one long, loud cry, the whole
fleet echoes it, and four great triremes burst from the
mass bearing Magon and Himilcon.

The galley of Magon, long and slender, with sweeping purple sails rounding to the breeze, and the dark
oars breaking the water in a stately cadence, is a wonder
of barbaric splendour.

See! how it glitters with brass and gold! A gilded
sea-horse at the prow, with outstretched legs seems to
paw the waves. On the deck Moorish guards, covered
with fine scaled armour, and scarlet mantles surround
the chief; behind are ranged the slingers and darters,
in tight-fitting breastplates, with rough coarse hair, and
heavy barbaric features.

Nor is this gorgeous sea pageant all.

From the west, tramping across the plain by the
Helorian road and the banks of Anapus, marches the
Punic army, three hundred thousand strong, with three
thousand horse, led by Himilcon in person. Himilcon
pitches his tent within the Temple of Jupiter Urios, on
the Olympeium. He cares nothing for Jupiter. He would
spit on the image of the God, if he thought of it, and
any African about him would do the same. All creeds
and all races are the same to Himilcon.

Himilcon's is a religion of amulets and charms, of
maledictions in burnt hair and flesh, incantations, potions,
and the bloody rites of Baal. According to circumstances Himilcon sacrifices to the stars or adores the
sun.

He believes in nothing but in destruction and in
death.

Behold him within the columns of Jupiter's peristyle,
his eyes fixed on the smoke of a thousand fires, lighting
the blazing ruins on the plain; long pendants are in his
cars, and his black beard lies thick and matted upon
his breast.

Upon his head glistens a coronet of pearls, shaped
in many tiers, like a mitre; on his neck are strings of
blue stones, engraved with cabalistic signs.

A black robe flowered with gold, flows down, and he
wears bracelets and anklets of uncut gems.

Behind him, a negro holds a golden fringed sun-
shade, and slaves wave palm branches to keep off flies.

Around the vast host lies encamped an army of many
nations.

Gigantic Libyans, with frizzly hair and handsome
features; renegade Greeks to be recognized by their slim
figures and clean-shaven faces; Bruteum peasants, clad
in sheep-skins; Gauls, with long hair drawn upon the
top of the head and fastened with an iron pin; Egyptians,
broad-shouldered and thick lipped; archers of Cappa-
docia, their faces stained with the juice of herbs; Ly-
dians in flowing robes, covered with vermilion, and
wearing yellow slippers; Ligurians, Lusitanians, Ethiops,
and fugitive Romans,—a motley multitude speaking
languages as mixed as their nations.

Some lie supported by cushions, dressing their
wounds; others stretched full length on their backs, relate

their past adventures to each other; a Gaul erect against a tree, passes round the wine-cup to his fellows; and a Roman archer throws arrows at random as the sea-gulls sweep by;—all more or less are in repose according to their nation and habits, yet all ready at the trumpet's shriek to rush into action.

For thirty days Himilcon's mercenaries ravage the whole city.

Achradina is taken. The Necropolis there and at Polichne are rifled by his Egyptians for treasure.

Not only are the tombs of Gelon and Demareta destroyed, the temple of Ceres and that of Proserpine burnt, but the whole of Syracuse is over-run.

And where is Dionysius all this time?

Why does he not defend the city of cities, and the temples, and the tombs?

What of his Pentapylæ? His arsenal and magazines of arms for seventy thousand men? His walls on Epipolœ down to the Hexapylum?

Is he afraid? Is he paralyzed? Or is it the calm of a great general shut up within his walls biding his time?

Neither—Dionysius is only waiting for reinforcements from Greece; and while he waits he leaves it to Anapus and its pestilent ditches, oozing pools, and malarious vapours, the stagnant lake of Lysimachia, parched-up, rocky Plemmyrium without springs or water, slimy harbour shores soft with black mud, to do their deadly work upon the strangers.

Suddenly, no one knows how, Himilcon's arm is seized with sudden panic.

Spectres of hideous Gorgons pursue the soldier through the night. Phantom-Chimeras hover over the camp;

Medusa snake-heads seize them, and "the monstrous serpents called Pythons." The whole brood of Cyclops and Titans escaped from Etna, to fight their battles with gods over again, amid the Carthaginian tents; the earth trembles, and pale funereal lights play upon the horizon.

It is said by the priests in Syracuse, and the rumour gains ground day by day, that Jupiter and Demeter, in their wrath, have given over the African host to destruction.

A pestilence breaks out.

It begins among the light-clothed Egyptians encamped in white tents along the ridge of Plemmyrium, passes to the Libyans and Numidians on the plain, and, from these, spreads over the whole Carthaginian fleet and army.——

This year the summer heats are long and excessive. In the marshy ground about the harbour, the morning sun brings forth poisonous vapours, to be dried up by the heated miasma of the burning noon.

Dry winds raise up showers of dust, which penetrate the hot skin, poisonous insects abound, and lack of rain exhausts the fountains.——

It is for this moment that Dionysius has waited.

While he attacks Himilcon by land, the whole Syracusan fleet steers down upon the Africans. It is an exact reproduction of the battle between Gylippus and Demosthenes; the same locality, the same movements, the same surprises, and the same results.

And now Dionysius, seeing some of the larger Carthaginian galleys intact, and making a feeble resistance, thinks, "It is time it should finish."

"Torches! Torches!" he cries to the guards about him: "Bring handfuls of torches! Burn what is not sunk!"

A brisk sea-breeze fans the flames, and carries them with fiery tongues from ship to ship. By a general impulse, the whole population of Syracuse comes trooping out of doors.

It is an awful sight which meets their eyes. A cincture of fire surrounds Ortygia. That terrible fleet that was to starve and destroy them is ablaze!

Himilcon and Magon escape by making a secret compact with crafty Dionysius, who foresees that his turbulent Syracusans may prove too much for him by-and-by, if the power of Carthage be utterly broken.

So the Carthaginian chiefs sail swiftly and stealthily away, and eluding the pursuit of a few Corinthian soldiers who have perceived their flight, gain the open sea.

The miserable Carthaginian army on Plemmyrium, abandoned by their leaders, throw down their arms and beg for quarter.

Their Sicanian allies, from about Lilybœum, make a rush for the mountains, and so save themselves.

The heterogeneous mass of mercenaries—Ethiopians, Libyans, runaway Romans, Iberians, and Gauls—spared by the pestilence, surrender at discretion.

Such are my day-dreams on the Marina of Syracuse.

I can see it all—the flight of the Athenians across the plain, the Carthagenians by land and sea—Noto, the Latomia!

If I can call up these pictures to the eyes of others, as they stamped themselves on mine, I have not mused in vain.

CHAPTER XL.

Castle of Maniace.—Temple of Juno.—Bronze Rams.—An Unlucky General.—The Normans Revenge Themselves.—General George turns Traitor.

BEYOND the Fountain of Arethusa, the modern town of Syracuse ends on a low point of black rocks, where stands a mediæval castle. Opposite are the long lines of dark Plemmyrium, now called Isola. Between flows the blue sea.

I should not care about this mediæval castle at all (a square pile of mellow-tinted limestone) occupying the site of what was once the Temple of Juno, with round towers of no particular architecture at its angles, and singularly confused as to loopholes and windows, were it not that here I meet my old friend, General George Maniace, whose acquaintance I made at the Signor Duca's, near Bronté.

At Bronté, General George was fighting against the Saracens in the centre of the island, under the snows of Etna. At Syracuse he has conquered them; bridled them so to say, and put this castle-bit in their mouths. But only for four years, be it remarked. In four years the Saracens, spite of Maniace and his castle, were back again in Sicily as victorious as before.

Nor is this mediæval castle improved by a trim new battery attached to it, with Bersaglieri on guard, pacing up and down in bright uniforms, and abundant black plumes waving from their hats; nor by the trim little light-house rising out of the sea close by.

Ma come si fa? One must take things as they come, especially in Sicily.

General George was a very fine fellow in his way. In many respects equal to Belisarius, only he was unlucky; not only unlucky in war, but unlucky in coming upon the world, at the very moment when those incredibly romantic Normans, altogether engrossed European interest.

At Syracuse you cannot overlook Maniace, although only a Byzantine, or modern Greek.

Not only has he a street named after him, running down from the Cathedral towards this rocky point (a street shabby and dirty enough in all conscience, as are all the streets of Syracuse), but also this castle, in a prominent position at the mouth of the harbour.

Altogether, therefore, Maniace is one of the *Genii loci* of Syracuse, to be placed on a par with Diana the protectress and Minerva the guardian; or even with Dionysius and Santa Lucia; only the valiant and elegantly-nurtured Byzantine might object to such an ill-mannered colleague as Dionysius.

Now the Castello di Maniace is by no means to be mistaken for the site of what Plutarch so wisely calls "the Acropolis" (seeing such never existed at all), or of the Pentapylæ of Dionysius, situated on the opposite or land side of the "island."

Maniace's castle, on the foundation of Juno's Temple, was built by himself, A.D. 1038, remarkably stout and thick as to walls, and serving well as a fortress against those roving Saracens, carrying on the same old foray between Africa and Syracuse, begun in the time of Gelon. In fact, it is quite a modern building in dim, far-off Syracuse, with nothing ancient about it but those two famous rams of Archimedes, turning on pivots and bleating to the wind, brought back by General George from Byzantium to the city of their birth, and set up here over his gateway,

Pray, let not the curious traveller look for these rams here now.

One has been lost; the other removed to the museum of Palermo. In their place observe the fat coat-of-arms and imperial crown of Charles V. of Spain, as obtrusive and prominent here as on the three drawbridges and three portcullises.

About the removal of the rams there is a very dismal mediæval story, in which a certain Marchese Gerace, the ancestor of Prince Gerace of Naples, figures very little to his credit.

Gerace appears to have received the famous rams as the price of a treacherous massacre of Syracusan notables, from his master, Alfonso, King of Arragon, as great a blackguard, apparently, as Gerace himself.

How one ram found its way to Palermo, I do not know.

What banquets and carousals of the good old sort, with swords on hip, helmets and nodding plumes on head, sword and dagger in belt, and tankard in hand, were held in this fine old castle-hall, with its vaulted wooden roof, carved shafts, and huge fire-place!

For the sake of picturesqueness we must hope the hall existed in Maniace's time; only I fear it did not.

What is more certain is that General George, a heartless, elegant Greek—I can picture him with an atmosphere of imperial courts about him, clad in a suit of inlaid Byzantine armour—having built this castle, could afford to do without his friends the Normans, whom he accordingly cheated of their share of "half the spoils and half the conquered towns."

They had their revenge, however; not only by com-
passing George Maniace's natural death, but by clean
snuffing his name out of history! You must come to
Sicily, or read Gibbon, to know that such a man ever
existed.

At all periods of his life General George was unlucky. Yet he served his master, Michael Paleologus,
well, and was just about to make some great coup which
would win Syracuse from the Saracens, and restore it
once more to Byzantium, when he was recalled to Constantinople.

At last, wearied by ill usage at home, and exasperated by the persistent attacks of his Norman ad-
versaries abroad, he turned traitor, proclaimed himself
Emperor of the East, and ended miserably by the hand
of an executioner at Durazzo.

After all, should his ghost "revisit the glimpses of
the moon," it may be gratifying to find that his name is
still preserved in a ducal dwelling at Bronté, a dirty
street at Syracuse, and in this same hideous yellow-
faced castle on its bed of black rocks—a perfect eyesore
on the azure sea-line of the Great Harbour.

CHAPTER XLI.

Minerva's Temple.—The Doctor's Lamentations.—Diana's Temple.
—A Tempest Shut Up.—How the Sea Roars!—Hotel Miseries.
—The Doctor's Anxiety.—An Historical Subject.

IT is an inexpressible disappointment to find the
great fluted pillars of Athena's Temple sunk into the
stone-work of the Cathedral wall. An inattentive person
might literally pass through the piazza without observing
them.

Not only built into the wall all round, but, on the south side, absolutely concealed and embedded; all except the Doric capitals, which peep out discomfited at the summit.

But, what is even worse, is a double row of *battlements* round the flat, plain roof, giving the grand old sanctuary, grey with accumulated ages, the aspect of a commonplace fortress.

Dennis says the Temple of Minerva was converted into a Christian Church in the seventh century, during the reign of Theodosius the Younger, by Zosimus, Bishop of Syracuse. Butler, in his "Martyrology," says Zosimus was a monk of Palestine, and mentions a meeting in the wilderness, beyond Jordan, between him and a certain St. Mary of Egypt, "a short, sun-burnt woman, with white hair;" going the length of relating what St. Mary said on this occasion, and what Zosimus answered. Indeed, Butler is so much occupied with St. Mary, that he forgets to tell us anything about Zosimus, or how he got to Syracuse.

A bell-tower—horrid sacrilege!—added to the indignity of the castellated roof, was erected, but fortunately thrown down by an earthquake.

The same earthquake also slightly displaced some of the great columns, as we still see them.

Modernized without, the building is Christianized within, out of all knowledge.

Yet the old pagan frame frowns down, naked and forlorn, in a dumb majesty, pathetic to behold.

All down the Cathedral nave are chapels: chapels to saints, as in the old time there were shrines to deities.

San Marziano, of the Norman church in Achradina, has one chapel, with a curious portrait on a gold panel; and Santa Lucia another.

The Chapel of Santa Lucia (her town residence) is tapestried with offerings—faded flowers, wreaths, votive candles, legs, arms, and hands in effigy, with little daubs of pictures in between representing death scenes and horrible accidents, in which she was successfully invoked.

The Doctor, who goes in specially for classic ruins, passes hours, I believe, in a kind of mute lamentation over these grand remains, seated, like Dante at Florence, on a stone in a corner of the ugly piazza, the Grecian "market-place," mentioned in Cicero "Upon Verres."

"If they had only left it a ruin," he sighs, quite low and pitiful. "What a monument! Built by the Gamori, six centuries before Christ; the Acropolis, if you *like*, only Syracuse never had an Acropolis; Doric, of course, and limestone—all the temples in Sicily are Doric and limestone; but this one, so old, the architecture is almost Archaic—as large as Pæstum and Segesta, which means, as any in the world; and in such a noble position!

"Now, many other temples may have been glorious, but *we know* that this one was.

"A man like Cicero does not go into tall talk for nothing. He speaks of the golden doors, covered with reliefs in ivory and gold, as marvels of beauty.

"It is incredible," the Doctor goes on to say, "how many Greeks have left written accounts of those doors. There were the spears, too, made of brass. 'It is sufficient,' says Cicero, 'to have seen them once, to understand what they were.'"

Then the Doctor passes on to quote the elaborate description given by Dennis: the walls inside covered with portraits of the Sikel kings, as well as twenty-seven wall paintings of Sicanian history, the subjects not specified; and the lofty pedestals between the columns, each bearing the image of a god in bronze, silver, or ivory.

In the cella sat the armed Pallas, "purple-robed Athena, a plumed helmet upon her head, a spear in one hand, in the other a shield, with Medusa's head engraved upon it." Here Physic breaks off to observe that "it was only Leonardo da Vinci and the cinque centists who made Medusa beautiful; the Greeks represent her as a hideous Gorgon.

"Minerva was partial to the wild olive-tree, so fresh branches were laid around her altar, and an owl, a serpent, a cock, and a dragon, represented at her feet. The roof was of gilded plates, the cornice of marble."

Here Physic again interrupts himself to tell me what I knew, namely, that the Sicilian temples are all built of limestone, and that it was only at Athens that marble was used.

"In the highest part there was a great bronze shield cased in gold, to reflect the morning sun."

"Yes," I put in, "as Ducetius saw it, when he came across the plain a fugitive to Syracuse."

"Ducetius!" Physic took me up quite sharp. "I do not care for those Sikels; they have no history."

"The Syracusans considered this shield as a good omen, especially the sailors. It was their custom to take some burning ashes in a cup from the fire on Juno's altar, and sprinkle them upon the waves as they sailed out to sea, their eyes fixed on the shield.

"The temple was raised on three broad steps—a stylobate, they call it (a good place for the beggars! for my part, I think all Sicilians are beggars)—six Doric pillars," pointing to the embedded columns, "in each portico, and a peristyle with fourteen pillars, the pillars twenty-eight feet high, and fluted.

"There is a bit of the architrave and a frieze left on the further side—[we will go and see it]; but the rest was destroyed to make way for Saracenic battlements. Devil take them!

"The Saracens should have been flayed alive!

"Even Marcellus spared this temple. Never touched the treasure or the ornaments—he, a conqueror and a Roman!

"Then that scoundrel Verres——" an expression intervened which I omit, as it might be deemed too strong on paper.

"After the Romans came the Byzantine Greeks, the most effete nation in the world, and turned it into a church, about the time of Belisarius.

"Look at that florid façade of glaring yellow stone; is that a thing to cover an historic temple? The façade was put up by a rascally Neapolitan bishop in 1754. What a beast! A statue, too, of the Virgin! Mercy on us!

"Then there was an earthquake. Two, I believe."

"Perhaps the earthquakes were worse than the Saracens and the Neapolitan bishop?" I suggested.

"Not at all." The Doctor is uncommonly obstinate when on his hobby-horse. "How many buildings have survived earthquakes? Nothing to do with earthquakes!"

The Temple of Diana, in the Vico San Paolo, is literally nothing but a few piled-up fragments of pillars and blocks of buff-coloured tufa, below the level of the street, in an open space, between two house-walls. Yet this temple of Diana was almost as splendid as that of her sister Minerva.

These are the two sanctuaries of the maiden goddesses in the island (the Temple of Proserpine was, as
I have said, on the mainland), but neither of them
could have stood out conspicuous objects in Ortygia, as
did the Shrines of Ceres and Proserpine at Girgenti, or
even those at low-lying Selimonte and Pæstum.

Juno's Temple was on a low cape. Diana's in a
hollow, and the shrine of Minerva (the Cathedral) but
very slightly elevated.

The island of Ortygia was sacred to Diana from
the landing of Archias. If Ceres was the great mother
of Sicily, Diana was the protectress of Ortygia; some
coins of the time of Agathocles show this. Minerva was
the guardian or president, wiser than Diana, yet less
beloved.

Diana's sacred grove, where the Oceanides herded
the sacrificial goats and deer, browsing among fields of
poppies and dittany, shadowed downwards to the water-
edge, beside the Fountain of Arethusa.

A single carobia now its only memory.

Here Diana reigned in her effigy—a statue with flowing hair, uplooped robe to free her naked limbs, a
many-coloured crescent on her brow, and buskined feet.
In her grove maidens and matrons sought her, to offer
up the toys of childhood, and to invoke her aid in marriage and childbirth.

Of the Hexacontaclinus, or House of Sixty Beds,
the Palace of Hiero II., occupied by the Roman Prætors,
Timoleon's Hall of Justice, and other national monuments, not even the traditionary sites remain.

While I write, I am sitting in a dark room at the
Hotel of the Sun (!), with a view over house-roofs. It
20*

has been pouring all day. Alas! People say it will rain for a fortnight!

Can one believe that this dusky canopy of heaven is the same glorious dome which has shed such heat and effulgence upon us?

Bank after bank of storm-clouds come riding up from the south, bringing a deluge of rain! And the wind!

I have one window; it does not shut by an inch, and there are holes in the plaster into which I can thrust my fist. A small tornado is passing through my room; I feel chilled to the very bone, and sad.

There is my bed, covered with a patchwork quilt; my glass, out of which all the quicksilver has fled; a dirty paper on the wall, and two washed-out prints.

I speak of a small tornado in the room; but what is that to the real tornado without?

How the sea must dash and roar against the rockbound coast of Achradina, and howl in those sea-caves, among the bones!

What banks of tossing and seething waves are rushing in at the mouth of the Great Harbour, between Maniace's Castle and Cape Plemmyrium!

How Anapus must swell and foam under the white bridge of San Giuseppe, and papyrus and arundo dorax bend under the blast!

And that gloomy lake at Lentini—Styx, or Dead Sea, or whatever it is called—loneliest or horridest. How its gloomy waters must froth and clamour upon its dreary banks!

How the tide must tower in, mountains high, in Agosta's Bay—by old Thapsus—and the plain about Catania ooze like a moist sponge!

Heaven send there may not be another trasborgo on the rail, and prevent my departure!

Having, for once in my life, come to Sicily, is it not intolerable to be shut up for two whole days, doing nothing? My two companions alone give me fortitude to bear it. In this respect I am blest. The excellent doctor strides about, spite of the weather, the very essence of good humour; his broad face framed into a continual smile, his cheery, English-toned voice waking echoes in the damp rooms. S.—intellectual, suggestive, artistic, with his books and his knowledge of books, his gentle, invalid ways, and his heavy sighs (as from a loaded heart), is immensely sympathetic.

After dinner, we meet in a central room, from which our various bedrooms open, as in a stage set-scene. We talk and we speak of what we have seen, thought, and read, display our respective "notes," and discourse history.

Not that we discourse history all day; Heaven forefend! As intermezzo there is the old joke of Tennyson's *In Memoriam*, well aired since our day in Epipolœ; of this Physic is never tired. Then he abuses the Smart young man, or treats us to a page of his travels, which, being chiefly in savage lands, are not specially interesting. S—— reads out Shelley—(the Doctor will not hear of Tennyson)—and I——, I describe the latest encounter I have had with my maid.

Furiosa, who, highly indignant at being brought to such an hotel, is grotesque in her insolence.

Then S——'s state of health seriously exercises the good Doctor's mind. Many is the times he takes me aside to ask me in a whisper, "What I think is the matter with him? Is it heart? or lungs? Or neither, only *mind?* An aching heart, which no medicine can reach?"

"How I wish I knew!" This is the phrase with which all our confidences end.

Another day! And the rain has not ceased for one instant battering against the window-panes, nor the sirocco left off howling! Even a man could not go into the street to-day unless he swam! So, to pass away the time, we agree to make notes for an historical subject, a Biography, which I am to put together and read aloud in the evening.

After much discussion, "The Life of Agathocles" is selected.

So I retire to my room and to my books, and am no more seen until dinner-time.

CHAPTER XLII.

I Compose the History of Agathocles.—Arrival in Syracuse.—How He Rises to Power.—A "Double" of Dionysius.—The Carthaginians Again.—A Happy Inspiration.—Ho! for Africa.—The Burning of the Ships.—A Perfect Eden.—Will Carthage be His?—Hamilcar's Head.—Returns to Syracuse.—Africa Once More.—Both Sons must be Abandoned.—The Result of a Message to Menon.—Conclusion.

DRAMATIS PERSONÆ:—The Doctor, S——, and Myself, holding a paper; several old chairs; a horsehair sofa; a table with three legs; a lamp that splutters; an old dog that creeps in for company; the wind outside.

All are of one mind about Agathocles, and all equally regret that not a stone remains to mark the site of his Hexacontaclinus, so lofty that the gods smote it with lightning as soaring above their temples.

The so-called Casa d'Agathocle in the walled up enclosure of a grassy garden in Achradina, between

Santa Lucia and the Capuchin Convent, is nothing but a ruined Roman bath, or Nymphæum, with long, subterranean passages, paved with *opus incertum.* This "Casa d'Agathocle" meaning, I presume, the House of Sixty Beds, is in Achradina; it is at least the legendary site; why, therefore, Dennis places the Hexacontaclinus in Ortygia, I am not prepared to explain.

The Doctor has just given it as his opinion, that Agathocles is "a wretch all round"—a sentiment carried by acclamation, during a furious gust of wind, which seems to roar for the express purpose of seconding us.

Then I commence reading the "Life of Agathocles," which I have put together.

About the time that Timoleon beat the Carthaginians at the Crimissus, Agathocles, eighteen years old, and beautiful as a god, came into Syracuse with his father, Carcinus, from Sciacca (Thermæ Selinuntinæ), near Girgenti.

That father and son both worked as potters was a mere blind, to avert suspicion. As Greek strangers coming from a Carthaginian settlement, they would naturally be objectionable to the oligarchy established on the death of Timoleon, a feeling well-founded, we know, for Agathocles was for years in secret correspondence with the Carthaginian leaders, Hamilcar and Bomilcar.

At Syracuse, Carcinus opened a shop, to which the excessive beauty of Agathocles soon drew customers and patrons.

The vileness of his early life cannot be detailed.

We are not surprised to find that Agathocles' next step is to become a soldier. Henceforth he is to be chiefly occupied in fighting. His strong point is courage —unless it be his cunning. He had, moreover, those two qualifications specially adored by the Greeks—beauty and strength. No one had such god-like features; and he could have wielded the bow of Ulysses.

Twice he was banished, and twice he became so formidable as a brigand chief, that he was recalled; the second time as Strategus.

At break of day, he summons the chiefs of the oligarchy to meet him at the Timoleonteium.

As a General, Agathocles is surrounded by his soldiers.

No sooner do the unfortunate chiefs appear than they are cut down; the gates are closed, and Syracuse given over to plunder.

Six hundred of the oligarchy are executed with horrible barbarity; also four thousand citizens, the richest and the most powerful. The temples cease to be sanctuaries, and no man who appears in the streets is spared. Six thousand Syracusans manage to escape by the roofs and the walls.

At the end of three days, not an enemy remains.

Then Agathocles calls the people together, declares the city "purged of the enemies of liberty," and modestly requests to be allowed, like Timoleon, to retire and live as a simple citizen.

A general clamour declares this impossible.

"You have no right to abandon us, after what we have done," cry the people. "Now you must rule us!" And Agathocles, who has divested himself of the purple chlamyde and the golden circlet of Strategus, is pushed violently forward by the mob.

Physic. The hypocrite!

Myself. "I will govern alone, or not at all." This is the only reply vouchsafed by Agathocles to the friends who are urging him to accede. Everything he asks is granted. Before he resumes the vestment of command he is in fact a king. Then he retires.

S——, in an analytical mood, leaning back on his chair, his thin white fingers raised and pointed together. "What strikes me forcibly in all this," he says, "is how wonderfully history repeats itself. Dionysius did precisely the same thing before, on pretty much the same spot, and Julius Cæsar came to do it afterwards at Rome. You remember Mark Antony:

> " 'You all did see that on the Lupercal;
> I thrice presented him a kingly crown,
> Which he did thrice refuse!' "

"Agathocles repeats the part of Dionysius. He has the same cunning, courage, and perseverance."

"Both willed in youth to be King of Syracuse under the most absurdly adverse conditions, and both took the same means. Both pretended to be democrats; both loved building and magnificence; both passed their lives in fighting the Carthaginians.—Here my comparison ends. Dionysius knew where to stop."

The Doctor.—"As for doubling parts, they all double Pisistratus. You have to live a long while before you can compass what is in the heart of a Sicilian. They are a mixed race. Now, how can you pronounce upon the eccentricities of mixed races?"

Myself.—In two years Agathocles was master of Sicily, all except the western coast at Lilybæum and Panormus, when an African fleet under Hamilcar appeared in the offing.

What led to this disruption between old friends is not clear. Possibly Agathocles had become too powerful, or as king he had no longer need of Punic support.

In the struggle that ensued, Agathocles fought like

a lion; but in vain. He was defeated at Himera with the loss of seventy thousand men, deserted by his allies, and nothing left to him but the strong walls of Ortygia.

Then came that wonderful inspiration of carrying the war into Africa, a *coup de main* worthy of Alexander the Great.

His measures are quickly and secretly taken. He coins the consecrated vessels of the temples into money, seizes upon the jewels of the women, and keeps a fleet in readiness day and night.

One day, when the harbour mouth is for a moment clear, after handing over the government to his brother, he hurries on board, drags after him a member of each of the chief families whom he had massacred as hostages, and rows out into the open sea. Surely, think the Carthaginians, Agathocles must mean battle!

Not at all! With all sails set he steers straight ahead for Africa, nor can the astonished Carthaginians catch him up till he is almost on their shores.

A fight ensues, half in and half out of the water; but the Syracusans, alive to their desperate condition if they fail, beat off the Africans with loss.

And now came a bold stroke on the part of Agathocles,—a stroke worthy of his audacity.

To his good Syracusans, he declared in a set speech, "that before leaving Syracuse he had vowed to the venerable Demeter and to Kore, to dedicate to them the wood of his ships, in the event of his victory.

"What might not a brave army do," he demanded, warming as he went on—; "Did not victory and conquest lie before them?"

"Let every Hierarchus take a burning torch in hand, stand on his own deck, and fire his own ship. I myself will bear the torch to fire the royal galley," concludes Agathocles.

And so it was!

The Doctor.—"Now, as a traveller in Africa, may I be permitted a few observations? The shore upon which Agathocles landed is all barren enough now, and, God knows, has been for ages, but at that time it was a perfect Eden, crossed and recrossed by canals, and little streams paved with white stones and bordered by grass margins, in the Moorish fashion; water is so precious, every drop is preserved."

"The Africans were great cultivators; their farms fenced with cactus, and hedges of twisted reeds and rushes, the oxen's horns artificially bent and gilt, and the sheep covered with skins to preserve the wool. There were date palms, aromatic trees, and thickets of plane and sycamore. No lack of traffic on the main roads; bronze chariots drawn by mules, dromedaries loaded with wine-skins, and oil barrels, and droves of slaves lashed together. The temples dotted about had the same heavy pillars you see on the Nile, the towns and villages flat roofs and white walls, country-houses on the low hills (the African, like the Roman, had his *rus in urbe*, agreeable and elegant), bands of oily blacks working in the fields, and a continual going and coming of horses and horsemen; everything in fact, as rich and varied as ever Baiæ was or Tusculum."

Myself (exchanging glances with S——, at this long speech).

When after their first exultation at witnessing the burning of the Sicilian fleet, the Carthaginians saw Agathocles march quickly along the shore, in the direction of Tunis and Carthage, they clothed themselves in black, and sprinkled ashes on their heads, in sign of mourning.

Agathocles had no troops to attempt the siege of Carthage, but he besieged and took Tunis. With prodigious activity he rushed from place to place. Now he was on the sea-shore, then within the lake at Tunis, threatening Carthage, on the borders of the desert, or back again on the sea. Again he fought Libyans and Carthaginians, and again he beat them.

One ruse I must mention. On first going into action against Hanno and Bomilcar, he caused a number of owls which he had procured to be uncaged; these, settling on the helmets and bucklers of the soldiers, were hailed as a visible symbol of the presence of Pallas.

Had Agathocles now pressed his advantage he might certainly have taken Carthage. The whole country round that great sea-lake on which the city stood, was his, and the Africans undecided if to worship him as a god or invoke him as a demon.

The Doctor. "How about Syracuse and Hamilcar? Was not Hamilcar's head sent to Agathocles, like John the Baptist's to Herod?"

Myself. Yes. The Syracusans, informed of Agathocles' success by a swift galley, would hear of no surrender, and Hamilcar being taken prisoner in an attack on Epipolœ, his head was cut off and carried to Africa.

When the siege of Syracuse had lasted four years Agathocles returned as suddenly as he had left, leaving his two sons to take his place in Africa.

This brings me to another side of his character. As a father, he was unnatural.

A cry of distress soon reached him from Africa. The young Archagathus, without his father's *prestige*, is defeated. Agathocles decides to return.

By one of his clever *ruses* he eludes the Carthaginian fleet,—that hydra-headed nation having once more raised an armament against Syracuse; yet still he lingers.   At length he departs.

Archagathus had utterly failed.   Agathocles finds his soldiers in Africa, starving and in rags.   They are so degraded they no longer obey him.

"You have called me," he says to them, in a curt harangue, "I am here; I will lead you to victory."

He is beaten.   Then all he thinks of is—How to escape!

There are the same ships which brought him from Syracuse, but no transports for the army.

That does not weigh with Agathocles; he arranges to escape with his favourite son Heraclides, and to leave Archagathus and his army to its fate.   But his plan is discovered.

Then he abandons *both* sons and the entire army, and sails back alone to Syracuse.

From that day, Agathocles becomes an embittered and sour-hearted man.   On his way home he falls upon beautiful Segesta, destroys it, and puts the inhabitants to the sword.   Syracuse becomes a shamble.   There are no bounds to his lust of blood.

Such senseless cruelty rouses even the slavish spirit of the Syracusans.

The better to overcome them, and to secure his power, he stultifies his own actions, by signing a solemn peace with Carthage, which he ratifies by an oath.

What are oaths to him?   He is busy preparing a fresh armament, with which to sail for Africa, when a little accident occurs he did not reckon on.

About the Court is a young man called Menon—a very handsome Greek, and the favourite of the King. Menon hates him, and is devoted to the younger Archa-

gathus, who, in his turn, hates the grandsire, who abandoned his father and uncle in Africa.

Agathocles, a middle-aged man, now reigning for
twenty-eight years, is living altogether too long to please
his grandson. Archagathus, knowing Menon's mind,
sends him a message.

Menon replies, "He will take time to consider."

Agathocles is in the habit of using a tooth-pick after
eating. He asks Menon to fetch him one.

Menon obeys. The point is poisoned.

The King, whose teeth are bad, retains it longer
than usual, while talking to his guests. The poison has
time to penetrate into the blood. His body is racked
with mysterious pains. Spite of sacrifices to Æsculapius
and the skill of the Greek physicians of that day, the
pains increase. His mouth is full of ulcers.

Yet, marvellous to the last in constancy and courage,
he calls together an assembly of the people, accuses
Archagathus of poisoning him, and implores them to
avenge him.

"If Syracuse will do this for me," he cries, "I, the
King, will declare the state a democracy!"

But a democracy would not suit Archagathus and
his party at all.

While Agathocles still lives, they place him, too
weak to resist,—on a funeral pyre, burn him, and silence
him.——

Physic puts down his cigar, and draws out a book
from among some others placed on a table beside him.

"This is Polybius. I have been looking at him. This
is what he says of Agathocles: 'A great man, endowed
with extraordinary talents.' To leave the wheel, the
kiln, and the clay, come to Syracuse at eighteen years

of age, follow his designs with such success as in a short time to become master of Sicily, render himself formidable to Carthage; and, lastly, grow old in the sovereignty he has gained, and die with the title of King, are signal proofs of vast ability and power of administration."

Thanks are then tendered to me for my little composition, and apologies made for interruptions. I apologise in turn for the imperfections of my hasty sketch. I remind them that we proposed an historical discussion, and that that means material to discuss.

No sensational event marks the close of my narrative. S—— does not cough, nor does the Doctor harangue; the stray dog that has taken refuge under the sofa is turned out, and our supper brought in by the imbecile waiter.

Then we bid each other good-night, and separate through the doors on the set-scene.——

The next day, though rainy, permits of locomotion. The Doctor and I take the afternoon train back to Catania.

S——, who has been ordered to Syracuse for his health, remains behind, much to the Doctor's sorrow. I am not sure that he did not shed tears at parting.

We have all planned to meet at Palermo.

THE END.

PRINTED BY BERNHARD TAUCHNITZ, LEIPZIG

www.ingramcontent.com/pod-product-compliance
Lightning Source LLC
Chambersburg PA
CBHW060532030726
47498CB00004B/1171